A [illegible] to Die For

J. Lewis-Thompson

Beacons Hill Publishing

This is a work of fiction. Names, characters, places, and incidents are either the product of the author's imagination or are used fictitiously. Any resemblance to actual persons, living or dead, or to events, or specific locales is entirely coincidental.

For more information please contact:
info@jlewis-thompson.com

First paperback edition July 2020

Book cover design by Michael T. Skirving

ISBN 978-1-9160752-2-1 (paperback)
ISBN 978-1-9160752-3-8 (e-book)

www.JLewis-Thompson.com

This book is dedicated to the most important people in my life…

…you know who you are
xxx

1
February

He cursed; the back-door key refused to turn. It wasn't the first time. He wondered if it was worth the effort it took to gain access from the back of the property. Of course it was, he didn't want nosy neighbours spying on him, and there were plenty of them in this street. The house was damp, black mould skulked in the corners and along the window frames; a sure sign that no one had lived there for years. The poor state of repair was reflected in the low rent. It was obvious from the start that his landlady wouldn't be making improvements anytime soon.

'I don't usually rent to gentlemen of your…senior years,' she told him as they stood just inside the front door. She gave him a look that managed to convey pity and disgust at the same time.

…*good*…he thought…*exactly the effect I was aiming for*…

'I used to live on this street when I was a boy,' he lied, pulling the rotting net curtain to one side to look out onto the rain-battered street. The woman had already turned away from him. He shuffled through to the kitchen, recoiling at the smell that rose from the sink.

'Just as I remembered it…' he told her, forcing a smile.

'I'll need your bank details,' she shouted from the front room, 'unless of course you'd rather pay in cash, in which case…'

'Six months in advance?' he whispered; his mouth close to her ear. She jumped, unaware of his return. She shrank away from him, grimacing at the pungent smell. They understood each other well enough; cash, no questions, no paperwork. She peered at his face, suddenly curious. He turned away, unable to risk anyone paying him that much attention. His disguise was good, but it wouldn't stand up to too much scrutiny. She shrugged; she didn't care as long as she got her money.

'You did say four hundred a month, didn't you?' he asked her.

'Five,' she snapped, 'five hundred, with six months up front, as you suggest…that'll take you through to the end of April. I'll send someone round every month after that.'

…*bitch*…he thought…*she's pushing it now…if it hadn't been so important*…he took a deep breath. He could imagine the sort of 'someone' that would be calling round. He sighed theatrically. He could afford it, but he wasn't going to let her know.

'I'll need a rent book…' he said. This was like going back thirty years… 'any chance I could have the keys today? My son, he's got some time off…he could…'

'You'll get the keys when I get the money,' she snapped.

'I'll be back at four this afternoon,' he said. He was beginning to lose his temper with her. She glared at him; she was the sort that was used to calling the shots.

'I don't know…' she frowned. He suspected he might have pushed her too far.

'Tell you what,' he said, 'why don't we call it an extra hundred…for your trouble.' He moved closer to where she stood, smiling. She recoiled in disgust at the sight of his nicotine-stained teeth.

'Four o'clock, don't be late...' she held the front door open wide and almost pushed him out into the street, unfurling her umbrella. He watched as she locked the front door and crossed the street without giving him a second glance. She climbed into her silver Mercedes and drove away.

The location was ideal, he'd spent days walking around the streets. Very few of his immediate neighbours used the alleyway that ran along the back length of the terraced houses. In all, he'd spotted a few young kids sneaking a smoke, and the occasional couple having what was probably an illicit fumble. It was poorly lit at night; good cover if he needed to leave quickly. Anyone he had passed in the semi-darkness had paid him little attention.

He smiled as he thought about the curiosity his arrival had caused. So many curtains twitching as he pulled up in the battered old van. He hadn't made much effort with his disguise, no need, really, no makeup or false teeth that played havoc with his gums. He adopted the role of a much younger man, frayed jeans, old trainers, and a hoodie. The rain had kept most of his neighbours indoors, giving him the perfect excuse to keep his hood up as he worked. He unloaded a mishmash of aging furniture, the kind of possessions that an elderly man of limited means might have acquired over a lifetime. Within a few hours he drove back to the abandoned industrial estate where he'd kept his van for the last few weeks. He climbed into the back, swapped his clothes, and began to apply the heavy makeup that aged him by more than forty years. Just one more thing to do, then he could walk the few miles back to his hovel.

He watched from a safe distance as the van exploded.

…*what a waste*…he thought, shaking his head. It had to be done though. He grabbed the holdall, adopted the slow steady gait of an elderly man, and started walking. He spent the next few days settling in, managing to fend off callers by feigning a heavy cold. No one wanted to catch it in the middle of winter, and after a few days, they stopped calling. At night he drew the curtains and turned on the two-bar electric fire. The cost of running it was horrendous, he knew, but there was little alternative.

Anyway, he wouldn't be spending much time here, he had other places to be…other people to kill.

2

Ellie gripped the wheel of her car, trying to summon up the energy to get out. She couldn't understand why her mother had insisted on meeting here, of all places. Memories of her last visit to the Red Man Bar almost overwhelmed her as she stared at the entrance… her sister Ruth's favourite lunch venue, one of the last places...

*…you can do this, sweetie…*Ellie felt dizzy, she shook her head…

…can I…? can I really walk back in there when all I can think about is being so angry with you?

Was it really just a few months ago? Details of their meeting flashed into her mind. The day hadn't started well, she was busy, very busy. She'd been frustrated at having to meet Ruth, something she would always feel guilty about, but with the pressure she was going through at work…she sighed. What she wouldn't give to have the chance…if only she'd known…

*…you don't have to beat yourself up, Ellie…*Ruth whispered…*it was meant to be…you know that…*Ellie took a deep breath…hearing Ruth's voice so clearly was comforting. She wondered sometimes if it was real, or whether she was all in her imagination, overcompensating for the fact that she was…

…*dead?* Ruth offered…

…*don't*…Ellie said aloud…*I know it's true, but don't, not today…its difficult enough…*

…*get on with it then,* Ruth snapped…Ellie took a deep breath and got out of the car.

…oo0oo…

Despite her best efforts, Ellie had been unable to persuade Julia to meet elsewhere. Her explanation that the place held unhappy memories had fallen on deaf ears. Nothing could alter Julia's determination to be in control of the venue for their meeting.

Ellie sighed; her mother's insensitivity shocked her at times. Ever since Ruth's funeral, Ellie had become the sole object of Julia's attention. She shuddered, she'd never felt comfortable in her mother's company, it gave Julia too many opportunities to find fault with her. Making allowances for Julia's behaviour was hard, especially after losing Ruth and Max.

'I want you to be happy, Ellie,' Julia had announced at the funeral. 'I have some ideas I'd like to discuss with you.'

Ellie found her words incongruous under the circumstances. She had an overwhelming feeling of dread. Nothing good had ever come of being involved in one of her mother's initiatives. No matter how many times Ellie tried to avoid her that day, Julia seemed to be hounding her footsteps. They had a huge argument at the Hotel after the service, although Ellie couldn't recall what had started it. It centred around a list of complaints that Julia had raised about the funeral arrangements. The hymns weren't Ruth's favourites, the music was inappropriate, the readings didn't reflect any of Julia's precious memories of her daughter…and… why hadn't she been asked to deliver the eulogy? The list seemed endless.

Ellie was tempted to remind her that she couldn't have had that many memories because they were left pretty much to their own devices as they were growing up. On Sundays they would go to church on their own to allow her some *'privacy'* with whichever *'uncle'* was paying the rent. Ellie wasn't sure how she'd managed to keep quiet for so long, especially when Julia changed the subject abruptly to Ellie's personal life.

Julia homed in on the fact that she and Graham had kept their distance during the service. Why had he sat at the back? How come they hadn't spoken in the church, why had they avoided each other in the graveyard? Why had he left so suddenly? Her incessant questions became more intrusive; a result, no doubt of having downed several gins on an empty stomach. There was something about getting *'Ellie's rights'* sorted out now that she had abandoned her husband. How Ellie should remember that she was *'entitled'* if she was going to insist on a divorce. Unless of course, she was going to honour her marriage vows and go back to him. She should reconsider giving him the child he so obviously wanted and support him as he rebuilt his shattered life.

Ellie sat in silence, twisting her scarf around her fingers. She could feel her anger rising. She could stand any amount of criticism when it was justified, but this was a spiteful attack by someone who should know better. Eventually, unable to take any more of Julia's vitriolic bile, she exploded. Afterwards, shaking with emotion, she blamed the whole thing on Ruth's influence, something which she realised was becoming a convenient cop out. She couldn't remember thinking such things, let alone imagine having the nerve to say them out aloud. The look on Julia's face was one she'd never forget. It was too much to hope that her mother would give up and go home. Ellie dreaded what she would come up with next. She didn't have to wait long. Yesterday, out of the blue, Julia rang and asked to meet, she accepted no excuses. It was as though the argument they'd had had never happened. Ellie was swept along with her mother's plans, and within minutes she had agreed to today's meeting. It was typical of Julia that she had completely ignored Ellie's pleas that they should meet somewhere else.

Ellie took a deep breath, bracing herself as she pushed the door open. Her legs were shaking as she walked through the reception area. The restaurant was quiet. Breakfast service had finished, and the staff were busy preparing for the lunch trade. There were just a few customers taking mid-morning tea. A shiver ran through Ellie's body as she realised that her mother sat at the same table that Ruth had occupied. For a moment Ellie could almost see her sister studying the menu, her long auburn hair tumbling around her shoulders. The memory took her breath away.

*…what are the chances…*Ellie swallowed hard as she made her way across the room, swerving to avoid a 'wet floor' sign. Julia watched her approach making no effort to change her piqued expression.

…it's not like it would cost her anything to smile occasionally, is it? The corner of Ellie's mouth twitched; Ruth was right. Julia mistook this for a greeting, and she nodded as she shifted awkwardly in her seat.

'I've ordered tea,' Julia managed.

*…more mind games…*Ellie sighed. Julia knew that she always drank coffee. Ellie let it go.

'So, how are you?' her mother asked as the waitress arrived with their tray. Julia waved her away and busied herself setting out cups and stirring the teapot. Ellie detected a hesitancy in her Mother's movements and wondered if she too was remembering their argument. Julia cleared her throat.

'I've been thinking,' she said. Ellie felt her heart sink even further. That usually meant that her mother had already decided on a course of action. Ellie wasn't sure if she was ready for round two. 'I've decided to stay, at least for the foreseeable future,' Julia announced. 'I'm going to look after you, support you in *whatever* you decide is right.' She spooned two sugars into Ellie's cup. Ellie rolled her eyes; there was no point in saying anything. Julia wouldn't take any notice, even if she reminded her that she didn't take any. She watched her mother's face working, mouthing words that held little sincerity.

'Mom,' she sighed, interrupting her mother in full flow. 'I've told you before…'

'It's all arranged, we're going to see a house this afternoon, it's small, but we'll be perfectly comfortable there, at least for the time being. You know of course that we'll have to get Ruth's estate sorted out. I believe she will have left me something, as her next of kin, I am her…I *was* her mother, after all. It might take some time to sort, legally speaking, but there it is.' Julia cleared her throat, the words seemed to stick there, as though she knew that what she was saying was distasteful. Ellie was shocked.

…of course, this is why she was so keen to meet… Ellie thought…*Ruth's estate…she wants money…again…* Ellie hadn't given it much thought; she wasn't surprised that Julia had. Ellie looked down at her hands, they lay

clenched together in her lap. She took a deep breath, trying to control her rising anger.

'No, Mom,' she said quietly, 'I won't be coming to any 'viewing', today, or any other day. I've said my piece; you know how I feel. If you want to stay on, well that's your decision, but it's a bit late to start playing the '*loving mother role,'* you've avoided it for too long.'

Julia stared open-mouthed as Ellie stood up and gathered her things. Her disgust at her mother's avarice was evident. This wasn't the first time that she'd walked out of the Red Man Bar in a temper, she wondered if it would be the last.

…oo0oo…

Ellie drove back to the Retreat on automatic pilot. It seemed that one minute she was sitting in her car outside the restaurant, the next she was parking on the drive at the side of the great house. The decision to live here was one that she'd had to consider carefully, one that she'd initially shied away from. Once she overcame that feeling though, the atmosphere of the place had afforded her the comfort she needed. For obvious reasons, though, she avoided spending any length of time in the Great Hall. Besides, where else did she have to go?

…you never did thank me for introducing you to Odelia, you know? Ruth piped up. Ellie smiled. Ruth was right, Odelia's friendship, and that of her mother, Della Mathers, was helping her to deal with the loss of both her sister and nephew. Ellie couldn't imagine having to cope without their support, and she would always be grateful. After that dreadful night, during which she, Odelia and Della had been tortured by John Prothero, they had each been instrumental in their mutual on-going recovery.

Ellie hadn't told them what she'd experienced when she touched her brother-in-law that night, though. She couldn't even bring herself to think about the images she'd seen, and the stress of bottling them up was beginning to show. There were times when she thought that she might lose her mind as they replayed over and over, mainly in her dreams. She knew that at some point she would have to rectify the situation, but the thought of, recalling them in detail, maybe even recording them, filled her with panic.

*...and to think, you freaked out that day at the Red Man...all because I asked Odelia to lunch without...*Ruth went on.

*...okay, okay, ...don't try and build your part up...*Ellie conceded. It was true though, she had been angry with Ruth, not least because she was concerned that she was being used by some stranger to...she shook her head. What did it matter now? She had bigger things to think about, like their mother.

What the hell was it with Julia? Her latest crusade wasn't helping.

...don't kid yourself, sweetie, you know the real reason she's hanging on here...money...

Ellie had to agree, Julia was always hungry for money, her life seemed to revolve around acquiring it and spending it. Ellie shuddered, how much of her mother's behaviour in the last few days was genuine, how much an act? The bereaved mother and grandmother, weeping into her handkerchief...was it all for show? Uncharitable as her thoughts were, Ellie wouldn't put it past her. She couldn't allow her mother to insinuate herself into a position of control again, she'd had enough of that growing up.

How could she start to rebuild her life when someone was trying to do it for her? She'd had enough of being managed; she'd allowed it to happen for too long. Other people had controlled her for most of her life, including Graham. Yes, she loved him, but she knew the difference between loving him and *being* in love with him. During the last few weeks, she'd had to acknowledge that she'd allowed him to make all the important decisions in their life without questioning any of them. She'd always known that his plan was to move back to Anglesey to live and work, back to the farmhouse that he grew up in, within the community that he knew. Ellie had fallen in with all the plans he'd made for their future, without question.

They'd never discussed the subject of having children before they got married, for Ellie it wasn't an option that she'd considered. Within a few months of returning to the island, he'd raised the subject several times and tried to persuade her to feel the same. He'd even managed to coerce her into going through three rounds of IVF when they didn't conceive. She could have saved herself a lot of pain and discomfort by telling him that she'd had a premonition that she would never be a mother…but how would he understand?

When she thought about it, he'd micro-managed almost every part of their lives up until…Ellie stopped. If she started to dwell on what happened to Ruth and Max, she would be useless for the rest of the day. Maybe she was being unfair, maybe Graham just wanted a nice life, perhaps she was the problem? But then, there was the question of Kara…Ellie started to shake as once again the memories of what she'd seen when she touched John Prothero assailed her brain. Nowhere had she seen anything that linked him to Kara Billingham's death.

Despite everything else that he'd done, Ellie was certain that John hadn't been involved in it, and the knowledge scared her. If he hadn't been responsible, then the only other suspect was… that was the main reason she'd avoided him at the funeral. She was afraid that if she had any physical contact with him it might…she shuddered again. She was sure that it wouldn't take much to approach DCI Porter and suggest that he look at the case again. But what if she did, and Graham had been involved…the repercussions were too awful to think about?

*…you'll know when the time is right, sweetie…*Ellie frowned, what was that supposed to mean? She locked the car and walked towards the main door. She'd promised herself so many times that she wouldn't go down the *'maybe'* route, it threw up too many *'if only'* scenarios. Nevertheless, even though Kara had been…she swallowed hard…the woman that Graham had…she couldn't go there…all she knew was that Kara deserved better than this.

…I need to take some positive steps, I need to move on, she thought. She was sure she could hear someone cheering.

3

He sat in front of the electric fire, staring at the glowing elements. That's what he'd lost, his fire.

*...too long...*he thought*...it's taking too long...too much time to think...to beat myself up about...*he had to get past this, to move on, to stop blaming himself for his early mistakes. *...too much time thinking about the past...*

He needed to remind himself of what had set him on his path in the first place. He had to recapture the determination he'd had back then. He'd made himself a promise that he wouldn't dwell on how easy it had been for her to fool him. He would treat his mistakes, his failures, as part of the learning process. But every now and then thoughts of her would worm their way into his consciousness. He hated her for how she'd treated him, yet in so many ways, he was grateful to her for the revelations that had led him to embark on his quest.

...to hell with it... he thought*...what's wrong with a little reflection?* He took a mouthful of his drink, its warmth seeping into his body

...just once more... he decided *...just this once...*

He closed his eyes, conjuring up the past, he'd been so naïve. Even after all this time, the knotted feeling he got in his stomach when he thought about her, about both of them, hadn't faded. He couldn't get the words of that old saying out of his head...*fool me once, shame on you...fool me twice, shame on me*...it might have written it with him in mind. He was always uncomfortable when he remembered how easily they'd manipulated him, especially the first one.

He remembered every detail about the first time he saw her. She was walking towards the Staff Room as he came out, his hands full of books. The early morning light shone on her long blonde hair. Her clothes, only just the decent side of being appropriate for work, clung to her shapely body. He couldn't remember having felt that way about anyone in his life. He invented excuses to talk to her, to delay her at the end of the day, to have a *'quiet word'*. It wasn't difficult, she responded readily to his attention, he couldn't believe his luck. Occasionally she would allow him to buy her a cup of tea from the vending machine, pulling a face as they joked about how awful it was.

Her looks had dazzled him, distracting him from the focus of their conversations which had mainly centred on his past, he hadn't realised that until it was all over. She'd been incredibly subtle. He might never have suspected that she was up to something if he hadn't caught her flirting with that tall good-looking waste of space in the corridor one afternoon. He couldn't get the image out of his mind. She was standing a little too close to him, giggling at something in an easy way he'd never seen before. Jealousy had never been one of his faults, he usually got what he wanted, and he had wanted her...to himself.

He began to watch her intently. Her manner towards him hadn't changed, she was still friendly, flirty, but then he noticed that she was like that with most of the male staff. She had to be seeing someone, maybe that lad, the one in the corridor…she must be, he decided. He offered her a lift home a few days later. It was cold, and raining. *…you shouldn't have to catch the bus, not after working so hard all day…* he'd told her. She smiled and thanked him, refusing politely.

'I'm all right, but thanks,' she said, pulling on her duffle coat and scarf and bracing herself for the chill of the late afternoon. He seethed once she'd left. It seemed she'd rather freeze than accept a lift from him. Did the *'waste of space'* have a car, he wondered, had she gone home with him instead? He checked, no, no car, just a refusal of his kind gesture, somehow that made it worse. He followed her the next night as she walked to the bus stop. He grabbed a taxi as he saw her get on the number seventeen.

'My girlfriend just got on that bus,' he told the cabbie, 'can you follow it, I think she's cheating on me?' The driver smiled; he'd seen it all before. She got off several stops later. He paid his fare and followed her along a leafy street with imposing detached houses on either side, not at all what he'd expected. She'd led him to believe that she was sharing a crowded house with four others, one step up from a squat. He stood waiting, unsure of his next move. He crossed the road and walked up the path, hidden from the front window by a tall hedge. To be seen at this stage would be embarrassing to say the least. He waited at the side of the house for what seemed like hours.

…this is pointless… he decided, walking slowly back towards the pavement. He reached the corner of the house, stepping back as he heard the front door open. He'd never forget what she said as she locked the door behind her. At first, he thought she'd seen him and was

talking to him. He soon realised that she was on the phone.

'I'm not ready yet…no…not yet…' she said. He held his breath, flattening himself up against the wall for fear of being discovered. She sighed and lowered her voice. In the silence he could still hear her. She sounded different, harsh, not the voice she used to talk to him.

'…I'm not going to tell you, you'll have to wait, trust me it'll be worth it,' she laughed, a cynical snort that sounded nothing like her. There was so much that he hadn't noticed, was he so smitten that he'd chosen to overlook her faults? He felt like he was listening to a stranger.

'…you know, you're beginning to get on my nerves,' she hissed, 'I'm sorry I ever told you that I was working on…look I know you have no idea of the subject, do you really think I'm going to let a sleaze-bag like you get his hands on any of my material…no, I'm not being difficult... you'll get the story when I'm good and ready…I don't know, maybe by the end of the month… I just have to work on my source…okay, okay, just a few more details to check out…' he heard her swear under her breath.

She walked down the path, passing within inches of where he stood. He heard a beep as she reached the pavement. He edged his way to the end of the path and watched her drive away. She had a car; he didn't know that either. He let out the breath he hadn't realised he was holding. He had to get out of there, his legs were shaking, and he felt as though he was about to pass out. He'd come here to find out…what exactly had he come here for, he wondered.

Who was she…what was she? He hurried back to the main road and took a taxi back to work, where his car was parked. Back at his flat he entered her name on his laptop…nothing. Nothing on social media either. Sophie, Sophie Chilton. He checked the Electoral Roll, the house was owned by Maurice and Harriett Livesey, the only other occupant was their daughter, Alyson. He checked the age, it was about right, but the name…he searched for it on social media, his mind reeled as he saw photographs of Sophie, his Sophie, flash up on the screen.

He typed Alyson Livesey into a search engine, it didn't take him long to come up with several leads. A journalist…she was a journalist. But why…he wasn't newsworthy…was he? He hadn't won the Lottery, or donated a kidney to some dying child…there was that stuff years ago, when he was a kid, no one would want to know about that…would they? He had to find out.

'What's wrong?' she simpered as they sat in the canteen the next day, 'you seem tense. Is there anything I can do?' she reached over and put her hand on his, the warmth sent a tingle up his arm. He had to remind himself that she wasn't who she said she was, that she'd lied to him.

'I didn't sleep well last night,' he mumbled, 'thinking about the past, I guess.' She shifted in her chair; this was the first time he'd referred to his past, her eagerness for him to open up was obvious. He was angry with himself for not noticing it before. It only took a few minutes before he couldn't stand it any longer. He apologised and left, glancing back as he walked through the door. She looked perplexed. He had to find out why she was doing this, why him?

The next day he saw her walking towards the library. He'd watched her on so many occasions, that he knew exactly where she'd go, which table she'd make for. He was right, the furthest corner, behind a bookcase, away from everyone else. He positioned himself where he hoped she wouldn't see him and waited, unsure of his next move. He heard her phone ring, a whispered conversation; the Library had strict rules about telephone calls. He could tell she was angry. She swore under her breath as he saw her look towards the entrance, then back at her laptop. He knew she was calculating the risk of leaving it unattended. He held his breath as she looked around. She grabbed her phone and bag and walked towards reception. He knew he was taking a chance…if anyone saw him. He waited until he was sure it was safe, then crossed to where she'd been working. Her laptop was still open, the USB stick still attached, he grabbed them both and wrapped them in his jacket.

…*how stupid is she*?... he thought…was she so arrogant that she believed the warning notices about leaving stuff lying around didn't apply to her? He was grateful, thankful, that she was. This sort of thing happened all the time, she'd be unlikely to suspect him above anyone else.

It hadn't taken him long to piece together the whole story. Their meeting was nothing to do with fate, it was to do with a carefully choreographed plan to destroy lives, to sell her story to any salacious newspaper that would pay her enough to make it worthwhile. She was writing about him, about his family. Who knew what had happened all that time ago, more than forty years now, before he was born? Suddenly everything made sense, he'd always wondered what had driven the people in his life to treat him the way they did…now he knew; the knowledge started to change him.

He remembered the nightmare that had been his childhood. The sarcasm, the criticism, the snide remarks at his shortcomings, the fear…he was never good enough, was he? No wonder he'd resorted to…no, he wouldn't go there…he couldn't afford to beat himself up about that now. It was strange in a way, he hated Alyson for what she was doing, and yet he was grateful to her for providing him with the missing pieces of his life… at least now he knew why. It was a bonus that she hadn't referred to him by name, only as *'Source 2'* in most of her files, *'S2'* for short. At first, he wondered who else she'd been leading on, it didn't take him long to find out. Accessing her emails was easy, and as far as he could tell, she hadn't backed up her files anywhere else on her laptop. He took copies of her documents, doused the device in petrol and set it alight.

He'd been right about *'the waste of space'* as well. They had dated several times, while she sucked up to him for information about his past. The thought made him feel sick, but it had gained him sympathy at work, with several people expressing their surprise when the information leaked out in the press. In the end he realised that it took a lot of the spotlight off him as a suspect. He'd been bombarded with questions after the first reports. Had he known she was a reporter? What had they talked about? How on earth had she managed to get away with her deception for so long? He managed to shrug and shake his head, he had no idea, he told them, he was as shocked as any of them; besides, he wasn't the only one she'd talked to, flirted with. They nodded; he was right. After a while, they left him alone.

The police had only asked him a few questions, more than the others at work. He was at pains to point the finger at the *'waste of space'*. They didn't seem to be paying him any special attention, which surprised him under the circumstances, and after a while he began to relax a little. He spent the next few weeks scouring the news reports, looking for any mention of stories she might have been working on. There were none.

It didn't take long for his focus to shift back to the subject of her investigations. He couldn't overlook the game she'd played with him, with his emotions, leading him on like that…just like the other one, the one that looked so like her it took his breath away. He read and re-read her notes. Each time his anger increased until he decided that he'd had enough. Someone needed to start paying for the way they had acted all those years ago, for the way in which he'd been treated throughout his childhood.

He finished his drink. He couldn't afford to spend any more time thinking about the past. He needed an early night, tomorrow he would start putting the final touches to his plan. Strange to think that Alyson's actions had inspired him so much, when he hadn't been the focus of the article she was writing. He was just background information, details to bulk out the real subjects of her story.

But that was another tale, one he might write about one day.

4

DCI William Porter shook his head, he was fighting a losing battle. He wondered how many more times they would have the same conversation. Unravelling the complexity of the *'Puppet Master'* case was taxing the entire team; everyone was in the same boat. Who knew how many more people had been coerced or blackmailed into committing murder? Since the showdown at the Retreat, they'd been trying to piece together the conundrum that was the '*Puppet Master*' case. John Prothero had been devious, Porter had to give him that, and it frustrated him that up until now, neither he nor any of his team had been allowed to interview him.

'It stands to reason Ma'am,' he pleaded, 'if we can't talk to Prothero, we're going to find it difficult to proceed with the case.' Chetwynd shook her head.

'Bill, look,' she took a deep breath, knowing that he wasn't going to like what she had to say. 'I've told you before, Prothero is in no state to be interviewed at the moment.'

'Then when?' Porter demanded, forgetting momentarily who he was talking to; Chetwynd sighed.

'I don't know,' she admitted, 'it's not like I haven't tried to get some answers, Bill, it's just…' Porter had never seen his boss look so defeated.

'I don't understand…why the delay?' He demanded. He needed answers; he couldn't afford to let her off the hook. 'Look at it from my point of view,' he said, 'we can't interview Prothero, you've told me not to go anywhere near Ellie Shaw or her husband for some reason, and we've been instructed not to pursue several other leads. Who exactly is calling the shots around here?' Chetwynd shook her head.

'If I could tell you, I would,' she confessed, 'but to be honest, I don't know myself. I'm having to take direction on this one, Bill. I've got a feeling that the case is bigger than we imagined.

'But Ma'am…' Porter started.

'You're going to have to trust me on this, Bill.' Chetwynd sounded weary, as though she'd fought a long battle and needed a good rest.

…but then again… he thought… *who doesn't…?*

Chetwynd stood up and walked to the window, her back to Porter.

'I think you better go back to your team, Bill,' she said, looking out over the city skyline, 'they're going to need you. What happens from here on in… just know this… it isn't my decision. I fought against it, but…' she shrugged her shoulders.

'What are you talking about?' Porter demanded, 'I don't understand.'

'Go back downstairs Bill, they're going to need your support,' Chetwynd repeated. Porter shook his head. He couldn't make sense of what his boss was saying. They seemed to be going around in circles. He made his way back to his office; loud voices were coming from the briefing room. He watched as Mason, Connett and the rest of the team filed out into the corridor. Mason turned to him as he approached, her face suffused with a mixture of fear and panic.

'Sir… Sir, they're… they're taking the… the files, they're…' she stumbled over her words more than usual in her haste to tell him what was happening. Porter reached the doorway. Inside the room he could see several men packing files into large black boxes. He took a few steps into the room before one of the men blocked his path.

'You can't come in here,' the man bellowed. Porter took in the size of him, calculating in seconds that if there was an altercation, he would come off worse. The man was the size of a brick outhouse, his muscular frame straining the fabric of his suit.

'What the hell's going on?' Porter demanded. No one spoke as they carried on with their work. 'You can't do this, who are you?'

Someone stepped forward, a shorter man with an identical suit to the man who had stopped Porter from entering.

'Step outside, please,' he ordered, his voice low and powerful. He held Porter's arm and turned him around, guiding him towards the door. Mason and Connett watched as he turned to the personnel gathered there, each of them talking over the others, demanding an explanation. Porter's patience was wearing thin as he shrugged off the unwelcome contact. The man stepped back, raising his hands, pleading with them to calm down.

'Please, please,' he said, 'if you would all go to the canteen, someone will come and talk to you to explain everything, just go now, we'll be there as soon as we can.'

Porter could tell that arguing would be pointless. He led his team down to the canteen. Once there, the buzz of protests started up again, until he shouted for them all to be quiet.

'Look, I'm just as much in the dark as you are,' he admitted, 'let's wait and see what they have to say.' Something didn't feel right; he could sense it in his gut. Whatever was happening upstairs, he was powerless to stop it. It was over an hour later that the doors swung open. Heads turned in eager anticipation, most were disappointed when the only person to walk in was Celia Chetwynd.

...oo0oo...

It wasn't good enough. Porter's instinct told him that they were being fobbed off, and worst of all, fed a load of bullshit. He stared around his office; nothing had been left behind. Filing cabinets, index files, every sheet of paper...all gone. Computer leads lay on the desk, the towers carried away, they'd even taken the shredders. It was the same in the general office. Mason's meticulous records, the white boards... everything... gone. The place looked as bare as a field after an invasion of locusts.

Porter shook his head as he walked back to join the others as they stood around the room, mumbling to each other. They looked shell-shocked; he didn't blame them; he felt the same way. Chetwynd had made some lame excuse that the perpetrators of this raid had had orders to leave as soon as they had completed their task. She would try to get more information and speak to them all when she found out what was happening. In the meantime, they should go to the briefing room and wait there, she'd be back as soon as she could. She left as suddenly as she'd arrived, leaving them all in a state of stunned disbelief.

'Can I have your attention, please,' Porter shouted over the hubbub of speculation that swirled around the room. He waited until it died down. 'I know we're all wondering what's going on,' he said, thinking how inane his comment was in the circumstances. 'I know as much as you do at the moment. Let's try and be patient, the boss will no doubt…' he couldn't find the words. 'She's already told us that she'll be back to bring us up to date, so let's make ourselves comfortable for the time being.' He knew that his platitudes sounded pathetic.

He was grateful as Connett started to pull chairs down from the stacks at the back of the room, he pushed them forward as others joined him. Soon the room was set up for Chetwynd's briefing. Porter watched as they settled down, the hum of speculative conversation started once more, this time lower and more controlled. How much longer that would last, was anyone's guess. He retreated to his office, something bothered him, something Chetwynd had said to him before he left her office, before he'd found out what was going on down here. He thought carefully about the conversation they'd had earlier... what was it she'd said?

…I think you better go back to your team, Bill…they're going to need you. What happens from here on in, just know this, it isn't my decision, I fought against it, but…

That was it, she'd known about the raid all along. Why the hell hadn't she told him outright, why the subterfuge? His heart sank. He'd always had the utmost faith in Chetwynd, she was one of the straightest talking people he knew. He looked up as Mason opened the door.

'S-sir,' she stammered, 'she…she's here.' Porter got up and went to join his team.

…oo0oo…

Ten minutes. Ten minutes was all the time it had taken for Chetwynd to offer up her pathetic excuses for what had happened. Porter was frustrated, no, he was well beyond that, he was angry. It had taken her some time to get to the point, prefacing her briefing with pointless platitudes. They ran along the lines of how well they had worked together in the past, and how she hoped that they could see each other through any difficult times that might be ahead.

'I want you to know that I'm always available for you if you wish to talk about any aspect of police work,' she said, her eyes gliding over them as they sat watching her. She seemed to be avoiding any form of eye contact. She was making this up as she went along, Porter knew it. He watched her body language as she took a deep breath… here it was… the explanation. Even at this stage, he had to believe that there was a reason for what had happened, and that his boss would be able to set aside any doubts that he and his team might have. Chetwynd started to pace back and forth in front of the gathered officers. She cleared her throat before turning and facing them again.

'I'm sorry,' she pleaded, she held her hands up, palms facing them, her posture told Porter that she was desperate, and for a moment his heart went out to her. 'I can't give you any explanation for what happened this morning, I'm not sure I understand it myself.'

The wall of protesting voices surged forward. It didn't seem to matter that she was their senior officer, in charge of the whole department. The mob was unhappy, and Chetwynd was on the receiving end of their anger. Porter watched as she raised her hands to try and calm his colleagues down. Their voices rose with each passing second, he could hardly hear himself think.

'Quiet!!!!' someone shouted. Porter looked around, Mason stood on a chair at the back of the room, which fell silent in an instant. 'For crying out loud...give the boss a chance,' she shouted. He watched in fascinated shock as whatever courage she had managed to summon up quickly disappeared and she got down. They turned around as Chetwynd began to speak.

'Thank you,' she faltered, 'all I can tell you is that the Prothero case has been taken over by...another authority.' The low buzz of dissent started again as she went on. 'In no way does this reflect on the work that you've put in, in fact I've been asked to pass on congratulations to you all...' Chetwynd could see that she was losing them again. 'Look, I'll try to find out more, and if I do, I can assure you that I'll pass what information I can onto you...'

'This stinks...' someone shouted from the back of the room.

'What's going on, what the hell are they playing at...why can't we finish what we started?' someone else added. Porter stood up and walked to the front of the room. He scratched his head as he turned to his team.

'Look, we can sit here all day and ask why,' he told them, 'I'm as unhappy about this as you are, but the boss just said that we'll know when she does, and that's good enough for me.' He turned to Chetwynd who flashed him a grateful smile. She excused herself and left before anyone else could protest. Porter went back to his office; it was as empty as he felt.

...this isn't right, this isn't fair... he thought, his disappointment threatened to overwhelm him, along with a sense of betrayal that was growing by the second. To get this far and have the Prothero case snatched from

them…he could fully appreciate how his colleagues were feeling, no conclusion, no closure.

It was as though the case had never been theirs at all. He looked round at the empty office, now what?

5

Getting the job was a gift, a sign, if he needed it, that his quest was meant to be…*almost a message*…he convinced himself.

'…*General handyman, part time…some chauffeuring involved…use of accommodation when on duty…please contact Dale Walsh at Harrington Hall…*'

Perfect. The wages were low, he didn't mind, he didn't need the money, and once he'd achieved his goal, he would be gone. He had to choose a disguise. Not too flamboyant, he needed to blend into the background. He wasn't sure if any of the staff that worked at the Hall would recognise him, they were mostly locals after all. He'd done his homework, taking a tour back in December with a local coach company. He'd used his *'old man'* disguise; it amused him when the old battle-axe with the blue rinse flirted with him in the coffee shop. He'd also scanned the Hall's website just to make sure. In any case, if anyone recognised him, he'd abort the plan and start again.

He sailed through the interview and soon settled into his duties. He spent Monday to Friday at the Hall, returning to his terraced hovel at the weekends. He had fun creating *'Crawford'*, the character he had adopted. He made several minor tweaks to his 'old man' disguise. He intended to lose the walking stick and use a lighter touch with the well-practised make-up. He needed to look at least fifteen years younger, no one was going to give him a job if he looked over eighty. He kept the changes simple, a different pair of glasses, a slight accent. He spent as little time as he could with the other members of staff, sticking to his rooms above the garage. He soon gained the reputation of being stand offish. He had to be careful, familiarity bred contempt, not only that, it made one relax…one slip up would be all it took to unravel everything.

The work was basic, mainly dealing with the general maintenance of the staff quarters. It gave him the opportunity to find his way around the Main House. He carried out a few driving jobs for his Lordship and his wife as well. After the first week he found himself with time on his hands, time he couldn't afford to waste. He needed to familiarise himself with the grounds, not sit on his backside all day. His room was clean, but it was cold, he'd had enough of cold at the house he'd rented. So far, he'd avoided stoking up the old wood-burning stove…that was it... there was a lot of tree felling going on down by the lake…he grabbed his chance.

'Mr. Walsh,' he said casually at breakfast the next morning, 'I know this is going to sound a bit…I was thinking…' Dale Walsh carried on reading his paper as he talked. 'I'm up to date with the list of jobs you gave me,' he went on, '…I could go down and help clear some of the timber, by the lake, if you like…'

Walsh flicked the corner of his newspaper and cleared his throat.

'…what do you think?' he persisted.

'I'm sure they've got that covered,' Walsh answered, finally putting the paper down and looking in his direction. 'Bannerman's have been our tree surgeons for many years, I'm…'

'…to be honest, I could do with the exercise,' *…careful, don't push too hard.*

Walsh looked at him for what seemed like the first time since his interview.

'I tell you what you could do,' he said, 'it doesn't really come under your job description, but…' he bit his lip thoughtfully. 'Her Ladyship mentioned that she'd like to start renovating the walled garden in the spring.' He smiled, leaning forward, '…she calls it her 'Secret Garden'…' he chuckled and sat back. 'You could have a look in there, see if there's anything you could start on, in your own time of course, it can't interfere with your other duties.' Walsh went back to reading his newspaper.

*…that's it…*he thought…*job done…*

6

Graham Shaw had tried to keep a low profile since the incident at the Retreat, His efforts seemed to have paid off, but he couldn't help suspecting that eventually the events of the previous year would come back to haunt him. This morning he felt different, cautious, something wasn't right. Within days of his encounter with John Prothero, two men had arrived at the farmhouse asking to speak to him. They flashed ID that he didn't recognise. At the time he had been too shell-shocked to focus properly. He'd taken it for granted that they were police. He couldn't tell them much; he was still trying to process it all. They'd warned him not to speak to anyone but them. He hadn't thought to ask why. Since then he'd heard nothing.

His initial return to work had met with little success, how on earth could he function when his colleagues were obviously skirting around him, afraid to say the wrong thing? His affair with Kara Billingham was common knowledge at the Lab, now they had new gossip. His wife was living at the Retreat rather than with him. Even his assistant, Cathy Beresford, someone he felt had always had his back, had started to avoid him. Things had grown progressively worse since then, now it was all he could do to turn up each day.

The University had been swift to act in light of what had happened so many years before. A summons from the Head of Department made it clear, in no uncertain terms, that Graham's position was untenable. It was unlikely that his contract would be extended beyond the academic year. In the meantime, his workload would be divided up between his colleagues. Everything had been spelt out in a comprehensive report, a copy of which was handed to him on his way out. Graham didn't need to be told twice, he cleared his desk, then retreated to the library to read it.

'...behaviour of this kind cannot be tolerated...' it read, *'...our teaching staff have a 'Duty of Care' concerning our students...'* it went on in the same vein for about three more pages, in the end the words seemed to blur together.

...In other words... he thought... *I'm sacked...*

Graham missed giving lectures, he missed his students, their often-inane questions, he missed helping them with their problems. Most of all though, he missed the glimmer of dawning enlightenment when they grasped a concept that they'd been struggling with. Didn't he have a *'Duty of Care'* to them, to make sure they received all the help he could give them in order to progress in their studies?

*...No-one's fault but my own...at least I'm still welcome here...for now...*he thought as he finished his coffee and stood to leave. He watched as Emlyn Davies entered the canteen and walk towards him, his face creased with worry.

...Oh, God, what now...? he sighed.

'Professor Shaw, could I see you in my office please?' his boss asked.

...*Not a good sign*... thought Graham, Emlyn usually called him by his first name. He followed his boss out of the canteen, his stomach churning. His head began to swirl, a symptom he had become familiar with since that day at the Retreat. He knew it for what it was, the signs of an imminent panic attack, which would leave him gasping for air and fighting for the strength to remain standing. As they sat down, Emlyn passed a newspaper to Graham, who stared at it in disbelief.

'...PUPPET MASTER PROFESSOR IN LOVE TRIANGLE WITH MURDERED EX-STUDENT', proclaimed the headlines. *'GRAHAM SHAW QUESTIONED IN THE BILLINGHAM MURDER CASE...'* it was something that Graham had been dreading. He'd wondered for a long time how the papers hadn't found out about him being interviewed...

'Well?' demanded Davies.

'Well what?' Graham answered, 'you know what people are like...' Emlyn held his hand up. Graham sighed; he knew when he was defeated.

'I know, I know, I've heard the rumours,' Emlyn said, 'God knows in a place like this I'd have to be deaf not to. I just wish you'd come to me sooner, Graham, warned me of what was going...'

'...Kara Billingham and I had an affair when she was one of my students, it was a long time ago and...it shouldn't have happened, but it did...would you like me to go?' Graham demanded, interrupting his boss. An eerie calm had enveloped him, what more did he have to lose?

'Graham,' Davies cleared his throat, he seemed to be at a loss as to where to take this. 'Why don't you take some time off? No, don't give me that look. I knew about you and Ms. Billingham, she was at pains to tell me about your liaison soon after she arrived. It's just that now the papers have hold of it… I thought you'd like some time to yourself, clear your head so to speak.'

'Emlyn, the last thing I need is more time to dwell on what's happened.' Graham shook his head, desperate to hold onto the one thing that was keeping him sane. He had a sinking feeling that he wasn't going to succeed. 'Sorry Graham, the decision is out of my hands. You're on indefinite leave until this thing is sorted out, starting now.' Davies sighed, he enjoyed working with Graham, and he hated what had happened to him during the last few months, but there it was. He had to put the welfare of his department, not to mention its reputation before any personal feelings.

Graham realised that there was no point in protesting. He stood up to leave, his legs felt weak as he stumbled towards the door. Emlyn moved to his side, offering him a shoulder to lean on. Graham smiled weakly, he held onto his boss as he guided him back to the chair and poured him a drink.

'Thanks Emlyn,' Graham said as he downed the glass in one, 'I won't forget this.' Emlyn refilled his glass and poured one for himself at the same time. The liquid burned Graham's throat as he swallowed it. One thing he was sure of, he would have to lay the matter of who killed Kara to rest once and for all. Having an affair with a student was bad enough, being unfairly suspected of her murder would end any hopes of resurrecting his career for good.

…oo0oo…

Graham stared sightlessly towards the wooded area at the end of the garden. For the first time in many years he had nothing to do. This kind of enforced leisure didn't suit him, and without Ellie to talk to…the solitude was beginning to scare him. He had too much time to think, a dangerous minefield given everything that had happened over the last few months. Thinking led to introspection, which in turn led him to dwell on everything he'd lost, possibly forever. He'd made repeated attempts to contact Ellie…all in vain. He wanted to explain, try to make amends, if he could…if she'd let him. It didn't look as though she was going to give him the chance, he was convinced that he only had himself to blame.

He sat on the veranda that surrounded the farmhouse, wrapped up against the chilly morning air, the second coffee of the day warming his hands. Funny, he'd never had the taste for coffee until he met Ellie, he'd always preferred a nice cup of tea. She, on the other hand drank nothing else, gradually winning him over to its appeal. Now it seemed disloyal to stop drinking it just because…

He shifted in his seat, how much longer was Ellie going to make him suffer? She hadn't even looked at him during Ruth and Max's funeral. Didn't she know that he was going through hell as well? The seed of a thought that had planted itself in his confused mind was growing every day. It seemed to grow stronger the more he gave it his attention…there was always the possibility that she would never forgive him. The prospect of losing her for good caused him to catch his breath; life without Ellie was unthinkable.

He heard a knock at the front door, he groaned. His father had called him earlier and arranged to pop round, they needed to talk, he said. Graham dreaded another one of his lectures, but he couldn't think of a good enough excuse to put him off.

'Hi, Dad,' he said, opening the door. He was surprised to find a woman standing in front of him, holding on to a child. Graham couldn't tell if it was a boy or a girl. 'Sorry, I was expecting my…'

'…father, yes I gathered that,' snapped the woman. She picked up a battered suitcase, and pushed past Graham into the hallway, dragging the child behind her.

'Excuse me,' Graham followed her through to the kitchen, where she deposited the case, and turned to face him. 'Excuse me, where do you think...?' the woman didn't let him finish.

'Get the kettle on then,' she demanded, 'and find something for this one to eat, will you?'

'What the hell do you think...?' the woman interrupted him for the second time.

'You're just as rude as she told me you'd be. I never took much notice of course, never thought I'd be in this position, what with her being so young and full of life.' She looked around the room, out into the garden, assessing the surroundings, all the time dragging the child behind her. 'Still we all know what can happen when you play games with people's lives, don't we?'

Graham stepped in front of her as she tried to walk through into the lounge.

'I want you to leave, unless of course you want me to throw you out,' Graham couldn't think of anything less likely to happen, 'or I could call the police…' he stopped abruptly. The child was staring at him; his eyes narrowed. Those eyes, they reminded him so much of… the realisation of who he was looking at made Graham's blood run cold. He stepped back as the woman plonked herself down on the settee, finally letting go of the child's hand.

'My name is Jenkins, Lydia Jenkins,' she announced, 'this,' she pushed the scowling child towards Graham, 'is your brat, Karl…Kara's bastard.'

…oo0oo…

They'd gone. Graham had finally managed to persuade the protesting woman that he needed time to think. He'd given her enough cash for her and the boy to stay at a Bed and Breakfast in town, and the taxi fare that she insisted on. Having had to walk up the winding road to the farmhouse, she said, she didn't see why she should have to walk back down. Graham stared at the envelope that Lydia Jenkins had left on the coffee table. He would have to read it, to find out exactly what she wanted. At least he had some breathing space, forty-eight hours to come up with a plan. He could imagine the headlines, another nail in his professional coffin. As if being involved with Kara wasn't enough, he'd fathered a child...

Graham stopped dead. Was that his priority now, damage limitation? What was more important, what was his biggest fear? That his career didn't suffer any more than it already had, or that the papers would have a field day? He swallowed hard; he hadn't given a thought as to how this news would impact on his relationship with Ellie. How the hell was he going to tell her?

…very carefully... Graham looked around; the voice had come out of nowhere, telling him what he didn't want to hear, that he was in even more trouble. He tried to pick apart the bombshell that Lydia Jenkins had just dropped, unable to dismiss his curiosity about the child. If Karl was his son…well, that just went to prove didn't it, at least it wasn't his fault…Graham stopped, hating

himself for direction his thought were going. Ellie didn't deserve this. But for now, Ellie didn't know, did she?

...oo0oo...

Graham's father was used to hard work. Pottering around on the few acres that he and Mary had brought after they sold their farm to Graham, wasn't enough to satisfy him. He'd spent years managing the business and the staff needed to run it. He loved living according to the seasons...he missed it more than he would admit to anyone. His health had improved since he was given the '*all clear*', and he was eager to take on more of a challenge. Apart from that, he needed something to take his mind off what was happening to his son. How had Graham managed to mess up his life so disastrously in the last few months?

Jim had been planning something for a while. He ran it past Mary, who was only too eager to get him out from under her feet. The only one he had to get to agree was Graham, and this morning he'd arranged to speak to him. It was a simple plan; some of the acreage that Graham obviously didn't need could be sectioned off, Jim would start to work it again. He'd promised Mary he wouldn't take on too much, of course. He had no intention of going back to how things had been before he'd sold up. Just a bigger version of the miserable amount of land he had now. The proceeds from whatever he produced would then go to Graham, as rent. Unless of course Graham wanted money up front, in which case he was prepared to stretch to...well, they could discuss details like that further down the line.

…yes, he thought as he made his way up the driveway to the familiar house where he and Mary had raised both their sons…*he'll agree, I'm sure he will.*

To be truthful, Jim wasn't as sure as he pretended to be. Unlike his older brother, Graham had never been interested in farming, beyond collecting specimens and taking them back to his room to dissect. It was the start of an obsession that had taken him away from the island to study, in London, of all places.

Jim sighed as he thought of his eldest lad, then drew back, knowing that if he allowed his thoughts to wander in that direction… It always caused him pain, the thought that there was no one to follow in his footsteps now that Tudor was gone. He squared his shoulders as he manoeuvred around the next bend, only to jam on the brakes as the approaching taxi did the same. He backed down the drive, rules of the road had to be observed after all. As the other car drove past, Jim saw the pinch-faced woman glaring grimly ahead.

…what the hell has Graham done now…? he wondered as he reached the house and parked up. It didn't take long for him to find out.

…oo0oo…

Graham had never been able to hide anything from his father. Soon Jim knew all about the stranger in the taxi, and the child that he hadn't seen sitting beside her. He and Graham sat on the settee, both staring at the envelope that lay unopened on the coffee table. It seemed to ooze malice, neither one of them wanted to be the first to investigate its contents. Graham suggested a drink, a stiff one, much to his father's surprise. After the second glass, Jim sighed and pushed the envelope towards his son as though it was contaminated. Graham picked it up, wishing he had his latex gloves on.

Jenkins had pulled no punches. She felt she was entitled to a *'little something'* for all the years she had looked after Kara's brat. Graham suspected she'd already been well paid for her services, nothing he could prove of course.

'Karl was an impossible child,' Jenkins had told him, 'I've been at my wits end, watching him day and night, nursing him through his childhood illnesses, what with his mother…'

It went on and on but boiled down to the fact that once Kara had given birth, she'd employed Jenkins as a live-in Nanny. Graham knew that Kara had a substantial trust fund from her late parents. Paying someone to look after her son must have been more than affordable. After Kara had graduated, she'd been headhunted by at least five companies, and had headed off to work in the North of England, leaving her son, *their* son, to the tender care of his *'Nanny'* on a full-time basis.

Graham could only imagine what kind of a life the boy had had. He suspected that Lydia Jenkins was the very worst example of a neglectful employee left to her own devices. He wondered how Kara could have been so cruel to leave Karl with her, but then what did he expect? There were no other relatives; he remembered her saying as much. Something primordial clutched at his heart, as he imagined how lonely and unloved the boy must have felt. Jenkins' motivation was easy to guess, yet it still shocked Graham as he read the last page aloud.

'She wants money, Dad, or she's going to the papers,' he sighed. He wished with all his heart that he had something good to say to the old man, but there it was, more bad news. To his surprise his father smiled.

'I think I might have a solution,' he said, 'something I wanted to talk to you about.' He refilled their glasses, Graham took a swig, intrigued at his father's tone. They did the deal; Jim would give Graham the money he needed to pay off the odious Jenkins…twenty thousand pounds wasn't a lot to pay for the dozen acres or so of prime farmland that it would buy back.

'You know, Graham,' Jim said cheerfully, raising his glass, 'I've always wanted a grandson.'

Graham almost choked.

7

It had been some time since Doris Mason had taken any leave, she was used to keeping busy, her days meticulously planned out. The incident at the station had been traumatic, the effect on her greater than she'd anticipated. The more she thought about what had happened that day, the angrier she felt. Not only had the team's routine been interrupted, but every shred of evidence they'd collected had been taken away, stolen, from them.

*...that's not exactly the case, though is it...*she thought. How on earth was she going to tell Porter? It hadn't occurred to her until a few days after the incident, if she'd have gone to him straight away...but she hadn't, and now she would have to pick the right time. She shook her head, surveying the piles of books on her father's desk. If anyone needed help to sort out...but he didn't, did he? Not anymore, not since...she sat down on the armchair that stood in the bay window, the one he preferred to sit in to read his academic papers. She wouldn't have dared to do that when...she sighed. Driving him to St. Mary's Rest Home just after Christmas was the saddest day of her life. He couldn't be trusted any more, not after almost killing himself. He would insist on smoking in bed, she couldn't remember the number of times she'd reminded him to make sure his pipe was out before going to sleep.

'Don't lecture me, girl,' he snapped a couple of days before he'd left his pipe smouldering on his candlewick bedspread. 'Brian doesn't lecture me, why should I put up with it from you?'

'Brian doesn't live here anymore, Dad,' she answered quietly, not wishing to cause another scene.

'He might as well, considering he's always calling around lately…' the old man tutted, grumbling under his breath. 'I do have work to do you know, the least he could do is warn me when he's coming…

Doris shook her head, to her knowledge, the last time Brian had visited was just before Christmas, they hadn't seen him for weeks. Her father started to say something else, then seemed to lose the thread of the conversation. Professor Mason had displayed signs of forgetfulness for some months before the incident. Doris was surprised at the speed that it took hold of him. Only last semester he had been teaching regularly at the University in Bangor.

That night his bedroom had rapidly filled with smoke, he was lucky, the paramedic told her, that she'd acted when she did. She had no choice, she had to contact Brian and tell him what had happened, he was her brother, after all. He dismissed her fears, she was worrying about nothing, he told her.

'Give him a chance,' he suggested, 'perhaps it was a one-off,' Doris clung to his words, hoping that he was right…she doubted it. She also doubted that Brian would bother to visit, she was shocked when he did, and more than a little apprehensive. Her father seemed pleased, though, and surely that was all that mattered. Things hadn't improved since then, and she knew that her father's rapid decline meant that she needed more help.

It was sheer luck that she was home the day her father left the house through the back garden and wandered through the park. Brian had 'popped in' to see him; Doris left them to talk and kept to her room until he left. As soon as she heard the front door slam, she went down to make a drink. Her father was nowhere to be found. She saw the back door standing open. She walked quickly down the garden path and through the gate at the bottom. It led onto the local park. He'd done this before, a few months ago. Doris found him talking to one of the park attendants, arriving just in time to see him waving as he prepared to leave. He walked off in the opposite direction to his home.

St Mary's seemed like the best option. She viewed it alone, not wanting to bother Brian, the less time she spent in his company the better. She knew that if her father suspected what she was planning, she would have a battle on her hands. In the end she told him it was a hotel and that they were taking a short holiday. She helped him to settle into his room, kissed him goodbye, and cried all the way home.

Doris shook her head, this wouldn't do. Her father had asked her to bring him some books on her next visit. He probably wouldn't remember, but she needed to fulfil his wishes, if only to salve the guilt she felt for lying to him. She wiped her eyes and started to search through his extensive library. He'd been talking about cataloguing them for so long…that was something she could do, list her father's books. It might help to fill the hole that had opened up in her life.

8

He couldn't sleep, the digital clock cast a sickly green light… 02.17…this wasn't good; he needed his wits about him. Today was the day he'd been working towards, his debut. Today's goal heralded the first of many, the first one he'd planned, not like the others, they were clumsy in comparison. He sighed. They'd served their purpose, after all if it hadn't been for Sophie… Alyson's snooping, he would never have found out, would he? Strange, that she was called that…Alyson, strange, but not a coincidence, more like fate…this quest was meant to be.

He turned, dragging the duvet over his head. He really needed to get some rest, otherwise…his mind was racing; memories came flooding back again, bubbling their way into his mind, driving any thoughts of sleep into retreat.

…when was it…, he wondered, *…the moment I decided to kill her…?* He knew, of course, he'd always known. It was the day she didn't turn up at work. The *'waste of space,'* asked if he'd seen her, it was all he could do to stop himself lashing out and punching him. She hadn't phoned anyone to explain her absence, she just…wasn't there.

The next day was Saturday, he parked his car three streets away from where she lived and walked towards her house. He didn't even know if she was home. He waited across the street for as long as he dared. Any minute now, someone would ask him what he was doing; they did that in this sort of neighbourhood. It was no use, there was no sign of her.

He had to stop her publishing the article he'd spent several hours reading and re-reading, he wouldn't allow that kind of salacious gossip to be launched, not when it hit so close to home. If there was any kind of retribution to be gained, it would be him who decided what it would be, not the court of public opinion. He sensed that she was close to completing her assignment, the way she'd spoken to him, no longer asking questions, just making small talk until she was sure she had gleaned every bit of information.

He wondered how the loss of her laptop had affected her, it didn't seem to have made any difference. Maybe she hadn't been as undisciplined as he had believed her to be, she had to have copies of her work. He kept replaying the phone call he'd overheard the night he had hidden by the side of her home. She'd promised the story by the end of the month, he only had a few days left.

He spent a tense weekend formulating his plan, it all depended on whether she turned up for work on Monday. He was relieved to see her walking towards him as he parked his car. She waved a greeting, he ignored her as he turned and hurried inside. He made a show of avoiding her for the next two days, walking out whenever she entered a room, leaving the canteen if she was there. He wanted to make sure she got the message that he didn't want to speak to her. In the end she cornered him in the reception area. His plan was working.

Was he all right, what was wrong, had she done something to upset him? He found it hard not to laugh at that last question. He shook his head and turned to walk away, but she held onto his sleeve and insisted that they sat down to talk. He adopted an air of resignation as he allowed her to buy him a mug of tea.

'Now then,' she'd asked him, a caricature of sympathy, 'what's wrong?' He kept silent for a while. He was reluctant to tell anyone, he confessed. He'd been having nightmares, about his past, it happened from time to time. Did she know anyone who might be able to help him, in a professional capacity?

Something in his voice had piqued her curiosity, she offered to listen if he wanted to talk. He'd accepted, reluctantly at first, feigning fear at what he'd 'discovered'. The papers in the locked drawer…the diaries he'd found…the memories that they'd brought back, he wasn't lying about that part. He saw her eyes light up as she licked her lips; the prospect of getting her hands on such material was irresistible.

She was clever he had to admit it. She suggested that maybe it would be a good idea to destroy them, he hadn't expected that. He couldn't, he told her, someone would miss them. It would cause no end of trouble. He was having a difficult time, he confessed, coping with what had happened all those years ago. She murmured soothing words that rang false, considering what he knew about her. He brought all his skills into play to convince her that he was as sincere as he sounded. It was time to deliver the final temptation.

'…then there's the photographs…' he said quietly, rolling his eyes, '...and the letters…' he saw her eyes widen. She hesitated; he had that eventuality covered as well. He didn't know what to do, he confessed, his eyes welling with tears. He gave a faint laugh, watching for her reaction.

'I suppose I could put them back, pretend I never saw them, or…as you say, maybe it would be better if I destroyed them…if anyone was to find out…' He buried his head in his hands, hoping that she would believe that he was in despair.

He sensed the shift in her energy. The bait was too tempting, and she'd fallen for it, almost salivating, no doubt, at the prospect of an exclusive. She'd ended up suggesting that he do nothing for the moment, that she would talk to someone she knew, someone that she believed could help him. In the meantime, she would do all she could…

He thanked her as she hugged him. She was where he wanted her to be, on the hook he'd baited so carefully. They walked to reception together, she sighed when she saw the rain, the prospect of another damp journey on the bus. He offered her a lift; she hesitated for a split second, then nodded. It was only when he drove out into the countryside that she began to realise that he had lied, and that she might be in danger.

…oo0oo…

03.09…sleep was as elusive as ever. The thin fabric that covered his bedroom window wasn't enough to block out the streetlight. It was still a few hours before dawn, before he felt himself relax, almost falling…but no, just as he closed his eyes, he saw her face in the moment before life deserted her. After that he gave up all hope of sleep. He stretched before sitting on the edge of the narrow bed, reaching for a hoodie and some sweatpants. He pulled them on and crossed to the desk and switched on his laptop.

…notes always take notes, and pictures wherever possible… He could almost hear the voice of the man he regarded as his mentor, the man he had come to admire over the last year. He had waited so long for him to answer his

last email before finding out that he was lost to him. He was gone now; they would never correspond again.

...your notes are an important part of the process and will ensure that when memory starts to fade, one can use them to rekindle the moment... his mentor had stressed. Such wise words, so necessary when one was embarking on a quest as important as this. He sighed, wondering how many more lost souls there were out there suffering a sense of bereavement at John Prothero's absence from their lives. He missed their *'chats'*, he missed talking to someone that understood what he was planning, that his actions were justified. He was grateful that he'd had time to discuss his plans with Prothero, aka Puppenspieler74.

His arrest had shocked many people, not all for the same reasons. He'd known who the *'Puppet Master'* was before the news had been broken to the press, not that he had ever let on. He had a reliable source, albeit an unwitting one.

*...old habits die hard...*he thought. The source of his information had filled countless pages with snippets relating to the case. Working out possible scenarios, writing down details helped to clarify the mind, as his mentor had often stressed, but one had to be careful where one kept such information. His mentor had congratulated him on his plans; a few modifications were all that were needed to perfect them.

There was no doubt in his mind that he would have the control to take pictures, after all, he had already started to acquire the habit. He never overcame his reluctance to share details of his first two outings, though; they were too clumsy to admit to. As for having the ability to keep a cool head when taking a life, that was a quality he could never have imagined he possessed. It had been gratifying to note that his blood pressure had hardly altered, even as he had hurried away from the scene.

...*Prothero would have been proud*...he thought.

He understood the importance of recording and evaluating his achievements, but he'd never anticipated the overwhelming thrill of reliving the experience. The photographs he had taken were far from perfect, well below the standard he would have wished for. When it wasn't possible to take pictorial evidence, a detailed written account had to suffice, extricating himself from the scene as soon as he had dispatched his subjects was the most important thing.

He turned on his laptop and retrieved the USB stick that he kept hidden in a hollowed-out book. It lay alongside the one he'd stolen from Alyson. On it, he had created meticulous files relating to his intended victims, their daily routines, their history, and relationships. Each one included a detailed analysis of how and why he'd chosen them. They were arranged numerically, in the order in which they had to die...except for the first two. He banged his fist down on the desk...

...*always comes back to that, doesn't it*...*the first two*...he took a deep breath. Control, he needed to acquire it and then utilise it. Without it his quest would fail, and that wasn't something he could countenance. That was in the past, he'd killed them, he couldn't change that, he didn't want to. They deserved to die, both of them. He tried to imagine what his mentor would have said, if he'd had the guts to confess that this wasn't his first time...he shook his head. He tried to put himself into Prothero's mind-set. From what he knew about the man, he would no doubt put a positive spin on the situation, something like...

...look at it this way, you have a list, quite a long list. By sheer chance you have already dispatched two of the intended marks on that list, with complete success, I might add. I would suggest that you start regarding them as victories, not mistakes...

He smiled; he would never really know. The fact that they were out of sequence still annoyed him, strengthening his resolve that he would never again be so hasty. He opened the folder marked 'A.L.' and read through his account of their last moments together.

There was value in analysing what he'd done, and he'd worked hard on the critique of his 'performance'. He studied the pictures, some early on in their encounter, then later during those final days. The last few were taken when she lay dead at his feet. Prothero would have been right, he had done well. Not one shred of evidence left behind.

He sat back, feeling pride in his achievements, in a way he had never felt before. Just because he hadn't planned every detail in advance, didn't mean that he should be ashamed...it was, after all, his first time. It wasn't Alyson's death that he regretted, he admitted to himself, it was...he swallowed hard...the other one... He'd seen her sudden appearance last year as his chance to redeem himself...to make up for what he had done to Alyson.

His trophies, he needed to see them, they anchored the memory to the deeds. He kept them safe behind the panel that blocked off the fireplace. The biscuit tin was one he'd had for years; he could remember using it to keep his toy cars in when he was a child. It had a picture of the Houses of Parliament on the front and was faded and slightly battered. He placed it on the desk, and sat down, staring at it in for a few moments, in awe of what it contained. This is where he kept them, his treasures, his trophies. He took his time, bringing each of them to mind, there was no need to hurry, it was important to treat them with the respect they deserved.

He paused, his body buzzing with anticipation as it always did when he thought about…he took a deep breath, steadying himself, he reached out and removed the lid. He placed it to one side and looked into the tin. In the bottom was a small red silk cushion, padded so that none of the items would be damaged. Two small pouches lay on top, he reached for the larger of the two, holding it reverently for a few seconds with both hands.

The cord yielded to his touch, he tipped the contents into the palm of his hand, taking care not to allow them to fall onto the desk. He placed the pouch back in the box, removed a square of the same coloured silk and spread it out on the table, laying the object onto it.

The links of the charm bracelet were beginning to grow dull, that's what happened when silver hadn't been worn for some time. He reached inside the top drawer of the desk and brought out a soft cloth. He began to polish it, not too much, he didn't want the last traces of her to disappear. He started at the clasp and worked his way around, gently rubbing each link. First came the tiny telephone box, then the ballet shoe, the treasure ship, the genie, the miniscule streetlamp with the amber bead encased in its metallic folds, each charm separated by several links. He could feel his growing excitement as he completed his task.

…such a shame, he thought, *still,* he told himself…*this is almost as good as having her here*…almost. He placed the bracelet gently back into its pouch, then reached for the smaller bag. This…this wasn't such a happy memory. He tipped the earring into his hand; it had been the only

thing he could think to take from her. He didn't hold this in such reverence. He wouldn't even have bothered with it if it hadn't been…he placed the earring on the cushion and stared at it. It was a large stone, obviously worth something, she would never have worn a fake, he knew that much about her. If only she'd…

He needed to remind himself, to refresh his memory. He placed the earring back in its container and turned to his laptop. He opened the next folder, in which he had recorded an almost identical pathway to A.L., at least in the latter stages. There were differences, of course, this one hadn't planned to ruin his life with her clever expose of his personal life. Nevertheless, the similarities never failed to overwhelm him.

He remembered that day so well, he counted himself lucky that it had happened during the height of Prothero's rampage. It was convenient that her death had got lost in the long list of those attributed to another. In his eyes, it showed him up for what he'd been at the time, an amateur.

It was dangerous to indulge in regret, he couldn't afford that, not at this stage. He yawned…he needed sleep; he had to focus. He replaced his treasures in their container and returned it to its hiding place.

…oo0oo…

03.58… He lay on his back staring at the ceiling. He should chalk the memories up to experience and start preparing mentally for the day ahead, he told himself. Everything was laid out in the spare bedroom, he had only to pick up his bag and head over to Harrington Hall, too early yet…he sighed, at this rate…he turned over again, trying to get comfortable on the aging mattress.

It was no good, sleep wouldn't come. He looked across the room, the laptop was still open. What better way to prepare for today than to read her file?

It read like the opening chapter of a novel.

'Stillness drew a cloak over the scene… the air was suffused with tension, I could imagine the wind holding its breath; wildlife struck dumb with shock, a sense of watching eyes peeping from behind trees. This wasn't how I had pictured it ending after weeks of preparing for the first time we could be together, imagining how she would feel. I'd hoped that she would be flattered by my attention, excited by the prospect of a liaison, eager to get to know me, not like the last one…the one that lied to me…

I had taken the utmost care not to rush her, to show her how considerate, kind and gentle I can be, helping her to overcome any doubts that this was a meeting of soul mates; that we were destined to be together. I was shocked when I first saw her, she looks so much like Sophie…like Alyson, I could be forgiven for mistaking her, for believing that she had somehow returned to me, so that I could make up for what happened. But I knew the truth, and soon realised that it couldn't be, could it…?'

He stopped reading, overwhelmed by his own words, his teachers had been right, he really did have the soul of a poet.

'…After the initial shock, it was a simple matter discovering her identity, where she was staying, and her motivation for visiting the Island. It was ironic to find out that she was involved in the current investigations. I positioned myself so that she would see me, at the bar at her hotel, at the café where she called in for coffee on the way to work.

It has proved surprisingly easy to follow her without being discovered, on foot as well as by car. It isn't that difficult, especially in that bright red vehicle of hers. Her resemblance to Alyson is breath taking it reminds me of how I used to feel before discovering how she had deceived me. I saw it as a second chance, maybe I could make up for what happened. Progress was slow at first, we exchanged an occasional pleasantry, a few 'Good mornings,' a nod here and there. I was so sure that she was becoming more friendly towards me, I had every reason to be optimistic of a satisfactory outcome...'

He paused, knowing that the outcome had been anything other than satisfactory. He cleared his throat, he had to finish reading, his habits, which he acknowledged bordered on the obsessive, were too deeply ingrained to be overridden today of all days.

'...today I followed her out of town, she was oblivious to my presence. I noted, not for the first time, that she is an extremely erratic driver. She neglected to indicate that she was turning into a side-road, and I had to slow down suddenly to avoid her being alerted to my presence.

I parked up in the small layby and watched as she disappeared around a bend. I knew who lived there, I make it my business to find out these things...the road leads to the Shaw's farmhouse. I know that the woman is currently staying at the Mather's Retreat, but I can see no reason for the subject to be visiting the man.

I waited for some considerable time, I was about to drive off when I saw her coming back down towards the main road, pulling out without hesitation. She just missed another vehicle that had slowed down to turn onto the same side-road. I slid down further in my seat and waited until I was sure that I was alone.

It would be risky, but I felt the urge to follow her again. I drove slowly, holding out little hope of finding out where she'd gone, but then I spotted a flash of red in the trees. There is a small clearing there that I know is a favourite for holidaymakers, a picnic area that in the summertime is packed with families eager to get some 'fresh air', and let their little monsters explore the woods.'

He shivered as he recalled what happened next. He unlocked the top drawer of his desk and drew out an envelope...he carried it reverently over to the bed, sat down and placed it on his lap. He stared at it, knowing only too well what it contained. His hands shook as he opened it and withdrew its contents.

The picture quality was grainy, but every detail was already seared onto his brain. He picked it up, his hands shaking slightly. He looked down at where she lay, sprawled on the ground. Her clothes were inappropriate for the time of year. The flimsy blouse, the shoulder strap that had slipped down exposing her left breast. He'd ripped that strap during a clumsy attempt to kiss her. She'd pushed him away, screaming at him, her words almost incoherent… *'are you insane...you must think I'm desperate…'*

He tried to explain, tried to tell her that he just wanted to get to know her, to protect her, keep her safe. Instead, he'd watched as she ran towards the trees, screaming for help. Didn't she realise that there was no one for miles, not this late in the year? The woods into which she'd driven her car were deserted.

No, she hadn't known, she was, after all, just a visitor to the Island. If it weren't for the on-going investigations, she wouldn't have been there at all. Her ignorance had been her downfall, along with her rejection of him. It hadn't taken him long to catch her, her shoes weren't made for running through bracken.

…*Shame,* he thought, *she was so beautiful, just like…*he sighed.

'You know I can't let you go,' he'd whispered, gazing intently at her face which was contorted in terror, 'you'll tell, and I can't have that.' She tried to shake her head as his hands tightened around her throat.

'Sorry, Kara,' he'd whispered, 'I can't take the risk.' There'd been a split second, as her hands let go of his, as she stopped trashing about, when he'd wondered if it would be possible to make amends. The moment passed. If she told, they would investigate his past, and if they did that…they would find out what he'd done to the other one…to Alyson.

…*enough,* he decided, returning the pictures to their rightful place, *that was then, this is now…*

…time to get ready…he had work to do.

9

Ellie sat on the outcrop of rocks; her scarf wrapped around her neck against the cold. She knew that she wouldn't be disturbed, not since Della's decision to temporarily close the Retreat. It was bad for business, but Ellie was grateful for the solitude that it afforded her. She reminded herself, she wasn't the only one who needed to recover from the ordeal they had so recently experienced.

'Just until interest dies down,' Della told her, 'too many morbidly curious individuals out there. The world will survive if we take a break.' She winced at the unintentional pun, her broken arm still in a cast which was supported on a cushion. The three women had made remarkable strides in their physical recovery. Ellie knew that their mental scars would take longer to heal. The waves lapped gently as a background to her thoughts as she stared out to sea. She'd read the letter she was holding at least a dozen times. There would be an enquiry into Prothero's case, it informed her. It seemed strange that the letter referred to 'enquiry' rather than 'trial', there was a big difference.

*...it could be...*she thought*...that he might not be fit enough to...*she shuddered. The thought of having anything to do with John made her flesh crawl, not only because of what had happened to Ruth and Max, but all

that stuff with Howard Atkinson…would anyone believe her when she told them that John was possessed by him? She shuddered; she didn't know if she could go through with this…she carried on reading.

'…*you will, at some stage, be required to meet with one of our specialists…*' Ellie skimmed over the next few lines…*in order to explore the finer points of what happened'.* Why was it that that phrase kept on creeping into her life, what did it mean anyway, …*the finer points…*?

She'd been expecting this, John had done some terrible things, he had to be made to answer for them. She could only imagine how bad it was for the relatives of the other victims. She at least had some inkling as to his state of mind, or did she? She knew she would have to give evidence. Even so, she had to admit that she was hoping that it would all go away. The last thing she wanted was having to sit in a therapy room for hours on end with some stranger, exploring the horrors that were lurking in her brain. She tried hard not to dwell on them, to forget the images that had lodged themselves in her memory that day. It was proving almost impossible. Snippets of unimaginable horror assailed her dreams and she'd woken several times recently, bathed in sweat, screaming. Odelia had rushed to her side to comfort her more than once. Other times she had lain in bed shaking, forcing herself not to cry out, desperately trying to erase the vivid memories that didn't belong to her.

The sound of a gull screeching overhead made her jump, drawing her attention back to the official looking document. She would give anything not to have to respond. The last thing she wanted was to have anything more to do with her brother-in-law, even though she knew that he was only partially responsible for his actions. Uppermost in her mind though, was that the events of that night had forced her to accept that she had inexplicable abilities. If she were asked to place everything on record for the enquiry, which she undoubtedly would be, she might have to explain them. Most of what she knew was sketchy at best, unbelievable at worst. The prospect of recalling her experiences in front of strangers terrified her. Would she even be able to explain how she had obtained the information to them, when she didn't know herself? She shook her head as she considered the irony of the situation. Her biggest fear though, was that she would have to meet John face to face. That, she decided, she would not do, could not do, no matter how much they tried to make her. She sighed; she might be jumping the gun. It might not be that bad; somehow, she couldn't convince herself.

Ellie's phone buzzed; it was her mother. The last thing she wanted was to be drawn into another round of mind-games. The call went to voice mail. There was another call she needed to make; one she couldn't avoid. She keyed in the number at the bottom of the letter, her call was answered on the third ring.

'Marion Larch, may I help you?' Ellie paused…*if not now, then when*, she thought.

'My name is Ellie, Ellie Shaw, I'm…' she faltered, she had no idea how to start the conversation.

'Ms. Shaw,' interrupted Marion Larch, 'I know who you are, how can I help you?' Ellie stood up and started to walk back along the sand… *might as well get this over with,* she decided as she cleared her throat

'Can, can you tell me what I have to do, I mean with reference to the case?' she asked, the lump in her throat growing as it always did when she thought about Ruth and Max. Within a few minutes Marion Larch had put some of her fears to rest.

'Allow me to make things clearer for you,' she said, her tone bordering on the patronising. 'Mr. Prothero has yet to recover from his recent accident. We don't anticipate that he will be in any fit state to be interviewed for the foreseeable future. When he is able to talk to us, we will, of course start questioning him. In the meantime, we will keep you informed of any developments.'

Ellie felt her body relax a little. Of course, she would have to talk to someone, but from what she'd just been told it might not be for quite a while. Why then had she received this letter if the process was only in its preliminary stages? It was as though Marion Larch had read her mind.

'We felt that it was only polite to keep you in the loop, the enquiry team will arrange a venue within the next few months. It'll be somewhere local to you, if not the station itself.' Ellie was only half listening as she went on.

'…it would of course be helpful… would need to talk to a specialist…provide the people concerned with as much information as she could.' Ellie couldn't help but feel that she was making it up as she went along, almost as though they didn't have a clue how to handle the case. It took her a few minutes to realise that the woman had stopped talking.

'Will I have to meet him, John I mean?' There, she'd asked the only question she really needed an answer to.

'No, you won't have to meet him face to face, that would be unthinkable at the moment. We appreciate that this must be extremely distressing for you, Ms. Shaw.' There was a pause, Ellie searched for something to say.

'Was there anything else you'd like to know?' asked Ms. Larch. There were plenty of things that Ellie wanted to know, but she felt unable to vocalise them. The points she'd raised so far seemed pathetic, but she couldn't think of anything else to say. 'Never mind,' Ms. Larch went on, 'perhaps you could give some thought to the matter, maybe make some notes. We'll talk again soon. Enjoy your walk, the beach looks wonderful today.' The line went dead, Ellie stared at her phone for several seconds before realising what the woman had said, her panic levels gradually rising.

How did this Ms. Larch know that she was out walking on the beach? She took some deep breaths, quickening her pace. She wanted nothing more than to get back to the house, the only place she felt safe. The message was clear, she was being watched, although how, and by whom she didn't know.

What had Marion Larch meant… *you won't have to meet him face to face, that would be unthinkable at the moment,* it was the '*at the moment*' bit that Ellie was worried about.

…oo0oo…

Ellie was lying on her bed after lunch when Julia Morrison called her for the fourth time that day, she knew she could no longer put off the inevitable. There followed a tirade of complaints, mainly related to Ellie's rudeness. Her mother berated her for her thoughtlessness, and her selfish disregard of Julia's own grief and loss. Ellie listened in silence as her mother ran through her list of grievances. After what seemed like an eternity, she managed to interrupt.

'…Mom, Mom, Mom, listen, please,' she started, although she knew that she could seldom distract her mother once she was in full flow. This time, though, Julia stopped abruptly, a tactic that Ellie knew well. It was designed to throw the recipient of her diatribe into a state of confusion. It almost worked.

'I'm sorry if you feel as though I haven't been considerate of your feelings, I'll try harder, I promise,' Ellie managed, fighting to control her frustration. Her mother's response was a short silence before Julia came back, sounding like a different woman.

'Listen, sweetheart, I only have your best interests at heart, you know that don't you?' she simpered. Ellie wasn't fooled, this was Julia Morrison at her best, manipulative, cunning, sly. Ellie was horrified as she realised that she didn't like her mother at all, and that the sooner she went back to the States, and was out of her life, the better.

*...I'm with you on that one...*Ellie jumped. Not for the first time, Ruth's intervention seemed to give her the strength she needed to stand up for herself.

'Mom, I appreciate your concern for my welfare, but I need some time to sort out my feelings about what's happened. Besides that, I've been summoned to appear...' she started.

'Have you opened your mail today?' her mother asked abruptly, completely changing the subject, 'if not, I suggest you do so and ring me back.' The line went dead. Ellie sat for a few minutes, trying to work out what her mother meant.

Of course, she'd opened her mail, she'd had that letter from Marion Larch, hadn't she, and there was no second delivery. The post was always left on a small table just inside the front door. She slipped on her shoes and made her way downstairs. She searched through the few letters still there, the one addressed to her was covered by others in the pile. She tore it open, sighing when she realised what it was about.

...*Richardson and Ball, Solicitors*... she skimmed through the introduction...*please contact the office*...*need to speak to you with reference to Ruth Prothero's Last Will and Testament...now a matter of urgency*...*we have taken the liberty of contacting your mother as this matter concerns her as well*...*we trust that for the sake of speed*...*joint meeting*...

Ellie sighed; her gut told her that sorting out Ruth's estate wasn't going to be straightforward at all, especially with her mother's involvement.

10

Months of painstaking planning, nothing had been overlooked. He'd booked a few days off, and last night he made a big thing of saying goodbye to the rest of the staff as he left. A visit to see relatives, he told them, back on Monday. He couldn't take the risk of being needed at short notice. By leaving the estate altogether, there was no chance of that happening. No one had taken that much notice; they were all too busy with their own lives.

There was no shortage of gossip below stairs, news had circulated at the beginning of the week, that Harrington-Smythe wanted to use the new bathhouse for his next 'massage'. That was in five days' time. He had taken the opportunity to explore the building again, by offering to help with the cleaning. He'd been inside before, but that was a few weeks ago. Walsh was impressed, he liked the staff to go 'above and beyond'. The place was a mess, wood shavings and dust littered every surface. It had taken them hours to knock it into shape. Walsh was anxious not to make his employer angry, even he turned up in an old tracksuit and wiped down a table or two.

There was an underground passage leading from the Hall in the Main House to the basement of the

Bathhouse. It was a relic of the days before Harrington-Smythe had the Victorian folly knocked down to make way for his current monstrosity. A small fortune had been spent on its renovation, but it had to be made safe. He had considered using the tunnel as a means of access, but had decided against it...there were too many variables. Anyone could be coming in the opposite direction... he would stick to his original plan.

Despite his lack of sleep, he felt an energy that he hadn't experienced for months. He dressed carefully in a black costume, martial arts style. He stepped in front of the mirror. The outfit seemed appropriate, considering the method of despatch he had settled on for his victim. He pulled a hoody over to cover the top and a pair of sweatpants over the trousers. His trainers were well-worn, ones he'd worn when he'd helped around the grounds, ones he wouldn't miss when he disposed of his clothing after...but he was getting ahead of himself.

He picked up his bag. It was light, he didn't need that much, just a pair of gloves and the soft-soled shoes he knew would muffle the sound of his footsteps once he was in position. He drove carefully, it wouldn't do to get stopped for any reason, not today. He could feel the adrenaline surging through his body. His first one...his first planned one, anyway. He wondered how it would feel.

He was almost at the Hall when he saw a car in front of him. It was her, the masseuse...*if that's what you wanted to call her*...he thought. He had never seen her, all he knew of her was what he'd heard at the Hall, none of the staff had anything good to say about her. It was all giggles and innuendo...a bit sickening, really. Apparently, the old goat made her dress up in a costume. She indicated and turned left to drive through the huge iron gates.

Within minutes he pulled off the road onto a narrow lane and parked up, the vehicle hidden in thick woodland. Timing was important. He'd asked a few subtle questions over the last day or so, his victim was a man of regular habits. From what he had found out, he'd estimated that it would be an hour before his lordship arrived at the kill zone, he had to be in place well before then. He grabbed his bag and walked through the dense trees towards the boundary of the estate, he'd already located a gap where he could squeeze through the fence.

He approached the lake, skirting the tree line, then made a quick dash towards the bathhouse. Harrington-Smythe was in the process of installing CCTV, in the area surrounding the building, as yet it was unfinished. He'd left instructions that he wasn't to be disturbed, so the area was deserted for once, none of the usual sounds of building work. He stood still, flattening himself against the side of the building. If he had been seen he would soon know it. He waited for a few seconds, dreading the sound of approaching dogs, a deterrent that his employer favoured. Nothing, the only sound was that of the birdsong and the wind in the cherry blossom trees.

He smiled as he slipped inside and started his preparations.

...oo0oo...

The building work was well behind schedule, Harrington-Smythe was beginning to lose patience. He knew his expectations were unrealistic, but his impatience to make full use of the facilities that the replica bathhouse would eventually offer, had finally outstripped his patience. He was fed up with waiting, he'd waited long enough. He left instructions that Emica was to join him in his new treatment room and made his way down there, through the underground passageway.

He could feel his frustration building as he surveyed the unfinished rooms. He tried hard to relax and conjure up an atmosphere of serenity. He didn't seem to be succeeding. It wasn't easy when all he could see was the builder's dust which seemed to cover every surface. He had designed every room himself and was proud of the detail he'd included. He made his way to the treatment room. One corner had been sectioned off with a lacquered screen providing him with privacy to undress. Not that he needed privacy, but he'd been told that that was how it was done in Japan, so that's how he would conduct himself. He paused to admire the intricate painting that covered the front panel; the detail was quite staggering.

...and so it should, he thought, it had cost him a small fortune. He took off his clothes and folded them carefully, grabbed a large bath sheet from a pile on a bench and wrapped it around his waist. At least it was warm in here, a little too warm, maybe. He heard noises in an adjoining room. Emica, preparing herself for their session. He stood behind the screen, determined not to give her the impression that he'd been waiting for her. The door opened and he heard her walk in, her shoes making shuffling sounds on the mats that covered the wooden floor. He pressed the 'play' button on the stereo's remote and frowned as the music boomed out. Someone had altered the settings, he turned down the volume, cursing under his breath. He stepped out from behind the screen. Despite knowing what she was, and what she was paid to do, his heart gave a lurch. She really did look the part. Small, dainty, slim almost to the point of emaciation, with coal black hair swept up in an

elaborate comb. She was getting good at applying the makeup that he had instructed her to wear, her face white, her lips deep red.

...*One could almost forgive her for being a whore*... he thought as he stood appraising her. He could see her growing more uncomfortable. Even after all this time, after all the things he'd done to her...she kept turning up, didn't she? He couldn't be that bad. Anyway, why should he care, he paid her enough?

He grunted, pointing towards the treatment table, dropped his towel and clambered on. Emica stepped forward to start the massage. He wasn't in the mood to go through the preliminaries that they normally observed. Emica removed the Obi, the belt that secured her kimono. She folded it reverently and placed it on a side table. She removed the elaborate outer garment and placed it on a chair. She moved slowly, as he watched her. She rolled up the sleeves of her *'Juban'*, the white under-garment that gave her the appearance of a child dressed as a ghost.

She hummed the little tune that he'd taught her. He knew that it meant nothing to Emica, but he had insisted that she learn it and she was in no position to refuse. Soon the smell of lavender blended with frankincense permeated the room, as Emica mixed a generous measure. She poured some onto his back, and rubbed her hands together murmuring a few words in Japanese. She hoped they would sooth him. He felt tense, his well-defined shoulders were knotted, he winced as she applied pressure, cursing her aloud.

'So sorry,' she simpered, using the heavy accent that she knew he liked. He settled down as she worked gently on the tension in his shoulders, he managed to relax, and soon he fell asleep.

She'd been tempted to cancel their appointment. But she had to go, she knew that if she didn't her next visit would be difficult, he would make her pay in some way. Memories of what happened the previous week had kept her awake for several nights. Emica had found out early on in their association that what her prestigious client wanted above all else was 'an authentic experience'. As a result, she'd brushed up on her Japanese, badgering her mother to speak the language at every opportunity, the better to keep Sir Roger Harrington-Smythe happy. Even now, two years after she'd first come to the house, she was unsure when he addressed her fluently in the language she regarded as archaic. The strange words from the past didn't belong to the modern society in which she lived. Emica had developed a trick of smiling sweetly, distracting him to avoid destroying the illusion that she had spent her entire life in Japan.

It was all a charade and she wondered how much longer she could keep participating. Her surname was Webley, her father's name, not Wong, the name he knew her by. It seemed clever to use her mother's maiden name, at least in the beginning. She was sure it had secured her the position. Who would have thought she would end up with such a well-heeled benefactor, even though on many occasions the lines of the therapeutic had been crossed? She had allowed liberties that her college lecturers would undoubtedly have disapproved of. *'Happy Ending Massages'* hadn't featured in their classes. It was a term that Emica had never heard before and was an experience that she didn't particularly enjoy. She'd been naïve at the beginning, she knew that now, and more than a little afraid of him. But the money he paid her meant that she could save to start a small beauty salon of her own, the prospect was too tempting. She had grown used to his demands, even though lately he had become more aggressive. Last week he'd ripped an expensive silk kimono from her back, an experience that had frightened her so much that she'd started to reconsider their arrangement. He managed to talk her round, again, and so here she was.

She had to admit to being more than a little surprised when he told her of his intention to use the partially completed treatment room, the room that she had helped to design. She was used to the small area just off the gym in the main house, in which she would change into full Japanese costume before beginning the lengthy ceremony that would culminate in his massage. Today she'd been taken through the passageway to the new building by the lake, guided into a tiny changing room and instructed to prepare herself. Being that far away from the main house, and anyone that was within earshot if she needed them…the thought troubled her.

Her costume hung in an elaborate wooden cupboard, the door of which was carved with oriental motifs. A waft of sandalwood drifted out as she opened it. Her instructions were to go through to the treatment room next door and to standing quietly until she was acknowledged. She didn't have to be told; she knew the drill. Sir Roger offered no greeting as he stepped out from behind the lacquered screen, and Emica knew better than to say anything as she eyed the veneer of dust left behind by the workmen. She was afraid that floating particles could mix with the oils she was about to slather on her client's body, giving him another excuse to find fault with her treatment. She felt more nervous than usual, the new arrangement heightening her fear, but her face showed no emotion as she greeted him.

It was warm in the room, she started to perspire as she worked on her client's lower back. He'd been asleep for at least ten minutes, she hoped he would stay that way. Maybe then she would be able to avoid the inevitable conclusion to their session, but she soon realised that he was awake again. Emica sighed, except for a few words, cursing her for her carelessness, Harrington-Smythe had been silent throughout, which meant she could expect him to take whatever residual tension he was feeling out on her.

She wasn't wrong.

...oo0oo...

Despite Emica's ministrations, their session had done nothing to dispel his Lordship's mood. He pressed the corner of the cupboard door, it sprang open revealing a well-stocked drinks cabinet, along with mixers and crystal glasses of varying sizes. Whiskey might do the trick, the smooth one from his visit to the Suntory Distilleries on his last trip. He opened the freezer drawer...no ice, yet another detail that had been overlooked. No use having all this booze if he didn't have ice. Cursing at the oversight, he poured a generous slug of the fragrant liquid into the glass. The Japanese-style couch beckoned, and he lowered himself down gingerly. The girl had bitten him too hard, and his left buttock was still smarting. Roger rarely thought about his employees, they were there to service his needs, their welfare didn't concern him. Despite that, Emica was different. She tried that little bit more, gave him what he wanted, and lately had begun to anticipate his needs to a degree that surprised him.

...*Well,* he thought, *she's paid enough isn't she?*

He'd often fantasised about going the whole hog, adapting his entire home life to a Japanese style of living. Who better to keep the illusion going day after day than someone who knew what he liked? Emica could help him, she was well-versed in a few Japanese customs, and what she didn't know, he could teach her. She would make the perfect student. Roger turned the glass around, swirling the liquid, savouring the aroma. The view through the picture window was breath-taking, the cherry blossom trees that he'd had planted in front of the lake were beginning to flower in the sheltered location.

...*Good call planting mature trees*... he congratulated himself as he considered the progress made with the bathhouse. He settled further into the cushions, relaxing into their softness. He really would have to apologise to Emica next week, he'd been rough with her and she didn't deserve it. He snorted in disbelief, what the hell was wrong with him?

...*She's an employee, isn't she, an actress, and not a particularly good one, and a whore, don't forget that*... he took another swig of his drink. Now, if only he could go back to Japan for real, on his own this time, or maybe he could take Emica with him? Another visit to Nagoya Castle, maybe? He closed his eyes, lost in memories. He could swear he heard footsteps muffled by soft slippers, that typified the tranquil tone of the day. The beauty of the buildings, the craftsmanship, the décor. They'd moved him unlike any other experience in his life.

He remembered bowing formally to the guide as he bid them farewell, then letting himself down by stepping forward to take the old man's hand, shaking it enthusiastically. The guide had stared in shock, this was not the way in which visitors usually behaved, it had taken him by surprise. Still, this was no ordinary visitor, this was a Lord, a *'Shogun'* of the British Isles, and was therefore to be excused any lack of manners. Roger had his lapse in etiquette explained to him when they got back to the hotel. Since then he'd studied hard so that he wouldn't make the same mistake again. Apart from that one lapse, the day had been perfect, almost. Their guide had been impressed by the fluency of his VIP visitor, and as they said *'goodbye'* for the last time, bowing repeatedly. Roger wished that every person could be affected by the beauty of the surroundings in the same way.

His well-rehearsed farewell had taken him days to learn, he'd been eager to deliver it. At the same time he caught sight of his wife standing by the doorway, her arms wrapped around herself, oozing boredom. The moment was destroyed, Roger cleared his throat and took a step backwards, signalling for his interpreter to deliver his speech. He was furious that Trish had once again managed to spoil his day. As the interpreter's sonorous voice filled the silence, Roger had intoned the words to himself, wishing that Trish would somehow disappear.

'...goodbye I hope to be back one day, I would enjoy it very much if you could show me the newest renovations when I return.' The guide turned towards him and bowed.

'My Lord…Sir… Harrington-Smythe,' he faltered, hoping that his impulse to address his guest in English wouldn't cause offence, 'it is also my wish that I can do so…until we meet again…' he stammered. He bowed low, Roger beamed with delight, it was an honour to be addressed like this. He left the bathhouse and followed his wife towards the outer gate. Her attitude had annoyed him so much that he'd been silent during the return to their hotel. She chatted away, trying to dispel the air of negativity that had settled between them. She had been the only blot on the horizon; his wife, oblivious to the beauty of the castle. Her only concern seemed to be with getting back to the hotel and taking a long hot bath. She was no doubt looking forward to a relaxed supper, preferably at an expensive European-style restaurant.

'So, that was interesting wasn't it?' she remarked inanely as he checked his phone for messages. She slid across the backseat and stroked his arm, sensing that she might be in the doghouse. He brushed her off, annoyed yet not surprised at her lack of interest in his private obsession.

He had to get his own bathhouse back at home finished, he decided, but the project had been beset with problems. There had been numerous objections from conservationists, something to do with rare flora. The notices from *'Architecture Great Britain…'* or whatever it was called, on the demolition of the folly down by the lake would have to be answered as well. How was he supposed to get the thing built when there were so many obstacles to sort out? Still, a few well-placed bribes had managed to get the contractors to start work at last, just the threatened lawsuits to deal with and he could look forward to starting the decoration stage in earnest. He smiled, secure in the knowledge that he could sort out most things by throwing a modest amount of money at it. Some people were easily pleased, those who proved difficult could be dealt with in other ways. He had staff to deal with that sort of thing, and between them and his unorthodox style of business, they usually managed the most unpleasant of situations.

Unlike the squirming wretch currently sharing his name. Wasn't there a fashion weekend going on somewhere in the world, some expensive event that she could be enticed to go to? It would leave him in peace for a few days without having to see her simpering face. Getting her to leave was becoming increasingly easy as their relationship deteriorated to an all-time low. Whenever her presence became too much, he would dangle the prospect of a few designer dresses, an odd handbag or two maybe a pair of Louboutin's. That would keep her satisfied for a while. He could get on with his project in peace, savour the anticipation of its completion, which for him was the greatest high. He'd suggested such a trip on their way back from the castle. She readily took the bait, kissing his cheek and snuggling up to his side in a way that no longer held any pleasure for him.

…I must do something about this when we're back in the UK. How much will it cost to get rid of this one…? He wondered. The last one had held out for several million more than he originally offered, if only she'd had known that he would have paid double just to dump the bitch. He didn't anticipate much opposition from Trish though, tears first maybe, then denial. She would no doubt try to make amends, promising to change, begging, the *'how was she going to live without him'* ploy. Then aggression, threats to go to the press, promises that he would regret even suggesting that they part. It was nothing that he hadn't been through before. His previous three wives had all come to heel when they realised that the pre-nuptial agreement that he'd made them sign left them penniless unless they complied pretty quickly. He paid them off handsomely in the end and had even reached a degree of civility when their paths crossed.

All except the third Lady Harrington-Smythe, who had spoiled his forties by carrying out her threat to go public with details of their private life. Her indiscretion with that journo had dented his image at the time. At least she did the decent thing and committed suicide in the end. That was the story that the press was sold anyway.

But that night in Japan he'd said nothing. For the moment he allowed Trish to tuck her arm through his and snuggle up closer, anticipating with relish the moment he would tell her that she was excess baggage in his life. He ended up dumping her at the hotel and left to find more convivial company.

He smiled as he imagined the letter that had arrived for her that morning, the one from his Solicitor. She had always been one for histrionics, but even so, the screeching virago that she transformed into had caught him by surprise. Something wasn't right though; it was as though she'd known what he was going to say and had prepared for it, the thought had left him with a bitter taste. He was used to calling the shots, having her anticipate them wasn't part of his game plan. In the end she slapped his face and flounced off to her room. No wonder his session with Emica had been less than satisfactory. He would just have to wait now; see what kind of settlement her legal team would demand.

Right now, he wanted nothing more than to immerse himself in the energy of his new domain, even though it wasn't finished. The room was warm, the music soothing, if he allowed himself to relax, he could be in the real thing. He made up his mind, a quick phone call and his entire staff could stand down, at least that way he wouldn't be disturbed, he might even sleep here. The thought cheered him up as he rang the main house. His drink was getting low, he got up and crossed the room to replenish it. He staggered slightly, his head spinning.

...after one glass...? he thought, *...maybe I need to eat something after all...?* He shrugged as he poured himself another good measure, then added water. He wanted his time here to mean something, not to be fogged in a drunken stupor. He replaced the bottle in the cabinet and started to turn, he heard the familiar whisper of slipper clad footsteps...then a hiss, cutting through the air...

...sounds just like a Samurai sword, he thought...then...nothing.

...oo0oo...

The phone call that Harrington-Smythe had made was a bonus. No-one would dare to disturb him once he'd given instructions to be left alone. He'd taken care not to step in the blood that had spread out over the mats as he picked up his victim's head and placed it on a small stool. That damned music, what on earth had Harrington-Smythe found attractive about it?

...just a few photos... he thought, snapping the scene from a variety of angles. Yes, this was better, he had executed his plan precisely this time, proved that he could do a good job. All he had to do now was to wait until dark and he could leave. He didn't even have to hide...just wait. He had to get out of the room, though, he couldn't look at that face for much longer, not without wanting to rearrange its position. That was dangerous; he might make a mistake, leave a clue.

A movement from outside the building startled him, he froze...maybe he'd waited too long. His instinct was to duck down, despite knowing that no one could see through the one-way windows that Harrington-Smythe had installed. He watched as a figure walked past towards the lake…security doing their rounds. Just another hour or so…he took one last look around.

…hell…the memento, his trophy…he'd almost forgotten…he made his way over to the far corner of the room, side-stepping the pool of blood. He'd already decided what to take. He picked up one of the figures from the chess board, knocking over several other pieces. He didn't care, it didn't matter, he had what he wanted…how appropriate…the black knight.

11

Some joker had named the recent incident *'Raiders of the Lost Files'*, to Porter it was anything but funny. Every scrap of the evidence in the Prothero case had been taken. He wondered who had the kind of authority to confiscate confidential records during an on-going investigation. They were left with little else to do but hang around waiting for something to happen. Mason was beginning to get on his nerves, it seemed that every time he spoke to her, she jumped, muttering something about having to be somewhere before running off. At least that's what it felt like. He was beginning to think she'd lost it.

'What's up with Mason?' he asked Connett as she left the office for the third time that morning.

'Her father's gone into a home…' Connett told him. Porter sighed. He'd heard some gossip around the canteen but hoped that it wasn't true. Something about the old man setting fire to his bed. Poor Mason, maybe he should try and have a word. He looked up as Chetwynd strode into the room. She walked towards him, nodding towards his empty office. He followed her inside.

'I've just had some news,' she said, her voice faltering slightly. 'We… err…we'll be getting our files back this afternoon, and our computers, minus the information on Prothero…apparently,' she waited for his response. Porter shook his head; so far, she hadn't managed to come up with a good reason for them being taken in the first place. She had stuck consistently to the story she'd fed them since the raid, that the case was now classified, and they would be informed of the outcome if it were possible.

'Well, Ma'am,' he growled, 'we'd better have a tidy round then, hadn't we?'

Chetwynd shook her head and sighed. She walked back to his office door and closed it gently.

'Look, Bill,' she said, her voice tinged with resignation, 'how long have we known each other?' She didn't give him a chance to answer. 'In all that time, have I ever lied to you?' Porter shook his head. She was telling the truth, if there was one person in his career that he could count on to tell it like it was, it was Celia Chetwynd.

'…and I'm not lying now,' she went on, 'I really don't have a clue what's going on here…for God's sake, would it make you feel better if I made something up?' she shouted.

'…it might,' he bawled. They looked at each other, each as frustrated with the situation as the other. Neither of them heard the door open. It was Mason, she stared from one to the other.

'Sir…you need to come…there's been a murder at Harrington Hall.

…oo0oo…

The smell of resin reminded Porter of his backpacking holiday in Canada just before he joined the force... cedar pine, he would recognise it anywhere. Memories of travelling through the countryside came flooding back. He remembered the small hostels he'd stayed at, his backpack stuffed with tee-shirts, socks and underpants in various stages of cleanliness. The aromatic scent of the wood didn't mix well with that of congealed blood that assailed him as he entered the strange looking building. Forensics had arrived about an hour before. Porter scanned them to see who was in charge. He spotted Simon Daventree in the far corner of the hallway. He and his team were well into their routine. Porter sighed as he walked forward to greet them.

Daventree was more than capable of dealing with anything his profession threw at him, but Porter had to admit that Graham Shaw would have been his first choice to lead on a case. He wondered how long Graham's absence would last, he did have a lot on his plate. The University had a zero-tolerance policy when it came to a member of staff having an affair with a student, no matter how long ago it took place. Having Kara Billingham turn up dead shortly after moving to the Island…he stopped and turned away from an approaching Daventree. He walked back out onto the pathway that surrounded the building.

Kara Billingham's death... it had reminded him so much of the Alyson Livesey case. He wondered if the files relating to the two of them would be among the information being returned to them. Neither of the cases sat well with him, he would have to back over whatever information they had. He could have kicked himself that he'd had all this time to spare, and yet something so important had slipped his attention. Connett was deep in conversation with Daventree when Porter finally joined them.

'Nasty one, I'm afraid,' Daventree said, glancing towards a semi-open sliding door.

'Can I take a look?' Porter asked. He headed towards the room before Daventree could answer.

'Be careful where you step, I'd keep to the right if I were you…,' he warned as Porter slid the door across, until it was fully open. The floor was awash with blood, now partially congealed. The decapitated body lay in front of an open cupboard. The head had been set on a stool in the opposite corner; it bore a mask-like grimace.

Porter swallowed hard…*the rictus smile*…he thought, the grin of death.

'I take it that this is how you found…' he turned away; the mingling odours were starting to overwhelm him.

'We haven't moved anything, if that's what you're asking, this isn't our first rodeo you know,' snapped Daventree. Porter had the grace to look ashamed at his ill-chosen remark.

'There's some blood spatter,' Daventree continued, pointing needlessly to the red arc scythed across one wall, 'whoever did this was careful to avoid stepping in the victim's blood. There are no footprints, as you can see, so they came prepared,' Daventree shook his head, 'the perpetrator took their time.'

Porter ran through the usual questions, identity of the victim, approximate time of death, and how the murder had been committed. Daventree stared pointedly at a samurai sword that lay within feet of the body, its blade covered with blood.

'I'd venture a wild guess that that could have played some part,' he answered sarcastically. Porter rolled his eyes and dispatched Connett to assemble the staff back at the house, then stood assessing the scene, committing details to memory. He squatted down to gain a different perspective. A table stood in one corner, on top of which was a chess set. Porter was no expert, but it looked valuable, possibly jade with metal inlays and what looked like semi-precious gems. Several pieces had been knocked over. Porter took one more look around, then headed out of the room, eager to be free of the gut-churning smell. Daventree stood at the entrance, clipboard in hand, he turned as Porter approached.

'I'd estimate sometime between four and five yesterday afternoon,' he said before Porter could ask. 'I'll know more after I've done the post-mortem.' Porter nodded, Daventree wasn't one for long drawn out explanations.

'Thanks, Simon,' he said. The use of his first name caused Daventree to pause. He'd always known that he was Porter's second choice, he could detect his disappointment when Graham Shaw wasn't heading up the show. It had been like that ever since he could remember.

'You're welcome,' he said, 'I'll have a more detailed report for you shortly,' Porter smiled, it was time for old scores to be forgotten. Daventree had worked with him on the Alyson Livesey case, not one of their finest efforts. They'd clashed several times; the bad feelings between them had persisted. Porter turned to leave, then paused.

'I know this may seem random, Simon,' he started, wondering if it was the right time to bring the subject up. 'But I need to speak to you sometime, about the Alyson Livesey case.' He braced himself, waiting for Daventree's reaction. The man shook his head.

'It's not what you think,' Porter explained, 'I promise…it's just... I think I may be on to something, a hunch, you know how it is?' Daventree stared. He'd heard about Porter's hunches. If what people said was true, it might lay the matter of Alyson's murder to rest once and for all. Their failure to find her killer played as much on his mind as it obviously did on Porter's. They'd missed something, they were both sure of it.

'Strange you should bring that up, I was going over some notes a few days ago…phone me, we'll talk,' he said, 'in the meantime…' he waved his hand towards the bathhouse. Porter nodded, gratified that Daventree had similar doubts about Alison's death. But that would have to wait, in the meantime he had people to interview.

…oo0oo…

…Lord Harrington-Smythe, wonder who he pissed off this time? Porter thought as he headed towards the house. The beauty of the grounds was lost on him as he viewed them with a forensic eye. Here and there, cameras sat in branches. They'd been positioned discreetly; he made a note to obtain the footage. Anyone coming or going on the path leading to the bathhouse would have been recorded.

Porter knew something of Harrington-Smythe's history. He wasn't popular, in either his business or personal life. He suspected that there would be quite a few people who would like to see the back of him, he wasn't wrong. Connett stood in the enormous hallway, with what seemed like most of the members of staff gathered in small groups, mumbling to each other in shock. Connett handed him a list of the names, he skimmed over it, noting that at least twenty of them had been on the grounds the previous day. He handed it back to Connett.

'Check them off, let them know we'll need them to stay here until we've spoken to them,' he said.

'Those I've spoken to don't seem to have a good word to say about His Lordship,' he told Porter. 'I've asked someone called Reynolds if he can make a room available…might as well get on with the preliminary interviews.' Porter nodded; he was impressed. Connett seemed to have everything in hand. Porter knew several of the staff personally. Most of them had nothing but contempt for the man who, up until a few hours ago, had paid their salaries. They only stayed on, many admitted, because there was a chronic lack of work in the area.

He looked around the hall as Connett left. The person Porter really wanted to speak to was Harrington-Smythe's wife, Trisha. His mind wandered back a few years…Trisha, Patricia Johnson as he had known her…who would have thought…

Gossip about Harrington-Smythe had been circulating around the press for the last few years…but that was nothing unusual, his Lordship had offended a lot of people. Porter had no doubt that the list of suspects would be extensive.

The heat in the hallway was unbearable, the atmosphere seemed hostile. Porter stepped back outside and walked slowly around the terraced area, the cooler air refreshing his energy. It wasn't long before Connett joined him.

'Everyone on there is accounted for, except for the masseuse, girl called Emica, Emica Wong. She was with Harrington-Smythe in the bathhouse during the hours leading up to his death. I think there's more to her visit than anyone's letting on,' he turned the page of his notebook. From where he stood, Porter could see into the hallway over Connett's shoulder. Some of the staff who had gathered there earlier had dispersed, allowed to go about their business once Connett had warned them not to leave the estate. Those who remained were shuffling their feet, eager to get away.

'We've still got several people to speak to, but I thought you should know that there's a chauffeur, name of Crawford.' Connett told him. 'He booked a few days off, told the others that he intended to visit relatives. I'll get his contact details and investigate it. Reynolds, the butler, took Lady Harrington-Smythe out just before five o'clock yesterday, dropped her off at a friend's house, returning here forty-five minutes later.'

'Get a description of Crawford, find out everything you can about him, we need to account for everyone,' Porter said. He and Connett headed back towards the hallway. They entered just as tall young man walked down the stairs to join them. Porter noticed that his suit that would probably have set him back at least three month's wages.

'Dale, Dale Walsh,' the young man gushed, walking forward with his hand outstretched. Porter shook it, it was firm. Walsh reinforced his grip by placing his other hand over the top. He noticed the look on Porter's face and cleared his throat, he looked flustered. 'I am their Lord and Ladyship's Personal Assistant and Social Secretary,' he explained.

'Where is Lady Harrington?' Porter asked, annoyed at being kept waiting.

'You mean Lady Harrington-Smythe?' asked Walsh, his smile fading again as Porter sighed. After the scenes he'd just witnessed in the bathhouse, he was in no mood to play serf to her Ladyship. The lady of the house was in her rooms, he was told, she could spare them a few minutes, but just now she was resting, to compose herself. Porter stared pointedly at Walsh, who cleared his throat.

'I'll just... I'll just go and...' Walsh hesitated, leaving Porter in the hall. He returned a few minutes later wringing his hands.

'Her Ladyship is, as I am sure you can appreciate,' he whined, 'beside herself…' he glanced at Porter. 'She wondered if you could come back…' he knew the answer before Porter started to speak. 'If you'd like to come with me, I'll take you for something to drink, tea maybe?' Porter was beginning to like this guy; he was nothing if not deferential. Connett had rejoined them, he started to follow Walsh, only to be stopped by Porter's hand on his arm.

'Mr Walsh, if Lady Harrington-Smythe is unable to talk to us here, maybe she would like to come down to the station, where I am sure we can make her comfortable for her interview.' Walsh brought himself upright; he looked as though he was about to salute Porter. He muttered something about giving it one more try, then disappeared again.

Connett cleared his throat, 'You know Guv,' he started, 'she *has* just lost her husband.'

Porter sighed, 'Have you ever met her?' he asked, Connett shook his head, 'just watch when she comes down, you'll understand.' He paced around the hallway. The walls were lined with oak linen-fold panelling, the stained-glass windows illuminated the stairs in the weak afternoon sun. In one corner stood a suit of armour, it looked oriental. The metal details gleaming against a red and black lacquer screen. Porter thought how out of place it looked in this setting.

Within minutes Walsh was back. Her Ladyship would be pleased to see them in the study if they could wait a short while until she had composed herself. Porter sighed again, even though he knew Lady Harrington-Smythe of old, just how he should play this was anyone's guess.

One thing about Connett, Porter thought later that evening, he could take notes more accurately than any other DS he knew. No, wait, not as well as Mason, but somewhere near that. It made it a lot easier knowing that his conversation with Patricia Harrington-Smythe, the Lady of the House was being recorded word for word. She kept them waiting for over an hour in the end. Then, just as Porter had had enough and was placing his gold-embossed bone china cup and saucer back on the coffee table, she materialised through a hidden doorway in the bookcase. She cleared her throat to attract their attention. Connett jumped, clattering the priceless teacup onto the saucer.

Porter had to admit, she looked good, not at all like the shy young woman he remembered from the police admin office. …*it's amazing what expensive clothes and make-up can do*… he thought as he indicated for her to sit down. She shook her head, determined that if she had to talk to him, it was going to be on her terms or not at all. She stepped daintily across the thick piled Aubusson rug, standing with her back to the fire. She'd lost weight, he noticed, too much in his opinion. The expensive looking jacket practically hung from her shoulders; her face pinched into something resembling grief. No, not grief…anger, she was obviously angry at his insistence that she speak to him.

'DI Porter,' she said, her voice low and husky, not the voice he remembered from so long ago. He cleared his throat, tempted to tell her of his promotion. He decided not to; this wasn't the time.

'Would you like to start then; your questions must be particularly important if they can't wait?' Porter almost winced as her words dripped like acid. She forced a smile, possibly the most insincere smile he'd seen in a long while. She shook her head as he indicated once again that she might like to sit down.

'As you no doubt remember, Lady Harrington-Smythe, time is always of the essence in cases like these,' Porter smiled and altered the tone of his voice, conceding that she may well be in shock at the events of the previous day.

Trish nodded, 'Of course,' she agreed, she seemed to relax slightly as she moved over to a large leather armchair. It swamped her slight frame as she sank into it. She sighed. 'Please go on,' she murmured. Her answers told Porter nothing he didn't already know. Reynolds had picked her up and driven her to her friend's house just before five, they arrived at her friend's house at five fifteen.

'You were out all night, I'm told.' Porter said. Trish looked out of the window as she nodded.

'Yes, Cecily was kind enough to ask me to stay for the night. Her driver brought me back this morning.' Porter could see Connett scribbling away out of the corner of his eye.

'One of your staff told my colleague that you and your husband had an argument yesterday morning. Was that the reason you decided to stay with your friend?' Porter asked watching her intently. Trish's head snapped round; her face suffused with anger.

'Who told you that?' she demanded, Porter waved his hand, dismissing her question.

'We've been informed that you received a letter in yesterday's morning post, a letter that you were required to sign for, from your husband's solicitor, stating his intention to file for divorce.' Porter could see the change in her body language as he waited for her to reply.

'DI Porter,' she said, her voice almost a whisper, 'I believe I have been more than patient with you, under the circumstances. If you have any further questions, I suggest you contact my solicitor.' She stood up, paused for several seconds, no doubt, Porter suspected, to stamp her authority on the meeting. She reached across and pressed a button on a side table. He could hear a buzz in the next room, her actions reminded him of a scene he'd watched recently in a series about the Queen. He had to smile to himself. Within seconds Dale Walsh opened the door and stepped forward.

'DI Porter is leaving, Dale, please show him and his colleague out…' she said, the tone of her voice betraying something he couldn't quite identify…he turned and nodded to Connett. He was halfway out of the door when he turned back.

'For future reference, *My Lady,*' he said quietly, 'that's DCI Porter…' he didn't wait for her reply.

…ooOoo…

Connett was quiet on their way back to the station. Porter glanced at him as he negotiated the long driveway and pulled out onto the main road. It was only as they reached the bridge that he broke the silence.

'Something bothering you Connett?' he asked. Connett shook his head, still looking out of the window. Porter could tell that he was lying. He cleared his throat.

'There is something, sir,' he said quietly, 'it's just…I thought you were a bit hard on Lady Harrington…' he stopped, as Porter interrupted him.

'What did you notice, what stood out to you?' he asked.

'Well, she was...' Connett thought for a few minutes, 'upset, understandably so, she *has* just lost her husband.'

'I agree,' said Porter, 'but what else, come on, what else was she?' Connett shrugged his shoulders. 'So, she's just lost her husband, yes? So how come she's immaculately dressed, not a hair out of place, perfect makeup, and, apart from being pissed off that we insisted on talking to her, she's completely composed? How about not a sign of having cried since finding out that her husband had had his head cut off? Not a trace of grief?' he demanded.

Connett shuffled in his seat, *no*, he had to admit to himself, *he hadn't noticed any of that.*

'Perhaps she was just in shock?' he offered. 'People grieve in different ways.' Porter smiled; he could allow for that.

'Okay,' he said, 'let's just leave it at that, shall we. Just think about this, how many times have you had to break the news to someone their loved one has just met a tragic end? How did they react?' Connett shifted again, he was recalling the composure, no, the coldness of the woman they had just interviewed.

'If what you found out is true, if Harrington-Smythe was planning to get rid, as he has done with his previous wives, then Lady Harrington-Smythe the fourth has a reasonable motive for doing him in, possibly with the involvement of this Crawford character.'

Porter shook his head, he knew stuff about Trisha, stuff he didn't want people to gossip about back at the station. She wasn't a saint, but somehow, he couldn't believe that she was capable of murder. He wouldn't be surprised if there was something going on between her and Dale Walsh. He made a mental note to investigate his hunch.

'Maybe I'm not being fair, there's a lot about Lady Harrington-Smythe that you don't know.' Connett turned expectantly. Porter didn't elaborate; some things needed to remain private.

12

Ellie wasn't sure if Mr. Richardson's suggestion, that he see both her and her mother at the same time, was ethical. In any case, she didn't have the strength to argue. She sat opposite him in his dark, sombre office waiting for him to finish scanning Ruth's Will. Ellie's only recollection of having anything to do with the strange looking man was at the police station, when Alan Cooper had ended up stabbing himself. It was not an incident that she particularly wanted to remember.

Richardson placed the first page on his desk as Ellie wondered why it was necessary for him to study the documents in such detail. Surely, he was well acquainted with what it said, he had drawn the damn thing up… she sighed as she looked around the office. It was even more depressing than that of her ex-business partner, John Prothero, the thought made her shiver. The only light was from a desk lamp, under which Richardson was turning each piece of paper this way and that. He seemed to be stalling for time.

Ellie glanced to her left. Her mother sat bolt upright on the edge of her seat, her feet together. She was clutching her handbag which rested on her knees. She stared unblinking at the elderly solicitor. Ellie could only describe the energy surrounding her as 'eager anticipation'. The thought of it made her feel slightly queasy.

...she can't wait to find out what she's inherited, Ellie thought, she was sure she heard a giggle.

'Well, it's all very straightforward,' Mr. Richardson said at last. He cleared his throat as he launched into an official introduction. 'Ladies,' he glanced at each of them in turn, 'we are here today to read the Last Will and Testament of Ruth Hilary Prothero, nee Clifford...' Ellie sighed as he droned on. She wondered if he'd ever belonged to a Dramatic Society, such was the performance he was delivering. She was finding it difficult to concentrate on what he was saying.

'It starts thus... 'I, Ruth Hilary Prothero, nee Clifford...being of sound...' Ellie shuddered, she would give anything to turn back the clock, to have had the ability to stop this terrible thing from happening...she fought to overcome the rush of emotion that was threatening to engulf her. It was a few minutes before she realised that Mr. Richardson had stopped talking and was watching her intently. She swallowed hard and nodded towards him. He looked down at the sheet of paper in his hand.

'...shall we dispense with the rest of the preamble,' he said, 'and skip to the bequests?' Ellie nodded; she noticed a shift in her mother's posture as she leaned forward. 'Firstly then, the minor bequests, Mrs. Morrison...Mrs. Prothero's Will asks that you *'choose any painting from the collection at the cottage, known as'...'* he stopped speaking as Julia jumped to her feet.

'Painting, but...' she started.

'Please Mrs. Morrison, I haven't finished,' he said. Julia sat down again. Ellie sighed; this was going to be awkward. If her mother started to play up...she heard Mr. Richardson clear his throat and start again. "*...In addition to this...'*, it goes on, '*I would like my mother to have* *the vase that she gave to me on my wedding day.'* That brings this section of Mrs. Prothero's will to an end.'

Julia gave what Ellie could only describe as a shriek. She stood up and paced around the room, shouting, swearing. She leaned over the desk, her hands gripping the edge. If Ellie hadn't been so ashamed of her mother's behaviour, she would have laughed at the look on Richardson's face. As it was, something inside her snapped.

'Sit down Mom, for heaven's sake…' she hissed. Her mother spun round; a look of hatred distorting her features before she could mask it. Julia took a deep breath fighting to bring her temper under control. She smoothed down her skirt, and resumed her seat. Mr. Richardson gathered his papers, shuffling them straight as he looked at her in undisguised horror.

'Any more of that kind of behaviour,' he said gravely, 'and I will have to ask you to leave.'

'I'm sorry, Mr. Richardson,' Ellie began, shooting a warning look at her mother who appeared to be working up to her next outburst. 'I can assure you that it won't happen again.' Richardson cleared his throat and resumed.

"*…the remainder of my estate, herein detailed, I leave to my sister Elenore Rosemary Shaw, nee Clifford, with my deepest love…'* Richardson cleared his throat again, frowning at Julia before he continued. 'Would you like me to read you a list of the items that your sister left you, or would you like to take it away and study it in private?' he asked. Julia stared at her daughter, open-mouthed; Ellie could see her expression out of the corner of her eye. Julia was almost at the point of exploding as she squirmed in her chair.

...take the list and study it later, that'll really piss her off...! Ellie bit the inside of her cheek. Not for the first time the realisation that Ruth was still causing mischief crossed Ellie's mind, and she didn't know whether to laugh or cry.

'Thank you Mr. Richardson,' Ellie said desperately trying to control her emotions as she saw her mother battling to do the same, 'I think I would like to take the documents with me and read them in private if that's all right with you.'

Richardson nodded, he would be glad to get this meeting over and done with. He couldn't stand people who were unable to control their emotions. Good manners cost nothing, and he wasn't going to have anything more to do with Julia Morrison, not if he could help it. He shuffled the pages of the document back together and placed it inside the folder, which he handed to Ellie. Who would have thought that they were related in any way? This fine young woman had conducted herself in a way that would make him think twice about judging foreigners before getting to know them. She'd been through a lot lately, and still managed to behave herself. Ellie stood up and shook his hand, thanking him for his patience. She got as far as the door before she felt a tug at her sleeve, pulling her around.

'Well?' her mother demanded, 'aren't you going to tell me...'. Ellie held up her hand, cutting Julia short.

'I don't know what's in Ruth's Will,' she said, her voice low and controlled, 'whatever it is, it won't make up for the fact that she isn't here anymore.'

Julia swallowed hard, trying to find the right words to get the result she craved.

'I only wanted...' she stammered.

'I know what you wanted Mom,' Ellie managed, her control threatening to break at any moment, 'but you have to admit that whatever Ruth decided to do with her things has very little to do with you, does it?' Julia looked as though Ellie had slapped her.

'No, but…' Julia tried again.

'*When* I've read Ruth's Will I'll be in touch, *if* I decide that there's anything in there that you need to be informed about, is that clear?' Ellie could hear herself but wasn't sure how she had the nerve to say what she had. Julia took her hand off her daughter's arm and stepped back. Ellie had never seen her mother look so pathetic. She tried to soften her next words.

'Get some rest Mom you look tired. I'll phone you later.' She watched as her Mother took a deep breath and gathered herself up.

'*If* you have the time, that is,' she answered, then spun on her heel and walked away.

Ellie shook her head; it was what she'd expected.

…some things never change, do they…? Ellie had to agree

13

Porter was impressed, as he was whenever he reviewed one of Mason's boards. Her capacity to deal with paperwork and the minutiae of an investigation was breath-taking. He felt secure in the knowledge that, having all but taken over the responsibility of this part of the enquiry process, she wouldn't allow a repeat of the chaos that had existed when DCI Horton had been in charge. Not a thing got past Mason, and Porter was thankful that he had no ego to appease on that score. She could pull the most obscure details together, things that on the surface seemed unimportant, and her ability to think outside the box made her a vital member of the team.

Up until this morning, he couldn't have said as much about Connett, however much he wanted to find something he could relate to. After working alongside Horton for several years, Porter had been worried that some of his former boss's habits had rubbed off on him. It wasn't until recently that he was beginning to realise that he might have misjudged him. A slew of documents lay on Porter's desk, amongst them a detailed timeline of events. Connett had also arranged and carried out several preliminary interviews, the results of which were all typed up neatly, with additional comments. He picked up the first page, it made interesting reading, just a couple of things that needed clarifying. He opened the door to his office and looked around. Connett was nowhere to be seen.

'Mason, he asked, 'have you seen Dai?' Mason shook her head, a pencil held in her mouth made answering difficult. 'Send him in when he gets back, will you?'

Porter went to close the door, then turned back to Mason. 'By the way,' he said, 'well done on the boards, good job.'

Mason blushed, she tried to reply, the pencil still between her teeth, instead she nodded and looked back at the pile of papers she was holding. Porter sat at his desk and selected the first of Connett's interview reports.

Emica Webley, also known as 'Emica Wong'
Occupation: Masseuse
Connection to victim: regular weekly visits to conduct 'Massages'.Last appointment was the day of his death.
Timeline:
10.00: Ms. Webley arrived at Harrington Hall. She was escorted to the Bathhouse and instructed to wait in a small ante room.
15.45: (approx...) Lord Harrington-Smythe phoned the Main House and gave instructions that Ms. Webley should be taken back there and that his personal Doctor was to be called to attend to her. No explanation for this was given.
16.00: Member of staff, Nigel Reynolds, collected Ms. Webley and escorted her back to the Main House to a room in the servant's quarters. She remained in the room attended by a female member of staff.
17.15: Doctor Beale arrived at the Hall to attend Ms. Webley.
17.55: After she had been treated for several minor abrasions, none of which Doctor Beale considered necessitated hospitalisation, Ms. Webley was sent home by taxi, where she

stayed for the rest of the day, as corroborated by her mother and sister.

Comments: Ms. Webley described the victim's mood as quiet, but tense, he wasn't in the best of tempers. He wasn't particularly communicative, but that wasn't unusual during their 'interactions.'

Porter turned to the girl's statement. He shook his head as he read her account of the afternoon's events. It painted a picture of Harrington-Smythe not only a violent bully, but as a border-line sadistic pervert. The fact that Ms. Webley had endured his attentions for so long without reporting him, mystified Porter.

…maybe she was afraid to lose such a lucrative client, Porter thought, cynically. He berated himself for jumping to such an unsympathetic conclusion. The pictures attached to Emica's statement told their own story. Harrington-Smythe was anything but a gentleman if this was the kind of cruelty he could inflict on a young woman. He shuffled the pictures back into the folder. So far, he was more than impressed with Connett's newly displayed efficiency.

He leafed through the remaining sheets of paper and found a further note from Connett. Ms. Webley had made an official complaint relating to the victim, in which she described his treatment of her during the time she was engaged by him. When asked why she had waited until she had learned of his death to make the complaint, she stated that she had been too afraid to say anything as he had made threats in the past regarding her and her family.

…so, that explains it. Porter picked up the next statement, pausing to look up as Connett knocked on his door and entered the office. He carried a tray with two cups of coffee. Porter wondered how he'd anticipated his

need for a drink, then realised that the second cup was probably intended for Mason.

'Sit down, Dai,' he instructed, 'well done on the interviews, you've been busy.' Connett adjusted his tie and cleared his throat. He muttered something that Porter didn't catch. 'Just like to ask, have you got any other thoughts about Miss Webley?'

Connett shook his head.

'Nothing I haven't already put down,' he said, 'her statement is attached, those are just my own notes,' Porter detected a hint of pride, he was obviously confident that he'd covered everything.

'I was wondering about her name,' Porter asked, 'was she Ms. Webley or Ms. Wong?'

'Her name's Webley, apparently she used her mother's maiden name when she realised that Harrington-Smythe was obsessed with anything Japanese, thought it would give her the edge when it came to securing the job,' Connett explained.

'Talk me through the rest, will you?' Connett looked confused as Porter handed over the files. 'It's all there, boss,' he managed, slightly offended that Porter might be suggesting that he'd missed something.

'Indulge me.' Ported answered, his hands formed a steeple as he leaned back in his chair, 'something might occur to you, something that seems unimportant, it happens to me all the time.' Connett sighed, he wasn't sure what this was all about, his notes were thorough and comprehensive, was Porter trying to trick him? He opened the next file and cleared his throat.

'Nigel Reynolds, Butler and general factotum,' he read, Porter interrupted him before he could continue.

'What did you think of him?' he asked. Connett thought for a minute before screwing his face up. He hadn't been impressed by Reynolds, he'd seemed loyal enough, but there was something underlying, a kind of contempt for his employer. He told Porter as much, then carried on reading from his notes.

'At approximately three forty-five, Reynolds received a phone call from the victim instructing him to collect Ms. Webley and take her back to the main house. He told him to call His Lordship's Doctor, a Doctor Beale, if he considered it necessary. Reynolds said he called the Doctor, as Ms. Webley was obviously distressed. He wasn't present when she was examined, and therefore couldn't make any comments on any injuries she may have sustained. He told me that this was not the first time that such an incident had occurred.' Connett looked up from the file, Porter had his eyes closed and was still. For a moment Connett thought he was asleep.

'Go on,' Porter said, Connett read on.

'At approximately four thirty Reynolds was in the kitchen preparing an afternoon tea tray for His Lordship. The housekeeper, a Mrs. Blackburn, passed on a message that His Lordship wasn't to be disturbed under any circumstances for the remainder of the evening. Apparently, his Lordship had… *'made his own arrangements'*… Reynolds wasn't quite sure what he meant by that but knew better than to go against his instructions.' Connett paused, he took a quick drink of his coffee, then started again. 'Reynolds went into His Lordship's bedroom the following morning at seven-thirty and wasn't surprised to find that there was no one there. He prepared a morning tea tray and carried it to the Bathhouse. It was at this point that he discovered the body and phoned the emergency services.'

‘So,’ Porter said, ‘His Lordship intended to spend the night in the Bathhouse.’ He shook his head, he couldn’t understand why Harrington-Smythe would want to sleep on a narrow couch, in an unfinished building, when he had a luxurious bedroom just a few steps away. Sometimes the ways of the wealthy just couldn’t be explained. Connett picked up the next folder.

‘Lady Harrington-Smythe,’ he started. ‘Lady of the Manor.’ Connett took a quick glance at Porter, he blushed slightly, he had meant to alter that. Connett had taken a further statement from her, during which he discovered the way she seemed to treat most of the people she encountered. His previous sympathy for the woman had transmuted into a complete dislike for her. To his relief, he saw Porter smile, and carried on reading.

‘…wife of the deceased, although if statements from some members of the Harrington Hall staff are to be believed, not for much longer. Her Ladyship kept to her rooms for almost the entire day. Some of the staff reported that she and her husband had had a heated argument earlier that morning. Her maid, a Ms. Fletcher, said she spent almost the whole day in bed with the curtains drawn. She got up and took a bath around three-thirty. Ms. Fletcher helped her to dress, Reynolds picked her up just before five o’clock, due to her regular driver, Crawford taking some time off. She arrived at the home of her friend, the Right Hon. Cecily Fordyce, around twenty-five minutes later. They had afternoon tea together, then spent some time chatting, until around six, when she was invited to dinner and ended up staying the night. She was informed of her husband’s death the following day when she arrived back home just after lunch. She was driven home by the Fordyce chauffeur...’

He scanned the page, as Porter shifted in his chair. '...we're still trying to locate Gerald Crawford's whereabouts.' Connett paused again, took another sip of coffee, then continued. Porter's lack of input was unnerving him. His previous boss, DCI Horton had never kept this quiet when being fed information about a case.

'Lady Harrington-Smythe denies that she and her husband were about to part company. She admits that they were going through a difficult period, but that they were 'working it out'. This was contradicted by statements given by other members of staff, and by Lord Harrington-Smythe's solicitor, who confirmed that the victim had already sent his wife a letter stating his intention to file for divorce. This letter arrived on the morning of his murder and was sent Recorded Delivery and placed in Lady Harrington-Smythe's hands by Ms. Fletcher.'

'So, potentially we've already got several people who didn't get on with Harrington-Smythe, hardly grounds for murdering him, though,' Porter said at last. 'This chauffeur, Crawford, anything more on him? He booked a couple of day's leave, didn't he? Anyone seen him since the murder?'

Connett shook his head. 'No, he was due back the day after Harrington-Smythe was killed, but he didn't turn up. We're still trying to access the employee records, boss. That Walsh guy told me I could pick them up in a couple of days. Something tells me he's not keen to hand them over.' Porter slapped the table as he stood up.

'I want them this afternoon,' he said, 'we don't have time for niceties, they'll be asking for a warrant next.' He sighed, thinking about the relative lack of activity up until the phone call from the Harrington-Smythe Estate. …*be careful what you wish for,* he thought.

'Anything else that struck you, anything out of place, something that's niggling at the back of your mind?' he asked. Connett shook his head, biting his lip.

'There was something,' he said, 'a chess set in the Bathhouse, the pieces looked old, Japanese. A lot of them had been knocked over. Forensics said they couldn't find the Black Knight. I don't know if that's significant?'

'A trophy, maybe?' Porter suggested, Connett nodded, he was beginning to relax. He hoped that the reputation he had acquired, that of being Horton's lackey was beginning to recede, Porter was certainly proving easier to work with. He gathered up the files and walked towards the door. Porter called after him.

'Give Forensics a call, will you, never know we might be lucky…' he said.

'Rang them this morning,' Connett replied, 'nothing yet, you know what it's like, takes ages. We still have quite a few people to interview formally, and there are a few leads I'd like to follow up, if that's ok?' Porter nodded, reaching for another file. Connett felt short-changed, he hoped he'd made a good impression, but wasn't sure…*quit while you're ahead*…he thought.

'Then of course, there's the matter of the CCTV of the grounds. The ones by the lake hadn't been connected to the system, the others show no signs of anyone crossing from the house to the murder scene, also no one leaving after the estimated time of death.' Porter grunted. Connett had lost his attention. 'I've made an appointment with the Head of Security to find out if all the cameras were working,' he went on, 'but there's always the possibility that whoever killed His Lordship could have entered via the underground passage that leads from the hall at the main house…'

Porter stopped reading; his head shot up.

'Underground passage?' Porter snapped, 'why the hell has no-one mentioned this before, exactly when were you going to tell me?'

Connett wished he'd kept quiet.

14

You can't keep doing this, Ruth…' Ellie had walked for miles, trying to get Ruth to answer her. The further she got away from the Retreat, the more uneasy she felt. 'If there's anything else I should know…' she begged, 'please tell me. You could have saved me a lot of…' she shook her head. Her conversations with Ruth were usually fluid, more like thoughts than speaking out loud.

*…sweetie, this is the kind of thing that people deal with every day…*Ruth said at last.

'Don't you dare, Ruth, don't you dare,' Ellie shouted, her voice carried away by the wind. She could feel the anger welling up inside her, all she'd wanted to do was scream.

…I'm sorry, sweetie, I didn't think…

'That's just it, Ruth you didn't think, you never did, did you?' Ellie snapped.

…all I wanted was to…

'I know what you wanted, Ruth, you wanted to score one over on Mom, to see her face as she got played like she played you…us…' she sobbed, 'you wanted her to suffer…it's not like you Ruth, it's…unworthy.' Ellie stopped walking and sat down on a tree stump; her legs felt like jelly. She knew that her words had met their mark.

*...I'm sorry, sweetie...*Ruth said softly*...I promise...*

'Don't make promises you can't keep, Ruth,' Ellie whispered, 'be straight with me from now on, or...' she started to cry again. What could she threaten her sister with? Nothing that was as bad as what had already happened to her. Ellie's body shook inside her over-large coat.

'Don't play any more games with me Ruth, I don't know how much more I can take...' she pleaded, 'I'm all for standing strong against Mom, but please, give me some kind of warning, include me in any plans you have for her.'

*...no more shocks, Ellie...I promise...*Ellie sniffed, took a deep breath, and stood up. She was ready to go back now, now that she had got that out of her system. She smiled...

'Coming?' she asked...she shook her head as she heard Ruth giggle...some things would never change

.

...ooOoo...

It hadn't taken long for Graham to realise that his mother-in-law had lied through her teeth to get him to meet with her. For almost a week she had bombarded him with texts and phone calls, none of which he'd returned. He had enough to deal with, without getting caught up in her games. Julia had even taken a taxi to the farmhouse, banging on the door shouting '*...I know you're in there...*' to his shame, Graham had hidden upstairs until he was sure she'd left.

Eventually he gave in and agreed to meet her. He didn't like the woman, he never had, and it was obvious from the start that the feeling was mutual. He had long ago formed the opinion that the way in which Julia had treated both Ellie and Ruth as they were growing up, was nothing short of psychological abuse. He'd always believed that Ellie's chronic lack of self-belief had originated from her relationship with her mother, nothing she'd said so far had changed that view. As their meeting wore on, he suspected that Julia's *'urgent need to meet and discuss the situation',* boiled down to her uncontrollable urge to meddle in things that didn't concern her. Her sole aim, she had already stressed several times, was to see her only surviving daughter settled and happy. After all, how could she return to the States knowing that Ellie was miserable?

Graham listened as she explained how seeing them back together, becoming parents at last would bring her great contentment. Surely, he could see the importance of them reconciling, especially since there more factors to consider now that Ellie was, well…in the position she had found herself in. Graham wasn't sure what she meant. His imagination went into overdrive, he swallowed hard.

'What exactly are you trying to say, Julia?' he asked, his mind doing rapid calculations. Was she suggesting… 'are you…are you saying…is Ellie pregnant?' he managed. It was a shot in the dark, and he knew it, but still. Julia shrugged, she had an annoying habit of leaving a subject hanging, not answering directly, it had the desired effect.

'That's impossible, Julia, and you know it, Ellie and I haven't lived together for…' he stopped suddenly, his stomach clenched. If Ellie was expecting…was it even his? The thought that Ellie might have…he felt sick…she wouldn't…would she? He remembered everything she'd said…about moving on. Another thought wormed its way back into his mind, he'd managed to subdue it since that night at the Retreat. He took a deep breath. He could almost see John Prothero standing before him, taunting him…what was it he said…something about them having a lot of fun together before he arrived on the scene…what did that mean? What if John had…he swallowed hard. He felt dizzy, nauseous. Ellie, his Ellie…what if that was the reason she was so reluctant to come back. The prospect seemed to tip him over the edge. He sat forward, grabbing Julia's wrist, making her jump.

'What the…let me go…' she hissed, twisting her arm away in an overly dramatic way.

'So help me Julia, if this is one of your games…' Graham whispered, as she managed to free herself. He was conscious of the interest they were causing, and of the field day the press would have if they found out.

'You could do worse than ask her yourself,' Julia snapped, grimacing as she looked at the faint red marks. She rubbed them theatrically. Graham sighed; Julia knew nothing about what happened that night…unless of course Ellie had confided in her. Somehow, he doubted it. He tried to focus on what Julia was saying.

'Anyway, that's not the *only* reason I asked to meet with you,' Graham noticed the emphasis in her words. So, there might be something in his suspicions after all. He swallowed at the enormity of the implications.

'…and of course, it doesn't take a genius to work out that Ruth may well have been coerced into leaving her entire estate to…' she shrugged again, a gesture which she no doubt believed was an elegant one, designed to encourage her audience to fill in the missing words. To Graham it just looked contrived.

…After all, he thought, *if she made no actual accusations, she couldn't be accused of causing any trouble, could she?* She was

clever, he would give her that, but not so clever that he couldn't see what she was getting at. So that was what lay behind the urgency of their meeting, Ruth's Will. Pity he didn't have a clue what she was talking about. He settled back into his chair, she might not know how little he knew, but he was damned if he was going to give her the satisfaction of confessing his ignorance.

'So, you know then?' he said, enjoying the crestfallen look that settled on her overly made up face. She swallowed hard, her lips pursed, like a spoilt child deprived of her sweets. She picked up her napkin and flourished it into the air before laying in on her lap.

'I don't know what you're talking about, Graham,' she said, reaching over to select a sandwich, her movements betraying her uncertainty. She shook her head as she placed the food on her plate, her annoyance evident. She thought she would be the one to break the news of Ellie's inheritance. The prospect that someone might have beaten her to it irritated her. Graham was almost enjoying himself, mainly thanks to her discomfort. The possibility that Ellie might be pregnant, and that the child might be his was cause enough, annoying his odious mother-in-law was just icing on the cake.

'I wonder why she's acting like this,' he said, a perfect picture of innocence, 'after all, you would have thought Ruth would have…' he paused, imitating his companion, shrugging his shoulders in a perfect parody of her own movements.

'You would have, wouldn't you?' Julia had taken the bait he'd so carefully dangled. 'After all, I am her mother,' she corrected herself, 'I…I was her mother.' She looked down at her hands, now holding her napkin, twisting it tightly. Graham kept silent, he didn't know how long he could keep it up, but he was determined that she would speak before he did.

'...and then to find, to find that she hadn't even...that she'd left it all to...I mean, what's Ellie going to do with it all, that's what I want to know? There must be at least...' her voice faded as she saw the look of shock on Graham's face. The realisation that he hadn't known after all, finally hit her.

So, Ellie had inherited Ruth's estate, whatever that consisted of. Graham sighed, moments before he'd imagined them being reconciled, maybe at first for the sake of the baby if there was one. They could work things out, he would make sure that she and his child never wanted for anything. Now he had been told that she had money. He knew he was coming from an entirely selfish standpoint, and a sexist one at that, but the thought of them getting back together was one that had kept him going for the last few months. Now she might not need him at all.

...oo0oo...

Their meeting wasn't going as well as Julia had planned it. She had rehearsed every line prior to sitting down with the idiot she'd been forced to acknowledge as her son-in-law for the past ten years or more. Now he was off on some flight of fancy. That hint about a child, that was clumsy, especially as she knew full well that Ellie wasn't pregnant. It was obvious that she'd lost him, his focus was elsewhere. How could she hope to gain him as an ally if he wasn't even...?

Graham was fidgeting with his coffee cup, turning it round and round in the saucer. Julia had a sudden urge to slap his hand to make him stop. She had asked him here for a reason, to find out how likely he was to speak up on her behalf. Damn Ruth, why the hell had she left everything to Ellie? As her mother, Julia felt that she was entitled to at least something.

She'd been busy over the last few days taking stock of her finances. If she was careful, she had just about enough money to last her for another few weeks in this God-forsaken place. If she was successful in her bid to acquire a decent amount from Ruth's estate, she could go back to the States and pay off her debts, start living the life she'd grown used to with her third husband before his untimely death. Who would have guessed, from his expansive behaviour, that he was up to his neck in debt? All she needed was to convince Ellie that she should do her duty and share her good fortune; she would be safe, at least for a little while. She could always come back for more, after all.

'Julia, I hope you don't think this is rude of me…I'm leaving,' Graham screwed up his napkin and threw it onto the table, covering what remained of the food. He got up and pulled on his coat. 'I don't know anything about this so-called inheritance of Ellie's. I just hope she'll tell me herself when she's ready. In the meantime, have a great life and I hope you get what you want, but I won't be joining you in your sordid little games. Personally, I think Ellie would be mad to give you anything at all.' He took out his wallet, withdrew two twenty-pound notes and threw them down on the table.

Julia stared at him as he turned and left. He didn't look back as he walked out into the chilly afternoon, leaving her open-mouthed. She was frustrated that he'd guessed what she was after, money, property, something, anything from Ruth's estate. The waitress approached carrying an empty tray, Julia shot her a look that halted her in her tracks. She turned around and walked back to the counter, leaving Julia sitting bolt upright, her mind reeling as she replayed the last few minutes. She had to contact Ellie, she had to try to get through to her daughter, without letting her know how desperate her situation was. She sat still, seething at Graham's words.

...*Graham's words*...she thought, '...*I think Ellie would be mad to give you anything at all*' he'd said. Mad, mad, it would be pointless trying to prove that Ellie was mentally incapable, but what if she could prove that Ruth wasn't in her right mind when she made her will? What if she could prove that her youngest daughter had been incapable of making those kinds of decisions, that she'd been coerced into leaving everything to Ellie.

...*after all,* she thought smiling to herself as she took a bite of her sandwich... *it's worth a try.*

...oo0oo...

Graham walked away from the restaurant as quickly as he could. He'd rarely met anyone as avaricious as his mother-in-law. Her interest in Ruth's money bordered on the obscene, her attempts to draw him into her plot to gain some of it, sickened him.

...*for God's sake*...he thought as he approached the car park...*her daughter and grandson just died, and all she can think about*...he shook his head, trying to clear his growing anger. He needed to speak to Ellie, now wasn't the time to hold back. He was minutes from her office, why not now?

...*she's not pregnant*...he kept telling himself...*how could she be?* They hadn't lived together for so long...*unless*...an image of John Prothero flooded Graham's mind, he could see him looming over Ellie's frail body. He shivered; nausea rose in his throat. He needed to find out if there was any truth in Julia's suggestions. Before long he was in the High Street, heading towards Ellie's office. His heart thundered in his chest; not since the incident at the Retreat had he felt so nervous. She might see him, or she might ask him never to contact her again, either way he would know where he stood. Miss Pritchard stared at him in surprise as he entered. She stood to greet him.

'Mr. Shaw, how are you? It's been a long time,' she managed, shaking his hand, indicating the chair behind him. With everything that had gone on, she wasn't quite sure how to deal with his unexpected arrival. Graham shook his head. He wanted to get this over with as soon as possible.

'Is Ellie…is my wife in?' he asked. He was afraid that if he had to come back his courage would desert him.

'She's busy just now,' Miss Pritchard said. She could see that Graham was agitated; her heart went out to him. She needed to buy enough time to warn Ellie. 'Let me see when she'll he free,' she offered. He sat down, knowing that this was the best he could expect. Miss Pritchard knocked quietly and disappeared into Ellie's office. Within minutes she was back, Graham hadn't realised that he was holding his breath.

'She'll be finished soon; she's asked if you could wait in the other office?' Miss Pritchard said, indicating the heavy oak door at the opposite end of the room. She was improvising, Ellie had said no such thing; it took a couple of seconds before she realised what she'd said. The look on Graham's face was almost painful to see.

…John's office…? Graham shuddered. He hadn't considered how he would feel being back here, now memories overwhelmed him. Why had Ellie suggested that he wait in there, hell, what was she thinking, still

using this place after everything that had happened? She obviously had her own reasons; he'd probably never know. ...*too much*...he thought, shaking his head. Miss Pritchard waited unsure of what to do next.

'I'd rather not, if you don't mind,' he whispered, Miss Pritchard nodded, her ability to *ab lib* was limited.

'I was just about to make a drink,' she said, desperate to diffuse the tension, 'why don't I let you do that, and I can get on with my work?' Graham felt relieved. He could keep himself occupied, do something useful, anything other than wait for Ellie's door to open, or go into John's office. He thought back to his meeting with Julia, how much of what she'd said could he believe?

He didn't have a clue what he was going to say to Ellie. He knew that Miss Pritchard wasn't interested in him making drinks. She'd provided him with a bolthole, that was all. He leaned against the table, trying to calm himself, to place his thoughts in order. He didn't hear the door open, or Ellie walk in.

...oo0oo...

One thing that Graham was sure of after all these years, and that was when his wife was angry. Not only because she went a deathly shade of grey, but also it happened so infrequently as to be noteworthy...and she was angry... truly angry.

The atmosphere was stilted as they sat in her office, exchanging a few awkward pleasantries. He told her about his meeting with her mother that morning. What he really wanted to ask was whether she was carrying his child. Having opened with the subject of Ruth's will, and seen Ellie's reaction, he wondered if that was such a good idea. Ellie stood up and walked around her office, shaking her head. He watched as she turned around, would she be showing any signs by now? He could see that she was as slender now as he remembered her, more so. She'd lost weight during the last few months, he felt concerned over just how much.

'I knew that Mom was angling for some of Ruth's money, well, my money now,' she fumed, 'I didn't think she'd try to enlist your help to try to get it.' Ellie paced up and down the length of her office, she knew how devious her mother could be, but this…Graham kept quiet as she talked her feelings out, eventually collapsing onto her chair.

'Ellie,' he started, 'I, I think she might try something, she seems desperate.'

'My mother is always desperate when it comes to money,' Ellie sighed, 'she has champagne tastes, without the bank account to go with it.'

Graham thought back to the stories Ellie had told him about her childhood. It hadn't all been bad; there were periods when her mother had tried hard to make their homelife happy. But then there was her insatiable need for money. Three husbands, all wealthy, all unsuspecting that the attractive, vibrant woman they had become involved with was there only because of the lifestyle they could offer her. One divorce, one suicide and one fatal heart attack later, Julia was broke, and thought no one knew.

'I'm going to offer her something,' Ellie said, sharing a confidence that she never would have believed she would with her estranged husband. 'It's just that she wants everything now, she can't wait. Besides, there's legal stuff, you know, making sure that whatever Ruth left wasn't obtained illegally.' She sighed again, then looked at Graham, who was studying her intently.

'She did say something else, Ellie,' he said quietly, 'she hinted that you might be…' he hesitated, it was now or never, '…that you might be pregnant.' He heard Ellie gasp.

'Is that why you've come, Graham?' Ellie's voice was almost a whisper, she shook her head, disbelief etched on her face. Despite her calm exterior, Graham flinched as though she'd hit him.

'Ellie, I…' he tried to speak, she stood up suddenly, pointing to the door.

'Get out Graham,' she hissed, 'there was I thinking you'd come here to warn me of my devious mother, all you wanted to do was to check me out, find out if I was…get out,' she screamed. He knew that there was no point in arguing with Ellie. She wouldn't have heard him. He stood up, looked at her for the briefest moment, then turned to leave.

…oo0oo…

Julia had spent the rest of the afternoon trying to work out how she could challenge Ruth's mental state just before she died. Now that she had alienated both Ellie and Graham, she had to come up with an alternative plan to get her hands on some of the money. The hotel room was stuffy, no air conditioning, not even a fan. She opened the window and breathed in some fresh air to clear her head. She needed to find out if Ruth was seeing a therapist of some description, maybe a counsellor, then develop a case for her Will to be looked at again. Julia knew that Ruth had had problems during her marriage to John Prothero, and God knows she wouldn't have been surprised if she hadn't been able to cope. She was a delicate child, after all.

...Yes, that's good, I could make a case that Ellie coerced Ruth into drawing up...

She walked to the bedroom door, then back again, turning over possible scenarios in her mind. What about the Mathers women, maybe they had some kind of hold over Ellie? It was Ruth that introduced Odelia to Ellie, she had told her as much. What if Ruth had been persuaded by them to leave her estate to Ellie...yes, that was possible. Then they could work on Ellie and gain control over it themselves. Julia smiled, any one of a number of scenarios sounded plausible. She picked up the phone and dialled a number in the States.

...this isn't the end, Ellie, she smiled, *not by a long way.*

15

Anthea Harrold was almost asleep as the car pulled into the drive. It had been a long week and she was looking forward to slipping into a hot bath. The thought of getting back home, of relaxing with a nice glass of Merlot, was all that had kept her going during the interminably long hours of filming for her latest television series. Not that she didn't enjoy it. It was just that each episode demanded at least two or even three days of studio time. Then there was make-up, recording close-ups, voice-overs, learning dialogue…the list was endless. All to demonstrate to the public how simple it was to prepare delicious meals in the shortest possible time.

Being a celebrity chef wasn't all it was cracked up to be. Her fans had never appreciated how hard she had to work. Still, at least she didn't have to do all the prep work nowadays. Most of that was handled by a gang of lackeys secreted behind the backdrops in the faux kitchen they'd created for her programme.

She laughed when she thought of the millions of fans who still believed that the set was her actual kitchen. The French windows at the back of the stage let out onto nothing more exciting than the props and equipment area. Quite frankly, she didn't care, so long as the network kept paying her the inordinate amount of money her agent had managed to negotiate. She was more than willing to leave her home in Wrexham and travel to Cardiff for a couple of weeks at a time. The knock-on effect of a new series was that sales of her books would take a huge leap throughout the broadcast period, and for some months afterwards.

...it's amazing how many times you can recycle the same old recipes just by tweaking them and adding different photographs... she thought, yawning as she prepared to get out of the car. It was raining. She sat resolutely as the driver ran to the front door to unlock it. He switched on the hall light, then made his way around the back of the vehicle to open her door.

'I hope you don't think I'm getting out in this!' she hissed. He paused; it took him a few seconds to realise what she meant. He fetched an umbrella from the boot, then held it out to her. She looked at him in disgust and waited. The driver opened it, holding it up to cover her. Anthea stepped out, clutching her bag tightly at her side. The driver stumbled, the umbrella slipped, rain battered down on her head. She shrieked with annoyance as she grabbed it and ran towards the house, leaving him behind to deal with the car.

...that's it, she thought, *I need to stop dealing with these jokers...first thing tomorrow...*

Inside, the hall was cold. She called out, no answer. Larry must be out somewhere with his cronies; she knew from experience that he'd be gone all night. If he didn't start towing the line, she'd carry out her threat to cut off his allowance. How the hell had she allowed herself to be blinded by his good looks and his sweet-talking manners? What else did he have going for him...a bronze medal in some obscure Winter Olympics years ago. So, the guy was good at skiing and shooting a crossbow, was that enough to hold them together?

What little patience she had, had evaporated completely. She looked out of the hall window; she could see the lights of the car receding in the dark. Where were all her staff? She was tired and hungry, and there was no one about. She locked the front door and fastened the bolts as she kicked off her shoes and threw her coat onto the back of a chair. The kitchen was deserted. Down lighters reflected off every surface, the place was spotless, nothing less than she demanded. There was food in the fridge, but after a week of dealing with fiddly menus, the last thing she wanted was to start cooking again.

Shit...she thought, *that's the last time*...she stopped, a noise from upstairs. She waited, holding her breath. Perhaps there was someone in, after all. She listened for a few seconds...nothing. She looked around the kitchen. There were no notes, no messages written on the huge blackboard that covered at least half of one of the walls. She grabbed a piece of chalk and wrote on it in huge letters...

...new driver crap...get rid!!!...

She turned and threw the chalk across the room shaking her head. She hadn't met the idiot in question before tonight. Tammy would have to deal him after his inept performance. She wanted Paulson back, he knew exactly how to behave. She sighed; nothing she could do about it now, but in the morning, she'd make sure that this would never happen again. That was what she paid her staff for, to meet her needs, to ensure her comfort.

She snatched open the fridge door, grabbed a few crackers and sliced some Stilton. A glass of...she heard the noise again. There *was* someone here, she was sure now. She pulled out a meat tenderizer from the top drawer and headed towards the stairs, stopping only to pull her phone out of her bag. The thought of coming face to face with an intruder, that she could be in danger...

*...hell, no battery...*she remembered that she'd meant to charge the thing up during her return journey, but it had slipped her mind. She picked up the handset to use the landline, it was dead. That was all she needed. Her heart lurched as she heard a thud, thud, thud coming down the stairs. She laughed with relief as her cat ran across the hall floor towards her. It wound itself around her legs as she bent down to pick it up.

'Monty, what on earth are you doing inside, you know...' she stroked his long hair, at least someone was glad to see her. 'Come on I'll get you something to eat.' The cat nuzzled into her neck as Anthea bent down to fetch his food from his cupboard. She laughed, this stuff cost almost as much as her own. Maybe this was another area she could branch out into...pet foods. She'd get Tammy to put feelers out, her own range, or maybe she could endorse some other rubbish, could be worth a few grand.

She put the cat down and opened the tin, the smell made her heave as she emptied the contents into a bowl. Monty purred contentedly as she stood back and watched him eat. Her own snack stood on the counter; she placed it on a tray and carried it through to the lounge. The place was in darkness as she picked her way across to a side table and switched on a lamp. Light flooded the area, as she tried to make herself comfortable. The overlarge chair allowed her to curl up, her plate balanced on the arm. She slipped off her shoes and settled in.

...Tammy will have to do better than this, she thought as she cut the cheese into thin slivers and placed them evenly on the crackers. Now that it came to it, she didn't feel hungry. She took a swig of wine, swallowing it

greedily with none of the finesse she'd learned during her last holiday in France, she wasn't in the mood.

Anthea curled up, suddenly overcome with emotion. She had to admit it, she was lonely. What was the point of all this fame if every time she came home…? She stopped, there was the noise again. She slipped her shoes back on. If there was someone in the house, she wasn't about to stay there. She'd go to Paulson's quarters; he'd know what to do.

…*damn*…she thought, remembering that he'd texted her to say he was sick. She'd have to see if that new driver, what was his name…Crawford, was still in the garage. Her coat was wet, she pulled it over her shoulders, picked up her keys and headed towards the front door. Her nerves got the better of her, her hands fumbling slightly as she tried to the bolts. She was turning the key when she heard a mechanical noise. It was so familiar, but she couldn't quite place it. It was followed a split-second later by an excruciating pain in her back. She looked down and wondered why an arrowhead was poking out of the front of her chest. She watched as the red stain spread down her dress before her knees buckled and she fell to the floor.

…oo0oo…

Perfect, just as he'd imagined it. One more ticked off the list, the stupid woman hadn't even asked him for proof of identity when he picked her up from the studios. All he'd said was that he was covering for her regular driver, that his name was Crawford, and that Paulson must have let her know that he was…she cut him dead, she didn't want to know. She grunted as she climbed into the back of the Bentley. He didn't care either way, it suited him to have a taciturn client, fewer questions. It couldn't have gone any better. As soon as they reached the house and she'd gone inside, he drove the car into the garage.

Paulson was still out cold, trussed up in the corner, oblivious to the fact that his daily medication had been laced with a powerful sedative. Not that he wouldn't have finished him off if he'd needed to. Collateral damage was something that couldn't be avoided, but he didn't want to harm anyone unnecessarily. He wasn't a monster, after all. It was easy enough to gain access to Paulson's quarters, he'd visited Anthea Harrold's home several times posing as a delivery driver. He and Paulson had had several casual conversations, the weather, politics, their health. He soon discovered that Paulson took medication for an ulcer. Earlier that afternoon he'd delivered a parcel and asked to use the bathroom. Swapping one lot of pills for another was easy. Paulson was chatty, as usual, he'd had a few days off, he said, all the staff had.

'Can't last for ever, though,' he laughed, 'we'll all be back at it tonight…'

'Boss coming back, is she?' he'd asked, Paulson nodded. 'What time are you picking her up?' he asked.

'Six o'clock, sharp,' Paulson told him, 'outside the Studios.'

'Don't forget to turn the heating on then, don't want her complaining, do you?' he laughed.

'Thanks for reminding me,' Paulson opened a small cupboard and brought out two keys on a red fob. He slipped them into his jacket pocket, patting them to reassure himself that they were really there. After that it was just a matter of timing…timing again…how crucial it was. He waited behind the garage as Paulson left his flat and started preparing the car, humming as he checked the oil and water. Damn…the sedative should be kicking in by now. Paulson closed the bonnet; his footsteps echoing as he returned to the small room at the back of the building. After a few minutes he took a quick look through the grimy window.

Paulson sat at the table, his arms folded, his head rested on top. He picked up his bag, opened the door and entered the room; Paulson was out cold. He dragged him off his chair and into a corner. He brought a length of rope and a piece of fabric out of the bag. He worked quickly. Paulson would be out for several hours, more than enough time for him to complete his task…still, it wouldn't hurt to tie him up and gag him…just in case.

He stood back and looked at the unconscious man, covered him with a tarpaulin, and started to get ready. Paulson's uniform hung on the back of the door; his phone was in the pocket…perfect. He sent a text message to Tammy…

…message from the Boss…she's been held up…staying over one more night…she said to tell the others not to bother coming back tonight…picking her up after lunch tomorrow…

Within minutes Paulson's phone pinged…*OK, see you in the morning …Tammy.*

He sent another to Anthea Harrold…*sorry, not well, Tammy's arranged alternative driver. Name's Crawford…*

This time there was no reply. She was known for her sudden mood swings. He'd made a point of listening to the gossip in the local pub, and there was plenty of that. He'd even brought her P.A. a drink one day when she turned up looking harassed. Tammy hadn't been too indiscreet, just a general moan during which she let it slip that her boss could be unpredictable.

…good, he thought*…just how I like them…*

He took the house keys from Paulson's jacket; he'd need them later. His car was parked around the side of the house, out of sight. The rest was quite straightforward, really.

...oo0oo...

He smiled, already several miles away from the house.

...*nice touch*...he thought to himself...*using the husband's crossbow*...Anthea Harrold literally wouldn't have known what had hit her. Another icon crossed off the list, another trophy to add to his collection. He glanced down at the passenger seat; the corner of the book, wrapped in a polythene sheet, peeped out from under his hold-all. He knew all about its provenance, he'd made it his business. *'A Guide to Modern Cookery,'* a first edition, written by Escoffier. It was one of the most expensive recipe books in existence, presented to Harrold a few years ago by an adoring fan club. He remembered seeing her on the news that night, simpering as it was handed over to the collective gasp of her gathered sycophants. He thought about the other items in their hiding place, the bracelet, the earring, the ornate chess piece. He'd need a bigger pouch for the book, maybe he would wrap it in a square of red silk, tie it with a gold ribbon...yes, that would be appropriate for such a prize.

...*bring on the next one*...he thought, *this is easier than I thought. Soon be done, you old bastard. I wonder if you'll be proud of me then.*

16

Mason had been busy all morning, doing what she did best, dealing with paperwork. She ticked off the items on her list. Statements from the Harrington-Smythe murder had been collated, alibis were being checked, photographs pinned to the whiteboard. She sighed; she needed a break. With no one else in the office, she spread out her lunch on the desk. A bottle of filtered water, ham sandwich, low-fat crisps. She ran her fingers through her short dark hair… *I need to book in for a cut…* she though idly as she settled down to eat. She switched on the Internet; the only time of the day she would allow herself to surf without direction.

Doris Mason didn't believe in wasting time, she had too much to do. Long hours at work, time spent helping at church, then visiting her father at St. Mary's. Her father's protests at having to move from their large Victorian home to the other side of the Island was one of the most heart-breaking experiences of her life. His distress at leaving his house, books, and artefacts, was overwhelming, it was the accumulation of his life's work. Still, she wouldn't think about that again now. This was a brief oasis in her day, a chance to top up her reserves of energy by catching up on various trivia, her one guilty pleasure. She chewed on her sandwich as she clicked onto a news website, not exactly exciting headlines. She scrolled down until something caught her eye.

'*…Celebrity Chef in Murder Mystery…*' Doris read it through. She owned one of Anthea Harrold's cookbooks, *'Cooking for One'*. The report gave a few general details of the murder, committed at Harrold's home in Wrexham. Mason frowned…there was something stirring in the back of her mind… she shook her head as she typed the name into the search engine, then read another couple of reports. No more information than she already had.

She heard rather than saw Porter arrive, she hesitated as his office door slammed shut, then turned back to the screen. Wrexham was practically on their doorstep; surely Porter would be aware of the incident? He hadn't mentioned it… she wondered which station had been assigned to investigate. Mason left her desk and crossed to Porter's office, she knocked gently and stepped inside, unsure of her reception.

'Sir, I…' she hesitated, Porter sighed.

'Mason, I am not in the mood…' Mason cleared her throat.

'I wondered if you were aware of…' she swallowed hard, almost afraid to go on.

'See Connett,' Porter snapped, shuffling some papers without looking at her.

'No…No, sir, I think it's important,' she insisted. Porter looked up from his desk. He knew Mason well enough to know that she would never waste his time for anything trivial. He nodded, ashamed at his reaction. Mason sat down and began to tell him about the murder of Anthea Harrold. She had a niggling feeling, she said, that it might be something to do with the Harrington-Smythe case.

'So why do you think they're linked…how?' Porter asked. Mason blushed.

'I-I don't know, I mean, there's something familiar…' Mason said, 'I just can't put my finger on it right now. I recognise patterns…you see…' she shook her head…he wouldn't understand. Porter stared at her, something was brewing in her mind, a mind that people underestimated at their peril. He'd made that mistake in the past. It was not one he could risk making again.

...oo0oo...

It was the end of another long day. Mason hadn't made it any easier on herself by trying to uncover more about the Harrold case. She found out that it was being handled by officers at Llay Station, in Wrexham itself. They seemed willing to talk to her off the record, but she could tell they were touchy about her poking around in their investigation. Mason knew that if she could prove that the two cases were linked, then Porter and his team would be able to claim that they had priority, due to the timeline. She wasn't sure how Porter would have reacted if the Harrold murder had happened first, but she could imagine. She held back; it was the most natural thing in the world for the case to be dealt with locally, but still...

What was it about the two incidents that had fired her curiosity? She couldn't think, maybe if she relaxed, took a nice hot bath with some of those lovely bath melts she'd treated herself to last week, it would help? She blushed as she remembered how much they'd cost. She never spent her money on frivolous things, and yet there they were, waiting in their pretty glass jar on the shelf in the bathroom, smelling so delicious. But even they would have to wait, she had a visit to make first. She drove from the station across the bridge, her regular routine since her father had moved to St. Mary's. She was determined not to let him down, even when he forgot who she was, and started talking to her as though she was one of his students.

It started to rain as she approached the Home, the wipers moved hypnotically, the warmth of the car causing her to relax. The side-road leading to St. Mary's needed urgent repairs. Deep potholes presented an obstacle course each time she visited. It was little more than a track in places, one that would allow only a single vehicle at a time. An approaching car moved to the centre of the road, speeding suddenly towards her, the lights blinding her. Mason swerved to avoid it, ending up on a grass verge, the motor stalled. She sat clutching the wheel, her breathing ragged, as she tried to gain control of her senses.

Her father was asleep when she arrived. She placed the box of truffles she'd brought him in his locker and sat in the orange leatherette armchair listening to him snoring gently. Every now and then he mumbled something, what he said rarely made sense.

'…ridiculous man…no right to claim…the Knight…it came before…no discipline…' Mason sat up straight and looked at her father, his body seemed to have shrunk since he moved here, she hoped he was eating regularly. His ramblings always followed the same path…if only she could…she sighed. She was too tired for this, she needed rest.

She kept her visit brief, feeling the effects of the long day and the shock of being forced off the road. She tucked the edge of her father's bedsheet under the mattress and kissed his forehead. There was that niggling feeling again, a memory dancing away from her, one she couldn't nail down.

…oo0oo…

'…anything?' Mason jumped; she hadn't heard Porter walk up behind her.

'Sir?' she asked.

'A link, Mason, you mentioned…'

'Oh, no, not yet…' she faltered. She'd spent the best part of last night staring at the ceiling, trying to bring disparate facts together to form a viable link between the recent murders.

'Don't worry, Mason, if anyone can work this out, you can.' Mason felt herself blush. The recently acquired belief that Porter had faith in her abilities, was one she was still getting used to.

'Still no sign of Crawford, sir?' she asked as they viewed the white board. She underlined his name, as Connett walked towards them.

'No…' Connett said slowly, 'I've just spoken to Dale Walsh about him. The information he gave when he started work at the Hall doesn't check out. According to the digging I've done, there's no such person.' He glanced sideways at Porter, hoping he had redeemed himself for forgetting to tell him about the underground passageway. He'd had it checked out, there was nothing to indicate that the murderer had entered that way, but who knew?

'Get someone over there to check out his living quarters. He had a flat over the garage, didn't he?' Porter asked.

'Already on it, boss,' Connett said, 'if there's anything there, we'll find it.'

'Mason, we haven't had the recordings from the CCTV cameras surrounding the house. Let me know when they get here.' Mason nodded, she watched as Porter and Connett retreated into Porter's office.

…sometimes, she thought, *it would be nice to be invited to join in their discussions…* she couldn't blame them though, working on her own was her choice, after all.

…oo0oo…

It was just after six thirty when Mason arrived home, the phone was ringing as she opened the front door. She wasn't in any hurry, her ancient answering machine would pick it up. She never had any urgent messages anyway, mainly sales calls, so what was the point in tripping over herself to reach it in time? The machine clicked on as she placed her shopping on the kitchen surface and started to unpack her bag. A ready meal, vegetarian lasagne, a small pack of cherry tomatoes and a fruit salad. She sighed at the sight of so much plastic. It ran contrary to her New Year's resolution not to buy so much pre-prepared food. The answer machine beeped; Mason jumped as the sonorous tones of her brother's voice assailed the silence of the hallway.

'Doris, it's Brian, can you ring the Home as soon as you get this, please? Dad's had a fall.' Fear clutched at Mason's chest.

*…not Dad, please. Let him be ok, let him…*she grabbed the phone and dialled St. Mary's number. In the short time he'd been there, her father had developed a habit of wandering out of the grounds. The last time the staff had found him in the middle of a wooded area two miles from the house, only a few hundred feet from a rocky cliff face. Mason had assumed that they would keep a closer eye on him. This time, though, he had fallen at the Home and was found unconscious at the bottom of the stairs. He'd been taken to the Accident & Emergency Department in Bangor. She phoned Brian to let him know.

'You'll have to go and deal with it, Doris,' he told her, 'I have a thing to go to tonight,' he cut the call short, before she could protest. She picked up her bag and made her way back to her car. Brian had always passed the buck when it came to their father, and apart for the last few months had kept out of their lives. She didn't care, it suited her. He was four years old when she was born, it was obvious from an early age that her father had wanted another son.

...*Girls were ok,* the Professor had told anyone that would listen, *but having a son, now that was different, that meant something. After all, what father wouldn't be proud of a strapping boy or two?*

For as long as she could remember, her father had been indifferent to her needs. Brian had made matters worse, playing up and throwing tantrums whenever their mother paid her the slightest attention. She was only a few weeks old when her cot was moved to the tiny bedroom at the back of the house. It was cold and musty, and needed decorating, details that her parents seemed oblivious to. As she grew older, she got used to the shabby furniture, but the worst thing was the loneliness. There was no one to reassure her when the sounds of the night invaded her childhood dreams, no one to hold her hand when she needed them. She had always felt *'second-best'* in her parents' eyes. Brian needed the bigger bedroom ...*because boys take up more space than girls, don't they?* Later he would need football boots... *she could do without ballet shoes, couldn't she...? After all he was so talented at sports, they had to give him a chance, didn't they?*

Mason accepted it all, never complaining, never asking for anything, it avoided disappointment. She went about her life keeping herself to herself, squashing any resentment she felt by focusing on her studies. By the time she finished secondary school, she was at the top of the class. After Sixth Form College her results gained her unconditional offers from several universities. She'd had her heart set on Oxford. Her father insisted that she should attend Bangor.

'It's close, he said, 'you can catch the bus every day.' She was sure she heard him mumble something about saving money on her living expenses. Doris had often fantasised about trying to change his mind, but she knew it would be useless to protest. She resigned herself to his decision. It turned out to be one of the best he had made, albeit unintentionally. Her years at Bangor resulted in a First-Class Honours Degree. She had sometimes fantasised that her father was secretly delighted with her success but knew that Brian's failure in academia had overshadowed her results. He hadn't even attended her graduation.

She rarely saw Brian these days, most of the time he managed to visit when she wasn't there. Not that his absence was a great loss…she shivered. Truth was she was relieved…she shook herself.

…no need to dwell on the past, she thought… *what's done is done.* Her main objective now was to get to the hospital and sort out her father.

…oo0oo…

Mason's head slipped from her hand, she woke up and stared around the side ward. For a moment she couldn't remember why she was there. Her father…she looked at him lying in the bed, he looked pathetic, somehow. The doctor had assured her that he would be all right, though, just a bump on the head, it could have been worse. Why he'd been upstairs in the first place was something they would have to watch out for if his balance was becoming a problem. She listened to the steady rhythm of his breathing.

'…thank you,' she whispered to no one in particular, '…thank you so much,' tears threatened as she absorbed the prospect of losing him. He breathed in deeply, opening his eyes. She edged her chair closer to the bed and picked up his hand.

'I'm here Dad,' she whispered, 'I'm here, it's me, Doris.' The old man turned his head. He looked straight at her, his eyes wide. His grip tightened suddenly causing her to wince.

'Don't let them get me, Doris,' he hissed, 'don't let them…' she could see that he was getting agitated.

'Shush, Dad,' she murmured, 'everything's all right, I promise.' He held on tight to her hand, shaking his head.

'They whisper to me…they tell me things…be careful cariad, be careful…' Doris pressed the call button, a nurse bustled into the room. She looked at Professor Mason holding onto his daughter's hand, his face agitated, his breathing ragged.

'I'll be back in a minute,' she said as she turned to leave. Mason stroked her father's hand. He started to calm down and soon he was asleep. Mason apologised as the nurse brought in something to calm her patient. She shook her head.

'Not to worry,' she said, and left. Mason felt her father's hand relaxing, she tucked it under the bedclothes and tried to settle into her chair.

…what was that about…? Doris wondered. Her father wasn't usually one for emotional outbursts, but then he was having other problems, wasn't he? She hadn't seen him this worked up since he had that row with a student a couple of months ago, the one where he was interrupted during his lecture on the…that was it…that was the connection…she could sense the pieces forming a tenuous link as the cogs meshed together. She'd have to talk to Porter as soon as she could, he needed to know… she swallowed hard; it wasn't the only thing he needed to know about, was it?

Mason swallowed hard as stood up and wandered to the window. Would it be so bad, admitting what she'd done? She'd thought about little else since that mob had ravaged her meticulous filing system. At first, she felt a sense of triumph, of getting one over on them, that soon evaporating at the thought that she might have overstepped her remit. But how could anyone accuse her of that? She wondered what Porter would say when she told him. How could she phrase it? She considered various elaborate excuses, discarding them all, they weren't her, they were too…contrived. That was it then, she'd tell him outright. She felt inside her handbag, she couldn't explain why she had hidden the USB stick there, only that something had told her it was expedient to do so.

…Such a small item… she thought, as she looked at it nestling in the palm of her hand, yet so powerful. …t*omorrow morning…*, she decided, *…I'll give it to him then, he can decide what to do with it…*

She felt better now that she'd made up her mind; it was the right thing to do. Porter would know how to handle it, she was sure he wouldn't be angry with her, well, she hoped he wouldn't be.

17

Ellie swiped her phone to reject the call. She turned down the volume and replaced it on the table. She knew that at some point she would have to speak to Julia, but right now she was trying to get her head around the extent of Ruth's estate, the total ran into several millions of pounds. Ellie was astonished as she realised how astute her sister had been. Her 'ditsy' persona had been a mask that hid the mind of a shrewd businesswoman. Ellie wondered if she had known her sister at all. For now, at least, Ruth was saying nothing.

…I wonder what a Psychiatrist would say… Ellie thought as she stared at the list of Ruth's holdings, *…someone waiting for their dead sister to talk to her, only she won't because of an argument they'd just had…?*

It had been a bad one, their argument, except that now it didn't seem so important. For the life of her Ellie couldn't remember how it had started. Something about it being a pity that Ruth hadn't let on about how much she had achieved during her life, and how come she'd left everything to her anyway? It seemed odd now, standing in a room, seemingly alone, the only voice that a passer-by would hear. Ellie, of course could hear both sides of the conversation, when she considered it, she had to laugh.

…as if we didn't quarrel enough while you were alive, Ellie thought, at which point she heard a muffled sob and Ruth apologised. Ellie started to well up at the thought that she had somehow upset her sister's ghost, at the same time she shook her head at just how absurd it sounded. The answer, once Ruth explained it, was both sad and sweet.

Ruth had always felt that she was a poor second best when compared with Ellie. She didn't see the point in telling anyone about her achievements. She'd had many 'experiences' that were like Ellie's but kept quiet about them. She'd seen people's reactions to Ellie when she'd told them about her *'glimpses',* she didn't want to receive the same level of attention or ridicule.

'You were protecting yourself?' Ellie whispered, knowing that she had guessed correctly.

…I wasn't as strong as you, I couldn't have dealt with their attention. Besides, Mom would have blamed you for getting me to tell lies, you know she would...

'I wish you'd told me, we could have supported each other,' Ellie said.

…someone would have found out; I couldn't have them taking it out on you Ellie.

'Why did you change your Will, Ruth?' Ellie asked, but Ruth had gone quiet. She'd asked her the question several times, so far Ruth had refused to answer.

'Enough for today, then,' Ellie whispered as she went back to reading the list furnished by Mr Richardson. In total there were fifteen properties, Ellie got as far as the fourth one and stopped. *Russell Grove*, John Prothero's former family home. She knew about it from the information she had gleaned during the incident at the Retreat. How on earth had it turned up in Ruth's Will though? She couldn't bring herself to read any further.

Ellie picked up Richardson's latest letter. It repeated the warning that nothing could be finalised until they'd confirmed that Ruth's estate was legal and not the proceeds of criminal activity. Ellie shuddered at the thought that any portion of Ruth's estate could have been procured by John during his murderous rampage.

...more waiting... she thought. Over the last few days her determination to get on with her life had been growing. The sting of betrayal, caused by those she had trusted, had started to wane. She even considered contacting Graham to see if they could talk, but something was holding her back from that. She was beginning to trust her intuition, after all it had made its presence known often enough, she just hadn't given it much of a chance to guide her actions.

The phone buzzed, the vibration moving it slightly, her mother again. Ellie ignored it and tidied up the papers she'd been studying. Reading them smacked of poor taste. Within minutes she'd made up her mind. She would find Odelia and suggest they go for a walk. Ellie hadn't spent much time with her since Julia had turned up. Come to think about it, Odelia seemed to be out a lot of the time. This time was no different. Ellie felt it was almost as though people were avoiding her. She shrugged; she couldn't afford to start feeling paranoid. She wasn't the only who wanted to move on with her life.

She smiled to herself; there was something she'd overlooked. Odelia had become very friendly with Gareth Wynne-Jones, the eccentric young man that had played such an important part during the show-down with John Prothero. If it hadn't been for him they might not have...Ellie shuddered. Just lately, he and Odelia had been seeing each other more frequently. Ellie was happy for her. Odelia certainly seemed more relaxed, and if

Gareth was the reason for that, well, good for them. She felt a small stab of jealousy, she wondered if she should contact Graham after all. She decided against it, for now. She had to clear her head sufficiently first, to sort out in which direction she should take her life. It wasn't easy, she admitted to herself, in the past few months she'd suffered acutely from the blinding migraines that had plagued her periodically since childhood. Then there were the recurring nightmares that left her in a cold sweat. Her instinct was telling her that she needed to get away for a while, but she felt that her commitments meant, for the time being at least, that this would be impossible.

…pressure…too much pressure… what she would give for a drink. She shook her head…

…don't go there, sweetie… she heard Ruth whisper…*you've got to keep a clear head…*

Ellie's phone buzzed again, she reached for it intending to switch it off, she didn't have the energy to speak to anyone, let alone fend off…

…*Rosa Pritchard* flashed on the screen. Ellie answered, within minutes she was pulling on her coat and heading towards the offices she'd shared with John Prothero.

…oo0oo…

Rosa Pritchard had always enjoyed the prestige that went with working for Professor Prothero. It was a role that her friends regarded with a mixture of reverence and curiosity. It imbued her with an air of mystery, and she handled her position with an expert balance. She never divulged anything confidential but couldn't help enjoying the frustration of her friends as they tried to guess what was going on behind the doors of her employers' office.

It had taken her a while to get used to Ellie, though. The young woman with the strange ways, was too modern for Miss Pritchard's taste. For the first few years of their association Miss Pritchard tolerated her at best, it was only in the last few months that her view of her young employer had changed to one of admiration and respect. Now she was at a loss as to how to handle the situation in which she found herself. She'd never had so many visitors, people who she hardly knew would *'drop in to make sure she was all right,'* each one asking, *oh so casually* about the case.

...nosey devils... she thought, on more than one occasion. She'd taken to locking the outer door and monitoring the visitors using the intercom that the Professor had...the thought brought her up sharply.

Ellie had rarely visited the office since Prothero's arrest. On those occasions she *had* called in, the two women avoided talking directly about the case, but they both knew that this situation couldn't go on forever. For one thing Miss Pritchard needed clarification about her job. Should she just pack up and stay at home, or would Ellie have anything she could offer her in the future? Acting on her own initiative, something at which she excelled, she'd turned up at the office every day since...she preferred not to think about what had happened at the Retreat. She focused instead on sorting out the mess that the 'visitation' had left behind. She still didn't know where they were from, only that they had the relevant papers to enter the premises and 'take any and all items connected with Professor John Prothero', that pretty much included everything in the place. The files, over which she had lavished such care and attention, had been decimated, there wasn't much to sort out. Miss Pritchard had never deserted her post, but there were only so many times one could do the *'Cryptic'* crossword or battle with her daily dose of Suduko without getting a little fed up.

Hence her phone call to Ellie. There was no need to call really, she could have suggested that Celia Chetwynd ring Ellie directly, but Rosa had seized her chance. Chetwynd's message had taken seconds to deliver once Ellie had arrived, leaving her wondering what the hell all the fuss was about. She'd presumed that Miss Pritchard's call was urgent, at least that's what it had sounded like.

There was something she wanted to talk about, Ellie could tell, although it took some time before Miss Pritchard could bring herself to speak. As Ellie sat listening, she began to appreciate the level of her secretary's anxiety, her uncertainty about the future. It may have been something about Miss Pritchard's obvious distress that drove Ellie to make her decision…she would concentrate on doing what she did best. Nothing and nobody was going to prevent her from getting back to work.

*…its funny, I thought that profiling was something I'd just dropped into by default, I never realised how much I enjoyed the challenge of the whole process… besides there's still Kara…*she cleared her throat…

'So, Miss Pritchard…bring me up to date,' she said, she shivered slightly when she realised that she'd used a phrase that John had said so many times in the past. The two women looked at each other for a second, Ellie saw the stress on the older woman's face. Miss Pritchard swallowed hard, then reached for her notebook.

'There are a few messages,' she said, 'quite straight forward, Celia Chetwynd of course… and DCI Porter has rung several times asking if he could arrange an off the record meeting,' she said, reading from her notes. 'I told him that I couldn't commit you to anything until I'd spoken with you…' she paused and cleared her throat. 'Mr. Shaw rang several times last week, but I haven't heard anything in the last couple of days, not since the boy arrived...'

'…what boy?' Ellie asked, then sat transfixed as a reluctant Rosa Pritchard broke the news.

…oo0oo…

The flimsy curtains did little to block out the daylight. Ellie sat at her desk, the closed the door against the outside world. How could he do this to her? How could he have let her find out this way? Why hadn't he told her himself? Questions crowded her mind, making her dizzy with a myriad of possible explanations. Only minutes before Miss Pritchard had dropped the latest bombshell, she had had a flash of clarity about her future. She wanted to stay on the Island, to go back to work at the station. Building a career that she really cared about was important to her. She'd even considered the possibility of meeting Graham to talk about trying to heal their relationship…now this. How could she stay now, so close to the man she thought had loved her, cared about her?

She would never forget the look on Rosa Pritchard's face when she realised that Ellie was ignorant of Karl's existence, and Ellie had no doubt that she would have given anything to have taken back her words. But there it was. Ellie hadn't seen the papers for weeks, she didn't want to read any of the dreadful things that had been printed, not only about Ruth and Max, but all the speculation about Prothero. Miss Pritchard had reluctantly fetched a selection from her desk, before making a tactical retreat, allowing her some privacy to read them. The headlines were worse than Ellie could have imagined.

'Local Forensic Pathologist in Love Triangle with Student', read one, printed the previous week, '*'Puppet Master' Pathologist investigated over Student Murder'*, said another, and finally one from only two days ago… *'Disgraced Pathologist Fathers Love Child with murdered Mistress'*.

Most of the 'revelations' were old news; Graham's affair, the fact that Kara was his student, that he had been suspended pending more investigations. It was the other revelations that struck like a dagger into her heart, even though she was sure that most of what she was reading were half-truths. One had suggested that Graham knew about the child, but kept it a secret from his wife, another, that he had refused to pay anything towards his child's upbringing. They stopped just short of saying that Kara's arrival on the Island to help in the investigation had somehow provided him with a motive for her murder.

…surely, he could sue them for that…? Ellie thought, then realised that she didn't care much one way or the other. She felt sick. She wanted to leave, to go home. But where *was* home? She heard a knock on the office door. Rosa Pritchard with coffee, another plaster to put over yet another injury. She shook her head, *no more*, she thought.

'Thank you, Miss Pritchard,' she said in a voice that sounded a lot stronger than it felt, 'I don't need more coffee. Will you get onto the estate agents again please? We need new offices.' With that, she pulled on her coat and left.

The High Street was busy. Ellie wandered blindly along the pavement towards the shopping centre. She needed to do something, something practical to distract her from what she'd just discovered. There were things she needed to buy. She hadn't been shopping for what seemed like months and she was running out of essentials. Everything she needed was available at the Retreat, but Ellie couldn't help feeling as though she was taking advantage, and it had to stop. She was procrastinating, she knew, at some point she would have to face the enormity of this latest bombshell…Graham had a child. She shuddered at the thought, had he known or…

…why it is I feel as though I've handed the reins of my life over to other people…? She thought as she made her way over to main entrance of the mall.

…because you have, haven't you, sweetie…? Ellie couldn't be sure if the voice in her head was her own or Ruth's. She rummaged around in her bag looking for her notebook, trying desperately to control the emotions that welled up inside. She regretted turning down Miss Prichard's offer of coffee, anything would be preferable to being out here, feeling exposed. She needed…what did she need? …a list, she needed to focus… it was difficult when her head was full of so many conflicting thoughts. The food court boasted several coffee bars. Ellie made her way over to the nearest one and sat down, only to be approached within seconds by a spotty teenager, who looked about fifteen.

'You can't sit there unless you order something,' he announced in a disinterested voice that varied in pitch, emphasising his youth. He held a pad and a pen in readiness.

'Don't you think it would be better if you asked me what I'd like, instead of …' Ellie stopped. She stared over the boy-waiter's shoulder as Graham and his father walked out of a department store, a young lad between them. Graham had his hand on the boy's shoulder, conveying a degree of closeness that made Ellie's heart lurch. Jim Shaw was talking, nodding his head as the boy looked up at him, drinking in his words. An air of camaraderie surrounded the three of them.

'…are you gonna order or what?' Ellie's boy-waiter persisted. Ellie hesitated, at that moment Graham looked up and saw her. He froze as his father and the boy continued walking. Ellie could feel her heart thundering, she felt light-headed, unable to answer. For a moment it looked as though Graham was about to walk towards where she was sitting. He stopped as he saw three men approaching him...reporters. They corralled him, one snapped away as he put his head down and turned to leave.

Ellie hadn't realised that she was holding her breath. She watched as Graham walked quickly towards the exit, in the opposite direction to his father. No doubt they would meet up later. The reporters followed him; she could hear them barking questions that he did his best to ignore and walked on. There was nothing Ellie wanted more than to be back at the Retreat. She had seen what it was like for Graham, how much more difficult would it be if they had seen her…what if she'd been recognised? They were both newsworthy people, the realisation made her shudder. She'd been lucky so far, no one had bothered her, she wondered how long her luck would last.

The boy-waiter had grown tired of hanging around for her order, he'd retreated to the counter to alert the manager. She walked towards Ellie's table. Ellie stood, muttering apologies about not feeling well. She picked up her bag, half expecting a tirade of abuse. She was surprised when a firm hand grasped her elbow and she was led over to a door behind the counter. The woman opened it and ushered her through.

'You may want to go down here,' she said, leading Ellie through a maze of corridors, 'turn left at the end, it'll lead to the staff car park. You can get back to the High Street from there.' Ellie started to thank her; the woman shook her head. She looked familiar, Ellie recognised her, one of her patients… 'I saw what happened back there, I know you've been through a lot,' she said, 'I hope you manage to sort it out.' She turned and went back into the centre, leaving Ellie alone in the deserted corridor. Ellie's legs felt weak; she flattened her back against a wall and tried to breathe slowly to quieten her racing heart. It was all very well trying to be brave; this morning had proved what a rocky road she had to travel. She'd felt so strong in the office, but out here…? She had to sit down; her legs wouldn't support her. The corridors were empty, nowhere to rest to gather her strength. She stumbled a few yards, then stopped and held onto a door handle, her head swimming. She gave up trying to fight the weakness that invaded her body and sat down on the floor in a heap.

…is this how it's going to be from now on…? she wondered… *if it is, then John Prothero might as well have finished me off as well…*

…how dare you…? Ruth's voice, as clear and firm as if she stood in front of Ellie… *how dare you say such a thing…? You have no idea, do you…? You don't deserve…I can't believe…after all I did…* Ruth's tirade, a mixture of anger and disgust. Ellie recoiled, as though Ruth had physically

struck her…*you'd better pull yourself together Ellie, if you think you've been through some shit already, let me tell you, it's nothing compared with what's to come…*

'I'm sorry Ruth…I'm so sorry…please…' Ellie sobbed. It was no use; she knew that Ruth had gone

18

Ronnie Bowers was exhausted. It had been a bad Christmas for the Chester store; the report he'd delivered to the board yesterday had been the final nail, giving him little hope that he could hold onto his position for much longer.

...what the hell did they expect...?

He sat down at his desk, staring at the pile of messages that his secretary had placed there, each one from an angry shareholder. He didn't bother reading them, he knew they were full of recriminations, accusations that he couldn't '*get his act together*' during one of retail's busiest periods. Ronnie sighed; his eyes strayed to the dark wood cabinet in the corner of his office that housed his favourite bourbon. He checked his watch, ten thirty-five...hell, not even he could justify drinking this early in the morning. What if the boss were to drop in unannounced?

Andrew Donaldson had stopped at nothing when it came to securing Ronnie's agreement to manage his retail outfits. Ronnie and his wife had been wined and dined, flown out by private jet for a holiday in Donaldson's villa, showered with valuable gifts...all for what? To convince Ronnie that he was invaluable to the future of the business. Less than three years ago he'd been hailed as their saviour. The seven Donaldson's stores, all in prime locations, had had their best trading figures in years. Both the public and the board seemed to believe that the newcomer could all but walk on water. Thoughts of the newspaper coverage his appointment had precipitated flooded back.

'...*The Man with the Golden Touch'*, one had called him... *'Bowers puts in the Hours',* another witty hack had commented...and he had. He had never worked so hard in his life. His efforts didn't go unnoticed by the staff. His arrival seemed to put a spark into every one of the store's *'associates'*; a renewed vigour into their efforts to reverse the trend of a downward spiral in High Street trading. He'd even won a prestigious award on the back of his results. It stood in the centre of his bookcase, a hunk of crystal engraved with his name and '*Businessman of the Year'* emblazoned on the front, confirmation of his achievements. Now it seemed to reproach him. He was being blamed for the fall in profits. It was all so unfair. When had it started to unravel?

...*don't be a fool, you know the answer*... he sighed. He was the one the buck stopped with, the one who would be blamed for all the ills that befell the stores. Donaldson had made sure of that. Yesterday's board meeting indicated that Ronnie would be tried, found guilty and hung out to dry.

...*I'm a fool*... he admitted to himself. He'd believed Andrew Donaldson when he assured him that he would stand by him...he hadn't. Donaldson had rounded on him. Bowers had expected better of someone with his reputation. He had placed his trust in a man he believed was not just his employer, but also his friend. He'd trusted Donaldson, but in the end...he sighed, at the end of the day they weren't friends after all, he was just another employee, not even that, he was a whipping boy. When 'The Board' caught the scent of blood, it was him that would be finished off by the pack, not his boss.

Maybe, if he could weather the next few weeks, make a big effort over the Easter period, maybe he could hold on. But did he want to? The looks on their faces yesterday were hostile, to say the least. Some even looked downright ugly; did he really want to be a part of this charade any longer? Ronnie shook his head, he had to think. What to do, how to mitigate his failure. He thought back to a phone call he'd had a few days before, someone from the Finance Department, he didn't know who.

…Just a heads up… the unknown caller had told him*…some discrepancies in the accounts relating to the pension fund, it doesn't feel right…someone is transferring large sums of money…* the caller rang off before Ronnie could ask him any questions. It was enough to make him think, though, to try to work out how he could access more information without raising suspicions.

What if that was the answer? What if the figures had been fudged to cover up…whatever? It wouldn't be the first time something like this had happened. The thought made him angry. He'd have to find someone he could trust, but who? There was no one. Ronnie took out his mobile, pressed his home number, the call went straight to answerphone. He swore, she wasn't answering…again. As if he didn't have enough problems already, he suspected Faye was having an affair, he just couldn't find out who with. She'd been very evasive during the last few weeks.

…screw it… he thought. He crossed the room to the cabinet. Bottles clinked as he opened it. A shot of *'JD'* would put him right. He poured a generous measure and added ice from the tiny freezer section. The cubes clinked against the crystal glass as he swirled the amber

liquid round, anticipating the effect of the first mouthful. He felt the warmth as the liquid hit his stomach.

Bowers was restless, he walked to the window. He had to get some air. Was it his imagination, or was it warmer in here than usual? He cracked the side window open a notch and loosened his tie, suddenly overwhelmed by the heat. He took another swig of his drink, gasping as it hit the back of his throat. With a bit of luck, it might help, a few more and he might not even care. He placed the glass on the windowsill and stood looking out down onto the main thoroughfare.

Chester High Street was quiet this morning, just a handful of people going about their business. Ronnie watched them, noting the time, setting the stopwatch function on his watch for five minutes. He counted how many entered the shop before the buzzer sounded. The result didn't lift his spirits…two, two elderly women, no doubt in search of the *'Buy one get one free'* breakfast deal he'd introduced to entice more mid-week trade.

What the hell was he going to do? He grabbed his glass and crossed to the leather Chesterfield sofa that ran along the opposite wall. He slumped down, almost spilling the remainder of his drink in the process. Back in the day, when he'd run his own business…he put his head back and closed his eyes, recalling how it had seemed like a lot of hard work at the time, now he appreciated how free it had felt. To be one's own boss, to choose what time you got up, what time you had lunch, whether you worked that day at all. There was no one to answer to then…true, he'd struggled to give Faye what she wanted, but he managed to provide her and the kids with most of the things they seemed unable to live without.

When Andrew Donaldson had asked him to come and help run out his stores, he'd been more than flattered. His salary would double, he would work fewer hours, both he and Faye were excited, they expected their lifestyle to soar. It took him less than six months to find out that Donaldson had lied. Every promise was overblown, exaggerated by a man he thought of as a brother, but who Ronnie was now convinced really wanted him as a scape goat.

The drink had softened the edges. Ronnie was beginning to feel human again. Maybe he could manage one more…the phone rang before he could replenish his glass. Andrew's PA…*could he be at Mr. Donaldson's house at three that afternoon…?* As if he had any choice… when his master called, he felt duty bound to answer. He confirmed the time. The room was still uncomfortably warm, he stood up unsteadily and crossed to check the thermostat, it was set to thirty, he turned it down. He never set it that high, and as far as he could remember, no one else ever touched it. The combination of alcohol and heat was suddenly unbearable. He strode to the full-length glass door and opened it wide, gasping as the cool air hit him.

Ronnie stepped out onto the narrow balcony. It was pleasant out there, a small table in the corner, where the area opened out as it met the corner of the building, a matching chair so that he could sit out in the summer…as if he had the time. His was one of only three offices that boasted such a feature. He felt the need to spend a few minutes there, just to clear his head. He ran his hand along the rail, his palm caught on something sharp. He looked closer at the metalwork, it appeared to have been partially cut through. He looked along the rest of the rail. Less than a metre away there was another cut.

...what the hell...? he thought. He stumbled forward as he felt a push in his lower back. He grabbed the rail to steady himself, remembering only at the last moment that it had been weakened.

Half a dozen people screamed as he hit the pavement.

...oo0oo...

*...no problem...*he thought, making his way down the back staircase. The door to the staff canteen opened as he passed, the low-level conversations suddenly becoming louder as a uniformed assistant came through. She almost collided with him as he pressed himself against the wall.

'Oh,' she shrieked, 'oh, I'm, so sorry, I almost knocked you...are you all right, you look a bit flushed?' he nodded, eager to get away from her. Being this close, she might see his make-up.

'Going home,' he murmured, taking a tissue out of his pocket, and dabbing his forehead. '...think I've got the flu.' The woman stepped away, quickly.

'Don't want that again, love,' she laughed, 'only just got over a bout. You get yourself tucked up with a nice hot toddy, sweat it out.' She laughed as she walked away.

He hadn't realised that he'd been holding his breath. He took a few moments to steady himself, then carried on down the stairs to the underground car park. His car was parked on the street but leaving through the entrance to the store might draw too much attention. He walked up the ramp and into the daylight. The air was peppered with flecks of snow that melted as soon as they touched anything solid. He fished a beany hat out of his tool-bag and pulled it onto his head. He hadn't anticipated that the warmth of Bowers' office would cause the hair dye he'd applied that morning to run.

*...nothing out of the ordinary...*he told himself, as he unlocked his car and got behind the wheel...*no sudden moves...nothing unusual, keep it low-key...*

He pulled out of the side street onto the main road, a small crowd of people had gathered in front of the store, a siren sounded in the distance. He drove slowly past the spot that he knew Ronnie Bowers lay, even though he couldn't see his body.

He was a few miles out of town before he stopped in a lay-by and allowed himself the luxury of looking at the trophy. A piece of crystal, not very imposing, considering the inscription it bore... *'Businessman of the Year'...Ronnie Bowers.*

...yes... he thought...*another addition to my collection...*Altogether a satisfactory afternoon. Just one thing annoyed him, he hadn't been able to get photographs of this one. He couldn't risk being seen leaning out over the street, nor had he had the thought to take the opportunity to join the crowd that had gathered around the body.

He hit the steering wheel, furious with himself *...I could have done it...I could have pretended that I was just passing by, then I could have got....* he wouldn't have been the only person taking pictures of a dead man lying in the street. He cursed aloud; this was sloppy. He couldn't get caught out again like this. Still, he could always check on social media later, someone might have posted their snaps by then. It wasn't the same though...

...next time, next time will be better...

19

Doris Mason's fork clattered on the table as she grabbed the radio's remote and turned up the volume.

'... tributes have been pouring in from many sources concerning the tragic death of Ronnie Bowers, the so-called 'Saviour of the High Street'. Mr. Bowers died this morning at Donaldson's flagship store in Chester, in an incident that is widely being regarded as 'suspicious circumstances. The police have so far refused to comment...

...Mr. Bowers' arrival at the store, three years ago, was heralded as a lifeline, his initial efforts in rescuing the ailing business had earned him several accolades. Andrew Donaldson, who now spends most of his time on his private island in the Caribbean, has paid tribute to Mr. Bowers, saying that his death would mean incalculable loss to both his family and to the business world.'

Mason shook her head as Donaldson's emotional speech echoed around the small dining room.

'...Ronnie Bowers...what can I say? He arrived at Donaldson's at a time when...I will be eternally grateful for his efforts...he was priceless...he brought benefit...to me as a friend and to my business...yes...benefit, great benefit...'

Mason shivered at his words; she'd heard them before. She sat still, going over and over them in her mind. She knew now, she was sure. All she had to do was to convince the others.

Chetwynd wasn't in the best of moods. She'd always prided herself on the latitude she gave to her '*troops*.' However, she didn't take kindly to junior members of her team taking it upon themselves to go behind her back. The repeated warnings she'd had from the higher ups rang in her ears as she made her way downstairs to the briefing room. Even so, a small part of her felt that Mason's actions, uncharacteristic though they were, might herald a new beginning for her team in the aftermath of the Puppet Master debacle. She'd had nothing to offer them, how could she, she still didn't have any more information about why…she sighed.

*…between a rock and a hard place…*she thought. For weeks she'd caught snippets of conversations around the station. Members of the old investigation had been moping, she could sense that their attitude towards her had changed. They resented being kept in the dark, she couldn't blame them, she felt the same herself. She'd spoken to Connett a couple of times, resurrecting the '*arrangement*' they'd had in the past, to be her eyes and ears on the ground. He seemed uncomfortable, though, as if with DCI Horton's exit, he expected to be let off the hook.

He confirmed her suspicions, most of the old team had been moaning to each other about lack of 'closure'. She couldn't blame them for that. Her orders were to say as little as possible, and only then to those she trusted the most. It said a lot that she hadn't spoken to Porter yet…she was still in shock. He probably wouldn't believe her anyway. She shook her head in disbelief. What was she worried about, anyway? In truth she didn't know anything significant about the Prothero situation. She could sense her carefully crafted relationship with the officers in her charge dissolving as each day slipped by.

One thing Chetwynd had been determined about, and that was not to go against the directive she'd received concerning Ellie Shaw. She had resisted Porter's suggestions that they could do with her help. He believed that her return would boost morale, and that she could prove invaluable in the Harrington-Smythe murder. Whoever had committed it had done so without leaving anything significant to go on. No DNA, no trace evidence, no fingerprints, nothing. Their main suspect was the man calling himself 'Crawford' who seemed to have disappeared without trace. They had even discussed the possibility that he might have been an associate of John Prothero.

Maybe, Porter suggested, if his team had been allowed to continue the investigation, they would have uncovered more of Prothero's associates, and Harrington-Smythe would still be alive. Their conversation had become quite heated at that point. It had ended in him bordering on insubordination, and her instruction that he calm down before either of them said something they might regret. Without doubt Porter was one of the most brilliant and hardworking DCIs she'd ever worked with, her only regret was that she hadn't appreciated how brilliant before now. She felt that Mason had overstepped the boundaries by inviting Ellie Shaw to the station to attend this briefing today.

Chetwynd knew she should have put a stop to it straight away. Still, she reasoned, if it went well the investigation could be wrapped up sooner rather than later. On the other hand, if it went badly, she could always attribute any failure to over enthusiasm on Mason's part. A part of her was ashamed at her own duplicity. As it was, she had agreed to join in, and made her way towards the briefing room.

The white board had been turned around, not, Porter knew, for dramatic effect, but to prevent the team's concentration being divided between it and whatever Mason had to say. He knew it wasn't in Mason's DNA to pull those kinds of tricks. The chairs were arranged in a horseshoe; they soon started to fill up. A low buzz of speculation circulated as Mason fiddled with a clip board, her nervousness was obvious. Connett was the last to arrive, having just returned from another round of interviews with members of staff from Harrington Hall.

Porter opened the briefing by welcoming Ellie back. He thanked her in advance for any input she might be able to give. He was surprised that Chetwynd hadn't done something to prevent her attendance. If she let this slide, then maybe he...they, could look forward to Ellie's permanent return. He recapped what little information they had. The room went quiet as he sat down, everyone waited for the next step. No one seemed to know what that was. Chetwynd looked round if that was all they had called her down for…Mason stood up and walked to the front of the room, clearing her throat. She hadn't told Porter anything about her suspicions as yet, she had one crack at this. Her face had gone a deep shade of red, mottled with pale blotches. She'd been preparing for this moment for the last two days.

'I, er, I,' she cleared her throat again, hesitating. What if she had this wrong? What if her suspicions were just that? No, she was sure, she had to tell them what she suspected, even if it was a load of rubbish. She opened the file as Ellie caught her eye and smiled. Mason managed to smile back, she looked terrified.

'Why don't you tell us what you've discovered, DS Mason,' Ellie said quietly, trying to instil her with some confidence.

'Um, well, I've er, I've been at the hospital for the last few days,' she began, 'my father had a fall,' there were murmurs of sympathy, Mason smiled weakly. 'He's getting better, thank you.'

...*God it's like pulling hen's teeth*...thought Porter, his patience wearing thin, his gut telling him that they needed to hear what she had to say.

'I spent most of the time catching up on news, reading...' she smiled weakly, sensing the tension. 'Two days ago, I was listening...' she heard someone sigh. She shook her head, reminding herself to be concise, not to waffle. She picked up a sheet of paper and started to read out the details of the Anthea Harrold's murder, followed by that of Ronnie Bowers. She turned the whiteboard around. On it were pictures of the victims she'd named. After a few minutes she stopped as she saw Porter shaking his head. His face said it all...*what the hell...?* She took another deep breath; feeling completely out of her depth.

Chetwynd stared at Mason, she wondered how it was that a junior officer was so up to date with what was happening within a close radius of their patch, when she wasn't. Why hadn't she been informed of these other events directly? She'd always believed that her relationship with senior offices from other stations was good, that any information that they had would be shared. Had she been so preoccupied with other matters, that she had overlooked the fact that not one of her sources had contacted her. She realised that she hadn't spoken to most of them since well before John Prothero had been arrested. Perhaps that was it, perhaps her so-called *'friends'* in other stations were avoiding her.

'So, what are your suspicions about these cases, Mason?' she heard Porter asking, cutting through her thoughts, '…and more importantly, why?'

'Sir, I have mentioned to you before…the possibility…I think…no, I'm sure, they're connected,' Mason said, standing up straight, looking a bit more confident. Ellie felt a prickle on the back of her neck. Something told her that they were connected, she was sure as well, although for the moment she had no idea how.

'I know this is going to sound…I have my reasons for suspecting…' Mason began again, Porter took a deep breath.

'How, Mason?' he asked.

'Sir, my father…he's…well he was,' she faltered. She shrugged… if she was right… 'my father was a Professor of English, he taught at both Oxford and Cambridge, he has several books published…' she heard Connett clear his throat.

…*God, I hate that bloke*…she thought screwing up the courage to go on.

'…he…he specialised in one area of study; he was quite an expert…' she stopped as she caught Porter's eye again.

'I think the three murders are themed,' she said more forcefully, 'and I think the theme is…'

'…*The Canterbury Tales…'* Ellie said, although for the life of her she couldn't explain why. She knew nothing about the subject, let alone how or why they could be linked with the murders. Mason looked at her with a mixture of surprise and relief. She felt as if she had an ally. If someone like Ellie Shaw considered her theory plausible…

Chetwynd led with the questions that followed. Ellie shrugged as some of them were addressed to her, indicating that they should be directed at Mason. Mason drew more pages from the folder and started to talk. Porter shushed the others as she tried to make herself heard.

'…Lord Harrington-Smythe, murdered at his country estate. We know that there was a missing item, a chess piece, the Black Knight.' Mason read from her notes. 'Anthea Harrold, a celebrity chef, a cook, murdered at her house. No details have been released relating to the circumstances of her death, but I'm willing to bet that something of significance relating to the nature of her work has been stolen. Ronnie Bowers, Manager of Donaldson's Department stores, died two days ago at his office in Chester. The press is speculating that his death was suicide, but there are reasons to believe that he was murdered.' Mason was warming to her subject, her nervousness dissipating as she appeared to gain more confidence.

'Apparently Bowers was facing a boardroom revolt due to failing sales at the stores. However, I think that he was murdered, and it had nothing to do with the business.' She could see the confusion on her colleagues' faces. 'He's *'The Reever'*, you see. A man who earns his living bringing benefit to his master. It's all there in the Canterbury Tales.' She nodded as though they, the rest of the gathering, would know what she was talking about. 'Not only that, whoever is responsible for the murders seems to be committing them in the order that some academics believe they were told, *The Knight's Tale, The*

Cook's Tale, The Reever's Tale...don't you see?' They didn't, she could tell.

'You'd better read these,' she said, with an uncharacteristic flash of irritation. She handed out a sheaf of notes to each of them.

'If I'm right, and I think I am, the next victim will be *'The Man of Law.'*'

...oo0oo...

'Sir, could I have a word?' Mason stood in the doorway to Porter's office clutching a file. Porter looked up, after her performance in the briefing room, he'd taken the files she'd prepared and was reading her meticulous notes.

'Of course,' he said, indicating for her to sit down. If he was sure about anything relating to Mason, it was that she wouldn't be bothering him for anything trivial. She closed the door behind her and perched on the edge of the chair. She swallowed several times, her discomfort was obvious.

'Are you all right, Mason?' he asked, she nodded, biting her lip. Porter could tell that she was anything but. She sniffed; he knew better than to interrupt her.

'I wanted...' she started, 'I, er, I don't know if I should...' Porter waited. 'You remember what happened a few...' she stopped again, aware of the enormity of what she was about to admit, 'when they raided...when they took all the files on the Prothero case...'

Porter watched as she battled with herself. She took a deep breath and closed her eyes.

'...I wasn't entirely truthful with them,' she blurted out, 'I said I'd turned everything over, that I didn't know of any...' Porter frowned, Mason was babbling something about the raid, about how she'd meant to be co-operative, it was just that she'd forgotten…

'Mason, Doris…look, calm down, I can't understand what you're trying to say,' he waited as she composed herself. She reached into her jacket pocket and brought out the USB stick, placing it in front of him like an offering at an altar.

'What's this?' he asked, the hair on the back of his neck starting to rise.

'A copy, sir,' Mason murmured, 'a copy of the Prothero files.'

It was the closest that Porter had ever been to wanting to hug one of his colleagues.

20

Graham stared out of the kitchen window watching the two figures in the distance. His father and his son… a sight he'd never imagined seeing. He sighed. He'd dreamed of this moment for so long, but…this wasn't how it was supposed to happen. Graham had always wanted a child, now he had one he wasn't sure how to deal with him. Ever since Karl's arrival at the farmhouse, dumped unceremoniously by Lydia Jenkins, Graham had fought to reconcile to the situation. On the one hand, he had the child he'd always longed for, on the other it almost certainly meant that his relationship with Ellie was over.

No matter how many times he tried, Graham couldn't understand how Kara could have kept the existence of their son to herself for so long.

…*who am I kidding?* He thought, not for the first time. *Kara is a consummate expert at playing games,* he shuddered at his slip-up…*she was an expert,* he reminded himself. During the long February evenings, a truculent Karl finally asleep in the guest bedroom, Graham had tried to work out what Kara's game plan might have been. Happenstance had resulted in her arrival on the Island during the Puppet Master enquiry, although Graham would have laid money on the likelihood that she had somehow engineered it. Her thinly veiled threat, to cause trouble between him and Ellie, had unnerved him at a time when they had enough problems to cope with.

*...I'm over analysing this...*he decided. It was simple really. She would establish herself in her new role, then torture him until he was at breaking point. Her coup de grace would be the revelation about their son. Graham shivered. He would never forget how he'd felt, the hatred bubbling up as she taunted him, how he'd even wished that she was...he shuddered again at the memory. The fact was that he had fathered a child with Kara was one more nail in the coffin of his marriage. But then again, he had a son...he couldn't describe his feelings.

...a blessing or a curse...? The question hung in the air.

Graham turned and walked into the hallway. Karl's backpack lay near the front door. The boy had stuffed some of his things into it, ready for his sleepover at Jim and Mary's that night. Graham sighed, was it wrong to feel relieved that he was going away? The last few weeks had been difficult, Karl had been almost wild on occasions. He screamed at Graham that he wanted to go home, that he wanted *'Jenny'*, his nickname for the odious woman who had played such a huge part in his childhood. Jenkins had almost run out of the house with her cheque stashed in her plastic handbag as Karl begged her to take him with her.

Despite their *'arrangement'*, she'd gone to the press after all. Graham had considered reporting her, but found he was too exhausted to bother. Besides, he couldn't take the risk that the press interest would become even more intense.

Graham picked up Karl's bag. He needed to make sure that the boy had everything, pyjamas, toiletries...he felt inside the front compartment and drew out a picture… Kara holding a baby… Karl. Graham stared at the expression on Kara's face, which was devoid of any sign of affection for the tiny bundle.

'Put that down…' Graham turned as Karl slammed his full weight into him, almost knocking him to the ground. Karl flailed at him, his fists beating on Graham's back. Jim ran towards them and grabbed hold of the boy. Karl screamed like a wounded animal as he turned on his Grandfather. It took Graham a few seconds to recover enough to pull them apart, by which time Jim's nose was bleeding profusely. Karl stopped suddenly, shocked at the sight of blood dripping down onto Jim's chest as he staggered back into the kitchen and sat down on the couch. Graham followed, pulling a tea towel off the side, and dousing it with cold water. He offered it to his father, then turned to Karl.

'…see this; see what you've done?' he shouted, pointing at his father. Karl stood in the doorway; his face drained of colour. He looked so small and pathetic as he stared at Jim; panic etched on his face. For a moment, Graham was sure he would turn and run.

'…don't Graham, can't you see the boy's upset?' Jim managed, dabbing his nose with the towel. Graham watched as Karl took a deep breath. He walked slowly to the couch and sat down.

'…I'm sorry,' he whispered, his thin shoulders shaking as he put his hand on Jim's arm. 'I'm sorry…Grandad…' Karl stared at his Grandfather as he fought to control his emotions. Jim smiled.

'Let's not say any more about it, eh?' Jim said, his voice almost cracking. He had asked Karl to call him *'Grandad'*, or whatever the lad was comfortable with several times. Up until now he'd had no luck. Jim leaned over and put his free arm around Karl, hugging the boy to his side. They sat for a few moments; Graham watched, regretting that his thoughtless actions had caused the incident. He was glad that they were bonding, Karl needed to feel safe, and Jim was wonderful with him. It was just…was he jealous? He had to admit that, yes, in a way, he was.

'I'll put the kettle on then, shall I?' he suggested, not sure how to move them on from what had happened.

'Good idea,' Jim said as he forced a smile, 'and let's have some of those chocolate biscuits, shall we?' Graham grabbed the kettle and filled it. He turned back to the sofa just as Karl looked up. The look on his face caused Graham to shiver. Karl reminded him so much of Kara. His expression was one of pure hatred.

…oo0oo…

Jim didn't tell Mary the full story. He was worried, both for the boy and for his wife. In the end he'd concocted a story that he'd bent down in the garden and hit his nose on a branch. He wasn't sure if she would believe him or not, he was never any good at lying to her.

*…she must have chosen to accept his explanation…*Graham decided as he locked the doors that night. At least he hadn't heard anything to the contrary. He'd spent the evening thinking about what had happened. He could understand Karl being angry at what he saw as an invasion of his privacy, but to fly into a rage like he had…that was something else, something that Graham couldn't understand. Jim, on the other hand, had demonstrated an amazing capacity to put himself into the boy's place. He'd suggested that it might be a good idea for Karl to spend some more time with him and Mary. Karl seized on his suggestion and headed to

his room to get the things he needed for his extended visit. Jim took the time to chat with Graham on the porch.

'I know you're angry,' he said, 'just imagine how the boy feels. We don't know what kind of poison that woman has been feeding him all his life. We have to be patient with him,' Graham sighed. He'd seen something in the look that Karl had given him. He needed time to try to sort out his head. It was as though Jim knew what he was thinking.

'Look, why don't we talk about this when the heat's gone out of it? Your Mom and I will look after him for as long as you need us to.' Graham had to admit there was wisdom in his suggestion.

'Are you sure about this, Dad?' he asked. Jim nodded in response. 'I've got a meeting booked for next Thursday, at the school in the village. I was wondering…it might be a good idea for you to come with us, if you're free?' Jim smiled.

'Graham, you've no idea how much it that means to your Mom and me, I'd be only too pleased. Don't give up on him, he's worth fighting for.' Graham could tell that his father was close to tears as he watched the boy struggle down the stairs with his bag slung over his shoulder.

The silence of the house, once they had left, was almost too much to bear. Graham sat staring out into the encroaching night before climbing the stairs to his office. He would give anything to be able to talk to Ellie about this, ironically, she was the last person that would want to take part in that particular conversation. He switched on his computer. There was someone he could talk to. He hadn't contacted her since…he thought back to the night that Ellie had overheard his Internet exchange all those months before. What had she thought he was doing, him watching porn? Talking to a lover, even to Kara herself? He doubted he'd get the chance to explain any time soon. She had said to him once that sometimes you needed to talk to someone who was one step removed from the situation. It was almost impossible, she maintained, to be a therapist to someone that you loved. An objective opinion was worth so much more than platitudes given by someone with an emotional attachment. That was all his Internet chats were, a chance to air concerns to a third party without fear that they were telling him what he wanted to hear, and not what he needed to hear. He logged onto website and entered the chat room.

…*typical,* he thought, no-one there he recognised. He sent a message instead

…*arrange a chat? Need to talk*…Graham stared at the screen, there was something else he needed to do, something that he'd decided that afternoon in the lab when Emlyn had delivered the news that he was on enforced leave. He opened his email account and typed in Simon Daventree's name.

…*I know this may be totally out of order, and I won't blame you if you feel it will compromise you in any way,* he typed, *but I really need to convince someone to investigate the Billingham case again. I know that it's not possible for me to be associated with it, can you help in any way?* There, it was done, he pressed send and closed down his laptop. He felt exhausted after what had happened earlier, he needed some sleep.

21

Chetwynd paced around her office; her hands clasped behind her back. She wasn't looking forward to her next appointment, not least because she would have to deal with the aftermath. It had been arranged at short notice two days ago, within hours of Mason's briefing.

...how could I have missed this? How had he weaselled his way back into a position of authority, after everything that happened last year...she thought ...*I should have refused... how dare he think he can manipulate me...who does he think he is, anyway...?* It was too late now, though, he was due in a few minutes, otherwise she might have cancelled altogether. Under the circumstances, she'd decided, it was the best she could hope for. She could imagine how Porter and the rest of her team would take the news. After the disappointment of not being able to close the last case, she knew it would come as a kick in the teeth.

It made sense that the murder of Anthea Harrold was being investigated by officers from Llay station, it was after all a local matter. She couldn't work out why they'd been asked to take over the Ronnie Bowers case as well. Chester was forty-seven miles from her station, forty-nine from Wrexham, nothing in it really. Her team was equally capable...something wasn't right. It had to be down to their performance in the Puppet Master case.

Perhaps it had been decided that Bangor had enough on their hands with the Harrington-Smythe murder. But to put someone like him in charge…it hadn't taken her long to realise why information had stopped flowing her way. He was up to his old tricks. She wasn't a fool, this was payback, but how the hell had he managed it?

She cursed herself again for not keeping her finger on the pulse. There was a time when she knew virtually everything that went on in North Wales, and beyond. Now, it seemed, she was completely out of touch. Despite her rationale that they had priority; she'd been met with a flat refusal to hand over any information unless certain criteria were met. She was disappointed, not to say furious that his conditions were being upheld. She shook her head. It was the effect on Porter and the team that she was dreading the most. They'd had enough to deal with, what with the incident with the files…there was a knock on the door. Chetwynd stopped pacing and smoothed down her jacket. She took a deep breath.

'Come in,' she said, picking up a clipboard, she needed to look busy.

'Good afternoon Detective Chief Superintendent Chetwynd,' a voice that oozed a malevolent satisfaction, a voice she'd thought she would never hear again.

'Good afternoon, please take a seat, DCI Horton.'

…oo0oo…

Horton's conditions were simple, a shared investigation, or he would insist on keeping the two murders he was now looking into, within his station. It didn't take Chetwynd long to suspect that despite his false bravado he was, once again, out of his depth. Knowing his history and the way he operated, she knew that once the murders were solved, he would claim all the credit and share none of the glory with his team. She also knew that her team had only to produce conclusive proof that the three murders were linked, and jurisdiction over the entire case would revert to her. Now, though, they didn't have that proof, only theories, suspicions. She studied Horton as he sat smug faced, his hands clasped across his considerable stomach.

...how the hell had he managed to talk his way back in...? She wondered. She thought he would have retired after what happened to him at the hands of his kidnapper last year. But no, he was here, like the proverbial bad penny. Chetwynd glanced at her watch. They were due downstairs in ten minutes. She felt duty bound to lay down some ground rules.

'I'm confident that you'll be sensitive of the need to keep to the point when we join the rest of my team, DCI Horton,' she said, knowing that she felt anything but. 'They've experienced an extremely difficult time following the inconclusive nature of the Prothero case, as I'm sure you are aware.'

'No, Ma'am I wasn't aware, please can you fill me in, after all I wouldn't want to say anything out of order, now, would I?' Horton grinned at her discomfort, his voice dripping with sarcasm. Chetwynd didn't believe that Horton was ignorant of what had gone on in her station, she knew that he would relish any opportunity to rub salt in the wounds. This had gone far enough, she decided, their game of cat and mouse had to end. She picked up the phone, dialled a non-existent number and waited for a few seconds before starting a one-sided conversation.

'DCI Porter, yes, Chetwynd here,' she saw Horton's face settle into a self-satisfied smirk, he thought he'd won. 'I've received some news I thought you might like to be made aware of. It seems that we won't be allowed to liaise on the two murders we believed were linked with our current case.' She almost laughed as Horton's face started to twitch, the grimace that passed for a smile slid as he sat upright, his hands clamped firmly on the arms of the chair.

'I will of course be bringing the refusal of the SIO to co-operate with us, to the attention of his station commander…' she stopped, cocked her head to one side, looking directly at Horton, 'unless of course I can manage to convince him to allow us to take the lead on the case.' Horton sat back heavily; he knew when he was beaten. The warning he'd been issued with when he was placed in his new post still rang in his ears. He was on probation. If he put a foot wrong, he would have to retire. Besides which, there were still some things that he didn't ever want anyone to find out, secrets that could do with being buried forever. Losing his job might mean a formal enquiry, he couldn't afford the risk.

He nodded reluctantly at Chetwynd, who still held the receiver to her ear, even though there was no one on the other end of the call. She knew how to play him, she had always known, going back to their days at training. Horton adjusted his tie, cleared his throat, and nodded to her again. She replaced the receiver and stood up, indicating that he should follow her.

…oo0oo…

Porter and the rest of the team were waiting in the Interview Room. He knew that Chetwynd was meeting with the SIO on the Harrold and Bowers murders, but that was all he knew. It was therefore somewhat of a shock when Chetwynd walked into the room with her 'guest'. Porter had to give her full credit, by the time she had finished introducing him in his new capacity, even he was impressed by what she'd said. She praised Horton's dedication to the job, returning to full-time duty, even though he had suffered considerably at the hands of his kidnapper. She spoke about his years of service that had stood him in good stead for the challenge they had been presented with. She thanked him for his unconditional co-operation and selfless action in allowing her team to take the lead in what they had dubbed the *'Canterbury Murders'*. His actions were admirable to say the least.

Porter laughed inwardly as he watched Chetwynd massaging Horton's ego, trying to place him in a flattering light, so that he would allow them to get on with their jobs and not interfere. Somehow, he couldn't see that happening. How had the old devil got away with it? At the very least he was guilty of serious professional malpractice; mistakes that might well have resulted in more victims than necessary in the Prothero case. Porter shifted as he realised that Chetwynd had finished speaking and was waiting for him to say something. He cleared his throat; his main goal now was to make headway in the current case. There had been enough killing in the area to last a lifetime, he didn't intend to allow his personal feelings about Horton to allow any more.

'I'm, er, I'm sure I speak for us all when I say that I hope we can work together,' he said, then sat down, arms folded. Chetwynd nodded. She was sure that she could placate Porter, and that the other members of the team would follow his lead. For now, that was the best she could hope for.

Porter's team had worked hard on their presentation, they'd pulled together a comprehensive summary that they could be proud of. Chetwynd tried hard to hide the look of satisfaction as she watched Horton try to keep up and promised herself that she would do all she could to stop him wrecking their chances of a swift resolution.

...comes to something when I have to watch my back against fellow police officers, let alone the villains... she thought, but there it was, and she had to cope with it, she just wished it was anyone but Horton.

22

Ellie had already apologised to Chetwynd, promising to get to the briefing as soon as she could. A call from Mr. Richardson the previous day had unnerved her. He had some distressing news that necessitated an urgent appointment, he told her, they couldn't afford to delay matters. Ellie sat in the Reception area, watching his secretary filing her nails, an action that was at odds with the sombre façade of the office that housed her. Ellie shook her head as the phone rang out several times, the girl tutted, eventually reaching out for the receiver. In the age of technology, Richardson and Ball had evidently chosen not to move with the times, and an outmoded telephone system still served their business.

Ellie checked her phone. Two calls from Graham, voice messages to match, a text pleading for a further meeting, four calls from her mother, one with an additional voice message, a curt demand that they discuss the situation before she took the matter further. Ellie sighed; she'd had enough of her mother's games. If Julia's sole aim was to acquire money from Ruth's estate, then maybe giving her something that would satisfy her and get her off Ellie's back for good. Sadly, she suspected that it wouldn't, and that within a short space of time her mother would be back asking for more.

'You can go through now,' the girl behind the desk announced as she resumed her manicure. Ellie muttered her thanks and walked down the dark corridor to Mr. Richardson's office. What was it with these dingy offices, did the British think that working in dark surroundings gave them more gravitas? She realised what it was that made her uncomfortable in her current offices...the lack of light, the air of secrecy that these old buildings generated. She needed light, space to move. What she had now was oppressive, heavy. She made a mental note to ask Miss Pritchard to double her efforts in her search for new premises.

'Ms. Shaw, thank you for coming in at such short notice,' Mr. Richardson stood to greet her, holding out his hand, she took it and noticed how firm his grasp was. He indicated a chair, and she sat down to face him. 'May I say how very well you're looking?' he murmured, the words seemed insincere, his smile never seemed to reach his eyes.

'Thank you, Mr. Richardson, shall we get on with it,' she didn't have time for this veneer of politeness. She realised, of course, her position had changed, she was now a person in possession of a rather large inheritance, and therefore someone that Richardson would no doubt like to keep on side, maybe as a potential client.

She sighed, ...*all this because Ruth died*... she thought. Richardson shuffled the papers, a habit that had always annoyed Ellie. He cleared his throat before speaking.

'We, er, I've had a letter from a firm of solicitors, er, should I say lawyers, in, er, Boston,' he started. Ellie sat upright, the hairs on the back of her neck had begun to stand up, a shiver travelled down her spine. She heard a gasp; she knew it wasn't her doing the gasping.

'It's my mother isn't it?' she asked, knowing the answer.

Richardson nodded, 'Yes,' he sighed, 'I'm afraid it is.'

…oo0oo…

During the time it took her to walk from Richardson's office to her car, Ellie tried to calm down. Her mother had pulled some tricks in her life, but none, Ellie decided, was as despicable as this. In light of what she'd just been told, her earlier decision to allow her mother a generous part of Ruth's estate was questionable.

…how could she? Ellie asked herself over and over, *how could she do this?*

*…you know how…*came the answer*…you've always known…*sadly, Ellie knew that Ruth was right.

The email that Richardson and Ball had received had been short and to the point…Julia Clifford-Harvey-Morrison had contacted them and asked them to act on her behalf. She intended to take legal steps to challenge the Last Will and Testament of her daughter Ruth Hilary Clifford-Prothero, on the grounds that her daughter was incapable of managing her financial affairs. There was a possibility, the source of which was impeccable they asserted, that Mrs. Prothero had mental problems and was seeing a therapist around the time that the Will was drawn up. They were also investigating claims that Ruth had promised her mother a substantial amount of money, as well as several properties, and some jewellery given to her by her late maternal grandmother.

Richardson had expressed his horror at this turn of events, not least because he had drawn the Will up himself. He did, however, have some words of comfort for Ellie regarding the likelihood of Julia succeeding in her plan.

'Firstly, your sister had the foresight to engage a team of experts to assess her state of mind. I have the reports they submitted on file; she was declared fully competent.' He made a sign in the air, as though ticking off the first item. 'Secondly, and this is perhaps the most important thing, no one else had a copy of Mrs. Prothero's Will, so no one could have known what was in it except her and, of course, me. At the time of reading the Will, I believe that not even you,' he indicated Ellie, 'knew that Mrs. Prothero owned any property. Your mother's claim that she is entitled to anything other than what was listed at the first reading of the Will, has no basis. People can promise the earth to expectant relatives and friends, but at the end of the day, unless those promises are included in writing, in the form of their actual Last Will and Testament, it unlikely that they will stand up in a court of law.'

Richardson finished his diatribe by banging his fist on his desk, a move so at odds with his usual sober demeanour, it made Ellie jump. She could see where he was going with this. Julia's claim about the properties were transparently false. It was true, not even Ellie had known about them until the Will was read, there in Richardson's office, only a few a weeks ago. She shook her head as she unlocked the car door.

...how could she...? She thought again, although the answer was becoming clearer with every passing moment.

Julia Morrison was a parasite, and one that Ellie could well live without.

Chetwynd was just about to wrap up the meeting when the door opened. Horton's mouth dropped as he watched Ellie Shaw walk in. Her entrance was not one that he had expected, no one had pre-warned him that she was back on the team…*but then again…* he thought…*what did I expect…?*

Horton's sense of being tolerated, almost patronised had grown during the last few hours. Everyone kept referring to the cases as the '*Canterbury Murders'*, he was finding it hard to keep up with their theories. The growing sense of being out of his depth increased as he listened to the members of Porter's team reporting their findings. The least Chetwynd could have done was to have forwarded him some notes on their progress. He had to keep reminding himself that his position was a fragile one. He needed to be seen to be working with Chetwynd, not against her, at least if he wanted to keep his job. Maybe he should have brought a few members of his own team to back him up?

Chetwynd watched him struggling to keep up. She needed to include him soon, otherwise he would start causing problems. Grandstanding was Horton's way of deflecting attention from his shortcomings. They didn't have time for any of his theatrical machinations. She waited until Mason had finished speaking.

'I'm aware that this meeting has caught people on the hop, so to speak,' she said, 'DCI Horton, didn't I see that DS Rowan is your second in command? It might be prudent to arrange a further briefing with her present.' Horton grabbed at the lifeline she'd thrown him.

'Yes, she, er, she couldn't be here today, problems at home, the kids or something…' he rolled his eyes to the ceiling, not realising how patronisingly sexist his remark sounded. Chetwynd, for one, knew that DS Janet

Rowan, who's career she had been watching with interest over the last few years, didn't have any kids.

'Well, I'm sure we can arrange something soon. Her input would be extremely valuable, not to say vital.' Chetwynd went on, nothing that Horton said would surprise her, she wasn't going to let him off the hook without sending the message she wanted him to absorb…*we know who's doing all the work, buster, and it's not you…!*

Horton shifted in his seat; Chetwynd knew him too well. She knew all his shortcomings, he only hoped that he could convince her to say something complementary in her report. He wasn't sure if his discomfort was because of this, or the fact that Ellie Shaw hadn't taken her eyes off him since her arrival. Either way, he knew when he was beaten. Playing power games with Chetwynd was one thing, having to cope with Ellie Shaw as well…he couldn't take the risk.

Chetwynd had given him a way out and he intended to take it.

…oo0oo…

Ellie gathered her things; it hadn't taken her long to sum up the situation in the briefing room. Horton was back, and with his arrival all the insecurities she had felt during the early days of the Puppet Master case had resurfaced. She grabbed her coat and headed for the door, hoping to avoid a face to face encounter with him.

'Could you spare a few minutes?' Ellie turned round. Porter stood behind her; he could sense her unease.

'I, I don't think…' she started. He nodded.

'Coffee?' he suggested, 'there's something I'd like to discuss if you…'

'Yes, coffee would be great,' she agreed, 'but not here, much as I love your canteen manager, she can't make a decent cup.' They both laughed nervously. Ellie was conscious of being watched as Porter held open the door and they left the room.

They walked towards the High Street in silence. Ellie thought about the repercussions of Horton's return as they entered the tiny Coffee House. She sat down as Porter walked to the counter to order. Seeing Horton again was the last thing she needed. He was a reminder of John Prothero, of how she had felt undermined during the early days of the case. If he was going to be part of this team…Porter placed her cup on the table, she murmured her thanks.

'First of all,' Porter started, 'I don't think we have to worry about Horton too much, Chetwynd can deal with him. I'm sure she knows that we have too much to prove to allow him to ride roughshod over this investigation, especially after…' he paused and took a sip of his drink. Ellie realised that he was feeling as trepidatious as herself. Horton's appearance had rattled them all. It was a few moments before she realised that Porter had started talking again.

'…every faith in you. Which is why I have a favour to ask.' Ellie watched as he fiddled with a bag of sugar.

*…don't you just love it when…*Ruth chimed in.

*…hush Ruth…let the man be…*Ellie couldn't help but smile.

'Why don't you just ask?' she said. 'I can always say 'no' after all.' Porter threw the sugar down and sighed.

'I know you've only been back a short while, but…this case, I was wondering if you could…if you'd consider coming…' he shook his head. 'We have so little to go on, I thought maybe you could…'

*...put him out of his misery for crying out loud...*Ruth screamed inside Ellie's head.

'Actually, I've been thinking. It might be helpful if I could go with you to view one of the crime scenes... Harrington Hall, maybe,' she suggested. Porter nodded.

'That's just what I had in mind... you never know, perhaps...' he cleared his throat.

*...he doesn't want to admit it...*Ellie thought...*the things I can do, the things that he's witnessed...he doesn't want to acknowledge that he believes I can do them...*

...no more than you do, do you sweetie...? Ruth reminded her...*because admitting it makes it real, doesn't it...?*

'I'll come with you, just tell me when,' she said. Porter nodded, his relief evident.

*...I can do this...*she thought. She shuddered as a wave of energy passed through her.

23

Porter pulled up on the gravel parking area. Memories of the last time he had been at the Retreat flooded back as he walked towards the huge oak door. For the life of him he couldn't understand why Ellie was still living here. Then again, where else could she go? At least here she had friends, people who cared about her, who could help her to recover from what she'd been through.

Since Chetwynd had sanctioned Ellie's return to the station for Mason's briefing, Porter had watched her with awe. He had to remind himself that it had only been a few months since she'd been in hospital suffering from the aftereffects of John Prothero's night of torture. Her recovery had been nothing short of miraculous. Whatever was going on here, he was glad it was working.

He remembered the first time he saw her after that night. She was even more emaciated than she'd been before. It made him speculate as to whether she could stand up, let alone come back to work. She'd proved him wrong, though, turning up every day, attending all the briefings and making valuable contributions to the investigation. He was only sorry that Horton's attendance seemed to have thrown her. He had his doubts about today, but with such a lack of leads…Ellie might be able to give them something to go on, although what that could be, he could only imagine.

The heavy door groaned as Porter pushed it. The hall was dark after the morning sunlight, and he blinked as he stepped inside, his eyes gradually becoming accustomed to the gloom. He was about to ring a bell on the side-table when he stopped. For a moment he was back to the night that he'd orchestrated the raid that had culminated in John Prothero's arrest, and the three women he'd held captive being rescued. He'd taken no direct credit for how the event had unfolded; he was just grateful that they'd managed to resolve the situation without further loss of life.

A side-door opened, Ellie jumped when she saw him standing in front of the door, his identity cloaked in shadow. She relaxed as she realised who he was and let go of the breath she was holding.

'Sorry,' he murmured, 'didn't think…' she shook her head.

'My fault,' she said, blushing, although she couldn't explain why.

'Ready?' he asked curtly as he turned and headed back out of the door, leaving her standing in the hallway. She grabbed her bag and jacket followed him out into the morning brightness, hurrying towards his car. Since her return to work she'd been involved in all the briefings at the station, but up until now she had never found an opportunity, or the right words to thank him for what he'd done. She had to admit to feeling somewhat nervous of what they would talk about now that they were alone together.

'Thank you for coming today,' he said as they made their way towards the bridge. 'We're, err, we're meeting a DS Rowan at the Hall.'

'That's Horton's officer isn't it?' Ellie asked. Was it her imagination, or was Porter just as nervous about today as she was?

'Mm...' he said by way of a reply, 'look, I just wanted...'

'...by the way, I just wanted...' they started at the same time. Porter stopped talking, he nodded towards her. Ellie took a deep breath; they had to get this hurdle out of the way.

'...I didn't get the chance, I mean, I haven't been able to say this...oh, hell...' her words stumbled out, she shook her head.

...oh, for crying out loud...just thank the man... Ruth's voice screamed inside Ellie's head...*I'd thank him myself, only it's a bit difficult*...Ellie smiled, Ruth certainly had a way of reinforcing her courage when she needed it, and she really needed her help right now.

'Thank you,' she managed, 'you and all your team for what you did. I can't begin...' Porter nodded.

'You're welcome, I'm glad...' he stopped, Ellie could tell he was grasping for the right words, '...I'm glad you said that, about the team, it wasn't just me...'

'Well thank you anyway,' she said hesitantly. Porter seemed embarrassed at what she'd said. She suspected that he would give anything for her to talk about something else. She cleared her throat. 'Could you go over what we're aiming for today?'

Porter sighed, not in exasperation, Ellie knew, but in relief. The hurdle, she believed, had been well and truly dealt with.

...oo0oo...

DS Janet Rowan shivered as she walked through the tunnel towards the bathhouse. She couldn't imagine anyone considering using it as a means of escape, too narrow, too risky. Forensics had combed every inch of it without finding anything relevant to the case.

… *waste of time*…she thought. Anyone with an iota of sense would know that. Still, procedures had to be followed, and Porter and his lot were on the ball. In the few days since her arrival at Bangor; she had started to appreciate the 'tight ship' that Chetwynd and her team were renowned for. It was a pity that the *'Puppet Master'* case had been such a disaster.

If gossip was to be believed it was mostly down to '*…he who shall not be taken any notice of…*' as one of her colleagues had joked. She recalled Horton's pathetic attempts at trying to organise her and her fellow officers. Things had gone from bad to worse since his arrival, his reputation had preceded him…he didn't stand a chance really.

Llay Station's investigation into both the Bowers and Harrold murders had been well underway before they'd been told that they had to share them with another station…she shook her head. Chetwynd and her team would be taking over the lead in this case, that was all there was to it, even though evidence of this so-called link was tenuous at best. At least she was in the forefront and not Horton. Acting as liaison between the two teams was demanding, but then again, she'd always been up for a challenge. She could understand the protocol that Horton had been forced to follow. Bangor station did seem to have precedence over the current investigation, but as for having a weirdo involved in profiling the suspect… she thought back to the conversation she had had with Horton just after he returned from Bangor. His instructions were brief. She would be his eyes and ears on the case, reporting directly to him every day, rather than to Chetwynd or Porter. He would then relay that information back to Bangor, insisting that any new information uncovered at Llay Station would go through him. At first, she thought he was joking, either that or he'd lost the plot. It took her several minutes to realise that he was serious. He had placed her in an impossible position, asking her to do her job with one hand tied behind her back. She had no intention of colluding with him in a game of one-upmanship against Chetwynd, she valued her career and her integrity too much for that. Horton was walking a thin line. One false move and he'd be obliged to retire. It wasn't anything she hadn't heard before; it was just that this time it made sense.

It was as if he had a huge sandwich board around his neck that read *'…I botched the Puppet Master case up and no-one is sure if my incompetence caused more deaths in the long run…'* she got the picture. She couldn't work out why he was still in a position of authority though. No matter how many of her colleagues she spoke to, or how much digging she did, neither could anyone else.

What really made her angry was that she had been in line for a promotion to DI before he waltzed into the station and caught everyone off guard. Word from above was that any changes would have to be placed on hold until he settled in. The last thing he seemed to want was someone, anyone, to gain a promotion after his recent experiences. She had wondered if he was one of those people who craved success but wasn't happy unless people around him were seen to fail. Horton seemed only too happy with things as they were, leaving Rowan more than a little frustrated, and now this, this… what should she call it? A crazy outing with DCI Porter and his ghost-busting sidekick.

Even though Rowan had mixed feeling about being seconded to Porter's team, she had to admit that she was curious to see what all the fuss was about. Chetwynd had given her only the slightest inkling of what she could expect at their last meeting, and Horton…he was rude to the point of being offensive about Ellie Shaw and her involvement in the Prothero case.

She shone her torch along each side of the tunnel as she walked. The neon lighting was low, it gave the passageway a dingy, yellow colour. She wasn't sure what she'd find that Forensics had missed, probably nothing. The path ended in a short flight of steps, a door at the top. She opened it and stepped out into a small hallway.

She could hear voices from the next room, Porter and the Shaw woman must have arrived before her. Damn, she wanted to be there before them, she wasn't sure why. Rowan slid the screen door to one side. She could see Porter standing by the window. He raised his finger to his lips as she stepped inside the room. As far as Rowan could see, he was alone. He pointed towards the ornate lacquer screen that stood in the far corner. Rowan cocked her head to one side and frowned…what on earth? She walked over to where Porter stood and kept as still as she could.

They stood silently for several minutes before Ellie stepped out from behind the screen. Rowan immediate impression was one of shock, she found it hard to believe that the diminutive figure was the subject of so much gossip. Ellie walked around the perimeter of the room, her hands held together as though in prayer, the tips of her fingers underneath her nose. She seemed to be focusing on the floor, as she walked past them for the third time. Rowan could see that she wasn't focusing on anything at all.

Porter watched as Ellie raised her head and looked out of the picture window. He was beginning to wonder if this was all a waste…Ellie took a deep breath and closed her eyes. Her hands dropped down to her sides.

'…he was angry…things weren't going the way he wanted them to go…' she said. Rowan started to speak; Porter put his hand on her arm to stop her. '…he took his anger out on the girl… he…he hit her…she screamed, she begged…' Ellie shuddered. The image of a man in a bathrobe, a young girl, heavily made up, her hand raised in a defensive pose flickered across her mind. '…he…he tore her clothes,' she said, shaking her head.

Ellie walked to the doorway and into a smaller room beyond, the scene of the murder. Porter and Rowan followed, watching as Ellie repeated her actions, circling the area several times. Forensics had long since finished in here, but Porter was annoyed that the place had been sanitised without letting him know. He wondered if it would have any bearing on Ellie. She stopped in front of the table; the chess set had been removed.

'He sat here,' she said pointing to the cushioned area, he was still angry. '…he was in pain…his buttock, it was injured…I don't know…a bite…?' Porter nodded; he'd kept several key pieces of information from Ellie, just to test her… he looked over at Rowan. She shook her head in disbelief. She knew what Porter had done; in fact, she had suggested doing it. Ellie stepped to the side, she pointed to the cabinet.

'He had a drink…he felt dizzy…he decided to spend the night here…' she turned round to face them, '…a man…came into the room, he'd been waiting since before the girl arrived, downstairs…he was wearing a black outfit, it looks like…martial arts…black mask, his head covered in a black scarf…' Ellie's face changed…

she could see the man coming through the door…Porter noticed the shift in her as an expression of panic suffused her face.

'It's all right Ellie,' he said, trying to reassure her, 'it's not real… it's a memory…'

'…he's…he's got a sword, a Samurai sword…he…' she stepped back, holding her hand up in front of her face. To her the vision was real. She screamed and dropped to her knees a split second before Porter and Rowan stepped forward. Porter hesitated as Rowan knelt by Ellie's side. She put her hand on Ellie's back. Ellie reacted as though she'd been struck.

'Get your hands off me…' she screamed. Rowan sat back in shock. She looked over at Porter, he shrugged… it took him a few seconds to recover. Ellie had curled up in a foetal position on the rush matting, her hands covering her head. Porter knelt by her side.

'Ellie,' he said gently, '…Ellie, can you hear me?' he waited… she nodded. 'Take your time, Ellie…don't move until you're ready…do you want us to leave you alone, or shall we stay?' Whatever had just happened to her, it had shocked both him and Rowan. Porter wanted Ellie to feel as though she was in control.

'…stay…' Ellie whispered, she reached out her hand. Porter held it as he sat down on the floor and sighed.

Whatever 'gift' Ellie Shaw had; they couldn't put her through this again, not without seriously considering the effect it would have on her.

…oo0oo…

Rowan watched as Porter's car pulled out of the car park. If she hadn't been there, she would never have believed what had just happened. She remembered Porter's words … *it's not real…it's a memory…* She was convinced that, at least to Ellie, it *was* real, it wasn't just a memory. Rowan had decided that whatever was going on here, and she couldn't figure out what that was, for some reason, Ellie was able to 'see' things that she and…she stopped. Since when she had believed in the supernatural…the paranormal? Yet there had to be something to it.

She made her way back to the station, how on earth was she going to write this one up.

…very carefully… she decided.

…oo0oo…

Porter sat in his car. Ellie had slept for most of the journey back to the Retreat. He'd helped her back into the house, asking her repeatedly if she thought it would be a good idea to see a doctor. She smiled weakly.

'I don't think a doctor would be able to help me…do you?' she asked. Porter shook his head.

'Thank you, for what you did back there,' he said. Ellie sighed.

'I didn't really do anything, though, did I? I just told you things you already knew,'

'You'd be surprised,' Porter told her, she started to feel uncomfortable as he stared at her. They both turned as Della Mathers walked into the hallway.

'Everything all right?' she asked. Porter was sure she knew that something had happened. 'Why don't you both join me…we could have some…?' Porter cleared his throat.

'I need to be getting back to the station,' he said. Della nodded.

'Ellie, you go through, I'll see DCI Porter out.' Ellie nodded to Porter and made her way through to Della's lounge. Della turned to Porter; he could sense her concern.

'You need to be careful, Bill,' she said, 'Ellie might give the impression that she's ready to move on, the truth is she's not…'

Porter nodded. It wasn't until he was almost back at the station that he realised that her words could be taken in more than one context.

24

The call of a Barn Owl was amplified in the silence of the night. Della Mathers stood looking out of her bedroom window, onto the moonlit gardens. She'd tossed and turned for hours, chasing sleep that refused to be caught. Something was wrong, something was bothering her. Things had changed since the show-down with John Prothero, they would never be the same again. No matter how philosophically she looked at events, which she believed happened for a reason, what they had experienced at his hands would take a long time to get over.

Tonight, though, tonight felt different. She'd been overwhelmed by a need to double-check everything downstairs, to make sure that things were as they should be. She'd tried to resist the urge to climb out of her warm bed, but the pull was too great. In the end, she had succumbed and drew on her dressing gown, wincing as she tried to ease it over her arm. She stood for a few moments, closing her eyes, calming her breathing.

...what now...? she asked silently. A light frost had highlighted the branches of the trees, reflecting the moonlight. Every leaf seemed to shine, giving the scene an ethereal quality. Della gasped as the owl swooped across her field of vision, its wings outstretched. It was

so close that she could see its talons flexing as it prepared to snatch its prey.

*...go downstairs...you need to go downstairs...*Della looked around. No one there, not that she expected to see anyone. This was how it always was. A voice, a guide, a feeling. The landing was silent as she made her way to the top of the staircase, the full moon sending beams of light onto the polished oak floorboards. They creaked gently as she padded along. She anticipated every sound the floor would make and greeted them like old friends. Occasionally she heard the shifting wood, contracting as it cooled from the ancient central heating. It was cold, very cold, and she shrugged the shoulders of her dressing gown, trying to gain as much warmth from it as she could.

A noise...someone was humming, low but resonant, something almost without melody, the kind of sound someone makes when they're afraid and trying to comfort themselves. A figure stood in the hallway, arms wrapped around their waist, rocking backwards and forwards, their face turned upwards towards the ceiling... Ellie. She knew better than to call out. If Ellie was sleepwalking it might be dangerous to wake her suddenly.

Della came down the stairs as quietly as she could. Ellie was oblivious to her presence as she turned around still humming. Her eyes were wide open, her thin arms held tightly around her body. Della held her breath as Ellie looked straight at her and started singing a few words...

...and a hay harvest breeze...swing, swing together...other will fill our places...

...those words...Della knew them, but she couldn't place them. Ellie stopped, she sighed as she turned towards the door of the Great Hall and walked forward.

She pushed open the door and stood on the threshold, her silhouette outlined in the moonlight. Della knew that Ellie avoided this room whenever possible, it held nothing but bad memories for her. She watched as Ellie stood motionless for several minutes. Gradually, she turned her head to the side and looked down to the floor.

…*she's waiting for you*…a whisper.

Della took a few steps forward. Ellie gasped as she ran to the centre of the Hall to the spot where John Prothero had placed her on the night…Della shivered, knowing that all she could do for the moment was watch. Ellie knelt in a parody of the position she'd been forced to assume by their tormentor, her arms thrust out in supplication. She stared towards the windows, now divested of their coverings. The moonlight bathed her body in a celestial spotlight.

Della caught her breath, she knew that Ellie had lost weight over the last few months, now she realised how much. Ellie was almost skeletal underneath her nightgown, her arms looked skeletal as she reached out towards the bay windows. A movement stirred the curtains to the right side of the window, drawn back to their very limit. Della, still in the shadows, pressed back against the panelling. She could see Ellie breathing heavily as she sat back on her heels, her head dropped to her chest as though someone had flicked a switch. Della jumped as she felt a faint breath on her neck.

…*I didn't come for Ellie, I came to speak to you, she needs your help…I…need your help…*

'I know Ruth,' Della answered, 'just…tell me what to do.'

Ellie was still asleep the next morning as Della sat in her lounge sipping sweet tea and eating toast. She thought over the events of the night before. Ruth was right, Ellie needed to regain her independence, but how to suggest it to her without making her feel that she was being abandoned?

In the end it wasn't that much of a problem. The message that Della had received from Ruth the previous night, had been the first thing that Ellie talked about when they met up later that morning. By that time Della was being driven almost to distraction by the memory of the tune that Ellie had been humming the night before. She knew it, she knew it so well, and yet? In the end she managed to turn her attention elsewhere, hoping that if she did, the memory would come back to her. *'Back burner thinking'*, she called it. Della was in the greenhouse when Ellie found her. She allowed her to drive the conversation.

'Della, you know that I've been here for quite a while now,' Ellie was stalling, 'it's just that, I think, it might be time, you know, for me…' she stopped. She didn't want to sound ungrateful for all that Della had done for her, but she'd woken up this morning with the urge to move on. She was sure that this was the right move, after all she couldn't stay here for ever. Della was preparing a seed tray, filling the compartments with compost. She sensed the need to keep the tone of their conversation casual.

'If you feel you're ready, Ellie, then I think it would be an excellent idea,' she said, 'could you pass me the trowel, please?' Ellie moved one of the trays from the edge of the bench and reached for the trowel. 'Had you got anywhere in mind, to live I mean?'

'I was thinking, maybe, Ruth's cottage,' she shivered as she spoke. In truth, she'd thought nothing of the kind, it was an idea that had just popped into her head, but then she shouldn't think that way, should she? Nothing was a mistake, everything was meant to be, she could sense Ruth's amusement. Della nodded.

'I think that would be as good a place as any,' she said carefully. She was more than aware that if Ellie's experiences at the Retreat were hard to live with, then moving back to the cottage might prove even more problematic.

'Look, I know what you're thinking…' Ellie started.

'I should hope so by now,' Della joked, she smiled at Ellie.

'I'm going to give it a try, Della, I have to.' Della could sense Ellie's emotions welling up.

'Well then, that's settled. We'll help you to get things moving…but you need to know, Ellie, you'll always be welcome back if you decide…'

'I know, Della, and thank you. You and Odelia have been more like family to me than you know.' She moved towards Della, as the older woman held out her arms. This was something Ellie would miss. The closeness that had built up between them over the last few months meant so much, especially in the light of her own mother's coldness.

'I have every faith in you, you're stronger than you know, sweetheart,' Ellie held on to Della as though her life would depend on it.

In some ways it would.

25

When Ellie thought about it later, she admitted to herself that it was the only place she could go. She felt sad when she realised that almost all her links on the Island had been broken. She couldn't go back to the farmhouse, to Graham, that wouldn't work…too much water had passed under the bridge for that to work.

She manoeuvred the car around the twisting bends, the sight of the cottage clutched at her heart…what was she been thinking? She hadn't been back here since the day that Ruth and Max…she swallowed hard. Memories of the times that she and Graham had visited them came flooding back. Ruth preparing a sumptuous meal, Max showing her his latest toy, John…

…this was a mistake… she thought…*I should never…*

*…don't be such a scaredy cat…*Ruth teased her…*this was my home, now it's yours…*

Ellie knew she was right, this had always been more Ruth's cottage than…she couldn't bring herself to think about John, not now. Odelia had offered to come with her, but Ellie insisted on going alone. She needed to take the first step. She promised to arrange a get-together as soon as she'd settled down, but for now…she had chosen not to call it a *'housewarming'*, although time would tell.

The front door was hard to open, the wooden surround swollen with damp. Ellie pushed against it with her shoulder, and all too soon she stood in the hallway. Memories came crashing in as she recalled the last time she was there. The noises, Ruth calling, Max shouting down the stairs. The crack of the gun as…this wasn't such a good idea, she'd find a hotel room, make other arrangements. She picked up her case, then felt a gentle push in the small of her back.

…you'll be fine, nothing to fear, Ellie…welcome home...

The cottage was damp, a musty smell had developed during the winter months. A thin layer of mildew bloomed on the leather furniture in the lounge, the aroma was unmistakable. Ellie knew that John had been back there briefly when he had come back, just after… He'd made a half-hearted attempt to clean up the mess left by the Forensic team, but evidence of what had happened still stained the floor tiles. The residual smell invaded Ellie's senses, causing her to retch at the invasion. She ran out onto the front porch, her emotions battered by her memories, and held onto a tall wooden pillar as she tried to clear her thoughts. Eventually she turned and walked slowly back to the front door.

…good, now that's out of the way, let's get some work done, shall we…?

Ellie sighed; how could Ruth be so matter of fact about the whole thing? Was it always going to be this way?

*…admit it Ellie, there is a funny side. Who'd have thought you'd end up living here with your dead sister's ghost...*Ellie shook her head, if there was a funny side, she couldn't see it just now. She carried her bags through to the lounge. She'd forgotten how much effort Ruth had put into decorating the place. A strange calm settled around her, she felt like she was coming home. It was a feeling she hadn't had since she lived at the farmhouse with Graham.

…first things first… she thought. Practicalities had to be addressed if she was going to stay here for any length of time. She kept her coat on as she explored the ground floor. The electricity was still on, but the place was freezing. Ellie set to work, cleaning out the log stove, lighting a fire, which instantly gave the place an aura of comfort. Her stomach grumbled…damn, she was hungry, nothing to eat since breakfast. She found some tinned food in the cupboards…not enough to last. Then she remembered Ruth telling her that she'd laid in stores for the Christmas period.

…food that she never got to enjoy… thought Ellie.

She had to give Ruth her due, the cellar was laid out like the larder of that stately home that she and Graham had visited a few years ago. Bottles of fruit, jars of sauces, vegetables, and soups, all lined up and labelled in Ruth's meticulous handwriting. Dried pasta, lentils and beans packed in vacuum bags were stored in sealed boxes, Ruth had even arranged them alphabetically. Ellie laughed as she realised that she could live off Ruth's stockpile for several weeks.

…always did underestimate me, didn't you sweetie…?

Ellie relaxed a little, she could do this, she was strong enough, she knew it. Somehow being back in the cottage where her life had begun to unravel didn't seem so daunting with Ruth's reassurance.

…oo0oo…

Ellie stood in the garden, hands on hips. She looked around at the mass of weeds that had invaded during the few months since Ruth's death. Already that morning she had cleared most of the vegetable garden, they were young weeds, they hadn't had time to take hold. She'd remembered the lessons her grandfather had taught them back in New England, where the climate was like that of the Island. She could recall longer winters, and much lower temperatures there, but nevertheless remarkably similar. She and Ruth had learned about gardening from an early age, and both had their own miniature gardens almost as soon as they could walk.

By the time she made her way back inside the cottage, Ellie was exhausted. What she needed was a hot bath and something to eat. It was the first time in a long while that she felt genuinely hungry. Her falling weight had started to worry her, and part of her new regime included plans to eat more. She brought out some of Ruth's lentil curry from the freezer and put it to thaw in the microwave while she ran a bath. Steam filled the bathroom as Ellie stripped out of her gardening clothes and pulled on her bathrobe. She stopped as she caught sight of her reflection in the full-length mirror. What she saw made her gasp.

Her body wasn't her own. She was taller, heavier, more curvaceous. Her hair was long, blonde, matted with blood. Tight legging clung to shapely legs, a diaphanous top almost see-through with thin shoulder straps, one hanging halfway down her right arm, which was covered with ugly bruises. One shoe missing, the other with the heel broken. Ellie stared as the image raised its head and looked directly at her, she knew who it was…Kara Billingham.

…it's wasn't him, she heard quite clearly… *it's wasn't Graham, he didn't do it, Ellie. I'm sorry, I'm so sorry…*

The image faded; the mirror fogged with steam. Ellie held the bathrobe around her, her body shaking, unable to move. An overwhelming need for a drink consumed her. She made her way downstairs to the kitchen, holding on to anything that would support her. She heard a noise as she drew near to the kitchen door. The old rocking chair that Ruth had salvaged from a junk shop a few years ago was squeaking rhythmically. Ellie grabbed a walking stick from the large blue and white ceramic pot that sat by the front door. It was an ornate antique, one of many that Ruth had collected during her obsession with '*English Traditional*'. The noise got louder as Ellie edged towards the kitchen door, trying to see through the gap at the side. She couldn't see into the far corner; she pushed the door open slightly as she entered the room.

In the chair sat Della Mathers. She stared at Ellie, the look on her face unreadable. Ellie shuddered. Try as she might, she couldn't come up with a reasonable explanation for Della's undetected arrival. How she'd entered the house without Ellie's knowledge was a mystery. The front door was locked and bolted; all the windows were secured.

'It doesn't matter how I got in, Ellie. I needed to make sure you were all right. What just happened?' Della asked pre-empting Ellie's question. Ellie sighed, she could feel the earlier surge of adrenaline waning, any minute now she would start to shake, low blood sugar, there was nothing she could do but…

'Sit down, Ellie,' Della was on her feet, steering Ellie to the rocking chair. She reached for a crocheted blanket and wrapped it around Ellie's legs, then fetched orange juice from the fridge. Ellie sipped at it as she watched Della re-heating the defrosted curry. She wondered idly where the fresh bread had come from. She didn't really care, she was ravenous, far hungrier than she'd been in a long time.

It took some time before she was ready to discuss what had happened in the bathroom.

...oo0oo...

Ellie was looking for an excuse to get out of the cottage. The last few days had been a mixture of determination to carry on as if nothing had happened, and a futile attempt not to dwell on her vision of Kara Billingham. Della was wrong, she'd made a mistake...her explanation was one that Ellie didn't even want to consider. Even so, their conversation had left her with a lot to think about.

'The very least you need to do is ask for guidance,' Della had said 'things are happening to you Ellie, you need help to cope the changes with. You know what to do, you've done it before...just ask,' she repeated as their conversation was winding up and she rose to leave.

It wasn't the first time that Della had offered her this advice but so far Ellie had resisted taking it. She'd spent most of the next day doggedly directing her attention on the garden. She had cleaned the greenhouse; measured up the cold frames for new glass and started clearing the tangle of weeds that had invaded the front borders. She knew she was procrastinating. Real life was out there, and she had to face it sooner or later.

Ellie's back was aching as she straightened up. She looked around in surprise as she realised that the sky was growing dark. She threw her tools into the wicker basket and grabbed the battered spade. Her grandfather had always insisted that she and Ruth tidy up after themselves, no matter how tired they were. She placed the tools in the shed and walked back to the house.

...are you done, or are you going to find something else to distract you...? Ellie heard Ruth's voice as she pulled off her boots and stepped into the kitchen.

*...leave me alone...*Ellie snapped.

*...sure, if that's what you really want...*Ruth answered...*but if I go, I'm gone for good, and then where will you be...?*

Ellie didn't answer. She locked the doors and hung up her jacket. Ruth was right. Once the evening had set in, once she was curled up with a coffee, the lights out, the log burner stoked up, she had no other distractions. That was when her mind had nowhere else to turn. She cleaned herself up, poured some coffee, and sat considering her options. Things were happening, and if Della was right, and she usually was, they were meant to happen. Resisting the inevitable was useless. What more of a disaster could she make of her life, anyway? Doing things the same way, thinking the same thoughts, and expecting different results...hadn't someone already observed that doing that was a form of madness.

*...at last...*Ruth chimed in. Ellie sniffed; she'd never liked to concede the possibility that her little sister could be right.

...okay... she decided, setting her coffee cup down on the side table...*let's give it a go, shall we...?*

She uncurled her legs, setting her feet squarely on the quarry-stone floor. The chill of the tiled surface sent shivers through her body. She closed her eyes, placed her hands in her lap and took several deep breaths, trying to relax. She could almost hear Odelia's voice. Their meditation sessions had been a huge part of Ellie's life at the Retreat, a part that she missed more than she'd realised. She acknowledged the thought, then let it drift away. She inhaled again, another deep breath. It had been a while since she had tried doing this *'asking'* thing that Della kept urging her to practice.

...I really don't know how to do this, so I'm just going to ask...she thought, feeling slightly foolish...*whoever it is I'm supposed to do now, can you help me, please? I need guidance, anything at this stage*...there, it was done.

Ellie felt nothing; she hadn't expected to. It had taken less than a few minutes to carry out the exercise; even her coffee hadn't had time to go cold. She reached for it, as the memory of an incident at the Retreat came back to her. It was the only other time that she had asked for help, for a sign. The sound of Graham's voice echoed in her head. He had rung her every night to check on how she was doing. She shivered as she remembered his revelation of the letter signed *'Jacob'* that he'd found on the kitchen floor at the farmhouse. Jacob...her childhood friend, her *imaginary* childhood friend...she had taken it as the sign she needed, she'd trusted then, why did she find it so difficult now?

...probably because of what I've discovered between then and now... she thought...*because of the lies that people have fed me, and I've believed them, even when my instincts have told me otherwise. How could I have been so...lies, that's what they've fed me, people I've trusted... lies... a box of lies...*

Ellie was close to tears. What had she gained from her attempt to get clarity, except confirmation of how little she knew about what was going on with her? Hell, she didn't even know what to call it. She got up and crossed to the stove, intent on more coffee. She stopped; her mind was already in overdrive, maybe coffee wasn't such a good idea after all. Perhaps something to eat? She opened the fridge, she needed to go shopping, but after her last attempt she was loathe to...an idea hit her.

…a deal, she needed to negotiate a deal…with her mother. Deals were food and drink to Julia, she lived for them. Ellie had grown up with them, her current situation was no different. Deals were the only thing her mother seemed to understand. She had bargained her way through her life for as long as Ellie could remember, everything was conditional. *…do this, and I'll do that… get this grade in school, and maybe I'll be proud of you…*it even extended to the way in which she had treated her husbands…and her other relationships. *…buy me something expensive and I'll be nice to you…*

Ellie shuddered; she couldn't imagine Julia agreeing to anything less than a small fortune. Whatever she offered, it had to be a one-time payment, legally drawn up and signed in front of …that was it. She would draft an agreement tonight, send it to Mr. Richardson and get him to make any alterations he deemed necessary. That way she could present it to her mother…*tomorrow if possible…*she thought, she was certain that the prospect of acquiring money would draw her mother to the meeting at short notice, Julia could never resist the lure of monetary gain.

…well now, that wasn't so bad, was it…? Ruth sounded almost smug, Ellie shrugged, reluctant to agree. She worked long into the night, considering the best way to word the document. She needed to create a watertight agreement that would settle a reasonable sum of money on her mother, worded so that she couldn't come back for more in the future. There was no denying the truth, Julia wanted cash, a lot of cash, she would stop at nothing to get it.

As the night drew on, Ellie grew more determined to get her mother out of her life once and for all. She sent an email to Mr. Richardson, attaching the draught agreement. She knew that this matter had to be laid to rest sooner rather than later.

...the sooner she leaves me alone, the better... she thought.

...yeah, like that's going to happen... Ruth chimed in.

26

Porter's insistence that Mason should take the day off both touched and annoyed her. Her objections had come to nothing.

'We've got everything in hand here,' he told her, sounding a lot more confident than he was feeling, 'it's your day off, take it.'

Mason sat in her father's study drinking her second cup of tea. Porter had no idea that she would rather be at the station, feeling useful, than contemplating another empty day. She heard her mobile ring and made her way into the front room to answer it. Maybe it was work…

'Doris, hi, I wondered if you had planned to visit your father today?' Doris was surprised.

'Odelia? …it's... it's nice to hear from you…no, I wasn't planning to…is anything wrong?' she answered.

'No, no, sorry if I gave you the impression… it's just that Mom and I are going over to St. Mary's this afternoon, it'll be the first time since…well, you know…and I thought maybe we could sit with you and your…'

'Yes, oh yes,' Doris answered eagerly, 'that would be lovely.'

'…see you there, then…around two?' Odelia asked. Doris stared at the phone as she hung up. She'd been meaning to ask Odelia if she could visit her father for some time, it hadn't seemed appropriate given what they were going through. Now this…now she had some structure to her day.

…oo0oo…

Their habit of making regular visits to a variety of different Care Homes had taken a back seat since the incident at the Retreat. Odelia wasn't convinced that her mother was strong enough to resume the appointments, but she knew better than to argue, once Della had made up her mind. St. Mary's had been a regular venue for as many years as Odelia could remember. It was Della's way of giving something back to the community, that, and visits to the local hospice. Ellie had mentioned that Doris Mason's father had moved there during one of their late-night conversations. Odelia liked Doris, she couldn't image what she was going through. When Della suggested that they visit St. Mary's, Odelia saw her chance. The residents were sitting in the Dining Room as she and Della walked in, some of them called out as they made their way over to sit down.

'Now then, who have we got here?' Audrey Fellows said in her sing-song voice as soon as she saw them. There was a chorus of greetings from the others as she laughed with pleasure. 'We didn't expect you, so soon…nice though…' she walked across to both women and hugged them in turn. 'Been a long time…you two…all right?' She didn't wait for them to answer as she turned to the hatch and called for two cups of tea. Audrey had worked at St. Mary's for as long as Odelia could remember.

Odelia smiled, it was nice to be doing something again. Della was right, she usually was. She scanned the room. An elderly man she didn't recognise sat in the far corner. He was drinking from a teacup held by a young man, Odelia assumed that he was one of the care assistants. She watched as the older man tried to turn his head away from the cup, the younger man seemed to become more aggressive as he tried to get him to take a sip. Odelia stood up and walked towards them.

Almost immediately, the younger man stood up and placed the cup back on its saucer. He skirted round the table and headed towards the serving hatch. Odelia turned and saw him change direction, he made for the door, taking the cup with him. She looked back at the old man. She knelt by the side of his chair and placed her hand on his arm. He looked at her, his eyes darting from side to side, trying to focus on her face. They were clouded, panic-filled…he shook his head.

'Don't want it…tell them…don't want it…can't think, please…' he begged. Odelia put her hand on his arm, she could feel him shaking. Audrey placed a mug of tea on the nearest table.

'Everything all right, love?' she asked. Odelia nodded.

'Who was that Audrey, the man who just left…is he one of the staff?' she asked.

'Oh no, that's Simon, Simon Collins, he volunteers here a couple of afternoons a week, real gem, loves all the old ladies…why is there something wrong?' Odelia didn't answer. She sat with the Professor until Della came over.

'What is it?' she asked, searching Odelia's face.

'I'm not sure, Mom,' she answered, 'but I think we need to have a word with the Manager, ask him if there's anyone here qualified to take a blood sample from Professor Mason.'

...damn them.... damn, damn, damn...if they...he gripped the wheel tightly as he sped away. He should have known they'd start their visits up again, but not yet, not so soon after... He had to calm down...to try to come up with an excuse. He'd heard about them, about their visits, of course he had. The Retreat, the Mathers women, they were the subject of a lot of gossip, especially after what had happened last year. If they suspected...his plans...he would have to move them forward...make them less ambitious, after all he wanted to make a point...

...damn, damn them, he could feel his blood pressure rising, the knot in his stomach tightening. He pulled into a layby and switched off the engine, trying to calm down. What could they do, he wondered, would that fool of a manager listen to them? He had to get some air. He got out of the car and walked back along the side of the road. He heard another car approaching, he turned his back to the road and stood still. With a bit of luck, the driver would think he was relieving himself. He waited until it was out of sight, he had to calm down, losing his nerve now was not an option.

...even if they listen to the old goat, they wouldn't take him seriously...he had to believe that, or...he walked back to his car. His plans would have to be pared down to fit in with what had happened... he would have to bring the showdown forward, all that it meant was the High and Mighty Professor wouldn't get as many sacrifices as he deserved...

...oo0oo...

...disgusting...Mason thought as she passed the tall man using the layby as a toilet. He was the only person she had seen as she drove towards St. Mary's. The

visitor's book lay open on the table in reception. Mason could see that Odelia and Della had been there some time, she hoped she hadn't kept them waiting. Audrey Fellows came bustling around the corner as she headed towards her father's room, her face red, she was sweating.

'Oh, Doris,' she said, 'I'm so glad you're here…no don't look like that…there's nothing wrong with your Dad.' She took Doris's arm and ushered her in the direction of the Manager's office. Doris could see Odelia sitting with Mr. Edwards. He was shaking his head.

'Miss Mason,' he said as she walked in, 'please sit…'

'What's happened,' she asked, 'is my father…?'

'Your father's fine,' Odelia assured her, 'it's just…Doris have you ever spoken to Simon, one of the volunteers here?' Mason shook her head.

'Not to my knowledge,' she said, 'please I want to see Dad…'

Odelia walked to the Professor's room with her. Mason was eager to get there; she didn't ask any more questions. Della sat by the Professor's bedside, her hand on his. He was asleep, the sound of his breathing was reassuring. Doris walked over and touched his forehead, he moved his head, muttering something as he turned over.

'What on earth is going on?' Mason pleaded as she sat down by his bed.

'Nothing to worry about, I'm sure,' Della said as she caught the faint sound of a melody…she raised her finger to her lips as Doris started to talk. 'Hush, what, what's that?' it took them a few seconds to realise that Doris's father was singing softly in his sleep…Della shivered…it was the same tune as Ellie had sung a few nights ago.

Professor Mason shifted slightly, he started muttering some words…

*…and a hay harvest breeze…swing, swing together…other will fill our places…*she looked over to where Doris was sitting.

'I know this,' she said, 'I remember this…it's…my father, he…he was at Eton when he was a boy…it's the '*Eton Boating Song*'.

Della shuddered, Professor Mason wasn't the only person she was aware of that had attended Eton, she knew for a fact that Howard Atkinson had also been a student there. Was that why Ellie knew the tune, and those words?

27

Ellie sat on the tall stool in the kitchen, staring through the steam rising from her coffee. Eating wasn't an option; her stomach was tying itself in knots at the thought of how much she had to do during the next few hours. She couldn't decide what she was dreading the most. The first appointment would be easy, a catch-up with Miss Pritchard at the office; the second not so much. She dreaded the prospect of another showdown with her mother. Mr. Richardson had been able to fit them in later in the morning and much as Ellie wanted to get this thing dealt with, she still wasn't looking forward to it.

*...things do tend to come in threes, don't they...*she thought. Yesterday had been a crazy day, between the phone calls and the emails, she hadn't had a minute to think. In a few short hours she'd arranged several appointments, all within hours of each other.

*...be careful what you wish for...*Ellie thought as she studied the list...*I suppose I should have known better...* First, her office to collect the paperwork that Richardson had asked her for. Miss Pritchard had called her minutes later. She wanted to discuss some premises that looked promising.

*...kill two birds with one stone...*she thought, she heard a giggle.

...oh, Ellie, you could use a more appropriate phrase... Ruth's voice brought Ellie up short. That was all she needed, Ruth telling her what she could and couldn't say...

...I was joking, Ruth said...*you're going to have to lighten up Ellie*...Ellie smiled; the irony of the phrase wasn't lost on her.

'Sorry Ruth,' she whispered, 'big day ahead.'

...I know, sweetie... Ruth murmured...*just don't lose your nerve...*

Her appointment with Mr. Richardson was at eleven, just time to check over the document that they'd worked on. They would be joined by Julia at eleven-thirty. It wasn't something that Ellie was looking forward to, but she wanted to get this matter sorted out. With everything else that was going on, it was one more thing she didn't have time to worry about. If she had to wait for letters to go back and forth across the Atlantic, this situation would drag on for months, even years. She only hoped that her decision to ask Julia to the appointment was the right one.

...don't forget to take time out for some lunch, sweetie...Ruth reminded her, her concern was touching, it made Ellie smile.

DCI Porter's call later in the afternoon had surprised her. He had beaten around the bush for several minutes, thanking her again for going to Harrington Hall...was she all right, had she got over...? She ended up interrupting him.

'I'm fine,' she assured him, 'it was just...it was strange...' she heard him clear his throat.

'I, err, I wondered...I'm going over to Donaldson's store tomorrow afternoon...would you consider...I wouldn't ask, only...' he stopped. Ellie didn't know what to say, her experience at the Hall was one she'd hadn't been keen to repeat. Now that she'd had time to think about it…

'Yes,' she said, surprising herself at how much she wanted to go, 'I'd be happy to. I'll meet you at the station at one, it's the earliest I can make it, I'm afraid.' Porter had mumbled something about how grateful he was and rang off.

Ellie checked her watch, seven forty-five, too early to leave for the office. She'd been awake since six, showered, dressed, briefcase packed. She could feel a tight sensation in her stomach. No wonder she couldn't bear the thought of food. She thought about her meeting with Richardson, him she could deal with; it was her mother that was the problem. She knew, of old, that she would have to play hardball with her. Providing Julia with multiple possibilities was dangerous, she could pick and pick away until she wore down whoever she went up against. They usually gave up just to gain some peace and quiet. Ellie knew that she would have to give something in order to gain something back, that's the way her mother worked.

She ran through the carefully worded document again. Would her mother be tempted by the amount she was offering her? More importantly, would getting her to sign the agreement ensure that she would leave Ellie alone to get on with her life? There was only one way to find out. Ellie gathered her things. She was as ready as she would ever be, she supposed. All the same, she couldn't help but feel like she was about to enter the dragon's den.

…okay…focus…one thing at a time…

Miss Pritchard's search for new premises was proving difficult. Nothing she had seen so far had met the list of criteria that Ms. Shaw had drawn up; she was beginning to feel as though nothing ever would. She sighed as she looked at the clock… eight fifty-five. Ms. Shaw would be here within the next half hour, she didn't have the heart to disappoint her again. In the past few weeks Rosa Pritchard had noted the fluctuation in Ellie's energy levels, she tried her best to cheer her up, but there was only so much she could do, wasn't there?

…*One more try*… she thought. That pub, *The Rose and Thistle*, on the edge of town. She had the feeling that it would be ideal. It was reasonably priced, and convenient enough for clients to get to, should Ellie decide to resume her face-to-face consultations. The details from the agent included a schedule of work already carried out by the previous owners, who had had plans to turn it into a suite of offices themselves. It still needed quite a lot of money spending on it, but for some reason it stood out from the rest of the prospects. She dialled the estate agent's number, it was early, but she had to make sure it was still available before offering it up for consideration.

…*yes, the property was still available, no, they hadn't had any offers yet.* Miss Pritchard noted down the details; she would ring back to make an appointment to view. The young woman cleared her throat, choosing her next words carefully.

'There may be a hold-up in the sale,' she said. Rosa could almost hear her holding her breath, thoughts of any commission she may have earned for closing the deal evaporating as she spoke. 'Apparently the owner has just died, we're waiting for clarity about who has inherited …may I suggest that you call back in a few weeks to find out if the situation has changed?' Miss Pritchard sighed, more delay. She left her details and asked to be kept up to date.

…what now…? She thought. She *had* hoped that she could give Ms. Shaw some good news for a change. Her progress in her quest to find them alternative accommodation for the business was the main reason for asking her boss to come in today. She felt foolish at having jumped the gun. Still, nothing she could do about it now. She busied herself for the next ten minutes, though in truth she had little else to occupy her time.

Ellie's appointment diary lay open on the desk, two hours blocked out for their meeting…what on earth did she have to say that would last that long? Rosa sighed, it wasn't like this in Mr. Prothero's day…she gasped, realising where her thoughts were leading her. She was still in shock, that's what it was. She still couldn't believe what was being said about him. He hadn't even been tried for…the door opened, and Ellie came in, something about her made Miss Pritchard stare. Something had changed. She nodded to Rosa as she placed her bags on the sofa, then crossed over to the desk.

'I've got rather a busy day today, Miss Pritchard,' she said, her voice sounding stronger than it had for a long time. 'Could we perhaps cover what we need to before ten-thirty?'

'Yes, yes of course,' Miss Pritchard replied, imagining that the great gaping timeslot had shrunk at least by a small amount. 'Shall I make you some coffee before we start?' She fiddled around with the pens lying at precise angles on her blotter. Making coffee would take her at least ten minutes…fifteen at the most. She looked up; Ellie was staring at her.

'That would be nice,' Ellie said, 'do you have any of those biscuits as well?' Miss Pritchard jumped up and walked quickly to the tiny kitchen, the rapid movement at odds with her usual sedate habits. Ellie smiled as she took her things through to her office.

'Make two cups, Miss Pritchard,' she called, 'we can talk and drink at the same time.' She picked up the post laid out on her desk, a few larger envelopes that she suspected contained sympathy cards, she'd received a lot of those in the last few months. Most were from strangers both local and from other areas of the country, even a few from abroad. It was surprising how many people had taken the time to contact her. She'd read them all in the beginning, some of them had affected her deeply, others not so much. She wondered why she sensed a difference, maybe the depth of the sender's sincerity? She'd mentioned it to Della, who suggested that she hold each of them in turn and see what she could pick up. Ellie hadn't managed to summon up the strength to try. Sometimes just handling the envelopes gave her a surge of emotion that she found difficult to handle.

As she sifted through the remainder of the post, she felt a jolt, almost as though someone had punched her, causing her to drop the last few envelopes. The memory of that night at the Retreat flooded back into her mind. She looked at the scattered items that lay on her office floor, almost afraid to pick them up. This was crazy, why would she allow...she knew why.

One of them was from him... from Atkinson. How she knew, she couldn't tell, but one of them...she bent down and picked up the closest one...nothing. She reached for the second, still nothing. Her hand hovered over the third, she felt uneasy as her hand hovered over it. She touched it again, snatching her hand away quickly. Ellie stared at the envelope for several seconds, she stood up and walked out of her office, almost colliding with Miss Pritchard. She crossed to the kitchen and opened one drawer after another, extracting a pair of kitchen tongs from the third one. She retraced her steps and looked in her desk for something to put the card in. Miss Pritchard watched from the doorway as she withdrew a plastic bag, picked up the envelope and placed it inside. She folded over the top and put it on the desk. She held the bag with the tongs as she examined the post mark…somewhere in Ireland.

She felt Miss Pritchard's eyes watching her as she cleared her throat. She wasn't in the mood to explain what had just happened. She couldn't think of a rational explanation in any case. She indicated for Miss Pritchard to sit down as she fought to control herself.

'Miss Pritchard,' she started, 'I've been meaning to speak to you for some time, about our arrangement.' Miss Pritchard remained standing. 'To be honest, I'm not entirely happy with our…'

…here it comes, thought Rosa, *the 'it's been nice to know you, but'…*

Ellie took a deep breath. 'Look, I appreciate that you've been trying your best…I've been thinking about it, and I wondered…'

…yes, I was right, she's giving up, I'm out of a job. Miss Pritchard looked at the floor. Ellie could sense her despondency.

'What I mean to say is,' she took a deep breath, 'are you still comfortable working with me, you know, here, considering…?' she looked up and saw the look on Miss Pritchard's face.

*…she thinks you're giving up…*Ruth whispered…Ellie shook her head...

'Let me explain,' she went on, 'I'll be continuing my work at the station, but I can't imagine it will be easy to carry on seeing clients here. I don't think I could deal with people who only want to find out what went on that night…' she took a deep breath.

'Ms. Shaw,' Miss Pritchard said, shifting her weight from one foot to the other, 'are you trying to tell me that my services are no longer…'

'No, no of course not,' Ellie replied, shaking her head, 'I'm not making myself understood, am I? This place has a lot of… I don't want to make things uncomfortable for us both by staying somewhere so full of unpleasant memories. I know that you've been doing your best to find us somewhere more suitable, it's just that I don't know how much longer I can work here. I still think we should move, but I want it to be the right location. I really don't know which direction I'm going to take, with my work, I mean, but I'd like you to stay on and help me with …'

'Yes, oh, yes please. I really thought…' Miss Pritchard sat down with all the grace of a wounded duck. Ellie had to force herself not to laugh... Was this stalwart of the office really crying? Not out loud it was true, but discreetly, into her lace-edged handkerchief.

'How is the search going, anyway? Any luck yet?' Ellie asked. Miss Pritchard hesitated, the point of their meeting had been based on her anticipation of delivering some good news about the only real contender so far, The Rose and Thistle. Her conversation with the agent earlier had put a hold on that option, but maybe some news was better than none. She handed Ellie the file, waited a few moments, then cleared her throat to speak. She hesitated as she saw a change on Ellie's face.

'Well, if that's not...' Ellie said shaking her head, 'you might not believe this, Miss Pritchard, I find it hard to believe myself...this is one of the properties that Ruth left to me.' She swallowed hard as she heard a distinct giggle.

...oo0oo...

Mr. Richardson launched into a long, and in Ellie's opinion, unnecessary explanation of the document they had drafted between them the previous day.

'What you are doing,' Mr. Richardson pointed out to Ellie, 'is *'gifting'* this money to your mother out of the goodness of your heart, so to speak,' he made quotation marks in the air. It was so out of character that Ellie bit her lip; she could hear Ruth giggling again. She knew what she was doing, she didn't need Richardson to explain it to her, but she let him carry on. 'I have worded the document in such a way that she will have no come-back, legally, you are, in fact...'

'...buying her off.' Ellie interrupted, although she knew it would steal his thunder. The look on Richardson's face as he absorbed the reality that this chit of a girl knew exactly what he was talking about, was enough to make her want to scream. She wondered if she could work with him in the future...she doubted it.

Richardson check his watch; Julia was due to join them shortly. They'd arranged to meet half an hour before so that they could thrash out any potential glitches in the agreement. Richardson was obviously proud of the document that he had prepared, which had in fact been written mainly by Ellie herself. It was one that would ensure that Julia would have no further call on Ruth's money. Ellie read the agreement through again. It had to be watertight, she couldn't stand the thought that she would have to go through this again sometime in the future. She nodded to Richardson as she handed the piece of paper back to him.

'You've covered everything, Mr. Richardson,' she said as he placed the agreement back in its folder, 'I just hope that my mother doesn't prove too troublesome.' Richardson cleared his throat, not, she suspected, because of any obstruction there, but merely to re-establish his authority. She'd watched him do this at the station, with Alan Cooper, she shivered at the memory. Richardson's phone rang, Julia had arrived, should she be shown in? He was about to agree when he caught sight of Ellie's face. Ellie saw his eyes narrow.

'No,' he answered, 'she's ten minutes early, ask her to wait, please.' He replaced the receiver and nodded towards Ellie, a slight smile managing to establish itself on his careworn face. She smiled back, she was impressed, as if seeing him for the first time as the wily negotiator that he was. It felt to her as though they were conspirators in a game, a game that she had no doubt that she would win, with his help. Something about his manner reassured Ellie that he was good at what he did, maybe she would be able to work with him after all.

'While I have the chance,' he said, 'I would ask you to consider talking to my partner, Mr. Ball, he dealt with many of Mrs. Prothero's business interests, you could do worse than discuss them with him.'

...*I agree*...Ruth chimed in...

Richardson soon reverted to his formal, detached manner. Ellie listened as he droned on. He seemed to make such a meal of everything, as though he considered mete mortals to be incapable of understanding the nuances of the legal profession.

'…and so, Ms. Shaw, Mrs. Morrison, despite the sad circumstances under which we find ourselves…' Ellie turned her attention back to Richardson as he cleared his throat for what seemed like the fortieth time since her mother had joined them. He paused and looked at them in turn over the rim of his glasses. '…as I said, incredibly sad, no, tragic circumstances…'

Ellie shifted in her chair. She hadn't slept much the previous night, if it wasn't for the coffee that Richardson's secretary had just served, she might have fallen asleep.

Julia sat at right angles to her, perched on the edge of her chair, her body alert. Mr. Richardson avoided looking in her direction. He heartily disapproved of Julia Morrison. In his opinion her actions over the last few weeks had been reprehensible to say the least. He could understand why Ms. Shaw had asked for her mother to be included in their meeting, she wanted to sort this unpleasant situation out and get it over with as soon as possible. The prospect of never having to be in the same room as Julia Morrison again was extremely appealing to him as well.

If Julia had been surprised to see Ellie sitting in Richardson's office, she managed to control it. Only the most observant of individuals could have detected the hint of shock as she'd walked in and taken her seat. Richardson looked from mother to daughter. A less likely pair he had yet to meet. Ellie sat still, as he savoured his pronouncement a moment longer. He shuffled the papers unnecessarily, selecting one and placing the remaining ones down on his blotter.

'Firstly, we come to the matter of whether Mrs. Prothero's estate was the result of criminal activity,' he paused.

...what a drama queen...! Ellie almost giggled as Ruth whispered in her ear. They'd already had a conversation about the subject. Ruth had assured Ellie that she'd amassed her fortune by legitimate means. Ellie felt she could hardly use her reassurance to inform Richardson, under the circumstances.

'I am pleased to tell you, Ms. Shaw, that it appears that your sister's estate was amassed legally, and that all her business transactions were above board,' he nodded emphatically.

...why couldn't he have told me this before now...? Ellie wondered...*it would have been nice to have been informed officially...*

...like I said, he's a drama queen...he needs an audience, the bigger the better. Besides, it lets Mom know that you own the whole shooting match, doesn't it...? Ruth pointed out in the mischievous way that Ellie remembered so well. She was once again forced to stifle her amusement.

'Mrs. Morrison,' Julia almost jumped as Richardson turned his attention to her. 'With regard to the attempt made by you and your legal team to declare Mrs. Prothero's Will null and void. I believe you have received notification of the steps that she took to confirm her mental health prior to making her Will?'

Julia nodded, Ellie could see that she was biting the inside of her cheek, a habit she had when she had more than enough to say but felt constrained to keep her mouth shut. She'd been warned; make a scene, and it would be the end of the meeting, and of her chance of being offered something out of Ruth's estate. So far, she had kept her own counsel; Ellie knew that it was taking a great deal of effort.

'Given that this would render further accusations that you could make futile, are you now willing to sign this document to that effect?' Richardson pushed a piece of paper towards Julia, she snatched it up and began reading, her face growing dark as she began to comprehend its meaning.

'This says that I accept the findings of these so-called experts and renounce all claims to my daughter's estate, except for…' she gasped. 'Does this mean…?'

'…that you will inherit only that which Mrs. Prothero detailed in her Will, and nothing else.' Richardson announced. He glared at Julia, almost daring her to continue down the path which led to confrontation. She sighed, she was beaten, and she knew it. Ruth had ensured that she couldn't challenge the Will. Her youngest daughter had been more astute than Julia had realised. Her body language conveyed her feelings. In her opinion, this was all a setup; she was being side-lined. Ellie could sense that her mother was working up a head of steam. She cleared her throat. Julia turned towards her; her face suffused with malice. Ellie was shocked into silence, broken only by Richardson's intervention.

'Ms. Shaw has, however, instructed me to make you the following offer,' Julia turned back to face the loathsome man, who she saw as the architect of her thwarted plans. He reacted to her withering look by taking a deep breath and consulting his sheaf of papers once more. Julia waited patiently; she was prepared to sit there all day if it meant that she would come out of this encounter with a decent settlement. Her reaction, she'd already decided, would depend on how great the offer was.

'Ms. Shaw has instructed me…' Richardson began again, 'to offer you the sum of twenty thousand pounds. I think you will agree that this is a substantial amount of money, offered on the condition…'

Julia jumped up, turning towards Ellie, her face twisted in a grotesque grimace. Ellie almost recoiled at the hatred emanating from her.

'…twenty thousand…you ungrateful little…' Julia snapped, stepping towards Ellie, her hands balled up at her side. Ellie was used to Julia's temper, having experienced it many times as she was growing up, but this was something different. Ellie stood up and faced her mother, head on. She stepped back as Julia advanced towards her, she felt a strange sensation of rising up from her body, watching from above, a growing surge of energy rising within her. She saw herself hold out her hands, her palms towards her mother, as if to fend her off. Julia flinched; her body jerked violently as the air was knocked out of her. She staggered backwards, a mixture of surprise and fear on her face. She groped for her chair and sat down.

Ellie watched her mother as she fought to regain her composure. She shook her head as she came to her senses. The feeling that she was floating had gone. She stared at her hands, then sat back down herself, wondering what on earth Mr. Richardson would make of what had happened. Both he and Julia were staring at her, their mouths open, their faces frozen in shock, and something else…fear. Whatever *this* was, she had to leave it for now, maybe Della could enlighten her later?

…another thing to add to the list… she thought. Richardson's voice was tremulous as he started to talk, choosing to act as though the interruption had never taken place. The only hint that he was affected in any way was the slight hesitation in his voice.

'...o…offered on the condition,' he went on, 'that you accept said offer today, and refute all further claims. If you decide that this amount is not acceptable, or, or attempt to extort any further benefit, it will be withdrawn, and no other offer will be made. I have a document here to that effect. This offer will expire at the end of this meeting.' Richardson looked from mother to daughter once again, neither was taking much notice of him. They stared at each other for several seconds before Julia turned back to him. She straightened the front of her blouse, a gesture that afforded her a few seconds to settle herself down.

'Where do I sign?' she asked.

28

Donaldson's car park was located underneath the store; it was cold and damp. Janet Rowan shivered as she leaned against the side of her car, her briefcase on the floor beside her. She looked around as a car pulled into the entrance. The staff area was small, just enough room for twenty or so cars. She watched as Porter reversed into the only remaining space. She walked towards his car, taking a deep breath as she got closer. She was surprised as Ellie emerged from the passenger door. After their visit to Harrington Hall, she hadn't expected to see her again.

Ellie smiled as she held out her hand. Rowan fought hard not to gasp as she felt the heat emanating from Ellie's palm, and the sensation of tingling that travelled up to her elbow in a matter of seconds. It reminded her of the time her brother had been given a magic kit for his birthday. His favourite trick was a device that mimicked an electric shock to whoever he had managed to persuade to shake his hand. Rowan fought to stop herself from snatching hers away from Ellie's grasp. She managed to recover enough to pretend that she felt nothing, but the sensation remained with her for the next few hours.

'Thank you for your help, the other day,' Ellie said, 'I'm sorry if I was short with you…'

'Don't mention it…' Rowan murmured nervously.

Ellie looked around the imposing entrance of the store. Her only other visit here had been a few years ago, a Christmas shopping trip with Ruth and Max. She'd bought a scarf for her father-in-law, a pair of fine leather gloves for Mary, and an obscenely expensive after-shave for Graham. The store was buzzing having just re-opened after the events the previous month. Pressure from Andrew Donaldson, who obviously had some powerful contacts, had been effective in persuading the authorities to allow trading to resume. The public's curiosity had fired their enthusiasm to shop there.

'Isn't it a bit early, you know, considering…?' Ellie whispered to Porter as they got into the lift.

'I thought that,' he said, 'but then that kind of decision isn't up to me.' He shook his head. He'd had a conversation with Chetwynd on the subject the previous day. She agreed with him. It was, after all, still a crime scene, but they weren't the ones making the decisions. Every surface that could be investigated, had been, and the victim's offices remained cordoned off. He'd had to make do with that.

He had no doubts that the murder of Ronnie Bowers was connected to that of Harrington-Smythe and Anthea Harrold, even if the only basis for this so far was a tenuous link. It was more the lack of forensic evidence at each of the murder scenes that had convinced him. In short, there was none. No fibres, DNA, fingerprints, nothing. He could accept that someone could just about pull that off, but if the cases weren't linked, then they had three perpetrators displaying expertise way beyond anyone he'd brought to justice before…and that wasn't feasible. It was the main reason he wanted Ellie to visit the crime scenes with them; maybe she could detect something other than physical evidence, maybe she would even be able to come up with a description. He felt that her performance at Harrington Hall had helped a great deal, even though she didn't believe it. At this stage, anything was worth a try.

Ellie shivered as she walked to the centre of Bowers' office. It was light and airy, the morning sun streamed through the window as she looked round. A faint coating of fingerprint powder covered almost every surface. Numbered signs identified spaces that once housed Bower's computer and other confiscated items. The officer on the door handed each of them latex gloves, giving everything they touched an artificial feeling. She felt nervous, if her experience at Harrington Hall was anything to go on…

Porter talked them through the timeline of events. Bowers entered the office at 10.15, as observed by his secretary. Less than half an hour later, several witnesses saw his body hit the pavement. Porter crossed to the glazed door that led to the balcony and looked out. Incident tape criss-crossed the gap in the railings. He indicated that Ellie should join him. She shook her head.

'I can't… I… heights… I can't,' she whispered. Porter shook his head; what use was she going to be if she couldn't even…? He stopped, the look on Ellie face had changed. She held the back of a chair to steady herself. Her eyes were semi-closed, the lids flickering.

'A man,' she murmured, 'dark hair, big, looks like he works out. He's wearing overalls, like the janitor's…er, caretaker's, green, dark green. He's kneeling…on the balcony…a saw, a…a hacksaw. He's cutting the metal rail…'

Porter watched as Ellie shook her head. Forensics had told him that the rails had been sawn through so that only a small amount had stopped the whole structure from collapsing before the weight of Bowers' body had caused it to give way. But Ellie hadn't been told, that was something else he'd kept from her, as far as she knew, Bowers had gone over the rail, not through it. He remained quiet as she carried on talking. Rowan stood in silence by the door, she held her breath as she watched Ellie struggling. The atmosphere in the room had changed, she watched, mesmerised, as the scene unfolded

'The man, he, he was inside the office, just before…he walked up behind Bowers…he pushed him…' Ellie swayed, the images flashing across her mind, the feeling of falling making her gasp. Porter reached out and caught her as she grabbed onto his arms. Rowan snapped out of her reverie as Porter sat Ellie down and called for a glass of water. He knelt in front of her, holding her hands.

'Ellie,' he said gently, 'can you tell if it's the same man as the one you saw…' Ellie nodded before he finished speaking.

'Yes, yes, its him, I'm sure I know him, there's something familiar…' Ellie said, 'I just can't remember…' she sipped some water as Porter held the glass to her lips. Within seconds she stood up, determined to conquer the weakness that had overwhelmed her.

'I'm ok,' she insisted, the concerned faces before her making her even more determined to overcome her emotions. 'Just give me a minute.' Ellie walked towards the window. She took a deep breath, pacing back and forth as she gathered her thoughts.

'He was in here before Bowers arrived,' she said. 'He was waiting in the bathroom,' she turned and pointed to the door at the far corner of the office.

'He was lucky that Bowers didn't go in there,' Rowan observed.

'…he had a bag with him, a bag of tools. An excuse to be here…repairs, something like that. Bowers wouldn't have suspected… in any case, he would soon be lying on the pavement, so he couldn't have told anyone, could he?' Porter frowned, shocked at Ellie's matter of fact assessment. She continued her pacing. 'The heating, it was cranked up, Bowers opened a window. He took a drink, loosened his tie. He was still too hot, he turned the thermostat down, then went over to the door and opened it. He stepped out onto the balcony, the murderer waited for him to lean on the railing, then…' she stopped, shrugging her shoulders.

'…he came up behind Bowers and pushed him, the railing gave way, just as he'd planned…' Porter finished off her summation.

'How did the suspect get out of the room?' Rowan asked. 'Bowers' secretary was at her desk, he would have had to pass her to get out, wouldn't he?'

'She said that Bowers phoned her and asked her to bring in some papers for him to sign, that's when she saw that the balcony door was open. She went across to it look for him,' Porter said, 'she saw the gap in the railing, leaned over and saw him on the ground.'

Ellie walked back to the door that connected Bowers' office to that of his secretary. She closed her eyes, breathing steadily, in full control of herself.

'He hid here when she came in,' she said, opening the door and stepping behind it. 'Anyone walking straight into the room wouldn't be able to see him. He waited until she was at the window, then went through to her office and down the corridor to the service staircase.'

'What about the phone call?' Rowan asked, 'Bowers couldn't have called his secretary and be lying on the pavement at the same time?'

'Is Bowers' secretary sure it was him? It wouldn't have been difficult to imitate him, especially if he only said a few words,' Ellie suggested. 'What did he actually say to her?'

'I'll check,' Rowan said, making a note. Any doubts she might have had about Ellie's abilities were rapidly fading. 'He took a hell of a risk, though, didn't he? If she'd turned around and seen him…'

'She would probably have joined Bowers,' Ellie said, still mulling over the images that she'd just seen. The feeling that she recognised the murderer persisted. She chewed on her thumbnail as she considered and discarded several possibilities. She couldn't put a name to the face that shimmered just the wrong side of recognition.

'Relax,' Porter told her, his voice charged with concern, 'you've already been more than helpful.' He placed his hand on her shoulder and gave it a gentle squeeze. Ellie didn't know whether to feel praised or patronised, either way, she felt uncomfortable.

'The man…he was wearing…a mask, some kind of…no, no he was wearing make-up, thick make-up…and his hair…dyed…it had started running…' Porter watched as she struggled to describe the assailant.

'When we get back to the station, I'll get Connett to arrange a photo fit session so that you can give us a better idea of what the murderer looks like,' he said, indicating that their time in Bowers' office was done.

…Connett… Ellie thought, *…why did his name cause her to feel uneasy?*

Porter had toyed with the possibility of asking Ellie to go out to the scene of Anthea Harrold's murder, the next day. The only thing that stopped him from suggesting it was the look on her face as they stepped back into the lift. She looked worn out. The events of this visit had obviously taken their toll.

'You need to eat,' he said as he pressed the button marked *'Café'*. Ellie nodded.

'I think you're right,' she agreed. The lift rose two floors before coming to a halt. The doors opened, revealing an Art Deco style room, complete with palm trees in pots, and sumptuous black and gold décor.

'No wonder Donaldson's were having money trouble,' Porter said, reaching for his phone. He saw Ellie smile as he rang Rowan's number.

'When you finish up there,' he told her, 'we're grabbing something in the café. What do you fancy?'

'Nothing, sir,' she answered, 'I'll make my way back to station, I'll see you back there. There's one or two things I need to do.' Porter shrugged as he hung up.

He knew that Rowan was having a hard time dealing with what had just happened. He couldn't blame her. He watched as Ellie walked over to a huge pillar in the centre of the room. It looked like black marble; the gold coloured veins gave the structure a sumptuous appearance. It reached almost to the ceiling; the top sported a festoon of gold feathers that cascaded down the sides. Around the base was a circular seating area, upholstered in black and gold fabric. The seats were supported by the heads of black peacocks; their features picked out in gold leaf. The effect was both elegant and garish. Ellie walked around the pillar, touching the column, she looked as though she was sleepwalking, her eyes narrowed. Porter wished he'd had the foresight to lead her to a table, at least he could get her to sit down.

'There's something else going on here,' Ellie murmured, almost too quietly for Porter to hear. 'I think, I think you need to get someone to investigate this place, they can't afford to spend this kind of money…' she stopped, 'someone's stealing…fraud…' she shook her head. Porter watched as she took a deep breath and walked over to a table. It was as though the last few minutes hadn't happened. Ellie picked up a menu and started to study it as Porter sat down opposite and did the same. He glanced up, almost afraid to ask. If she was right, if someone here was dipping into the company money and Bowers had found out about it…it was a powerful motive to murder someone. But if it was the motive, it cast the link they were trying to establish into doubt. Harrington-Smythe and Anthea Harrold had nothing to do with Donaldson's, at least not that he was aware of. He hoped Ellie was right, that the murderer was the same man she'd seen at the Harrington Estate.

Something else he would have to sort out.

…oo0oo…

It was late afternoon when Porter got back to the station. Ellie had been quiet for most of the return journey. She'd ordered a sandwich and coffee in the end, and she had only picked at that. The coffee was burnt, she said, pulling a face. He'd laughed, only an expert could tell, he told her. He tried to cajole her into eating more but realised that he sounded like a bossy parent and gave up.

'You mustn't worry about me,' she said quietly, 'it's not like I'm going to starve myself to…' she stopped, wiped her hands on her serviette and finished off her drink. Porter saw a shadow cross her face; a slight shudder passed through her body. He knew that look. It was one he'd seen many times before. It was an expression he called *'the look of recollection'*. It had happened many times when someone he was interviewing remembered something unpleasant about their past, maybe not even connected with the matter in hand. He wondered if he should ask, he decided not to.

She stood in front of the house as he drove away. He was beginning to realise how little he knew about Ellie as he made his way back towards the bridge. The little he did know was what he'd been told, he wanted to know more, exactly why he couldn't say. The station was quiet when he got back, most of the team were out following up leads, a few were sitting at their desks, some were typing up reports. DS Rowan had appropriated an empty desk in a quiet corner. She was studying the notes she'd taken that afternoon and didn't hear Porter as he walked towards her. She jumped as he cleared his throat.

'Can I have a word, please?' he asked, she knew it wasn't a request. She followed him into his office, taking her notebook with her. Porter sat down and motioned Rowan to do the same.

'Well,' he started, 'what do you think?' Rowan shook her head.

'About what?' she asked, although she had her suspicions. She sighed. 'Not for me to judge, is it?' she said.

Porter suspected that she had been doing nothing but judging since the moment she'd arrived at the station. His silence was beginning to make her nervous.

'Okay,' she said, 'I'm impressed, freaked out, but definitely impressed. She obviously has…' she stopped, searching for an appropriate definition of what she'd witnessed. 'I don't know how to…what makes you so sure that we can take what Ms. Shaw says with anything but a pinch of salt?' she asked.

'I'll tell you more about the John Prothero case. Maybe that'll tell you more about her, and her abilities.' He told Rowan as much as he could, given that he hadn't been prepared. As he spoke, he realised again how little he knew about Ellie. He could see the scepticism on Rowan's face. When he'd finished, he could have sworn he'd heard Rowan snort in disbelief.

'So, do you really believe in her, one hundred percent?' she laughed.

'Ellie Shaw doesn't believe in Ellie Shaw one hundred percent,' he said, 'let's just say, I've never known her to be wrong, and leave it at that.'

'It's just that DCI Horton said…' she started. Porter could feel her eyes on him, he wasn't used to this kind of intense scrutiny, except from maybe Chetwynd. There was a lot about Rowan that reminded him of his boss. He shivered, one Chetwynd in his life was more than enough.

'Horton's a dick-head,' he snapped, Rowan giggled, it was the first time he'd heard her laugh, it wasn't an unpleasant experience. He paused, there was a distinct possibility that any conversation they had might get back to Horton.

'You don't need to worry about me, or any of the officers at my station,' Rowan sighed, 'they all have the same opinion of him…same as yours I suspect.' She stared out of the window. 'Things have gone downhill since he arrived, but I did hear a rumour,' she stopped, wondering if she had overstepped the mark, after all, she hardly knew him.

'You can't stop now,' he urged her, smiling conspiratorially.

'Okay, but first I have to tell you something. I don't know if you're aware, but I was up for promotion just before Horton arrived, about to be made acting DI.' Porter shook his head. 'The boss told me that it would have to be put on hold for the foreseeable, down to him being drafted in.' She stopped; Porter got the impression that she regretted starting this conversation. She was obviously antagonistic towards Horton for putting the brakes on her career…a case of sour grapes maybe?

'Go on,' he said. Rowan sighed.

'I heard, through the 'grapevine', that his performance is being closely monitored; he's virtually on probation. If he puts a foot wrong, he's out. As you can imagine that makes things a bit awkward.' Porter shrugged, he wanted her to tell him in her own words, not put them into her mouth.

'I'm not out to discredit him in any way,' she sighed again, 'after all, I hardly know the man, but I've seen enough to know that he's inept. If Llay Station drops the ball during this investigation, it won't be because either me or my team have given any less than we can. I want whoever killed these people put away every bit as much as you do,' Rowan took a deep breath, she was taking a risk, and she knew it.

'Sir… I've heard of Horton's reputation for taking the credit without doing any work. It worries me that he could pass this so-called probationary period, then be let loose to run our station, which I'm positive he isn't capable of.'

Porter had kept quiet, his eyes narrowed. Her body language said everything.

'Tell you what,' he said at last, 'how about we solve the case, then we'll worry about Horton?'

Rowan nodded; it was only then that Porter realised she was on the verge of tears.

29

The faint sounds of his ringtone filtered through to Graham as he rinsed the last vestiges of shampoo from his hair.

…*sod it*… he thought, …*whoever it is can wait.*

The days were beginning to drag, to merge into one another; he'd begun to believe that his exile would never end. He turned the thermostat to cold, hoping it would stir him from the lethargy that had settled into his everyday life. He gasped as jets of icy water hit his back. Within seconds he'd had enough, he wrapped a towel around his waist. The urge to find out who had called him drove him into his office. Graham retrieved the message, then pressed the hash key to call the sender…Emlyn Davies.

…*could he drop into work on Monday…?* Could he? He was going crazy cooped up in the farmhouse on his own. He wasn't sorry that Karl was staying at his parents' place, he hadn't managed to wrap his head round the fact that he had a son, let alone developed the skills to deal with him. He had nothing to do, no one to talk to. He agreed at once, although why couldn't he go back now, he asked, it was only Tuesday? Emlyn kept the conversation official.

'Monday will be fine,' he stressed, a hint of '*you want to be thankful you're coming back at all,'* had crept into his voice. Graham agreed, he didn't want to jinx an opportunity to be back where he belonged. Being out of the loop had been tortuous, but it had given him some time to think.

'I don't want you to read too much into this, Graham, this might be a short-term thing. We need you to go through some of the paperwork on the cases you were working on before…' Emlyn cleared his throat. The last thing he wanted was for Graham to think that everything had been swept under the carpet, there was still the matter of what had happened to Miss Billingham. He told Graham as much.

Graham stared at the phone long after their conversation had ended.

*…okay, it's not much, but it's something…*he told himself, trying to put a positive spin on what Emlyn had said. It wasn't easy. He had behaved like a fool. To believe that he could do what he'd done without karma biting him in the backside, was naïve to say the least. Ellie had forgiven him for his dalliance with Kara, or at least he thought she had, now he wasn't sure. The University had been less understanding. If Kara had been a colleague they might have understood, but a student? No, even Graham had to concede that that was expecting too much. He could understand the position that his bosses at the Lab had taken as well. While there was even a hint of suspicion that he was involved in Kara's death, however far-fetched the prospect was, he couldn't carry out his job without compromising anything he touched…yes, he could understand the logic behind every sanction that had been taken against him.

So why were they asking him to come back now? He didn't want to know, just getting back there was enough right now. What he couldn't understand was how

Kara's death had been investigated, or rather how it hadn't been. During his enforced leave of absence, he'd begun to realise how many aspects of the '*Puppet Master*' case had been left hanging in the air. He knew that Porter was dissatisfied, he'd heard the rumours. If he felt that way, how had the rest of the investigating team taken it? No closure, not for them or the relatives of the victims. Now that he had the opportunity to return to his job, he would make it a priority to clear his name and perhaps go some way to ending their misery.

His phone bleeped, a text. Simon Daventree's name flashed on the screen. He'd never managed to create much of a rapport with Daventree, who he regarded as a bit of a cold fish, so the message surprised him.

...looking forward to seeing you on Monday...the place hasn't been the same without you. Must have that meeting you mentioned, I have several ideas I'd like to discuss with you. Suggest that we meet before you return...tomorrow, three o'clock, The Talbot Inn... Graham re-read the message several times, it was unlike Daventree to be so cloak and dagger, maybe he was working on something...*steady*...he thought...*don't push your luck...*

Still, it was nice to have the feeling that someone was on his side.

...oo0oo...

Porter stood at the bar waiting for his pint. The place was quiet, three o'clock on a Thursday afternoon was the perfect time to arrange their meeting. He was curious though. Apart from delivering his findings on the Harrington-Smythe case, Daventree hadn't spoken to him. Porter thought back to the first time they'd worked together, the difficulty he'd had in trying to convince Daventree that his methods were slightly outdated.

They'd rubbed along through several investigations before the Alyson Livesey case, but that had been their stumbling point, professionally speaking. Thereafter he'd preferred to work with Shaw, he realised now that he must have made it obvious. During the last few weeks, however, Porter had found out that although Simon had none of Graham's flair, he did a damn good job.

During what little free time Porter had, he'd gathered all the evidence he could on the two cases. The USB stick that Mason had handed him held very few details on the Livesey case, just a few crime scene photographs and a couple of interview statements from some of her workmates. He knew for a fact that there had been more paperwork. Kara's records were even sketchier, photographs, again, and some details of her movements during the few hours before she died, that was about all. Porter's plans to acquire Daventree's records had also drawn a blank. Emlyn Davies had been forced to hand over files, just as Chetwynd's team had. It seemed that every time he made a move, his progress was blocked.

Porter hated relying on memory. It wasn't as though he could get the details of either case out of his mind, but memory wasn't always infallible. From what he *could* remember, there were too many similarities to allow for coincidence. Both women found in thick woodland, both beaten and strangled. If that wasn't a link, then the physical similarities between them was something that couldn't be denied. Kara could have been Alyson Livesey's twin, if not that, then certainly her sister. Both tall, slim, blonde, Kara even had a mole on her chin in almost the exact same place as Alyson. If his suspicions were correct, and the same person had murdered both victims, then Graham Shaw was indeed innocent. He'd done his homework on that one. Graham and Ellie Shaw had been on holiday in the States when Alyson was killed, which was why Daventree was assigned the case, no doubt. If Graham hadn't murdered Alyson, and they were linked, then…he looked round as the door opened drawing a blast of cold air into the warm room.

Daventree walked towards him, followed by Graham Shaw.

…oo0oo…

'This is off the record,' Porter stressed, knowing that what he was about to say was pointless, but he felt as though he had to say it anyway. 'I'm sorry, I have to ask this Graham, I'm sure you understand. Did you have anything to do with the death of Kara Billingham?' he sat back. There; it was out.

Graham felt two pairs of eyes boring into him. He sighed. They'd worked together in the past, for many years, he was disappointed that Porter felt the need to ask, but he could understand. He picked up his drink and took a swig... a scholar of body language might have accused him of playing for time. He didn't care, what did he have to lose?

'If you mean would Kara be dead if I'd never had anything to do with her all those years ago,' he answered, 'then yes, I suppose I did have something to do with her death. She claimed that she had come to the island because of the '*Puppet Master*' case, we couldn't cope, if you remember. But she had an ulterior motive.' He sighed again, hoping that they would understand. 'Kara liked nothing more than playing games with people's lives. We were dealing with a landmark case, but she was more concerned with the chaos she could cause between myself and…' he paused, swallowing hard at the thought of what he'd lost. 'She wanted to split us up, Ellie and me, I'm convinced of that.' He sat back in his chair. The fact that he had finally managed to voice his opinion of Kara's motivation out loud was a mixture of relief and exhaustion.

'What happened that day Graham?' Porter asked, his voice low, reassuring.

Graham told them, every detail. How Kara had come to the farmhouse, how she'd tried to seduce him, her little tricks, her snide comments about Ellie. He told them how she'd acted as though their lives had merely been placed on hold all those years ago, and she was finally picking up the reins once more.

'She left, more than a little annoyed that she hadn't succeeded in getting her own way,' Graham told them, 'that was the last time I saw her, I swear.'

'You do understand why we had to bring you in, don't you?' Porter asked. Graham nodded. 'Miss Billingham had your DNA under her fingernails…and with Prothero as your only alibi, no wonder…'

'I know,' Graham interrupted, 'I'm guilty of a lot of things, Bill, but killing Kara isn't one of them.' He took another long swig of his drink. 'You know, I can't believe I'm going to suggest this, but there is one person that would be able to help sort this out…' Porter knew what he was going to say before he said it.

'We'd better hope she's willing to give it a try then, hadn't we?' he said, wondering if Ellie would put her principles above her emotions. Despite everything, he had the feeling that she would. Now all they had to do was ask.

'Aren't you going to ask me why I invited you both here, then?' Daventree asked, his tone seemed slightly peeved. Porter frowned; he'd almost forgotten that Simon was there. Daventree opened his briefcase.

'I thought you might need these,' he said, placing a manilla folder on the bar. Porter reached over and picked it up.

The label read 'Kara Billingham.'

'Sorry I didn't have the foresight to copy the Livesey one as well,' Daventree grinned as Porter closed his eyes and sighed, holding the folder to his chest... it was a start.

30

Doris Mason had processed so much paperwork in the last few weeks, the last thing she needed was more. Porter felt guilty. He sat in his office surrounded by the information relating to both the Livesey and the Billingham murders, wondering how he could approach Chetwynd about the possibility of re-opening two more cases. First, though, he would have to explain how he had acquired them. But was this the right time? He sighed; he knew the answer. The matter would have to wait until the '*Canterbury Murders*' had been dealt with.

…*then*…he promised himself… *then we'll investigate them.* He started to gather the files together just as Chetwynd walked into his office, followed by Mason. His first prayer was that his boss was just passing, and that she wouldn't notice the picture of Kara Billingham on his desk. His second was that she wouldn't ask him where it had come from.   Neither prayer was answered as she picked up the photograph and studied it for what seemed like hours. He could see Mason shifting uncomfortably from one foot to the other.

'Where…' Chetwynd said, turning the picture round. She picked up the file and opened it.

…*here it comes*…he thought, calculating the odds that she wouldn't know he was lying.

'...did these come from?' Porter could have sworn he heard Mason give a little squeal of desperation. Chetwynd turned around; Mason blushed.

'I asked DS Mason to look out the files on...' Porter started.

'I can see who the files are on, DCI Porter,' Chetwynd snapped. 'how is it that you have them in your possession, given that everything on the...' she was beginning to lose it, he could tell. She took a deep breath, ' more importantly that that, do they have anything to do with the current case?'

'Err, no Ma'am,' he stammered. If Chetwynd's only beef with him was that he appeared to be distracted, he could take that. Chetwynd sighed.

'Look, Bill,' she said, placing the file back on his desk, 'it might be politic, in view of what happened in the Prothero case, to focus on the murders currently being investigated. I appreciate the need to look into the Kara Billingham case, and the...' she stopped and picked up the other file and flicked through it. She paused for a few seconds as the similarity between the two women became evident. Her natural curiosity, and the need to see justice carried out seemed to take over. '...Livesey,' she said, almost to herself, 'I remember her...Alyson Livesey, wasn't she...'?

'A-Alyson,' Mason stammered, Chetwynd and Porter both turned and stared at her. She stood blinking, at them. 'Sorry...sorry Ma'am, did you say Alyson? I knew there was something...it can't be...I'm...I'm such a fool...' Mason shook her head. 'No, that's not possible, that's not right, that would be out of order...' Mason muttered to herself. She turned and almost ran back to her desk. Chetwynd and Porter followed close behind.

Mason typed *'Canterbury Tales – order'* into a search engine. Within seconds she read from the screen.

'...although there is no definitive order to the Canterbury Tales, it has long been believed that the original intention was for them to be told in the order of the class of the character about whom they were written. It is widely believed that the 'Knight's Tale' was the first to be told, followed by 'The Miller's Tale', 'The Reever's Tale', 'The Cook's Tale' and 'The Man of Law'...' Mason stopped.

'I knew it...' she hissed, turning to look at a bemused Chetwynd and an equally mystified Porter. He shook his head...what did she know? Mason took a deep breath, she no longer read from the information on her screen.

'In the second edition of *'The Tales'*, published in 1483, William Caxton suggested the order in which they should be told. This has been disputed by scholars ever since, my father wrote several papers, in fact he was in quite a nasty argument between him and one of his best friends about it. It caused no end of trouble at the time, they actually stopped speaking in the end...in fact his friend...' she stopped as she saw the look on Chetwynd's face. She was losing them, and she knew it. 'Never mind...' she said, shaking her head. She stood up and crossed to the white board where she had already pinned a list of the Tales.

'Firstly, *'The Knight's Tale'*...that's obvious, Harrington-Smythe. But then we come to the *'Reever's Tale'*, Ronnie Bowers, or so we thought. The Reever's Tale is actually the third in Caxton's list, the second is...' she waited in vain for an answer.

'... *'the Miller's Tale',*' she pointed to it on the board, and drew an arrow placing it at number two.'

Porter shook his head. 'But we don't have a Miller, do we?' he said, he was totally lost.

'Actually, the Miller's Tale tells the story of a carpenter and his wife,' Mason answered, 'the carpenter's name was John, his wife…' she placed a picture of Alyson Livesey underneath that of Harrington-Smythe, '…was called Alyson.'

Porter sat down on the nearest chair if what Mason was saying was right…

'But you said our murderer was killing his victims in the order the Tales were told,' he said, his face registering the enormity of her suggestion.

'That's just it, Sir, no one can agree on what that order was.' Mason explained. 'When I said that, I was using the common belief…it's hard to explain. My father would…' she stopped abruptly. Her father was the last person that could help them.

Chetwynd had been studying the board, she'd fetched the picture of Kara Billingham from Porter's desk and placed it next to that of Alyson.

'If, as you suspect, these two murders are linked, why would the murderer want to kill both Alyson and Kara?' she asked, 'if each murder represents one of the *'Tales'*, then why bother killing two women who appear identical?'

Mason thought for a moment, running through information gained long ago in her childhood. Chetwynd looked at Porter who shrugged, she opened her mouth to ask another question, Porter placed his hand on her arm. His instinct told him that Mason needed some time to flex that awesome memory.

'… *'The Wife of Bath'*…of course,' she said, 'her story isn't listed until much later, but I'm sure…' she looked at the board. Number nine on the list… *'The Wife of Bath,'* she circled the title and looked around.

'I'm sorry, Mason,' Porter pleaded, 'I'm lost. That one is even further down the list you made.'

'It is,' Mason confirmed, 'but that's not the point. My father always maintained that *'The Wife of Bath's'* name was *Alys*, but she was also known as Alyson…there were two of them, perhaps he needed to kill Alyson twice. Kara didn't have the same name, but she was practically Alyson Livesey's double,' Porter shook his head.

'Get the team together,' Chetwynd said, 'I want chapter and verse on this before the end of the day.'

Porter wasn't sure if her pun was intended.

…oo0oo…

'…all known associates, where she worked, who she saw socially, everything we can find out about her movements in the few weeks before her death.' Porter mentally ticked off the team's list of actions, as he'd done so many times before. Mason was handing out photographs of both Alyson and Kara as Chetwynd joined Porter at the front of the room. She nodded towards Mason.

'Is she still worried?' she asked. Porter sighed.

'When isn't Mason worried?' he said. 'I wouldn't be surprised if the worry gene was implanted in her DNA.'

'Tell her not to be,' Chetwynd replied. 'Without her input…' she stopped talking as DS Rowan walked towards them.

'Ma'am,' she said, acknowledging Chetwynd before turning to Porter. 'I wondered, if we're linking the Livesey and Billingham murders to the others, well, shouldn't someone inform Graham Shaw? I mean, he was brought in after Kara died, wasn't he?'

'Next thing on my list, Rowan,' Porter told her, 'in fact I was about to pay him a visit. Want to come?'

Chetwynd watched as the two of them walked out of the room. She smiled; she really did have some fine officers in her team. She turned to examine the white board. The body count was building. This felt like the Prothero case all over again. Was there a connection, she wondered? If there was it would have to be a tenuous one. Perhaps a copycat, or one of Prothero's sycophants carrying on the work he'd started. She shook her head, there were obvious differences. Prothero got his kicks by coercing a disparate group of strangers to commit the murders, based on obtaining revenge for some past action. With this enquiry, if everything that Mason had suggested was true, there was a common, almost theatrical theme.

...Mason's father...? I wonder... How much of an expert was he? Who were his peers during his academic career? Maybe...she walked across to where Mason was printing off more copies of the photographs.

'Well done, Mason, you really are an asset to the team,' she said, patting her on the arm. Mason blushed; Chetwynd cleared her throat.

'Your father,' she started, 'I hope he's settled into his new surroundings...' she hoped that Mason wouldn't get too upset. Chetwynd knew what it was like to have to make the kind of decision that Mason had recently taken. 'You said that there was an argument...about the order of the *'Tales'*, who was the argument with?'

Mason thought for a few minutes, once more pulling information from her past. She shook her head, Chetwynd sighed. Maybe this was a dead end.

'…Blackstock…' Mason said suddenly, 'Edwin Blackstock, he and my father studied at Eton together, then at Oxford…I don't know much more, only that there was a falling out. Blackstock committed suicide…I'll check my father's diaries, if he'll allow…' she stopped as she suddenly realised that he was in no position to prevent her from examining his papers. Chetwynd patted her on the shoulder, she could see how much the realisation had upset Mason.

'If you could do that, please?' she asked quietly, 'anything that we can find out, well, it's bound to help isn't it?' Mason nodded.

'I'll have to ask him first, though,' she whispered, 'even though…you understand…'

Chetwynd nodded…she understood completely.

…oo0oo…

Graham stood staring out of the kitchen window; the smell of fresh coffee permeated the air. It was late afternoon, just growing dark, he could see the kitchen reflected in the window. The two officers sat in silence, waiting for him to speak. It took some time for Porter's words to sink in.

'…let me get this straight,' he said, 'you've made a connection with a current investigation…' he could feel his emotions getting the better of him as he struggled to absorb the enormity of the news. Now perhaps he could get back to work full-time, now he could tell anyone that accused him to…

'The downside is,' Porter said, clearing his throat, 'we can't let this new development be made public just yet. If we did, it might jeopardise our investigation and…'

Graham turned back to face him. He shook his head in disbelief.

'There's a boy out there who believes that I killed his mother,' he snapped. 'My family have been put through hell by way of a trial by tabloid, my wife…my wife…' he turned around, putting his hands on the window to steady himself. Rowan crossed the room in a few strides, she put her arm around Graham's shoulders, and cupped his elbow in her hand.

'Come and sit down, Mr. Shaw,' she urged. Graham shot her a look of desperation. Porter watched as she guided him to the sofa. He was in a worse condition than Porter had suspected, but then what had he expected, given the circumstances.

'Graham,' he said gently, 'I'm going to contact Emlyn Davies to let him know. I'm aware that you're helping out with paperwork now, but it may be that…' he glanced at Rowan. She had no idea about the meeting that he, Daventree and Graham Shaw had had, he wasn't sure if she would approve…at this point, he didn't really care. 'It may be that given this new information, you'll be able to resume your position…'

'…thanks,' Graham mumbled, he sat with his elbows on his knees, supporting his head in his hands, as though it was too heavy for him to hold up.

'Is there anything we can do, Mr. Shaw?' Rowan asked. The last thing they needed was for him to do something desperate once he was alone.

'No, I-I'll be fine,' Graham said, 'I just need some time for this to sink in, that's all.' He sat upright, inhaling deeply. He hadn't realised how much being under suspicion had affected him. Now that was lifted, perhaps life could get back to normal…somehow, he doubted it. He ushered Porter and Rowan to the front door. Rowan stopped abruptly, she reached into her pocket and drew out her card.

'If you need anything,' she told him, 'call me…us,' she corrected herself.

Graham nodded as he watched them walk to the car. He couldn't wait to be alone, to try to think through what had happened. He realised with a shock that he was sub-consciously trying to put a spin on it that would look good in Ellie's eyes.

*…I think that boat has sailed, sweetie…*he heard, Graham had to agree.

…oo0oo…

Rowan sat at the kitchen table typing up her daily journal. It was a habit she had developed during her training, and one she had stuck to ever since. Some days there was little to record, others, like the past few weeks, went on for several pages. She sat back and read through the last few entries. If nothing else, they made for extraordinary reading. Her experiences at Bangor had been a rollercoaster since her arrival, she had begun to wonder what might happen next. She shook her head as she closed her laptop. Some supper and then bed, she wanted to be up early and at her desk before Porter arrived the next morning. She frowned as her mobile rang and Horton's name appeared on the display. He was the last person she wanted to hear from. She swiped the phone and answered the call.

'Okay, so why haven't I heard from you?' he snapped, she sighed. She had managed to stick to her decision not to play Horton's games, despite his texts and emails demanding constant updates. 'Are you still there?' he demanded.

'Yes, Sir,' she said, she had the feeling that he was going to get the information he needed, with, or without her help. She had an idea. 'I've asked Detective Chief Superintendent Chetwynd to provide you with a rundown of the progress we've made so far…' she paused, she could hear Horton breathing heavily, she could tell that he wasn't happy.

'You mean to tell me that you've…that Chetwynd knows…' he blustered.

'I don't think you could have a better person to let you know what's happening, Sir, do you?' Rowan said, her voice the epitome of innocence. 'I'll get her to email you tomorrow, if that's all Sir, I'll say goodnight.' She swiped the phone and ended the call before Horton could reply.

There would be a price to pay, she knew, but just for now she felt triumphant.

…oo0oo…

Rowan had been true to her word. An email from Celia Chetwynd, outlining the progress they had made so far, had arrived at five minutes past nine that morning. Horton had waited for it to arrive, expecting some scathing comments from his nemesis. There were none, just the information he had requested.

'Keeping you informed,' it said, 'as agreed in our initial meeting...' He read through the notes, nothing much, nothing that he needed to…

…*oh God,* he thought, as he scrolled down…*Alyson Livesey*…somehow, he knew that that case would come back to haunt him. Horton read the email several times before the implications started to sink in.

…*shit*…he thought…*what the hell do I do now? If this gets out…if anyone finds out.*

He should have done something about it, he should have filed the reports that had been passed on to him. How was he going to get out of this one? He took a deep breath and tried to remember the details of the case.

Porter had been heavily involved, he remembered that much. He'd sent Connett to interview Alyson's parents, they hadn't known what she was working on, just that she was excited about breaking a big story. Some of her friends hadn't seen her socially for weeks. Apart from that there was just the matter of…Horton swallowed hard. The reports, the ones he'd destroyed rather than let anyone find out that he'd neglected to file them. Porter would be looking for them, now that they had a lead…he shook his head.

…*this could be it*… he thought, *this could be the one that brings me down*…

31

Something was wrong. Connett should have left for the station by now, everyone was working overtime, so why hadn't he left home yet, and why had his wife taken their kid to school? For the last few weeks he'd kept a record of Connett's movements. Sometimes he would park just down the road from his house, other times he would stand across from the station car park and watch him stroll towards the entrance. He had to know that the main players were in their proper places; he didn't have the time to follow them everywhere.

He had to know what was going on…if Connett was ill, then he had a valid reason to stay home, but what if…what if he wasn't…what if he'd found out…he couldn't take the risk. He looked at his watch, five more minutes and he'd make some excuse to ring the doorbell, he'd have to take the risk.

The minutes ticked by; his head started to swirl. This was no good, he needed a clear mind to…he held his breath as a delivery van pulled up outside Connett's house. He got out of his car and walked towards it as the driver pulled a large box from the back. He stood on the pavement opposite and watched him approach the front door. It was several minutes before it opened and Connett stood in the entrance.

'Morning, not at work today?' called the driver as he held his clipboard towards Connett.

'No, got the day off, haven't I?' Connett replied.

'Good job you were in or I'd have had to leave you a card again,' the driver laughed, he handed the parcel to Connett. 'See you soon, no doubt…' he chuckled as he walked back to his van and climbed in. Connett glanced up and down the street and stepped back inside the house.

*…like hell, he's got the day off…he's distracted…he doesn't look ill…*a myriad of possibilities flooded his mind. He walked back to his car. He needed to work this out, maybe even re-jig his plans. Keeping tabs on Connett hadn't proved to be that difficult, he was so predictable, it was the other one that had proved to be more challenging. *His* routine seemed non-existent.

Still, the occasional visit to the Bell and Hammer had revealed a wealth of information so far. He'd done his homework after studying Alyson's research; it was all there, in her notes. She certainly got around; he'd give her that…lying little bitch. He wasn't surprised that she had someone else for a fool as well as him.

…oo0oo…

Connett had phoned in sick that morning. It wasn't the result of a bug, or anything he'd eaten, just a dread that had been building up over the last few days. The only sickness he felt was in his stomach. He'd taken on board Porter's latest pep talk stressing the importance of the team pulling together, but there was something he needed to do, and it couldn't wait. A hollow feeling had taken up residence in his body, and it wouldn't go away, no matter how much he tried to reassure himself that his suspicions were unfounded.

He should have known better; he should have listened to that small voice that had whispered to him the first time that Mason had voiced her suspicions of a link. How long ago was that? A week, a month…it didn't really matter, all he knew was that the feeling that things were spiralling out of control had grown stronger after yesterday's meeting at the station. Before that he'd only suspected, but now… with the discovery that the cases might be linked to the Livesey and Billingham murders…damn Horton, damn him to hell. He'd begun to believe that that episode in his life was over.

He knew that he was the only one that Horton had confided in, anyone else would have had the sense to report him long ago. The fact that his old boss had destroyed witness statements that he had 'forgotten' to file, had never sat well with him. He'd let it go for too long, he knew that. Reporting Horton after keeping quiet would mean…Connett had already decided one thing, if he was going down, then Horton was going with him, he wasn't going to carry the can for him again. First, though, he had to deal with the other matter.

He waited until his wife had left for work, taking their youngest daughter with her. She grudgingly agreed to drop Vicky off at school, being as he couldn't manage it this morning, her annoyance at being made to change her usual routine was obvious.

Connett lay in bed, he hadn't meant to cause this much inconvenience, but she needed to believe that he was sick enough to stay home. He waited for an hour, trying to put off the inevitable. He pulled on an old sweatshirt and jogging bottoms and stood gazing at the hatch in the landing ceiling for what seemed like hours.

He sighed, this was getting him nowhere, he shook his head, there was no use trying to avoid it. He fetched the pole that stood in the airing cupboard and slotted the hook through the ring on the loft door. He pulled down the ladder and started to climb up towards the darkness above. He stopped as he heard the front doorbell ring.

…shit, what now? He backed down the ladder and went downstairs. He could see the distorted figure through the glass as he snatched the door open.

'Morning, not at work today?' said the delivery man as he pushed his clipboard forward. Connett sighed, yet another parcel, he would have to stop this. If it wasn't his wife ordering stuff, it was Vicky.

'No, got the day off, haven't I?' Connett replied, as he scrawled his signature on the drivers list. He could have kicked himself. He'd seen this driver before, he was a regular. What if he told Margaret, what if…he shook himself… *comes to something when you're afraid of your own wife,* he told himself.

'Good job you were in or I'd have had to leave you a card again,' the driver said, laughing. He handed the parcel to Connett. 'See you soon, no doubt…' he said, chuckling as he walked back to his van and climbed in. Connett glanced up and down the street, without paying much attention to the people he saw. He sighed and stepped back inside the house, hoping he wouldn't be disturbed again.

It had to be done, he had to know, one way or another. He climbed up the ladder again, until he could feel around for the light switch. The neon strip buzzed into life, flooding the roof space with a sickly glow. He shuffled over to the boxes in the far corner. He hated the loft; it was musty, and he'd never trusted the flooring that had been laid by the previous owners. He only ventured up there when it was unavoidable, like fetching down the cases for their holidays, or storing the Christmas decorations. The place needed sorting out, some of the boxes dated back to the time he was training, all out of date now.

He saw the box he was looking for and debated whether he should take it downstairs to look through. He thought better of it, found an old cushion to sit on, and started to examine one folder after another.

The years slipped away as he read the contents of the files, only now could he appreciate their significance for the first time. He had to talk to him, to find out if his suspicions were correct. He would know, just by having a conversation, he would know for sure. He stared at the number that he hadn't used for years. It was now or never. It rang twice before kicking over to voice mail. Connett hesitated, then left a message.

'…it's me, Dai, I err, I need to talk to you, can you call me?' He hung up and started to tidy the papers and re-file them. A photograph fluttered to the floor, landing face down. He bent down to retrieve it, his heart dipped as he saw the faces of his mother and father, their arms around each other, taken on their honeymoon. He'd forgotten he had it.

He stared at his Mother's face, she was so like…he shook his head and placed it back in the box. He took the file with him as he climbed down the ladder and folded it back into the space above. Within an hour he'd showered and put his clothes in the wash. He spent the rest of the day reading and re-reading the file. He hoped he was wrong, and that his suspicions were unfounded. He had a feeling that he wasn't, and they weren't. The phone rang, he recognised the number and snatched it up.

'I hoped you'd ring back,' he said, 'I was wondering if it would be okay to call round, maybe this afternoon?'

'…and why would you want to do that?' a voice asked sharply.

'Well you know, it's been a long time, we could catch up, maybe go out for a drink?' He was improvising. Connett cursed himself for not preparing what he would say if he got a response. The silence seemed to last for an age.

'All right,' came the reply, 'but not today, I'm busy. Meet me at the café on Amlwch Harbour at ten-thirty tomorrow.' The line went dead. Connett sighed, he prayed that his suspicions were groundless. Too many people could be hurt if he shared them with anyone at this stage, not least, himself.

…oo0oo…

He had no choice. He had to take the risk. He stood so close to his target that he could almost touch him. The voices in the bar grew louder with every drink. It wasn't long before he found out what he needed to know. Among the obscenities were the complaints about the copper…his brother.

'Doesn't contact me for years, then rings me up out of the blue and asks to meet me for a drink…' he shouted.

'Hope you told him where to go,' one of his mates roared.

'I did that…Amlwych Harbour…ten-thirty, tomorrow morning…the least he can do is buy me breakfast…' he banged his glass down on the bar as the whole group roared with laughter.

'You want to be careful what you say,' laughed another of the men, 'he might cotton on to your little side-line...' it was obvious that they were all in on some sordid little secret. He wasn't interested, the only thing that concerned him was that the two didn't get together and compare notes.

'...families, eh, who'd have them?' he heard, in the general melee of voices. He knew who had spoken, he was still watching carefully. '...especially brothers...take mine for example...both of them...please...' his cronies roared again, '...who'd want them, I say...' he laughed along with his mates. So that was it... he knew...

He had to think quickly, Connett was the most problematic, if he found out the whole story, made the final connection, he would almost certainly report his suspicions, being a copper. He had to stop them from meeting the next day. He couldn't shake off the feeling that he was being backed into a corner.

Getting rid of Connett would enable him to tick another character off his list. The flaw in that plan was that Connett wasn't the person he'd earmarked as the '*Man of Law*'.

It couldn't be helped; he didn't have a choice. He couldn't shake the feeling that if the two of them got together...he couldn't take the risk. He left the pub and made his way over to Connett's house.

...oo0oo...

Connett's wife tutted as she dressed for work. This was the second morning that she'd had to take Vicky into school, it was out of her way. She suspected that her husband wasn't as sick as he made out, she knew for certain that he had been out of bed the previous day.

Then there was that incident last night, his car alarm had gone off, not once but three times. He'd been well enough to sort that out, hadn't he? The door banged as she left the house and she revved her car several times, just to let him know how annoyed she was.

*...can't be helped...*Connett thought as he showered and dressed...*especially if*...he stopped, swallowing hard. Did he want to prove his suspicions correct? No, he decided, that was the last thing he wanted. He checked the time, 9.15, he would have to leave within the next few minutes if he wanted to be there on time.

He grabbed his wallet and made his way to the car, praying that the battery wasn't flat. It started first time, just the early morning traffic to deal with now. It wasn't as bad as he'd expected. Once he was out of the traffic, he drove faster, there were some tricky bends, but he was afraid that if he was late...he may not get another chance.

Connett swore to himself as he took the next corner, he knew that he was driving too fast and cursed as he applied the brakes. They didn't respond. He pushed down on the pedal again, he heard something... that didn't sound right. He hit the patch of oil before he knew what was happening, the brakes were unresponsive. The car spun round, hitting the boards, breaking through as he held his hands up to his face.

The air bag deployed the instant the nose of the bonnet hit the ground, forcing him back into his seat, taking his breath away. The car turned a full summersault, landing back on its wheels, knocking any remaining air out of his body. His head was wrenched back and hit the headrest. He felt a sharp sensation in his leg as something pierced his thigh. He closed his eyes as the pain seared through his body.

Everything went silent…he could smell something, it didn't register what it was at first, then it came to him, all too familiar…petrol. The tank had ruptured. He fumbled for his seat belt and managed to open it, he reached for the door handle. The door resisted as he struggled to open it, he tried to ignore the searing agony in his shoulder as he pushed his weight against it. It wouldn't budge. The smell of petrol grew stronger as he summoned his remaining strength, and wrenched it open, just wide enough to climb out.

Connett howled as he moved, something metallic was sticking out of his thigh. He placed his hands under his leg, screaming as he tried to raise it. His head swam as he fought to remain conscious. He managed to swivel round in his seat, a shooting sensation bringing him to the point of collapse.

He dropped sideways out of the open door; his shoulder screamed as he hit the ground. He dragged himself a few yards before looking back. A pool of petrol was spreading over the ground towards him. He knew that he had to get further away, he struggled to get up onto his good leg, dragging the injured one. He hobbled a few yards before the blast hit him, knocking him to the ground.

…oo0oo…

DS Rowan sat in the briefing room, staring at the white board, trying to make the pieces of evidence fit together in a coherent way. Her temporary desk was littered with notes about the visits she'd made with Porter and Ellie.

Sleep had eluded her since then, as she tried to get her head around what she'd seen and heard. She had managed to snatch a few hours last night, before she started once more on the merry-go-round of questions that she couldn't find answers for. She'd given up around dawn, showered and returned to the station, her early arrival surprising the duty officer.

Now, three hours later, she was still none the wiser. She needed something to eat, she decided as she stood up and tried to stretch the weariness out of her body. She was confident that Porter ran a tight ship, and she would kill to have someone like Mason working with her at Llay. Not that Mason would consider the possibility. Was she mistaken, or did the strange looking DS have a secret crush on Porter? She couldn't blame her; he was quite attractive.

She jumped as the phone rang, snatching up the receiver. Within minutes she went to find Porter, they needed to get to the scene of the accident as soon as possible. She bumped into Mason as she raced down the corridor.

'Have you seen DCI Porter?' she asked her. Mason shook her head, then bent to pick up the files that had skittered out of her arms, spilling pages all over the floor. She tutted; she would have to re-file everything now.

Rowan turned as she heard Porter talking to Chetwynd. They were standing on the landing that lead to Chetwynd's office.

'Ma'am, sorry, I need… DCI Porter, a call,' she gasped for air. 'It's Connett, … an accident.' Chetwynd nodded to Porter, who motioned for Rowan to follow him. They headed out of the City and towards the bridge that led to the Island; the traffic was light as they sped along.

Rowan noticed how expertly Porter handled the car, his reflexes undiminished as he speculated on any number of possibilities for what had happened. Porter knew the road where the accident had happened; he knew the statistics on how many people had skidded off there during the years he'd been in traffic.

He also knew that Connett was more than familiar with the dangers that it represented. He would have been cautious when driving along it, but who knew? Maybe his bout of sickness was more serious than they had been led to believe. In which case, why had he ventured out this morning, and not taken another day to recover?

He pulled up a short distance from the gap in the reflective fencing, shattered from the impact of the car. Police incident tape bridged the space it had created. Porter and Rowan flashed their warrant cards to the Constable standing guard, they looked down the side of a steep slope to where smoke spiralled into the sky.

They started their descent, Porter stopping to make sure that Rowan was keeping up. She was as sure-footed as a mountain goat, he noted, ashamed of himself for doubting her. As they reached the bottom of the slope, he heard a familiar voice.

Graham Shaw was directing operations, Porter sighed, it was good to have him back. Graham had seen Porter's approach and walked over to him, nodding to Rowan, she nodded back, feeling a little awkward. After their visit to his home, he'd rung to thank her for her concern, the conversation had been more than a little stilted.

'Welcome back Graham,' Porter said, looking around the scene, the car smouldered in the background, 'is Connett…?' Graham shook his head.

'Haven't found him yet,' he answered. 'There's blood a short distance from the car, so he must have managed to get out before it set alight, we've got…' they heard a shout, people moved to its source, running over to where the tree line ended.

'He's here, quick, he's here…' Paramedics rushed towards the voice, Porter could see a group of people close to the water's edge.

… *'the Man of Law'*…whispered a woman's voice close to his ear. He turned around, but the nearest person to him was Graham, and he was a long way away.

Porter shivered as he watched. It seemed like an age before anyone spoke.

'He's alive,' someone shouted. Porter gasped with relief, the day had grown darker, colder, he had to put an end to this, he had to.

…oo0oo…

*…damn it…damn it to hell…just when things were starting to go according to…hell…*he punched the wheel with his fist…*I had to do it; I had no choice...* he shook his hand to ease the pain.

He'd regretted his actions as soon as he saw Connett's car spin round on the oily road. It was all wrong now, Dai Connett wasn't supposed to be *'The Man of Law',* he reminded himself. It was wrong…all wrong. The whole thing was a mess, he'd panicked as the sound of an approaching emergency vehicle caused him to flee from the scene. He ran as fast as he could towards the lane in which he had parked his car, fumbling with his keys as he unlocked it. He drove further on.

The lane led to a main road, once he was on it, it was less likely that he'd be followed. He had to be quick…it was wrong…all wrong…he felt sick, he had to stop, no matter how risky it was. He turned up a side road, he didn't know where it led, only that he had to stop the car as soon as he could.

A vision of Connett lying unconscious on the ground almost overwhelmed him. He hadn't meant…it wasn't right…He pulled the car over and sat hunched over the steering wheel. Connett wasn't just anyone, was he…? He tried to regain control of his emotions. This wouldn't do, what would his mentor think if he could see him now.

He breathed in deeply…one…two…three…he could feel himself starting to calm down.

…*assess*…he thought…*assess the situation, make small changes…if things don't go the way I want them to, reframe them…it might all work out for the best*…He replayed the last couple of hours, waking up, getting dressed, driving to Connett's house, waiting until he got into his car to drive to his meeting.

…*why did I choose him…?* he wondered…*why not the other one…?* He had no answers…or did he? *'The Man of Law',* perhaps that was it, the appeal of killing two birds…no, he couldn't believe it could be that simple. All he knew for sure was that if Connett had found out about him the days of his *'Quest'* would be numbered. Perhaps it *was* all for the best, the thought cheered him up. He began to relax a little.

…*focus*…, he thought, … *it wasn't all bad.* He thought about the photograph he'd taken after dragging him to the water's edge. Connett looked as though he wasn't long for this world, there had been no reaction when he'd fished around in his jacket for the trophy.

He could kick himself that he hadn't had the guts to finish him off. His thoughts darted about…he had to get a better camera, the quality of the pictures he had taken on his phone weren't good enough. *Invest in the best equipment possible*…he could almost hear his mentor's words. He reached into his jacket pocket, pulling out the small wallet that housed Connett's warrant card... a memento to add to the collection. He would need to do something about the quality of his pictures, though, he knew just how to address that.

Good, he felt better now. He had to get out of here, put as much distance between himself and the incident as he could. He'd done well, given the circumstances, the short timeframe that he'd had to work with. He pulled back onto the road and made his way towards the main road. He could feel himself relaxing, he had other issues that needed to be addressed, like retrieving his camera... *no time like the present*...he decided.

All the same, he couldn't shake the feeling that he'd killed the wrong one. He needed to do something about the other one now...

...oo0oo...

It felt strange, going back to the place where it all started, where he'd discovered that Alyson had fooled him.

It was late in the afternoon as he drove to the building where he'd spent most of his working life, the staff had already left. He entered the building and walked down the corridor without being challenged. The lack of security hadn't changed. He made his way towards the staffroom, still dingy, paint peeling off the walls. The smell of stale body odour turned his stomach. He was confident that his stuff would still be in his locker. He'd sent in regular sick notes, his colleagues would probably still believe that he was ill.

He walked over to where the lockers stood, next to the notice board. He stopped suddenly, the hair on the back of his neck standing up.

It was her, Alyson, and…Kara, pictures pinned to the board. A notice, a police notice…he read the text. An appeal for information about the two women… *'Please contact…'* he snatched it down as the door opened, he spun round as a familiar voice filled the room.

'…what the hell?' Mr. Freeman, the caretaker, 'oh, sorry, it's you, I didn't know you were…'.

'Mr. Freeman,' he said trying to sound casual, making light of the situation, 'how are you, how's your son…Luke, isn't it? I just popped in to collect some stuff, sorry if I startled you,' he was improvising, not very well.

'I wondered when you'd be back, I've waited for you. Police were here a few days ago,' Freeman said flatly, a strange smile creeping onto his face, 'wanted to see everybody about your friend Miss Sophie, only she's not Miss Sophie, is she? She's that there Alyson Livesey, isn't she?' he nodded towards the notice board. 'Asked me questions, about people, people who weren't where they were supposed to be. I didn't tell them nothing of course, I know when to keep my mouth shut.'

He swallowed hard. Freeman knew something, otherwise why had he called her *'your friend',* and looked at him with that sneering expression? It took a few moments before he realised that Freeman was staring at him intently.

'Got her stuff, I have,' Freeman said, his smile turning into something altogether more sinister, 'read most of her notebooks too. Interesting, what she had to say about…but you know all about that, don't you?' his voice slid into silence as he nodded. He felt sick as he gritted his teeth

He opened the door of his locker and reached inside. He turned back to face Freeman, who stood watching him by the open door.

'Do you remember Christmas, Mr. Freeman,' he asked, 'when we all got a bottle of whisky?' he held up the bottle, smiling. 'Let's go down to your 'office' and crack this open, shall we? I'm sure we can come to some kind of arrangement; you know what I mean?' Freeman's eyes widened at the prospect of a free drink and a reward for his silence. He smiled again, this time it held no malice, and held the door open.

'By the way, Mr. Freeman,' he said as he slung his camera case onto his shoulder and they made their way down the stairs, 'it's lovely and warm in here, you got the boiler going have you?'

32

Connett's wife handed over the file that her husband had locked in his desk. The fact that she had made a point of telling Porter that she had a copy of the key, and that her husband didn't know about, spoke volumes about their relationship. She was more reluctant to part with his laptop, though, surrendering it only when she was reminded of how serious the situation was.

...Not entirely sure there's a lot of trust between them... Porter thought as he left their semi-detached house. He could hear Margaret Connett snapping at her daughter as she fussed around carrying the tea things back into the kitchen. She hadn't exactly been co-operative. The impression Porter got was that it was more of an inconvenience to her than a potentially life-threatening incident for her husband. He remembered thinking the same thing about Trish Harrington-Smythe. To be honest he was glad to leave, he felt sorry for the child though.

...Demanding parents, they seem to find fault in the very air they breath. No wonder they could scar a kid for life, he thought, drawing on personal experience. He headed back to the station; the techies could deal with the laptop; he'd get Mason to read the file. He knew that they would have made little progress if it hadn't been for her. Still, early

days. They would have to go through this new information carefully, but Porter was confident that with Mason in charge, nothing would be overlooked.

The station was buzzing as he walked through the reception area. What had happened to Connett had galvanised everyone into action. The past, along with Connett's association with Horton, was forgotten as every officer felt empathy with one of their own. Mason was sitting at her desk as he walked into the office, head down, pouring over statements. He'd asked her to check everything while he was away, he had no doubt that she had followed his instruction to the letter. Porter felt almost guilty about asking her to do even more work. He cleared his throat, making Mason jump.

'Sorry,' he mumbled, 'stuff from Connett's place,' he explained, 'there's more, but this was the only one he bothered to lock away.' Her expression was hard to read, Porter tried to figure out what it was, then it came to him…hunger. Mason was hungry for more information that could give the team clues, any clues to follow. He realised again, as he left the file to Mason's tender ministrations, how much of an asset she was to the team. His office seemed like a quiet haven after the buzz outside. He sat down just as the phone rang, shattering the peace. It was Graham Shaw. Porter braced himself.

'DCI Porter?' he could hear the noise in the next office rising and falling, the sound of his blood drummed in his head. 'Just a word, it's about DS Connett.'

'He's not…' Porter asked, almost a whisper.

'What? No, sorry, I didn't think…' Graham paused, 'as far as I know he's still being assessed…it's just that, from what I saw of the injuries he sustained, he couldn't have got that far away from the car on his own. There are signs of drag-marks on the ground between the car and the water's edge. I think someone moved him before we got there.'

...oo0oo...

Celia Chetwynd walked back to her car; she was needed back at the station as quickly as possible. That was the message she'd received less than twenty minutes ago, as she sat beside the bed in Intensive Care Unit, the sound of the monitors, rhythmically pulsating in the background.

...*Damn it,* she thought, *one of my troops*. She watched as the ventilator, acting in lieu of Dai Connett's autonomic nervous system, supplied him with oxygen that his body couldn't deliver. She had to admit, he looked awful. Despite her position, she couldn't get any information out of the doctors. She knew she could pull the *'...I'm the SIO officer in this case...'* card, but the truth was that Connett was still being monitored, the full extent of his injuries was yet to be uncovered, and she would have to settle for that. Chetwynd was grateful to the young nurse who had furnished her with even that much information. Besides which, she was experiencing a numbness she had rarely felt before. This is what shock felt like, and she didn't like it. When the text came through from Porter, she was relieved to have an excuse to leave.

...*Not that Connett would know one way or the other,* she thought as she gathered her bag and coat. She could at least salve her conscience by telling herself that she was the only one from the station that had visited him, but then that was her role, wasn't it, part of her responsibilities?

The last six months had shaken Chetwynd's belief in herself to the core. What sort of a senior rank was she,

Horton running around like a headless chicken, her giving him the latitude she would never have allowed anyone else, and now this? The Prothero case had been enough to unsettle the most confident of station commanders, let alone having to deal with a new series of murders. Dai Connett lying at death's door…she stopped, standing still in the middle of the car park. That was unthinkable, losing a colleague…

She started forward, quickening her pace. Porter's message had insisted that she return to the station immediately, something wasn't right, and she needed to be there.

…oo0oo…

Chetwynd's secretary had already settled Porter and Mason into her office. Mason sat, staring at her hands, which she clenched in her lap. Porter stood at the window looking out onto the car park.

'She's back,' he said as gently as he could. He heard Mason sigh and tried to place himself in her position, he failed. Within minutes they were both standing as Chetwynd entered the room. She murmured a greeting, then removed her coat and hung it behind the door. The atmosphere was charged as she sat down. Porter shifted slightly. Chetwynd cleared her throat. Whatever this was, she had a feeling she wasn't going to like it.

Mason sat down, her legs felt heavy, and she'd begun to feel slightly nauseous. Porter saw the change in her and without asking, poured her some water. He took a seat next to her. Chetwynd looked from one to the other, wanting to know what the hell was going on, but sensing that she had to give Mason time. Mason sipped the water, fighting with her emotions. Porter cleared his throat, hoping that she would take his cue, and start talking. Eventually she took out a handkerchief and dabbed her mouth.

'I, er, I really don't know where to begin, Ma'am,' she started. Chetwynd knew that to hurry her at this point would be a mistake. She nodded, hoping to instil the woman with some confidence. It seemed to work.

'This afternoon…' Mason began, 'this afternoon, after DCI Porter visited Dai Connett's house,' she glanced across at Porter. 'he, he brought back a folder, I read through it, as he asked me to, that's when…' she stopped, swallowing hard, '…Ma'am, I'm so sorry,' she went on her voice trailing into a whisper. 'I didn't know anything about…' She looked down at her hands, her handkerchief twisted around her fingers so tightly that Chetwynd thought for a moment that she would cut off the blood supply.

'Whatever it is, Doris…' Chetwynd started. The use of her first name seemed to dissolve down whatever control Mason had left, she shuddered as she wept silently. Chetwynd looked to Porter for an explanation. He cleared his throat, he always felt uncomfortable when in the presence of distressed people, male or female.

'I asked DS Mason to go over one of the files that I collected from Connett's house,' he confirmed. Chetwynd looked from him to Mason, who seemed to be mustering the last vestiges of strength. She sat up straight, took another drink of water, and a deep breath.

'I read most of it,' she went on, 'it's mainly notes, some of them don't make sense, I can't…I mean…I didn't understand, at first…then…then I realised the implications of what I'd read, and asked to see DCI Porter,' her voice had regained a degree of strength as she spoke. 'As a result of what I discovered, I've asked DCI Porter to allow me to step down from the case, I hope you agree Ma'am.' Chetwynd sat still, staring at Mason, completely bewildered by what she'd said. Porter shook his head slightly; Chetwynd asked no further questions.

'I'm sure that DCI Porter will be able to fill me in on the details, DS Mason,' she said, realising that Mason could deal with authority far better than she could with familiarity, and kept her tone firm, though sympathetic.

'I will, of course, be only too glad to help you if you want me to…' Mason's voice began to falter again as she stood. It was obvious that she wanted to distance herself from both Porter and Chetwynd, at least for the time being. Chetwynd nodded. Mason turned and fled the room, closing the door with an accidental bang. Chetwynd stared after her, then turned to Porter.

'What the hell was that about?' she demanded. Porter sat back down, he sighed, then started to explain.

…oo0oo…

…*Sometimes,* Chetwynd thought, *I'm glad I didn't go in for all that relationship crap, especially when…*she sighed. Porter had left her office over an hour ago, during which time she'd read Connett's file for herself. The implications were serious, not only for the current case, but also for DS Mason's life.

So…Dai Connett had a brother, Ray. Nothing remarkable about him, got into trouble when he was a teenager, but apart from that, he led what could be described as a quiet existence. He worked as a builder, based in Beaumaris. Chetwynd shook her head, so much for her knowing the officers in her station. It seemed that Ray had changed his name in his early twenties, just after his grandmother had died. His surname was Blackstock, he and Dai Connett were Edwin Blackstock's sons. The same Edwin Blackstock that Professor Mason had argued with when they were young men.

Chetwynd's instinct that Mason's father was involved in this case had been spot on. But when had Connett started to suspect Ray of being involved in the current murder investigations? She was disappointed that he hadn't come to her at the first hint of involvement. It wasn't as though Connett wasn't aware of the feud that had existed between Mason's father and his own, his notes had confirmed it.

Chetwynd turned away from the window, standing there was purely a distraction, she'd hardly registered any of the comings and goings down in the street. Nor had she noticed when the light started to fade and the streetlamps flickered on, illuminating the pathway to the station car park. The rest of the folders that Porter had brought back that afternoon had been copied and delivered to her office. They lay on her desk in a neat pile. She knew the gist of the story of course, now she wanted to find out the details. There was only one thing for it she decided as she sat down and reached for the top file.

33

Doris drove straight to St. Mary's as soon as she left Chetwynd's office; it seemed the only thing she could do. She doubted that her father would be lucid enough to tell her anything, but Chetwynd had been right, maybe her father's papers could give them a clue into the murders. Doris didn't hold out much hope, after all this was…her father, he couldn't have had anything to do with them, he was too old to go around killing people.

The Professor was sitting in the lounge by the window. He seemed quite bright compared to her last visit. He was still vague though. Doris sat in the chair next to him. He drummed his fingers on the arm of his chair and looked out onto the garden. Every few minutes he turned to look at her, his face registering surprise at her presence. Once or twice her called her 'Emily', Doris swallowed hard. She knew she looked a little like her mother, but all the same…it was no use, she couldn't put this off any longer.

'Dad,' she said softly, her father turned towards her, trying to focus on her face. 'Dad, I wanted to ask you…'

'…read my papers,' he said, pre-empting her request. 'I want you to know, I want…' he turned away, staring out of the window again. Doris was confused.

'What do you want me to know, Dad,' her father turned back.

'…be careful,' he urged her, '…and cariad…try not to judge me too harshly…' he said, patting her hand. She nodded; she didn't have a clue what he meant. Before she could ask, she heard her phone buzz, it was Chetwynd wanting to check that she was all right.

'I'm at St Mary's,' she said watching her father as he put his head back on the chair. She knew that within minutes he would be asleep. Chetwynd started to speak.

'…yes,' Doris said, before Chetwynd could ask, 'he's agreed, in fact he suggested it…I'm going home, I'll start on them tonight.'

'Let me know if you find anything…' Chetwynd said, 'and Doris…don't…' Mason cut the call short. She turned and looked back at her father as she opened the lounge door to leave. Mr. Edwards stood in reception studying some papers.

'Miss Mason,' he said as she walked towards him, 'I just needed to confirm…'

'I'm sorry Mr. Edwards, it'll have to wait,' she didn't want to talk to him now, she wasn't sure if it was because of Chetwynd's call or because she couldn't trust her emotions. She scribbled her name in the visitor's book and left. Edwards shook his head. He stared after Mason as he watched her get into her car and drive away.

'Everything all right Mr. Edwards,' he jumped. Audrey Fellows struggled through the reception area, dragging a bag of laundry behind her.

'I think so,' Edwards replied, 'I wanted to have a word…still I suppose it can wait.'

'Anything I can do?' Audrey asked. He shook his head.

'Just wanted to have a chat with Miss Mason, about that new therapist that she hired to attend her father,' he said, 'haven't had copies of his qualifications come through yet. Never mind, at least I've got written confirmation from her…'

'I wouldn't worry about it then,' Audrey said as she walked towards the garage. She had a long afternoon of washing and ironing ahead of her.

Edwards shrugged. He'd worked through his lunchtime, he felt entitled to a few games of on-line poker before he got back to some work.

34

Mason sat in the lounge, her shoulders hunched, oblivious to the cold. Most of her remaining energy was being taken up with the simple act of breathing. She picked up the sheaf of papers that lay on the table in front of her. She was well aware that she had breached regulations again, copying confidential files seemed to be becoming a habit, but how else was she going to find out the truth, once she was away from the station?

She couldn't believe the things that she'd read in Connett's notes earlier that day...he and Ray were Edwin Blackstock's sons. Connett had obviously spent a long time working out various scenarios, but one aspect remained constant. He believed that Ray had carried a grudge against her father for decades, blaming the old man for what had happened to Edwin. Who knew what damage that sort of thing could do to someone? Connett had speculated on the possibility that Ray had taken matters into his own hands, devising a complicated revenge plot. Despite the personal connection, Mason had been fascinated at how much detail he had gone into. In the end he had talked himself into and out of several possible plots.

How long had he suspected his brother of being the *'Canterbury Murderer'* she wondered? He knew all about the feud between his father and her own. Why hadn't he said anything to anyone?

...why didn't he say anything to me...?

It took several seconds before she realised that the phone was ringing, the sound echoing in the sparsely decorated hallway. She realised that she was staring at the wall, the gathering gloom of the evening making it difficult to focus. The sound of the answer phone clicking on, registered in her confusion.

'Doris, Doris, if you're there will you pick up please?' her brother, Brian, she shivered. He waited a few seconds, then carried on speaking. 'Doris, you need to go and see Dad, as soon as possible, he's been playing up at the Home. You need to go and sort it out. I'm afraid I can't manage to...' Brian swore at something and the message ended. Mason sighed, the last thing she wanted was to have to go and see her father again. She needed time to study his notebooks. There were more of them that she thought. She'd spent most of the day sorting them into order. She grabbed her coat and her keys and walked to the door.

...no, she thought... *sod it... I need time, I need time. Everyone else takes time, why not me for once...?* She picked up the receiver and dialled Brian's number, her heart thundering. She wasn't sure if it was because she was about to break the habits that reached back to her childhood, or if it was anger. Brian answered on the second ring.

'Doris, so you were there after all...' he started, she cut across him.

'Sorry, it's not convenient right now, I've got stuff to do,' she snapped, ignoring him as he tried to interrupt her.

'But you need...' he began again.

'…what I need right now, Brian, is some breathing space. If it's that bad, you'll have to deal with it yourself, goodnight,' she replaced the receiver carefully, a heady mixture of panic and triumph fighting for dominance. She could imagine the look on Brian's face. He didn't like being second guessed on anything, nor did he like being denied…anything.

…*Tough,* she thought, *he'll just have to put up with it for once.* The surge of adrenaline she'd experienced moments before, started to subside, leaving her feeling weak. She hadn't eaten for hours, she had to address this situation before anything else. The practical skills that served her so well as a police officer kicked in, and she crossed to the kitchen in search of food. Scrambled eggs, toast and a pot of tea soon sat on the dining table. Food was the last thing she wanted; her common sense told her it was the first thing she needed. She managed to eat, all the while thinking about Connett's notes. They were mainly about him and his brother Ray, Ray Blackstock…she shivered as she said the name in her head. Connett had recorded important events in their lives in chronological order, but they were sketchy at best. She already knew about what had gone on between her father and Edwin Blackstock when they were colleagues, what was it about the prospect of learning more that filled her with such dread?

She picked up her teacup and returned to the lounge, turning on the lamp by her favourite chair. She settled back, placing her feet on the stool, pulling a crocheted blanket across her knees. She didn't want to think about Connett, or her father, but she had to, it was her nature to unpick puzzles; just because they impinged on her personal life didn't make them different…

…*Ok*… she thought …*let's look at this objectively, in so much as I'm able to...* She took a sip of her tea, the warm sweetness seemed to comfort her. She picked up the notepad and pencil that she had left on the side table. She lay back and closed her eyes, breathing deeply, her gift of instant recall and an eidetic memory kicking in as it did with all the cases she'd dealt with. She needed to cross reference Connett's files with her father's diaries. She looked at the neat piles in the corner of the room. One pile of books contained mainly notes that her father had made for his lectures, the others were his diaries. Books…so many…books she'd never dared to touch before, let alone read. It started with her father, she knew, all she had to do was find out why.

…*a few minutes rest*…she thought, that's all I need. She put the pad down on the side table and leaned her head back. How was it that people could keep secrets like these? She'd never even suspected…*but then I should be used to people telling lies, shouldn't I, in my job? …but family…* she thought…*my family*…despite everything, she could feel herself relaxing.

The brightness of the room woke her. She looked at the clock on the mantlepiece…six fifteen…she'd slept through the night.

…*must have needed it*…she winced at the phrase that her mother had used so often. Mason stretched the stiffness out of her body as she got up out of the chair. The list she had started the night before needed completing, she needed a shower and something to eat. It wasn't long before she was back in her father's study, she paused before sitting at his desk. If she was going to do this, she was going to do it properly, she decided. She reached for the first of his diaries, the sight of her father's handwriting still had the power to move her.'…*I cannot stress the depth of sorrow that I felt on hearing of Edwin's tragic passing…'* her father had written, his artistic handwriting, looping across the page. '*…no matter how much our friendship, which at one time was closer than that of brothers, had deteriorated, I never wanted our estrangement to go this far…'* Mason shook her head. She'd arranged her father's diaries into chronological order, she didn't want to miss any clues, only then had she started to read them. Despite his insistence that it was what he wanted her to do, she felt guilty, almost as though she was betraying him.

She reached over and picked up her notepad…she needed to summarise the facts, try to make sense of it all, if she could.

She had always known that Edwin Blackstock and her father had developed a close friendship when they attended Eton College. Their friendship had continued as they studied at Oxford, each gaining a First-Class Honours Degree in English. It was during this time that they developed a mutual passion for *'The Canterbury Tales'*.

Their passion became more of a rivalry as they each published conflicting theories on the subject. Eventually this had turned into a bitter conflict when Blackstock had accused Professor Mason of plagiarising some of his work.

She paused; she needed the bathroom. Within ten minutes she was sitting back at the desk. She picked up the diary she'd been reading and turned the page.

'*…I felt duty bound to visit Emily…'* her father wrote, '*…after all, she was an innocent party in this situation…I couldn't help a sense of guilt…'* Doris froze…Emily…her mother, how had her mother been involved? Surely all this had happened before her mother and father had married? She carried on reading, a knot forming in her stomach. The rest of the pages were ramblings, her father tended to make notes on his lectures in the most inappropriate places. She turned the pages, hoping that she could find out more about her mother…there was nothing.

She grabbed another notebook. The next block of entries had been written a few months later, detailing her parent's move back to the Island. She checked the dates he'd written on the front of it…there was one missing. Mason looked at the filing cabinet that stood in the corner of room. She tried the top drawer; it was locked, just as she expected it would be. She emptied the small jar he kept his bits and bobs in…no key.

Where would he have hidden it? It had to be somewhere that meant something to him. She picked up the framed photograph of her parents, taken just before her mother died. The gilded frame looked hollow, she dismantled it…nothing. Doris sighed; it could be anywhere, she realised. What was the most important thing to him…the *'Tales'*, it had to have something to do with the *'Tales'*.

She hadn't realised how many artefacts her father had collected over the years. She picked up one after the other, shaking them, listening for the sound of something inside. Her father's bookcase, crammed with books, pamphlets, magazines and…she smiled, that money box she'd brought him, a miniature version of the Cathedral at Canterbury …she picked it up, the chink of metal on pottery was unmistakeable.

…oo0oo…

It was early morning before she finished reading. Her eyes were stinging, she couldn't tell if it was because she was tired, or because she'd cried so much. Her parent's history read like a warped Romantic melodrama.

All the characters were there, except for one…the hero…nowhere in this sorry tale had she found anyone she could admire. Almost everyone had behaved despicably.

Most of the facts she already knew, the fall out between her father and Edwin. Blackstock had made accusations about her father plagiarising his work. Her father had always maintained that he had lied, that the charges were false. The University agreed with him and gave Blackstock a warning, he was furious that his academic reputation might be affected. The tension between them had escalated to such a point that the University suspended them both.

Doris had often wondered why her father had left Oxford and come back to the island. He told her it was because he wanted to be closer to family, but he had no family, now she knew the real reason. She picked up the missing diary, the one she'd found pushed to the back of the filing cabinet and carried on reading it.

'…I swear I didn't mean for it to get this far…' he had written, *'…but now we find ourselves in a situation which needs to be dealt with. When I first hit upon my plan to seduce Blackstock's wife, I didn't imagine that it would end in Edwin's suicide. It was only my intention to cause tension between them, after all, they had so much and I, I would have ended up with nothing after my career, my position was threatened. Who could have known that Edwin's jealousy of our flourishing relationship would lead…?'* Mason stopped reading, she felt sick. She shook her head as she placed the diary on her father's desk. Her father and Connett's mother had had an affair…she never knew…how could she? The diary seemed to pulsate as she stared at it. She wanted to destroy it, to erase the past and make it different…she knew she couldn't.

'…I have urged her to make a decision; I hope it is the right one for all of us…there is, of course, no question that I will stand by her, partly because of her current circumstances, but also because I have become very fond of her. She looks so downhearted when I visit, I know that she blames herself for Edwin's death. I try to cheer her up, but the fact that her mental health has deteriorated to the point that she needed to be incarcerated for her own protection…' Mason felt her stomach surge, almost as though someone had dealt her a physical blow…Connett's mother had been sent to a Psychiatric Hospital…she had to force herself to read on.

'…I thought that she was quite reasonable today…' the diary went on, *'she agreed that it would be wiser to surrender Edwin's sons to the care of her parents and signed the papers that I submitted for her approval. I think it is better this way, for all concerned, after all this way the boys will have the undivided attention of their Grandparents. It would be cruel to tell her that once she has relinquished her sons to them, they intend to prevent her seeing them again. It is obvious that her behaviour in this matter has turned them against her…'* Doris stared at the pages of the diary. She shook her head in disbelief… her father, her father had been party to …this, this terrible betrayal…what about her mother? Did she know anything about what was going on? She carried on reading…

'…we travelled to Beaumaris today, I thought it prudent that we take this next step away from the prying eyes of anyone who knows us…fortunately the child has not yet made a difference to Emily's slender figure…I have to say she looked almost ethereal as we waited in the Registry Office…I cannot wait to start our lives together, to try and make amends for all the suffering she has endured…if we have a son, I will suggest we name him Brian…' Mason gasped in shock. She shook her head…she read the last part again. Emily…her mother…Registry

Office…but that would mean…her father, he couldn't have…

Doris shook herself, …*none of this is my fault*…she thought, being unaware of the actions of others wasn't a crime, although right now it felt like one. She had an unreasonable sense that she should have known what was going on in her own family.

…*family*…she thought…*what family?* For so many years it had just been the Professor, Brian, and herself. Her mother had died when she was thirteen, she'd hardly seen her father from one week to the next, the running of the household had fallen on her shoulders. She remembered the long hours she had spent on her own while her father worked most days at the University. He chose to sleep in his office, rather than make the effort to come home at night.

Her life became even more solitary when Brian dropped out of his Engineering Degree and moved on to Performing Arts, much to the consternation of their father. He moved away to the Midlands to take his Degree at Worcester; their father never spoke of his change of discipline. Doris knew better than to discuss it. She was relieved when Brian left; given what he'd done…she shuddered, forcing the memory back. Apart from the three of them, there were no other relatives, at least that's what she'd believed, until…

35

It was late in the afternoon when Ray Blackstock walked into the station reception area, accompanied by two officers. They'd decided against handcuffing him, not enough evidence to go on for that. Their instructions were clear, tell him as little as possible, take him straight to an Interview Room, don't offer any kind of refreshment, and leave him to stew.

Porter and Ellie sat in the observation room, watching him over the next hour or so, Chetwynd soon joined them. Blackstock sat slouched in the chair, staring at the ceiling for the first twenty minutes. He stood up and walked around the table a few times, stretching nonchalantly. He sat back down and steepled his fingers, resting his wrists on the tabletop. Once or twice he sighed, altered his position, then went back to staring at the light fixture. After almost an hour Rowan joined them. She handed a sheet of paper to Porter. He didn't look pleased.

'Are you sure this is right?' he asked, 'we've double checked, I assume?' Rowan nodded. If the information was correct, the man next door was unlikely to have committed one of the three murders he was suspected of. If that was the case, and they were connected, then it cast doubt on him committing the others. Porter wasn't taking any chances though, considering what had happened in the Prothero case. Porter handed the information to Chetwynd, she read it and passed it to Ellie.

'Question him anyway,' Chetwynd said quietly, 'we need to know what he knows, which might be more than he realises.' Porter nodded; it was time. He knew just how long to keep his suspects waiting, and Blackstock was reaching that limit. Porter stood up, Rowan joined him, they had already decided that she should take the lead. He'd watch for any tell-tale signals that might be overlooked, but with Ellie watching, he was confident that he had all the back-up he needed. He turned as they left the room and smiled at her.

'Ready?' he asked her. For a reason she couldn't explain, she was taken off guard. She blushed, aware that Chetwynd was watching every move.

'As I'll ever be,' she cleared her throat, trying to avoid Chetwynd's attention. She picked up her notebook and clicked her pen. Porter closed the door as Ellie looked up to see Chetwynd still staring at her.

'Careful Ellie,' she said, then turned her attention back to the man in the next room.

Ellie wasn't quite sure what she meant.

…oo0oo…

The temperature in the Interview Room was carefully controlled. It was warm enough to avoid complaints from both interviewees and their legal advisors, but not too hot to promote lethargy. Blackstock had been sitting there long enough to become uncomfortable through inactivity.

'What the hell are you playing at?' he demanded as Porter and Rowan walked in, 'I've been here for hours, you can't keep me here like this.' Porter ignored him; it was nothing he hadn't heard before. Rowan apologised.

'I'm so sorry Mr. Blackstock,' she said, settling in opposite him and going through the formalities. His name, date of birth, address. He answered her, managing to convey a sense of boredom.

'Now then, can I ask you…' Rowan started. Ray leaned forward, staring at her.

'Aren't you going to tape this?' he snapped. Rowan turned to Porter, he shrugged. 'At the moment, we are just having a chat, Mr. Blackstock, but if you want…'

'I do,' he snapped, 'you lot could claim I'd said stuff that I didn't, I want this down on record.' It was what Porter had gambled on, Blackstock wanted to make this official... good. Rowan leaned over and placed a tape in the recorder and started the machine.

'Can I clear something up before we start, Mr. Blackstock?' she asked, Blackstock nodded.

'I think I know what you're going to ask,' he said smugly. She waited, expecting him to go on; he kept quiet. He was playing with them, she knew it. She cleared her throat.

'Could you explain why you and your brother, Dai Connett have different surnames?' Ray sat back in surprise; it was obvious that he'd had something else in mind.

'Not a mystery,' he said, 'our surnames were changed by my maternal grandparents; they adopted us when my father killed himself and my mother deserted us. They couldn't forgive either of them for what they had done. 'Connett' was their name, when I was older, I found out what really happened, and I changed mine back, simple as…'

'What did happen,' Rowan asked, 'when your father died.'

'Do you mean why did he kill himself?' Blackstock replied, 'simple really, he'd been betrayed, not only by his best friend, but also by his wife, my mother. That bastard Professor High and Mighty Mason managed to persuade her to hand over my father's manuscript. Not only that but…'

'But why would your father kill himself over…' Rowan started, unable to stand his smug expression. She heard Porter's sharp intake of breath. She'd broken the first rule of interviewing, never interrupt when someone was on a roll.

'No, no, you don't get it do you?' Blackstock shouted. 'my father didn't kill himself over some stupid book, he killed himself because Professor Mason and my mother were having an affair.'

In the next room Ellie watched intently, she was unsure of her feelings about Ray Blackstock. She could sense his internal rage, but something was nagging at the back of her mind. She remembered the images she'd seen during her visit to Donaldson's store, the vision of the man who murdered Ronnie Bowers. It had reminded her of Dai Connett, and family resemblance with his brother was striking. The same colour hair, similar profile…she shook her head, it wasn't either of them…something was missing, another piece of the puzzle…

'So, you arranged to meet your brother…' Rowan started.

'No…I didn't arrange to meet him…' Blackstock grinned, he seemed to be enjoying himself now.

'… you didn't intend to meet with your brother that day,' Rowan asked.

'I didn't say that,' Ray answered, 'we did arrange to meet, but he was the one doing the arranging. I phoned him just after nine-fifteen to tell him I was going to be late. Some bastard slashed one of my tyres during the night, I had to change it.'

'Did you replace the spare?' Porter chimed in. Ray nodded. He could check that out later. Porter was starting to feel uncomfortable; he could sense that Blackstock was setting them up for a grand finale.

'Tell me about the relationship with your brother,' Rowan went on. Ellie watched him intently as his mouth twisted into a wry smile.

'Which one?' he asked. Rowan looked startled, although she tried not to let it show. Something in Porter's stomach dipped. They'd obviously not done their homework well enough. He saw the look of smug satisfaction on Ray's face as he realised that he'd just dropped a bombshell.

'You didn't know, did you?' he gloated, the smile spreading over his face. 'Let me enlighten you, shall I?'

…oo0oo…

He watched from the shadows as Ray Blackstock walked away from the station. That was it then, they knew everything now, well, not everything. Not even he knew what he intended to do next… He had to get out of here in case anyone saw him. He needed to end this, sooner than he'd planned, but at least he was aware that they knew about him, and that they could come looking for him at any time. He had one last chance to get to present his offerings, his main goal…the kingpin…it was a pity there hadn't been a tale about him…what could they have called it? *'The Architect's Tale'*, perhaps…

He walked back to his car and drove towards his terraced home. He needed to think, to adapt his plans again. He locked the doors and drew the threadbare curtains against the cold of the night. He poured himself a drink and cradled it as he considered one possibility after another. He should have killed them both, he knew that now. Getting rid of Ray Blackstock as well as Dai Connett might have kept him safe, at least for a while longer.

36

Mason had always believed that she and Porter had a close working relationship, even though he scared her half to death. She looked up to him, he was everything she believed an SIO should be. This was the first time that her faith in him had been tested. She'd found out that Ray Blackstock, her half-brother, had been interviewed in connection with the *'Canterbury Tales'* murders, but the information hadn't come from Porter, a courtesy that she would have expected. It came from one of the civilian office staff that Doris had met in the car park as she made her way to the station to update Chetwynd.

Tina Foster was known in the office as a cruel gossip, with a vicious tongue. She relished being the first in the know and delighted in breaking news to any unsuspecting individuals that got caught up in the maelstrom of events that occasionally broke surface at the station. Under normal circumstances the vivacious brunette wouldn't have given Doris a second glance. These, she knew, were not normal circumstances. In recent days Doris Mason had become somewhat of a celebrity, her relationship to Connett a subject of fascination to the likes of Tina. It hadn't taken long for news of his revelations to spread through the station.

There was the matter of confidentiality, but Tina, ever eager to be the one to deliver bad news, didn't seem to understand the concept of keeping her mouth shut. She couldn't resist the opportunity to inform the gawky-looking DS of what was happening. Her announcement was casual, her eager anticipation at the prospect of Mason becoming emotional, evident.

Mason couldn't remember Tina's exact words as she walked away, her face burning, her mind whirling. Something about Ray Blackstock being interviewed and letting it slip that there was yet another brother that no one knew about.

'How come you didn't know, Doris?' she asked, feigning innocence. A stranger might have assumed that she was trying for sympathy, her efforts fell far short of the mark. Mason almost ran back to her car, the fear that she would break down and show herself up, almost overwhelmed her. She sat behind the wheel, her heart beating so rapidly that she thought she might pass out. She couldn't drive while she felt like this. She had to calm down.

Her phone rang… the Nursing Home, that was all she needed. She let the call go to voicemail. Doris closed her eyes and leaned back on the headrest, grateful that she'd parked in the furthest corner of the car park, the front of the vehicle turned away from prying eyes. She wouldn't have put it past Tina to have followed her to see how much havoc she had wreaked, but then again, the nosey cow wouldn't care.

She breathed in deeply, practicing the techniques that she'd learned in Odelia Mather's Yoga classes. That morning she had made an appointment to see her later in the week. She had to talk to someone. It was about time she took notice of that little voice that kept telling her she needed to spend more time on her own needs, how important self-care was. There was a knock on the window, Doris peered out before she opened it. A WPC she didn't recognise asked if she was all right, she nodded, hardly able to speak. The woman got into the car next to Doris's and drove away. Her phone rang… the Care Home again. She swiped to answer.

'Miss Mason,' a muffled voice, one she recognised as the manager, Mr. Edwards. 'I'm so glad I caught you, just checking…have you had any contact with your father this afternoon?' Doris gasped…not again. 'What's wrong Mr. Edwards, what's he done now?' Edwards paused before answering.

'Erm, I'm not sure, you see, we wouldn't have allowed the trip under normal circumstances, only that we received your letter confirming that you had given Mr. Lester authorisation…' Doris grabbed the steering wheel. Something wasn't right, her police training took over.

'Who on earth is Mr. Lester?' she snapped.

37

He ran through the plan once more as he drove towards St. Mary's. It wasn't the first time he'd had to change tack. After that incident with the Mathers women, he'd had to think quickly. It wasn't a problem; he already knew the routine at the Home. Lunchtime would be the best, when the staff were busiest, getting the residents ready to eat. Some were unable to wash or dress themselves, some needed to be lifted in hoists and lowered into wheelchairs to get them to the dining room. It was a lengthy process; he was counting on most of the staff being too busy to pay him much attention. He'd witnessed several incidents where visitors or delivery people had been allowed access to the place without being asked for I.D. In any case, Edwards was a fool, more interested in on-line gambling than ensuring the residents safety.

Access to the Professor had never been a problem, admittedly he had more opportunity before the move, but you couldn't have everything, could you? He had the suspicion that the old man knew who he was, just before the medication he fed him kicked in. It hadn't taken long for people to jump to the conclusion that Dementia had set in. The level of his confusion had increased rapidly. Not, as his doctor believed, because of aging, but something else for which he could take the credit.

Administering a sedative, had been easy, small doses at first so that the symptoms would be subtle. Gradually increasing the dose had ensured the inevitable decision to place him in the home for his own safety.

Gaining regular access could have been complicated, volunteering as 'Simon Collins'; an unpaid carer had solved that problem, at least for a while. They were constantly busy, and another pair of hands seemed like a blessing. No one had asked to see any references, easy. It was almost amusing to see the old man battling to understand what was happening to him. Every afternoon, his cushions plumped by the caring young man with the somewhat familiar face, Professor Mason drank his orange juice as instructed, then sank into a stupor which the staff at the over-priced home were too busy to notice.

He found that his visits had become almost therapeutic for him. He would sit by the old man's bed for hours as he snored gently under the influence of the unauthorised medication, watching him, whispering to him. Accusations, justifications, what he planned to do to him when the time was right.

…*enough*…looking back was all very well, now he had to look to the future. He'd had to change his plans more than once. Not long after the Mathers incident, he had dropped by and introduced himself to Edwards as 'Thomas Lester', an older man, suave, smart, an air of authority, a persuasive manner. He'd been engaged by the Professor's daughter, Doris, he told Mr. Edwards as he flourished a letter of introduction, supposedly written by her. It confirmed that she wanted him to visit her father and was to be given access to him on a regular basis. He was a therapist, who would assess her father's health and treat him accordingly.

Edwards had heard it all before. Yet another loving off-spring who wanted the 'best' for their failing relative. The pressure of running the place had made Edwards blasé about the strict procedures he and his staff were required to follow. His time as Simon Collins had come in useful, he was more that aware that Edwards had a predilection for logging in to gambling sites the minute he got into his office every morning. It was rare that he logged off before lunchtime. It meant he was only too happy to hand over the responsibility for the Professor to the persuasive newcomer.

Lester had arrived at lunchtime, helped Professor Mason into his coat, then popped his head around Edwards' office door and announced that they would be taking a 'stroll'. Edwards had been writing reports all day, trying to catch up with a backlog, he waved his hand in the air as the office door closed. He went back to his papers; he needed to update the records before the auditors came at the end of the week.

He was finishing off the last file when one of the carers popped her head around his office door and asked where the Professor was. The look on Edwards's face said it all… he had no idea. He glanced at the clock, the last he'd seen of them had been at least three hours ago. That wasn't long, was it? He'd give them another half hour or so, then ring Mr. Lester, just to check.

'Everything's quite all right, Lyndsey,' he said, feeling less sure than his manner suggested. 'We have authorisation from the Professor's daughter, Mr. Lester will no doubt be on his way back soon.' Edwards tried to concentrate on his paperwork. It was no good. His gut told him that something wasn't right, only then did he start to question what Lester had told him. He cursed himself, he should have checked directly with Miss

Mason herself, the story didn't hang true. Doris Mason was a junior police officer, since when could someone on her pay grade afford a private therapist? He tried to reason that perhaps the family had money, after all the Professor *had* been placed in one of the most expensive homes on the Island. Something niggled in the back of his mind as he dialled Lester's number… '*the number you have dialled is not available*'… Edwards's stomach lurched as he realised that something was wrong.

38

Okay, so we all know where we're going...' Porter shouted above the low hum of speculation. Rowan waited at the door; she was eager to get out of the station. Ellie sat in her office, studying the files yet again. Porter pushed her office door open.

'You ready?' he asked Ellie, she nodded as he grabbed her coat and held it for her. She slipped her arms into it, mumbling her thanks. She grabbed her bag and followed him into the Incident room. She was being watched; Rowan had begun to follow her every move during the last week. Ellie wasn't sure why.

...oh, come on Ellie, surely you can tell she's jealous...? Ellie couldn't tell, and she laughed at what Ruth was suggesting.

'You might want to get your phone,' Rowan called to Porter, who was halfway out of the door. He turned, and walked back to his office to fetch it, retrieving a voicemail message at the same time. Ellie saw the change in his expression.

'It's Doris isn't it?' Ellie asked. He nodded, no hint of surprise at her question.

'But Sir, what about...' Rowan started.

'If what I've just heard is correct, we won't need to try and find him,' he said. He shouted orders to the other officers, who grabbed their things and followed them out. Porter hurried towards his car, closely followed by Ellie and Rowan. He sped away from the station, two more cars following him.

'I want an ambulance standing by…paramedics… Mason's going to call us when she has more information…we may need an armed response team…' he barked at Rowan as she picked up the radio and followed his instructions.

'Sir, where are we heading…?' she asked, Porter shook his head. Mason just said to drive towards the St. Mary's Rest home, do you know it, because I'm damned if I do?'

…oo0oo…

Doris Mason did what she was told, as she had done when she was a child, as she had done every day of her working life as a police officer. Throughout her childhood it had been her father that called the shots, recently her senior officers.

Edwards' message had left her confused. Her father had been taken out from the home by someone who claimed he had been employed by her. Where they had gone, or whether the stranger, Mr. Lester intended the old man harm, Edwards didn't know. Nor, it seemed, did he have a procedure to deal with such an event. Doris cut his apologies short, she had no time for his grovelling explanations. If her father was in danger, and her instinct told her he was, then she needed to clear her phone line and get ready to hear from 'Mr. Lester'.

Her phone call to Porter was almost a reflex action. She regretted making it almost as soon as she'd finished recording her message. She had no proof, just a suspicion.

…Mr. Lester, Mr. Lester, where have I heard that name before? The sound of her ringtone made her jump. A number she didn't recognise showed on the display.

'You know who this is, don't you Doris?' the voice, the one she remembered him using when she was a child, the one she hadn't heard for years, the one that used to scare her in the night when he came into her room…she shuddered as he started to speak again, his own voice, equally as chilling…yes, she knew who this was, somehow, she'd always known…

'…the cliffs…his favourite spot on the island, do you remember? Follow the path,' he said, 'come now, don't tell anyone, just you.'

'Don't hurt him,' she pleaded, 'I know what he did, he…he…' she couldn't find the words.

'Come on now,' he insisted, 'there's a good girl. If you don't come now, it'll be too late.' Doris nodded, almost as though he was there in the room with her. She had to go, she had to go now, she only hoped that she could stop shaking enough to drive. Her stomach tightened as she drew near to the cliff top car park, the nearest access point she knew. Her instinct was to run straight to where he had told her to go. Her common sense made her dial Porter's number to tell him where she was heading for, where he intended to take her life, and that of her father.

39

Ellie sat in the back of Porter's car, her eyes closed, trying to focus on a myriad of images that flickered across her consciousness. The best she'd been able to manage was…*somewhere south-west of the island.* Porter had pleaded for something else to go on, Rowan placed her hand on his arm as he bawled at Ellie for the third time. He shot her a look of desperation as she half turned in her seat.

'Ellie,' she said, as calmly as she could, 'relax, just take a deep breath.' The situation reminded her of their visit to Harrington Hall, and the afternoon at Donaldson's. Ellie had been nervous while everyone's attention was on her, it was only when they allowed her some space that she'd been able to 'see' what had happened to the victims. She heard Porter's sharp intake of breath; she could appreciate the urgency to get whatever information he could, but placing Ellie under this kind of pressure…

'…A bay, cliffs…a lighthouse,' Ellie murmured. Porter stopped just before another outburst. 'The beach …a shingle beach, I can see a large rock, right in the middle of the bay…'

'Are there trees?' Porter asked, calmer, his voice steady.

'Pine trees…acres of pine trees…' Ellie said, 'a memorial of some kind, black marble…'

'Stanley's Point,' Porter hissed, 'get on the radio, tell the others,' he snapped at Rowan. He took a sharp turn to the right, and headed down a narrow lane, the two other cars followed him. At least now he had a general direction, it was then that Mason called.

Ellie was right, but then he knew that already.

...oo0oo...

Mason ran towards the promontory; two figures stood precariously close to the edge of the cliffs. Her father, his overcoat flapping in the wind, his captor holding onto him. He'd worked out the exact position, nothing was going to upset his schedule, least of all losing the Professor to an errant gust of air.

Tiny flecks of snow were falling, it was late this year, but then who knew what was going on with the weather these days? The crystals fell on Doris's cheeks, mingling with the tears that streaked her face, a response both to the vicious gale, and to the appalling situation she now found herself in. She could hear something, a whisper, so close, so clear.

...keep calm...help is on its way...they're nearly here... Doris had heard that voice before, she couldn't place it. She knew she could be seen, she suspected that it wouldn't be long now before he ordered her to slow down, not to come any nearer...she was right. His voice... almost lost on the wind. His own voice this time, no hiding behind his many characters, she realised that she found this more frightening than all the rest put together.

He stood at the very edge of the cliff, one hand holding a hammer, the other clamped firmly around Professor Mason's arm. The old man stared down at the ground, only moving when his captor shoved him perilously close towards the abyss, then dragged him back.

'I'll do it, Doris, I'll do it,' he hissed, 'it's no less than he deserves, is it?'

Doris stared at him, Mr. Lester, that was it, she remembered. Mr. Lester, the name of that Drama Teacher, the only person he had any respect for, her brother's favourite… Brian's inspiration. He'd used his name in the ultimate homage, as the captor and would-be killer of the person he hated most in the world, Professor Mason...

'Brian,' she said, her voice disappearing on the wind. 'Brian, why are you doing this? Why have you done all these terrible things?'

'I don't know what you mean,' he said, grinning inanely.

'You killed them, didn't you, all those people,' she shouted, the roar of the sea snatching her voice away.

'You'll never understand, sweetheart,' he shouted, 'not in a million years. You see I had to, I had to show him that I was as good at something… that I could succeed at something. I had to get his attention, what better way than killing the people that he loved the most, the characters he spent most of his time with?'

'I don't…I don't know what you mean, Brian,' she shook her head, 'what characters, what are you talking about?'

'Not so clever now, are you Doris?' he sneered, 'I though you were supposed to be the genius in the family, that's what he kept telling me any chance he got…the players in his damned book. We didn't matter, he wouldn't have missed us if we'd disappeared off the face of the earth, but God forbid that anyone find fault with *The Tales*.'

'Brian, Brian, we can talk about this, it doesn't have to be like…' she pleaded stepping closer to them. Brian moved further towards the edge of the cliff; Doris gasped.

'Don't come any closer, Doris,' he screamed, 'we both know how this is going to end, it's too late for you to try and play the concerned sibling.' She looked around, her mind trying to work out what she could do to stop him. She saw a large holdall by her father's feet. She pointed to it.

'What's in the bag, Brian,' she shouted, hoping to gain a few extra seconds. Brian's expression changed, he looked down to where she was pointing and smiled. She watched as he put the hammer down on the ground, his eyes never leaving her face. He bent down and picked up the bag, he held it out in front of him.

'These are offerings, they come with us,' he gloated, 'I took their most precious possessions.' Doris shook her head as he laughed at her confusion. He pushed the Professor again, Doris gasped…

'…you can't do it, Brian, please…he's your father…' she pleaded.

'He's *not* my father…' Brian snapped, 'don't you understand…Edwin Blackstock was my father. Our dear mother was pregnant when he killed himself, she never told him, she never told either of them…she was never sure *who* my father was, so she took the path of least resistance. She needed the money, couldn't manage without her poor late husband, and that's where the old man came in. They'd been having an affair for months, it was 50-50, really.'

Doris gasped again as he shook her father, causing him to skid on the shale that edged the cliffs.

'He split the family up, didn't he? Didn't want to be reminded that his beloved wife already had two sons…he made her choose…she chose all right, wanted to be looked after, didn't she, can't you remember, Doris…?' he sneered.

Doris shook her head…he was lying, it couldn't be true, not her mother…not her as well, how could she have lied…

'It's all making sense, now isn't it?' he shouted, 'all those times when he used to say, '*…sometimes boy, I can't believe you're my son…perhaps genius skips a generation…'* he knew you see, knew I was yet another Blackstock, the one he couldn't get rid of…took him a few years of course… Can't you remember, Doris, can't you remember the rows, can't you just hear him… '*…look at Doris, why can't you be more like her…why can't you be more like your sister…?"* he turned towards the Professor and shook him hard. 'I'll tell you why, you old bastard…because she's not my sister is she…?' the old man cried, covering his face with his hands. Doris couldn't tell if it was because he feared Brian, or because of what he'd just heard. All she could think about was how she was going to diffuse the situation. She took a step towards Brian and her father. Brian thrust his prisoner further towards the cliff. Doris stepped back immediately.

'No, Brian, please…don't,' she screamed. She had to play for time, there was a chance…she took a deep breath…flattery…Brian was always swayed by flattery. 'How did you find out?' she asked, 'about what happened all those years ago. It must have taken some putting together.' Brian looked back at her; his expression had altered.

'I know what you're trying to do, Doris,' he said, his head cocked to one side, 'it isn't going to work, you know…'

'You know me, Brian,' she improvised, this wasn't working, perhaps if she changed tack. 'I always had to dot all the 'i's', didn't I? Used to drive you mad, didn't it, me being better than you? Dad always pushing that down your throat every time you disappointed him.' Brian's expression changed again. He sneered as he looked at her.

'I never understood, that was all,' he hissed, 'someone…someone made me aware of what had happened.' He could see an image of Alyson, her eagerness when he spoke about the past, he remembered the impact that her notes had had on him.

'Once I discovered the truth, when I found out, it all made sense. I had to do something about it, Doris, I had to punish him…they were all he cared about…the characters in his damn *Tales'*. Pictures…I took pictures…' he looked at Doris pleading for her understanding…

…*ask him about Alyson*…the voice seemed to come out of nowhere…*tell him you know what she was doing*…

'It was Alyson, wasn't it,' Doris said, in desperation, the pieces were beginning to fall into place. She watched as Brian relaxed his grip on her father, 'she was a reporter, wasn't she, was she investigating the old feud? Touched a nerve, didn't she?' She was guessing, she hoped she was right.

'Bitch…' he screamed, '…she tricked me, not just me, she had proof… she had DNA results in her files…mine and theirs…my, my brothers…she was clever…if she hadn't…if she…' he shook Doris's father, '…this bastard made my childhood a living hell…'

'…and you made mine one…' Doris screamed back. Brian turned towards her; his face changed rapidly as he took in what she'd said. He knew what she was talking about, it wasn't something that he could forget.

'…I…I was young…I didn't know any better…you…' he stammered.

'…don't you dare try to put the blame on me, Brian,' she sobbed, 'you were fifteen, you should have known better…' she reached out and steadied herself, holding on to a tree trunk as her emotions overwhelmed her. She'd spent so much time trying to forget…finally saying what she'd wanted to say all these years…

'…he ruined both our lives, then, didn't he?' Brian hissed. Doris looked over to where he had stepped closer to the edge of the cliffs.

'Please…please come away…' she cried, 'you'll fall…' she realised that falling wasn't in his game plan. He meant to get rid of her and her father, and there was little she could do to stop him.

…oo0oo…

Porter's car skidded to a halt; they ran along the edge of the pine woods towards the cliffs. They were hidden for the most part, although Porter knew that soon the treeline would end, and they could be seen.

'Slow down,' he hissed, grabbing hold of Ellie's arm. The three of them dropped to the ground. The wind whistled through the trees, the snow, which until now had been light, had started to thicken.

'What now?' Rowan asked, looking round as several more officers approached them. Porter indicated for them to stay low, as he surveyed the scene. He could just about make out the figures a few hundred yards away. It looked as though the Professor could hardly stand. Doris Mason stood a short distance from her brother and father.

'I think we should…' Rowan gasped, 'Sir, look.' She pointed at Ellie who was walking towards the cliffs, in full sight of Brian Mason.

'What the f….' Porter hissed, 'what the hell…?' he hesitated. Any sudden move would surely send Brian Mason over the top, along with his father. He stared at Ellie, something akin to panic started to take hold inside him, how could she…?

*…she knows what she's doing…trust her…*a voice in his ear…the one he'd heard at the crash site. Porter watched as Ellie walked further towards the cliff top. The wind dropped; an eyrie silence descended as Ellie's movements changed. Her hips swung seductively; her figure seemed to grow more curvaceous as she sashayed forward. Doris had been staring at her brother intently, she saw the look of disbelief suffuse his face, watched that look turn to one of fascination, then horror. He dropped the bag, and let go of the Professor, who slumped to the ground. He snatched up the hammer, brandishing it in front of him.

'No,' Brian gasped, shaking his head, 'no, it's not…it can't be.' Brian stepped back, too close to the cliff edge for safety. Doris looked round; her mind did a double take. A woman was walking slowly towards them. She was dressed in tight leggings, and a flimsy top with thin straps that were just about holding it onto her shoulders. Blonde hair cascaded down around her neck. She realised with horrified fascination that she recognised her… Kara Billingham…but…

'Hello Brian,' the voice, deep, sultry, so loud it resonated back to the pine woods. He recoiled as though she had struck him. 'You didn't think I'd let you get away with it, did you?'

Brian Mason shook his head trying to clear his thoughts. Logic told him this wasn't possible…his eyes told him a different story. The apparition got closer as he raised the hammer above his head.

'This is a trick,' he shouted, 'don't think you can stop me, Kara…' he took a step towards Doris, who stood transfixed, unable to move. 'I'll do it, I will, don't think…'

'Not today, you won't, not if I can help it…' hissed Ellie. 'Enough…' she screamed. She thrust her hands out in front of her, as she had done on the day she'd fended off her mother in Richardson's office. A great surge of energy hit Brian Mason and he flew backwards, disappearing over the edge of the cliff. Porter heard Doris scream, he rushed forward, closely followed by Rowan.

Ellie stood still, staring out over the sea, surrounded by silence. In the distance she could hear voices, they got louder as Porter and Rowan reached her. She felt something being placed around her shoulders, a jacket, warming her as she shivered in the aftermath of something she couldn't explain. She allowed them to walk her back to the car park but drew the line at getting in the ambulance.

'There's nothing wrong with me,' she whispered at last. 'I just want to go home.' Porter nodded. Rowan helped her into Porter's car as they watched Doris Mason and her father climb into the ambulance.

The sound of a helicopter was the last thing Ellie heard as she fell into a deep sleep.

40

Doris sat in the corner of her father's hospital room, the steady bleep of the monitor punctuating her thoughts.

Brian, her brother, no, her stepbrother, one of three, he was the *'Canterbury Killer'*. The revelation, along with that of her father's questionable past, had turned her whole world upside down. Porter had promised that he would talk to her in the morning, to bring her up to date. She wasn't sure that she could wait that long.

How on earth had Brian done it? His teaching job, his social commitments, how had he found the time? She was horrified that it was easier to believe that he was guilty, than it was to accept that he could have fitted everything into the busy life he always maintained he led. She stood up, the cellular blanket fell to the floor as she made for the hallway and approached the nurse's station. The sister greeted her warmly, asking after them both. Doris muttered assurances, then asked if she could have some paper and a pen.

'Are you sure, poppet,' the sister simpered, 'why don't you go and get some rest while you can?' Doris shuddered; Brian used to call her 'poppet' back when…she shook her head.

'Please, I have to write things down, or I'll forget,' she lied, hiding the real reason for her request. The sister nodded and crossed to a side ward. A patient, discharged that evening, had left a writing pad and some pencils on the side-locker. She handed them to Doris.

'It's ok,' she said, 'a visitor brought them in earlier, I know for a fact he didn't touch them…no need to worry.' Doris took them gratefully.

'Is there somewhere I can sit and write…I hate to be a nuisance,' she said. The sister took her into the day room, switched on the lights and indicated the large crafts table that filled the centre of the floor.

'Will that serve?' she asked, smiling at the shrinking woman. She'd seen women like Doris before, ill-used by people at every stage of life. Her own cousin had been a victim…Doris cleared her throat. 'I'll get on now if that's all right?' she asked. The sister smiled and turned to leave.

'The tea-trolley will be around in a while, make sure you ask for a biscuit,' she said, then turned and left her alone. Doris started to write down individual events, some relevant, others maybe not. At first it was an effort to remember everything that had gone on in their lives, hers, and Brian's. After an hour though, she'd amassed a sheaf of information that had never made sense before.

The startling thing was that now they did. She had to see Porter, she needed to explain. Not only that, she needed to take her father's diaries in as part of the evidence.

…oo0oo…

Porter shook his head when he saw her sitting in reception the next morning.

'Mason…' he growled, 'you don't need to be here, I could have come to you,' she stood up, determined not to leave until she'd said her piece.

'Interview me,' she pleaded, 'I want to make a statement.' He stepped back in surprise; her assured attitude was so unlike her usual behaviour. She looked completely lost; he didn't have the heart to make her leave. He nodded, he would have to interview her eventually, why not now? Rowan joined them and they went through the preliminaries as they had done so many times before.

'I should have come to you as soon as I started to read my father's diaries,' she said, 'but…they didn't make sense at first. There was nothing in them that indicated… I was so shocked…and things…things moved so quickly, I didn't put the pieces together until…out there, on the cliff…I'm sorry, I'm so sorry…' Porter watched as she started to fall apart. Rowan reached out and took Mason's hand. The little control Doris had left seemed to evaporate.

'You need to know that I had no idea about…' Mason swallowed hard. They kept quiet as she fought to control her emotions. 'There's so much…it never made sense, but now,' she squirmed in her chair as she placed both hands under her legs trying to consolidate her position.

'Brian, he…he did things, to me when we were children. I, I've never told anyone…' she stared at the desk.

'Look,' Porter said, he cleared his throat, 'I think it might be best if…' Mason's head shot up.

'I'm not asking you to sit here and listen to the sordid details,' she snapped, 'I wouldn't put anyone through that, I've already decided to ask for help, but not from you.' Porter sighed, he knew could have handled this differently, with more understanding, but then again, he wasn't a therapist.

'Doris,' he said trying to appease her. He couldn't imagine what she'd been through as a child. 'What is it you wanted to tell me?' Mason shook her head.

'I'm not sure,' she confessed. 'I suppose I just wanted you to know that I had no idea what was going on, with Brian, with my father, let alone with…if I'd known, I would have told you, I wouldn't do anything to jeopardise an enquiry…you all mean too much to me for me to…' she stopped, the effects of the last few days had taken what little strength she had.

'If you think this is going to affect your position here, Mason,' Porter said, realising how much of her life she had invested in her career, 'then let me assure you, we can't do without you for too long.' Mason looked up, she searched Porter's face for any signs that he was trying to placate her. She sighed, he was telling her the truth, she knew him well enough to be able to detect any deceit in his words.

'Thank you, sir, you don't know how much that means…' she mumbled.

'In the meantime, it might be an idea to take some time off, I'm sure you're owed quite a bit, aren't you?' Porter suggested. Mason nodded. 'Then, when you're ready, come back and take over again. The place wouldn't be the same without you.'

'I've, er, I've written down everything I can remember, about Brian, I mean, not, not the other thing…' she said, 'it might be easier than trying to tell you…' she stopped and handed over a file that had sat on the table between them. Porter took it and thanked her.

'If there's anything I can do, Doris…' he asked.

'Not for the moment,' she said, 'I'm going to stay at the Retreat for a while, I know Odelia Mathers quite well, she and her mother have offered to help…' her voice faded away.

'That's good,' Porter answered, he didn't know what else to say. Mason stood up suddenly and held out her hand. Porter shook it.

'I'll be back soon, though,' she said with more strength that he believed she was feeling. 'Don't let Rowan mess up my filing system, will you?' she smiled. Later, as he replayed their conversation, Porter couldn't believe what he did next. As Mason walked towards the door, he called her back. He stood up and crossed to where she stood, he put his arms around her and held her close for several seconds before stepping away and muttering an apology. She shook her head, obviously effected by his gesture.

'No need, sir,' she murmured, and walked out of the room.

…oo0oo…

Porter edged his way through the crowded bar, two pints of craft beer threatening to disgorge their contents onto the Rugby fans enthusing over their team's victory. Rowan had managed to secure seats in a relatively quiet corner, she waved as he looked around for her. The mayhem continued, as anthems were sung one last time, backslapping and promises to meet up for the final exchanged, and travel arrangements made. The noise faded as most of the fans packed up and left, with only a few die-hards hanging on for the match analysis. Porter sipped his drink, opened a packet of crisps, and offered them to Rowan. She shook her head, she needed to leave, the prospect of a long-drawn-out farewell didn't appeal.

'So,' Porter started, 'how did we do?' Rowan was confused. Their debrief the day before had been long and tortuous, but they'd managed to fill most of the gaps, or so she thought. To her amazement, Doris Mason had turned up, bringing her father's diaries with her. Rowan was sure that if her father was anything like Mason, everything they were unclear about would soon be explained in detail.

'If you mean the case, sir…' she started.

'Not the case, Rowan, us, the station, the team,' he explained. 'How did we do, in your opinion? Think you could work with us on a more permanent basis?' Rowan paused, her glass halfway to her lips.

'Are you offering me a job, sir?' she asked. Porter smiled.

'Not me, Rowan,' he said, shaking his head, 'that kind of power is way above my pay-grade. Chetwynd asked me to pass the offer on, seeing as how you fitted in so well, but then of course, there's always the prospect of going back to work with Horton…' he chuckled at the look on her face.

'You know what,' she said, 'I might give it some serious consideration.' She raised her glass towards him. 'Cheers, sir,' she said, 'or should I call you 'Boss'?'

Porter shuddered, reference to his seniority always made him uneasy. He sipped his drink watching the shadow of unasked questions flicker over Rowan's face.

'Something you want to ask, Rowan?' he said, Rowan sighed.

'Lots of things, getting them is order is the problem,' she answered. Porter smiled, there were so many things still unclear about this case. At least they would be able to consolidate the evidence in a way they had been prevented from doing in the *'Puppet Master'* murders.

'It's a pity we can't ask Mason to collate the information,' he observed, 'too close to home, I really don't want her exposed to more trauma, not with her father…'

'…*I* could do it,' Rowan offered. She could have bitten off her tongue, becoming more entrenched within her temporary place of work would make moving on difficult, if she chose to leave. Her sense of wanting to see the job through to the end, to gain closure for the whole team this time had made her speak out.

'I'm not sure if that would be a waste of your talents,' Porter said, enjoying the flush of embarrassment his remarks caused, 'but then again, we are going to need someone who can look at the evidence with an impartial eye.'

Rowan cleared her throat; she took a swig of her drink. The last thing she wanted was to go back behind a desk, if she did accept his offer…she could feel Porter watching her.

'Any news of DS Connett,' she asked, trying to deflect his attention from her embarrassment. Porter smiled; he knew what she was trying to do. He could work with Rowan, he was sure of it, and with Connett's future uncertain…

'He's going to need a lot of physio, not to mention the psychiatric evaluations…it'll be some time before he's ready to come back,' he said.

Rowan hesitated, 'Did he know, sir, about Brian Mason being Edwin Blackstock's son, his other brother?'

'No,' Porter replied, 'he suspected Ray. He wanted to speak to him before he told anyone at the station, not the wisest move, although understandable in the circumstances.'

'He knew that he was related to Doris Mason, though,' Rowan observed. 'I think it's going to take some time before those two will feel comfortable in each other's company.'

'The ironic thing is that if Brian Mason had killed Ray instead of going after Dai Connett, it might have taken us a lot longer to find out who the *Canterbury Killer* was.' Porter said.

'What a mess,' Rowan sighed, 'all this because of some stupid row over books written centuries ago…'

'Wars have been fought for less,' Porter replied. 'Anyway, about this job, I spoke to Chetwynd yesterday, she mentioned that once this case was wrapped up, there might be an opening for a DI position, you wouldn't know anyone that might be interested, would you?' He watched as Rowan nodded slowly.

'I think I might…' she said, raising her glass. 'My round,' she said as she turned to go to the bar. Porter watched as she ordered their drinks.

*…she'd be an asset to the team…*he thought, they needed good officers. If only they could get some sort of closure on the Prothero case, but perhaps that was a bit too much to ask for. He watched as Rowan turned way from the bar, was it his imagination, or had the man deliberately bumped into her? She managed to avoid spilling the drinks as she recovered, shaking her head as the stranger apologised, then left.

'You all right, Rowan?' he asked as she sat down at their table.

'Idiot,' she said, grabbing a handful of serviettes from the next table to dab at the beer that had spilled on to her jacket. They lapsed into silence for several minutes, Porter stood up.

'Loo,' he said as Rowan looked up. He headed towards the door, and out into the corridor. The door to the men's room opened as he walked towards it. Porter watched as the man who had bumped into Rowan walked through, and towards the exit. He turned as he reached the outer door.

'You're Porter, aren't you?' the man asked, his voice a lilting Irish brogue, '…DCI Porter.' Porter frowned.

'Who wants to know?' he asked.

'Oh, I'm nobody,' the stranger answered, 'just recognised you from the newspaper reports, that's all. Good job by the way, catching that fellow…Prothero, was it?' Porter nodded. The man stared at him intensely. 'See you around,' he said as he turned towards the exit.

Porter shook his head…*what was that all about…?* he thought.

…oo0oo…

Miss Pritchard tidied her desk. It was time for her to leave for the night. She felt guilty as she packed away her *'Sudoku Page-a-Day'* puzzle book. She'd spent most of the afternoon completing today's challenge, once she'd finished reading the draft contract for the new offices. She placed the file in her desk drawer. She must remember to fax it over to Richardson and Ball tomorrow. After that she was free for the rest of the day.

She sighed, one more check in Ms. Shaw's office, then she'd be off. She switched the light on and walked over to the desk. She saw the envelope that Ms. Shaw had placed in the plastic bag. She must have forgotten about it, it was obviously important, otherwise why would she…Miss Pritchard shrugged, she'd have to ask about it the next time Ms. Shaw came into the office.

Who knew when that would be?

41

Della watched from her lounge as Ellie walked a well-trodden path in the garden. The previous week's events had almost pushed Ellie over the edge…Della's choice of words struck her as ironic. Ellie blamed herself for Brian Mason's death, no amount of reasoning could make her believe otherwise. She found it difficult to accept Della's assurances that the outcome couldn't have been different. In Ellie's eyes, she had caused his death. Her anguish was compounded by what had happened to her in the few minutes before he was knocked over the cliff edge. Della had to admit, if only to herself, that even she didn't know what had happened.

How was it, Ellie kept asking, that she had taken on the appearance of Kara Billingham? It wasn't only Brian that had seen it happen, Doris Mason, Porter, Rowan, they'd all made statements that confirmed that she'd seemed to change in front of their eyes. How was that possible? What frightened her the most, though, was the surge of energy that she'd directed towards Brian Mason, a result of the anger that had built up inside her.

Della knew that Ellie was battling with herself, she'd even suggested that she should be locked away for everyone's safety. It was then that Della had an idea, although how could she suggest it to Ellie without her thinking it was a cop out on her part?

'I think I know someone who might be able to help you,' she said that morning as they sat in her lounge. 'I don't know if he will agree to see you, although I have a suspicion he will when he hears about what happened.' Ellie shook her head.

'I don't want to see some stranger that will prod about in my past and tell me I'm a freak,' she said, causing Della to speculate on her childhood.

'Ellie, this is someone that I think you need to see, he's, well, let's say he helped me in the past, when I was in a similar position to you…' she watched as her revelation caused Ellie to sit up straighter; her curiosity peeked.

'Tell me about him,' Ellie asked, her instincts kicking in.

Della sighed as her attention focused once more on Ellie's progress around the flower beds. She'd been out there for hours, Della knew that she was engrossed in her thoughts, deciding her next move. She believed she already knew what that move would be.

…oo0oo…

Ellie hugged herself as she made her way around the grounds, always within sight of the house. She didn't know how long she'd been walking, only that she had replayed the scene with Brian Mason over and over in her mind.

…what's happening to me…? She kept asking herself the same question. It was the same one that she'd asked Della during their talks. She knew that Della didn't have the answers, just as she knew that Della believed that this

man, this Marcus Faraday could help her. But another question kept on repeating in the background of her mind…

…*do I really want to know…?* Every time she asked it, the same answer came back, she wasn't sure whether it was her that was doing the answering or Ruth.

…*it's not about wanting to know, it's if I can go through the rest of my life not knowing*…she imagined what her life would be like if she went on the way she was. She would have to go somewhere isolated, somewhere where she didn't have to mix with people, that way they would be safe from her, from what she could do.

…*like that's ever going to happen*…this time it was Ruth. Ellie felt angry at her intrusion. It wasn't as though she didn't have the money to carry it through. She could buy somewhere…somewhere far away from people…she shook her head. Ruth was right, she couldn't live the rest of her life as a hermit.

…*in which case*…Ellie stopped pacing, she had to know, even if it meant leaving the island, at least for now. She turned and walked back towards the security of the house. Della was already pouring the coffee as she entered. She looked up as Ellie sat down.

…*she already knows what I've decided*…Ellie thought.

'I'll make the arrangements…' Della said, as she passed her a mug.

…oo0oo…

The Puppet Master

The 1st book in the Ellie Shaw Series
by
J. Lewis-Thompson

The Island – a series of brutal murders terrorises an Island community, it seems that no-one is safe…

The Investigation – as the body count builds, the Investigating Team, led by an incompetent Senior Investigating Officer is being pressured for results…

The Solution – when expert profiler, John Prothero accepts a role with the Home Office, he recommends Ellie Shaw takes over his position in the investigation. No-one, least of all Ellie, believes that she has the maturity that taking the lead in the investigation needs. But she has something that her mentor never possessed…

…oo0oo…

A Tale to Die For

The 2nd book in the Ellie Shaw Series
by
J. Lewis-Thompson

An unpopular member of the House of Lords...
A celebrity TV Chef, author of several best-selling books...
The MD of a well-known High Street Chain…

All murdered, but how are they connected?

DS Mason can see a link, but can she make her senior officers believe her…

DCI Porter and his team are eager to provide the relatives and friends of the Puppet Master's victims with closure but are shocked when the case is taken out of their hands. With so many unanswered questions, DCI Porter is not happy. He and his team are soon swept up in a new case, with no time to pursue their grievances.

Betrayed by people she trusted; Ellie Shaw is almost overwhelmed with the changes in her life. Her life becomes more complicated as she deals with two new arrivals on the Island…but it is the increase in her abilities that frighten her the most…ignoring them is no longer an option…

...oo0oo...

Coming soon

By the Turn of a Card

The 3rd book in the Ellie Shaw Series
by
J. Lewis-Thompson

A man driven to distraction by the voice in his head…
The Head of a controversial Government Department,
who will stop at nothing to fulfil his own agenda…
A mysterious recluse obsessed with privacy…

Ellie Shaw's future balances on a knife's edge. Confused and afraid, she agrees to talk to Marcus Faraday, a reclusive and enigmatic mentor, hoping to come to terms with her growing 'abilities', and learn how to control them. Faraday's obsession with anonymity delays their meeting and places Ellie in further danger…

Since his unfortunate accident on the Island of Anglesey, Danny O'Neill spends every day in pain and most nights in terror. The voice in his head is growing stronger, tormenting him…

Despite their recent success in solving a difficult case, DCI Porter and his team are still smarting from having the 'Puppet Master' case snatched from them. Celia Chetwynd receives notification that an enquiry will be held into her station's part in the case, but it soon becomes clear where their focus lies.

…oo0oo…

ACKNOWLEDGEMENTS…

…to everyone who bought my first book
'The Puppet Master'
…your encouragement and positive feedback
has meant more than you could imagine

…to Liz, Chris, and Kate, who inspire me every day
…you are my greatest achievements

…to Emma, for her inspiration…a wise 9-year-old
…to Georgia who looks at me with such curiosity

…to Michael S., who designed the cover…
again…calmed me down when I realised
halfway through the book that the
plot wasn't working…
and fed me with delicious meals

…to Sue G., thank you for proof-reading again

…and not least to Mrs. McGorty, my English Teacher
…I did it again!!

J. Lewis-Thompson July 2020

Printed in Great Britain
by Amazon

45048948R00197